The Overcoat

and Other Tales of Good and Evil

I0887986

David Magarshack was born in Riga, Latvia, on December 23, 1899, and received his secondary-school education in Russia. Settling in London in 1920, he received the B.A. degree from London University in 1924 and is now a British subject. Among the books Mr. Magarshack has written are: *Stanislavsky on the Art of the Stage* (1950), *Chekhov the Dramatist* (1952), *Turgenev* (1954), and *Gogol* (1957). His other major translations include works of Chekhov, Dostoevsky, Leskov, and Ostrovsky.

Originally published in 1949 in London, this collection originally included "Taras Bulba." This story has been replaced in this edition by "Ivan Fyodorovich Shponka and His Aunt" and "The Nose" in new translations by David Magarshack.

Nicolai V. Gogol

The Overcoat

and Other Tales of Good and Evil

Translated with an Introduction

by David Magarshack

The Norton Library

W · W · NORTON & COMPANY · INC ·

NEW YORK

➤➤➤ W. W. Norton & Company, Inc. is also the publisher of
The Norton Anthology of English Literature, edited by M. H.
Abrams, Robert M. Adams, David Daiches, E. Talbot Donaldson,
George H. Ford, Samuel Holt Monk, and Hallett Smith; *The
American Tradition in Literature,* edited by Sculley Bradley, Rich-
mond Croom Beatty, and E. Hudson Long; *World Masterpieces,*
edited by Maynard Mack, Kenneth Douglas, Howard E. Hugo,
Bernard M. W. Knox, John C. McGalliard, P. M. Pasinetti,
and René Wellek; *The Norton Reader,* edited by Arthur M.
Eastman, Caesar R. Blake, Hubert M. English, Jr., Alan B. Howes,
Robert T. Lenaghan, Leo F. McNamara, and James Rosier; and
the Norton Critical Editions, in hardcover and paperbound:
authoritative texts, together with the leading critical interpretations,
of major works of British, American, and Continental literature.

PRINTED IN THE UNITED STATES OF AMERICA

2 3 4 5 6 7 8 9 0

CONTENTS

The Overcoat

and Other Tales of Good and Evil

Introduction

NICOLAI GOGOL was born in the Ukrainian township of Sorochintsky, Poltava Province, on March 19, 1809. His father was a small landowner and the author of a number of Ukrainian comedies which were performed at the country house of a local grandee, a former Minister of Justice, and a distant relative of the Gogols. It was at the house of this rich landowner that Gogol first came into contact with the world of art, for there he found a large library, a picture gallery, and a theatre.

Gogol was sent to school in 1819, first to a preparatory school in Poltava and then to a grammar school in Nezhin. Already as a schoolboy he had made up his mind to become a famous man. In a letter to a schoolfellow he speaks scornfully of the people in Nezhin who, as he expressed it, "have buried the high destiny of man under the rubbish heap of their ridiculous complacency. And among these people," he went on, "who merely vegetate I have to spend my days! I dread the thought that fate may cast me into some Godforsaken hole and make me play the part of a nobody in the world." Living among people "who merely vegetate" and being conscious of his future greatness, it is no wonder that Gogol, though fond of laughter, gave way to fits of depression and made few friends. "I have suffered more unhappiness than you think," he wrote to his mother shortly before leaving school. "I doubt if any other human being has ever experienced so much ingratitude or so much cold contempt. . . . You say I am a dreamer. No, I know people too well to be a dreamer. The lessons I have learnt from them I shall never forget."

His father died when Gogol was sixteen, and three years later, on leaving school, the young man went to seek a literary career in Petersburg. When he arrived there towards the end of 1828, he had already written an "idyll" in verse, which he published at his own expense shortly afterwards under the pseudonym of Alov. The hero of this juvenile poem bore the German name of Hans Kuechelgarten. He is a dreamer who leaves his home and his beloved Luise to wander all over Europe in search of "the beautiful." In his wanderings he visits Greece and on the ruins of the Acropolis comes to the conclusion that people everywhere are "contemptible creatures." Realising how empty his dreams are, he returns home and marries his Luise. *Hans Kuechelgarten* was a dismal failure and, characteristically, Gogol at that early phase of his literary career did what he was later to do in more tragic circumstances: he destroyed his book of verse and went abroad. He embarked for the German port of Luebeck, intending to emigrate to America ("the fantastic country of happiness and rational productive labour," as he told a friend), but came back within a few weeks. "The moment I found myself at sea," Gogol writes in his *Author's Confession,* "on board a foreign ship (the ship was English and there was not another Russian on board), I felt terribly depressed; I was so sorry to leave the friends of my childhood whom I had always loved that even before I felt the firm ground under my feet I was thinking of going back. I spent only three days abroad [he was, in fact, away for six weeks], and although I was beginning to be interested in the strange new things I saw, I hastened to return home, fearing that otherwise I might not return at all."

In Petersburg, Gogol was faced with the necessity of earning a living, for he had returned penniless, having spent not only his meagre allowance, but also the money his mother had sent him to pay the interest on the mortgage of their estate on his ill-starred jaunt abroad. He succeeded at last in getting a small and miserably paid job in the civil service, eking out his salary with translations of articles. In April 1830 he was transferred to a better-paid job in another ministry and spent his leisure time in the summer of that year attending a course of painting at the Petersburg Academy of Art. He also gave private lessons in rich houses, through the intercessions of influential friends, and in 1831 gave up his "idiotic" and "nonsensical" work in the civil service to take a job as history teacher at the Patriotic Institute for Young Ladies. All his free time he now devoted to writing. Having failed as a poet, he turned to prose, and in September 1831 the first volume of his *Evenings on a Farm near Dikanka* appeared and was universally acclaimed with the result that Gogol became a literary figure in Petersburg and, at the age of twenty-two, established a close friendship with Alexander Pushkin and the poet and translator Vasily Zhukovsky, as well as with other famous literary men. His financial position, too, had improved. The second volume of *Evenings on a Farm near Dikanka* was published in March 1832. This volume, which included the stories "The Terrible Vengeance" and "Ivan Fyodorovich Shponka and His Aunt," finally established him as a writer of genius.

In "The Terrible Vengeance," first published with the sub-title "An Old Legend," the conflict between good and evil, which is so characteristic of Gogol's writings even in what was later to become known as his "naturalistic" period, finds its most perfect expression. In it he seems to penetrate into the most hidden places of the human mind and reveal the most secret stirrings of the human heart. The two heroic figures in the story, the ideal hero Danilo and his ideal wife Katherine, are helpless against the evil machinations of Katherine's father, the sorcerer, who in his person embodies the two evils most dreaded by mankind: murder and incest. But the sorcerer himself is merely the instrument of a still greater evil: man's treachery to his friends.

The whole story is a remarkable example of Gogol's genius. Not a single fact in it stands up to rational analysis. Even Katherine's age presents the most insuperable difficulties, for, according to the story, she is at most eighteen, while if other facts, such as her father's long absence, his murder of her mother, her own memories of her mother, and so on, are pieced together, she would be at least forty. And yet the more incredible each single circumstance is, the more credible does the whole story become, for it contains a world in itself, a world in which the earth, the sun, and the stars, the wood-demons and the water-demons, the quick and the dead form one magic tapestry in which man's life is interwoven with the life of everything on earth —the rivers and the woods, the mountains and the valleys, the birds and the clouds. The whole story is sheer magic, a poet's dream, a fantasy that transcends reality. And the most remarkable thing of all is that against this background of supernatural forces, the forces of good spring to life with such an intensity that they make everything acceptable and credible.

The final triumph of good over evil in this story does not, however, solve the problem of just retribution: the "terrible vengeance" is so terrible because it is based on man-made justice; and if God acquiesces in it, He does so reluctantly, for it lacks the essentials of mercy.

If "The Terrible Vengeance" is the only story in the *Evenings on a Farm near Dikanka* which lacks the comic element, "Ivan Fyodorovich Shponka and His Aunt" is one in which the comic element not only predominates, but also approaches most closely to the humour of Gogol's greatest masterpieces. Indeed, "Shponka" differs radically from the other stories in the two volumes of the *Evenings*. Here for the first time Gogol perfected his typical method of creating character by making the most effective use of the most insignificant details in the daily life of his hero. The story only seems to be unfinished: there is nothing Gogol could have added to make Shponka more intimately known to his readers. His portrait has been painted with the assured brush strokes of an artist of genius.

After publishing the second volume of *Evenings on a Farm near Dikanka*, Gogol paid a visit to his mother's estate, only stopping for a short while in Moscow, where he made a number of friends among the local literary celebrities. He returned to Petersburg in the late autumn of 1832 with his two young sisters, whom he placed at the Patriotic Institute for Young Ladies. History now began to occupy his mind to the exclusion of everything else. He undertook a history of the Ukraine and in July 1834 got himself appointed Assistant Professor of Medieval History at the University of Petersburg. Gogol's career as a university teacher was perhaps one of the greatest failures of his life. Turgenev, who was a student of Petersburg University at the time, described Gogol's position in the lecture room as extremely comic. All the students, Turgenev declared, were convinced that Gogol knew nothing about history. It was easy to see that Gogol himself was bored and that he realised that his students, too, were bored. Gogol complained that his students refused to listen to his lectures. "I read my lectures," he wrote to a friend, "but no one listens to me. Oh, if only one student would take the trouble to understand me!" Gogol gave up his lectureship at the end of 1835. "Unrecognised I entered the lecture room," he wrote, "and unrecognised I left it. But in these eighteen months—inglorious months for everyone agrees that I have undertaken something I have no ability for—I have learnt a great deal. . . . Long live comedy! At last I have made up my mind to put one on the stage!"

The comedy was *The Government Inspector*. For, balked in his ambition to achieve fame as an historian, Gogol spent all his leisure time writing. In addition to *The Government Inspector*, he was working on his collection of short stories and critical essays *Arabesques*, published in 1835, and on his other collection of short stories, published in the same year under the title of *Mirgorod*.

The miscellany, *Arabesques*, included Gogol's stories "The Portrait" and "Nevsky Avenue," which, too, deal mainly with the problems of good and evil. In the original version of "The Portrait" the supernatural mechanism, so characteristic of Gogol's first stories, was given full play, but in the second version (included in this volume), published in 1842, Gogol had removed most of the "demonic" elements. While eliminating most of the fantastic features of the story, however, Gogol could not very well change its main feature, namely the existence of evil outside man and man's helplessness against it. Its influence on his hero's career, though, is confined only to supplying him with the means of his spiritual and ultimately physical self-destruction—money. The story, therefore, deals mainly with evil as expressed in man's lust for money and the dire effect this lust has on art, though the mysterious disappearance of the portrait of the evil moneylender does carry the idea of evil as a separate entity to its logical conclusion.

"Nevsky Avenue" marks a transition in the development of Gogol's art. Here the conflict between good and evil is shifted from man's blind subjection to the forces of evil to the incompatibility of man's idealised conception of life with reality. The idealist artist who falls in love with a girl he meets on Nevsky Avenue, whom he afterwards discovers to be a common prostitute, refuses to accept reality and prefers to live in a dream world of his own in which the girl he loves appears as the direct opposite of what she is —with the inevitable tragic results.

But this story is also important because here, as in "Shponka," Gogol emerges as the great realistic writer that he was afterwards to become. The artist, it is true, is still a highly romantic figure, but his friend, Lieutenant Pirogov, is no longer treated romantically. He is one of the most realistic portraits Gogol ever painted, and it is its realism that Dostoevsky admired so much. "This naive impudence and self-conceit of a fool," Dostoevsky writes in *The Idiot*, "are marvellously depicted by Gogol in his wonderful portrait of Lieutenant Pirogov."

Before going abroad for the second time (this time because of the storm raised by *The Government Inspector,* performed for the first time on April 19, 1836), Gogol wrote two more stories, "The Nose" and "The Carriage," both in his best satiric genre and both published in Pushkin's quarterly, *The Contemporary Review,* in 1836. "The Nose," a biting exposure of the snobbery, self-complacency, and stupidity of the Russian upper classes, Gogol wrote specially for the *Moscow Observer,* a new periodical published by some of his Moscow friends. But they sent it back to him because in their view it was too "sordid." This story brought Gogol for the first time into open conflict with the censorship. "If the stupid censorship should object to the fact that the 'nose' pays a visit to the Kazan Cathedral," Gogol wrote to a friend, "I might take him to a Catholic church. But I can't believe it has lost its senses to such an extent." But the censorship did object to the scene in the Kazan Cathedral and Gogol had to send his "nose" to the Shopping Arcade instead. The original text of the story has been restored only recently.

The subject of "The Overcoat" was suggested to Gogol at a tea party in Petersburg. One of his friends told an amusing story of a poor civil servant who had a passion for shooting game birds. Unfortunately, he had no money to buy a shotgun. For years he stinted himself, saving up all he could from his meagre salary till one day he had enough money to buy the gun he had so passionately desired to possess. But on his first shooting expedition in the Finnish Bay he dropped the gun into some reeds and was unable to retrieve it. The poor man took the loss of his gun so much to heart that he fell ill. He was saved from death by the generosity of his colleagues at the office who made a collection among themselves and bought him a new gun. The story made everybody laugh, everybody, that is, except Gogol. To the amazement of the whole company, Gogol lowered his head, looking sad and dejected; he felt pity for the civil servant. The plot of "The Overcoat" was already stirring in his mind. But he was not to write the story till 1841 during his second sojourn in Rome, and it was published in the third volume of the first edition of his collected works in 1842.

Gogol draws the character of the inoffensive civil servant, the hero of "The Overcoat," with a compassion, simplicity, gentle humour, and seeming casualness of style that makes it one of the greatest achievements of his genius. With this story Gogol began a new chapter in Russian literature in which the underdog and social misfit is treated not as a nuisance, or a figure of fun, or an object of charity, but as a human being who has as much right to happiness as anyone else. As regards what Gogol himself called "the fantastic ending" of the story, it does not, like the fantastic elements in Gogol's earlier stories, enforce a "suspension of disbelief." Indeed, Gogol's contemporaries seemed to have interpreted the stealing of the overcoat from the Very Important Person by Akaky's ghost as the fate awaiting the Russian ruling class if it did not repent of its ways, an interpretation that most certainly did not occur to Gogol but that seems to have been justified by the events of less than a hundred years later.

The last ten years of Gogol's life were bitterly frustrating. Gogol's literary career covers a period of only about eleven years, the first volume of *Evenings on a Farm near Dikanka* having been published in 1831 and the first part of *Dead Souls* in 1842. Gogol himself admits as much in his *Author's Confession*. "Several times, accused of idleness," he writes, "I took up my pen forcing myself to write a short story or any other literary work, but I could not produce anything. Almost every time all my efforts ended in sickness, suffering, and, finally, in such attacks that as a result of them I was forced to put off all my work for a long time. What was I to do? Was it my fault that I was no longer able to repeat what I had written in the days of my youth? And if every man is subject to these inevitable changes as he passes from one age to another, why should a writer be an exception to this rule? Is not a writer also a man? I never turned aside from my path. I always walked along the same road. My subject was always the same: my subject was life, and nothing else."

Gogol's illness seems to have been due chiefly to his inability to reconcile his belief in literature as a moral force with the fact that his own writings had not only failed to destroy the evils from which his country was suffering but had actually supplied the Russian radicals with ammunition against a system of society in which he believed. For Gogol himself was a dyed-in-the-wool conservative who believed in the sanctity of the throne and in what he conceived to be the patriarchal way of life. To him serfdom, for instance, was part and parcel of this patriarchal way of life, and he regarded its abolition as a step towards the destruction of that system. He therefore became obsessed with the idea that he could repair the damage his earlier works had wrought by the two remaining parts of *Dead Souls,* in which he would contrive to show how his country could be saved by a return to the Christian ideals of brotherly love. In attempting to do this, however, the artist in him came into violent conflict with the moralist. His work on the second part of *Dead Souls* did not progress, and in the summer of 1845 he burnt all the chapters of that part and started work afresh. In the meantime the feeling that the "high destiny" of which he had dreamt as a boy had not been fulfilled made him publish in 1846 his *Selected Passages from the Correspondence with My Friends,* a collection of essays in the form of letters in which he discussed politics, religion, and literature in the manner of a man laying down the law. This book produced a veritable storm in Russia. From his deathbed the critic Belinsky hurled a thunderbolt at Gogol's head, accusing him of black reaction and calling him "a preacher of the whip, an apostle of ignorance, a defender of obscurantism, and a panegyrist of Tartar customs." Belinsky's "Letter to Gogol," which was immediately suppressed by the authorities, was directly responsible for Dostoevsky's arrest and imprisonment in Siberia, Dostoevsky having read it to a meeting of radicals in Petersburg. Gogol's efforts to save his country certainly had the most unpredictable consequences. But the unkindest cut of all was that Gogol's political supporters in Russia had also turned against him. To them Gogol's rather naive blending of religious mysticism and politics at a time when the whole of Europe was in a revolutionary ferment was a political blunder of the first order, and they told him to mind his own business and leave politics to those who knew something about it. Gogol replied to these criticisms by writing his *Author's Confession* in 1847, but he did not publish it. At last the truth dawned on him and in a letter to Zhukovsky he ruefully admitted that "as a matter of fact preaching is not my business. My business is to speak with living images and not with arguments. I must present life as it is and not write essays about it."

Unhappily Gogol could no longer present "life as it is." For he was getting more and more obsessed with the idea that he had been called upon to regenerate Russia. His natural predisposition to melancholy and his mystical bent grew apace till they took entire possession of him. He had always been a valetudinarian and a melancholic. Now he became obsessed with his imaginary illnesses, rushing all over Europe in an effort to obtain a cure for them. He ended by going on a pilgrimage to the Holy Land, but to his horror he discovered that during the Easter service in the Church of the Holy Sepulchre his thoughts wandered and the spirit of grace did not descend upon him. He returned to Moscow in 1848, still pegging away at the second volume of *Dead Souls*. When his confessor, Father Matthew Konstantinovsky, a Rzhev priest, demanded that he should renounce his literary work and enter a monastery, Gogol replied: "Not to write means the same to me as not to live." And he meant it. For when on the night of February 12 he burnt for the second time the completed chapters of the second volume of *Dead Souls* he pronounced by this act a sentence of death on himself. Indeed, he immediately pro-

ceeded to starve himself to death. Neither the exhortations
of priests nor the efforts of his doctors were of any avail. He
died on February 21, 1852, a month before his forty-third
birthday.

D. M.

The Terrible
Vengeance

I

THE OUTSKIRTS of Kiev resounded to the din of a wedding feast. The Cossack Captain Gorobetz was celebrating the wedding of his son. A great many people had come as guests to the Captain's house. In the old days they liked to eat well, they liked even more to drink, and most of all they liked to enjoy themselves. The Dnieper Cossack Mikitka was among the guests. He arrived on his sorrel horse straight from a wild orgy in the Pereshlyaye Plain where for seven days and seven nights he had been regaling the Polish king's gentlemen with red wine. Among the guests, too, was Danilo Burulbash, the Captain's sworn brother, who came with his young wife Katherine and his year-old son from the other side of the Dnieper where his farmstead lay tucked away in a fold between two hills. The wedding guests marvelled at the fair face of Katherine, her eyebrows black as German velvet, her handsome dress of fine cloth and blouse of blue silk, her boots with silver-shod heels; but they marvelled still more that her old father had not come with her. He had been living for no more than a year in the Cossack country beyond the Dnieper. For twenty-one years there had been no news of him, and he returned to his daughter only after she was married and had borne a son. He would no doubt have told many wonderful stories of his adventures. He had been away so long in foreign parts that it would be strange indeed if he had no tales to tell! Everything is different there; the people are different, and there are no Christian churches . . . But he had not come. They gave the guests a strong drink of vodka and mead with raisins and plums and on a large dish a round white loaf of fine bread made with butter and eggs. The musicians tried the loaf first, concentrating their attention on the lower crust, for there were coins baked in it; and, falling silent for a while, they put aside their cymbals, fiddles and tambourines. Meanwhile the young matrons and girls, having wiped their mouths with their embroidered kerchiefs, stepped out again into the middle of the room; the young men, arms akimbo and looking proudly about them, were ready to dash forward to meet them—when the old Captain brought out two icons to bless the young couple. Those icons had been given to him by the venerable hermit, Father Bartholomew. They had no rich ornaments, there was no glitter of gold or silver on them; but no evil power dare come near the man in whose house they were. Having raised the icons, the Captain was about to utter a brief prayer, when all at once the children who were playing on the floor became frightened and began to cry loudly, and after them the people in the room shrank back, and they all pointed their fingers in alarm at a Cossack who was standing among them. No one knew who he was. But he had already danced through a Cossack reel to everybody's delight and he had raised many a laugh among the people who gathered round him. But when the Captain lifted up the icons, the Cossack's face underwent a sudden transformation: his nose grew longer and twisted to one side, his eyes began to roll wildly and their colour changed from brown to green, his lips turned blue, his chin shook and became pointed like a spear, a long tusk grew out of his mouth, a hump raised itself from behind his head, and in a twinkling the Cossack turned into an old man.

"That's him! That's him!" shouts were raised in the crowd as they all huddled together.

"The sorcerer has appeared again!" the mothers cried, snatching up their children.

Solemnly and with great dignity the Cossack Captain stepped forward and, turning the icons towards the sorcerer, said in a loud voice, "Vanish out of sight, image of Satan! There is no room for you here!"

With a hiss and a snap like a wolf, the mysterious old man vanished. A hubbub of voices rose in the room, like the roar of the sea in a storm, each expressing his own opinion or hazarding his own guess.

"What sorcerer is this?" young and ignorant people asked.

"There's going to be trouble!" the old men were saying to each other, shaking their heads.

Everywhere, in every corner of the Cossack Captain's spacious forecourt, the people gathered in small groups and listened to the story of the mysterious sorcerer. But almost every other man was telling a different tale, and no one knew anything certain about him. A cask of mead was rolled out into the yard, and there were gallons of Greek wine besides. Everybody grew merry again. The musicians struck up a dance tune; the girls, the young matrons and the brave Cossacks in their bright Ukrainian coats were soon caught up in the dance. The ninety-year-olds and the hundred-year-olds, having had a drop too much, jigged about too, not satisfied idly to remember the years that had passed. They feasted far into the night, and feasted as people no longer feast nowadays. By and by the guests began to disperse, but only a few went home. Many of them stayed to spend the night in the Captain's large courtyard, and many more Cossacks dropped to sleep, uninvited, on the floor, or under the benches, or by their horses, or near the barn: wherever a Cossack's head, heavy with drink, dropped, there the Cossack lay, snoring for all Kiev to hear.

II

A soft light shone all over the world: that was the moon which had appeared from behind a hill. It covered the hilly bank of the Dnieper as with a costly damask muslin, white as snow, and the shadows drew back further into the dense pine woods.

A large boat was gliding in midstream. Two Cossack oarsmen sat in front, their black Cossack caps cocked on one side, and from beneath the oars spray flew in all directions like sparks from a flint. Why did the Cossacks not sing? Why did they not speak about the Catholic priests who went about the Ukraine, converting the Cossack people into Catholics? Why did they not tell about the hard-won battle with the Tartars at the Salt Lake which had gone on for two days? But how could they be expected to sing or to speak of acts of bravery when their master Danilo sat brooding, the sleeve of his crimson coat trailing in the water? Their mistress, Katherine, was gently rocking her child, and not for one moment did she take her eyes off it, while the spray like grey dust descended upon her fine dress, unprotected by a boat cover.

How beautiful the high hills, the broad meadows, and the green woods are when seen from the middle of the Dnieper! Those hills are not hills: they seem to float in the air, sharp-pointed above as below, and under them and above them is the towering sky. Those woods on the hills are not woods: they are the hair which grows on the shaggy head of the wood-demon; under the wood-demon's head his beard is being rinsed in the water, and both under his beard and over his head is the towering sky. Those meadows are not meadows: they are a green girdle encircling the round sky, and the moon is taking a stroll in both the upper and lower halves.

Danilo gazed neither to the right nor to the left; he gazed on his young wife.

"Why are you so sad, my dearest Katherine?"

"I am not sad, Danilo. The strange stories about the sorcerer have filled my heart with dread. They say that when he was born he was a terrifying sight . . . and no small child would play with him. Listen, Danilo. They tell such dreadful things about him. They say he always imagines people are laughing at him. If he meets a man on a dark night, he immediately thinks the stranger is grinning at him. Next day that man is found dead. As I listened to those stories, I was filled with dreadful forebodings, Danilo; I felt frightened," said Katherine, taking out a kerchief and wiping the face of the child who slept peacefully in her lap.

Not a word from Danilo, who was scanning the dark bank of the river where, in the distance, an earthen mound could be seen rising like a black shadow from behind the wood, and behind the mound rose the dark pile of an old castle. Three deep wrinkles suddenly appeared above Danilo's eyebrows; his left hand stroked his handsome moustaches.

"It isn't that he is a sorcerer that worries me," he said. "What worries me is that he is here for some evil purpose. What did he want to come here for at all? I'm told the Poles intend to build some kind of fortress to cut off our way to the Dnieper Cossacks. There may be some truth in it. . . . I shall destroy his devilish lair if any rumour reaches me that he is using it as a hiding-place for our enemies. I shall burn the old sorcerer himself so that there won't be anything left of him for the crows to pick. I wonder if he has any gold or other treasures, though. Look, that's where the old devil lives! If he has gold . . . We shall soon row past some crosses—that's the cemetery where the bones of his wicked forebears are rotting. I'm told all of them were ready to sell themselves to Satan for a groat—soul, and tattered old coat, and all. If he really has gold, there's no time to lose: it's something you can't always get in war. . . ."

"I know what you're thinking of. I fear no good will come of it if you meet. But what's the matter? Why are you breathing so hard? Why are you looking at me so fiercely? Why are you frowning on me so?"

"Hold your tongue, woman!" Danilo said angrily. "Have anything to do with you, and before I know where I am I'll be talking and acting like a woman myself! I say, one of you lads, let me have a light for my pipe, will you?" he addressed one of the oarsmen, who knocked some hot ash from his pipe into his master's. "Not trying to frighten me with a sorcerer, are you?" Danilo went on. "A Cossack, thank God, fears neither devil nor Catholic priest. Much good would it do us if we started listening to our wives. Am I not right, lads? The best wife for us is our pipe and our sharp sword!"

Katherine made no reply. She turned away and began watching the sleepy river. The wind raised a ripple on the water and the Dnieper gleamed like a wolf's coat at night. The boat turned and kept close to the wooded bank. A cemetery came into sight; the tumbledown crosses stood huddled together. No guelder-rose grows among them, nor does green grass grow under them; the moon alone sheds its ghostly light upon them from high up in the sky.

"Do you hear the shouts, lads? Someone's calling for our help!" said Danilo, turning to his oarsmen.

"We can hear the cries, sir. They seem to be coming from over there," the oarsmen replied in one voice, pointing to the cemetery.

But everything grew quiet again. The boat turned and began to go round the bend of the projecting bank. Suddenly the oarsmen dropped their oars and stared before them without moving. Danilo stopped, too; his blood ran cold with horror.

A cross on one of the graves swayed giddily and a withered corpse rose slowly from it. A beard to the waist; long nails on the fingers, longer than the fingers themselves. The dead man raised his hands slowly upwards. His face twitched and was twisted. One could see that he was suffering terrible agonies. "Give me air! Air!" he moaned in a wild, inhuman voice, which cut one's heart like a knife.

Then, suddenly, the dead man disappeared under the earth. Another cross swayed and again a dead man rose up from the ground, taller and more terrible than the one before. He was covered with hair all over. His beard reached to the knees, and his claws were even longer. "Give me air!" he cried still more wildly, and disappeared under the ground. A third cross swayed; a third dead man rose up. It seemed as if only bare bones rose up high over the earth. His beard reached down to his heels; the long nails of his fingers pierced the ground. Terribly did he extend his hands upwards, as if he wished to seize the moon, and he shrieked, as if someone were sawing his yellow bones.

The child, asleep in Katherine's lap, screamed and woke up. The oarsmen let fall their caps in the river. Even Danilo himself could not suppress a shudder.

Suddenly it all vanished, as if it had never been; but it was not for some time that the oarsmen took up their oars again. Burulbash looked anxiously at his young wife, who, terrified, was rocking the screaming child on her lap, and he pressed her to his heart and kissed her on the forehead.

"Don't be frightened, Katherine! Look, there's nothing there!" he said, pointing in every direction. "It's the sorcerer who wants to frighten people so that no one should go near his foul nest. He'll scare none but women by these tricks of his! Come, let me take my son!" With these words, Danilo picked up his son and kissed him. "Well, what do you say, Ivan? You're not afraid of any sorcerers, are you? Now say, 'Daddy, I'm a Cossack!' There, there; stop crying! We shall be home soon, then your mother will give you your porridge, put you to bed in your cradle, and sing:

> 'Lullaby my own dear heart,
> Lullaby my own dear darling,
> Grow up, my son, to be our joy,
> To be the Cossacks' pride and glory,
> And our enemies to destroy!'

Listen, Katherine," he addressed his young wife; "it seems to me that your father does not want to live at peace with us. When he arrived he looked harsh and sullen, as though he were angry with us. . . . Well, if he's not pleased, why come at all? He would not drink to the freedom of the Cossacks. He has never dandled the baby! In the beginning I would have confided all my secrets to him, but for some reason I couldn't bring myself to do it: the words stuck in my throat. . . . No, Katherine, he hasn't a Cossack's heart. When Cossack hearts meet, they almost leap out of the breast to greet each other. Well, lads, how far is the bank? Don't worry about your caps. I shall get you new ones. You, Stetsko, I'll give you one made of velvet and gold. I took it off a Tartar, together with his head. Got all his trappings, too. The only thing I let go was his soul. Well, let's land here. Look, Ivan, we're home and you're still crying! Take him, Katherine!"

They all got out. From behind a hill a thatched roof came into view: that was Danilo's family mansion. Beyond it was another hill, and beyond that the open plain, and there you might walk a hundred miles and not meet a single Cossack.

III

Danilo's farmstead lay between two hills in a narrow valley that ran down to the Dnieper. His country seat was not large. His cottage looked like the cottage of any humble Cossack, and there was only one big room in it; but he and his wife and their old maidservant and ten picked young men lived there without feeling cramped. There were oak shelves high up on the walls, on which were piled bowls, pots and pans, silver goblets and drinking cups mounted in gold, both gifts and war booty. Lower down hung costly muskets, sabres, harquebuses, spears. They had come to him, willingly or unwillingly, from Tartars, Turks, and Poles. That was the reason why many of them were notched and dented. Each mark on the steel served to remind Danilo of some bitter encounter with an enemy. Along the bottom of the wall were smooth oak benches. Beside them, in front of the low stove, the cradle hung on cords from a ring fixed in the ceiling. The entire floor of the room was levelled smooth and smeared with clay. Danilo and his wife slept on the benches; the old maidservant on the low stove; the child played and was lulled to sleep in the cradle; and the fighting men slept one beside the other on the floor. But a Cossack likes best to sleep on the bare ground in the open air. He needs neither feather-bed nor pillows. He spreads a pile of fresh hay under his head and stretches at his ease upon the ground. He feels happy when on wakening in the middle of the night he looks up at the lofty sky studded with stars, and shivers at the chill of night which brings fresh vigour to his Cossack bones. Stretching and muttering through his sleep, he lights his pipe and wraps himself more closely in his warm sheepskin.

Burulbash did not waken early after the merry-making of the night before. When he woke, he sat on a bench in a corner, sharpening a new Turkish sabre he had exchanged for something or other; and Katherine set to work embroidering a silk towel with gold thread. All of a sudden Katherine's father came in, angry and frowning, with an outlandish pipe between his teeth. He went up to his daughter and began questioning her sternly why she had come home so late the night before.

"You'd better question me and not her about such matters," said Danilo, going on with his work. "Not the wife, but the husband is responsible. If you don't mind, this is our way here. In some infidel country perhaps it isn't so— I don't know."

The colour came into his father-in-law's stern face and his eyes flashed ominously.

"Who if not a father should look after his daughter?" he muttered to himself. "Well, I ask you. Where were you gadding about so late last night?"

"Ah, that's better, dear father-in-law! I can easily answer that. You see, I am no longer a baby. I can sit on a horse. I can hold a sharp sword in my hands. And I can do something else: I can refuse to answer to any man for whatever I do!"

"I can see, Danilo, that what you want is to pick a quarrel with me. A man who has something to hide is quite certainly hatching some dastardly plot in his head."

"Think as you please," said Danilo, "and I shall think as I please. Thank God, I've never been a party to any dishonourable action so far. I've always stood up for the Orthodox faith and for my country, not like some vagabonds I know who gad about heaven knows where while good Christians are fighting to the death, and then drop from the sky to reap the harvest they have not sown. They're much worse than the Uniats, I'm sure, for they never visit the church of God. It's such people who should be made to give an account of themselves."

"Ah, what a pity, Cossack, I'm such a bad shot; my bullet only pierces the heart at two hundred yards. I'm afraid I'm not much of a swordsman, either; I always leave some bits and pieces of my man behind, although it's quite true they are not bigger than the grits they use for porridge."

"I'm ready," said Danilo, making the sign of the cross smartly in the air with his sabre, as though he knew what he had sharpened it for.

"Danilo!" Katherine cried aloud, seizing him by the arm and hanging on it. "Think what you're doing, you madman! See against whom you're lifting your hand! Father, your hair is white as snow, and you're as hotheaded as a foolish boy!"

"Wife," Danilo exclaimed angrily, "you know I brook no interference! You mind your woman's business!"

The sabres clashed terribly: steel struck against steel, and the Cossacks sent sparks flying like dust. Weeping, Katherine went to another room, flung herself upon the bed and covered her ears that she might not hear the clash of the sabres. But the Cossacks did not fight so badly that she could smother the sound of their blows. Her heart was ready to break. Each sound made by the sabres seemed to go right through her. "No, I can't bear it; I can't bear it. . . . Red blood is perhaps gushing out of his body this very minute. My dear one may even now be bleeding to death, and I'm lying here!" And, pale as death, scarcely breathing, she went back.

The Cossacks fought a terrible, but well-matched battle. Neither got the better of the other. Now Katherine's father pressed home his attack, and Danilo gave way; now Danilo attacked, and the dour old man yielded ground; and again they were equal. But their blood was up. They swung their sabres, slashing out at each other with all their might, and, with a noise like thunder, the blades broke off at the handles and flew out of their hands.

"I thank you, I thank you, O Lord!" cried Katherine, but she screamed again when she saw that the Cossacks picked up their muskets.

They set the flints, drew the triggers. Danilo fired and missed. Katherine's father took aim. . . . He was old; he could not see as well as a young man, but his hand did not falter. A shot rang out. Danilo staggered. Red blood stained the left sleeve of his Cossack coat. "No," he cried, "I shan't sell myself as cheap as that. Not the left, but the right hand is master. There on the wall hangs my Turkish pistol; never before has it failed me. Come down from the wall, old comrade! Do your friend a service!"

Danilo stretched out his hand to take the gun.

"Danilo!" cried Katherine in despair, clutching his hands and flinging herself on the floor at his feet. "Not for myself do I beseech you. There can be only one end for me: unworthy is the wife who outlives her husband. The cold Dnieper will be my grave. . . . But look at your son, Danilo; look at your son! Who will cherish the poor child? Who will fondle him? Who will teach him to outstrip the wind on his black stallion, to fight for faith and freedom, to drink and be merry like a true Cossack? Oh, my son, you must perish, you must perish utterly! Your father does not care for you. Look how he turns away his head. Oh, now I know you! You're a wild beast and not a man! You have the heart of a wolf and the mind of a crafty serpent. I thought that there was a drop of pity in your veins, that there was human feeling in that heart of stone of yours! What a fool I was! I suppose it will make you happy, your bones will dance in the grave with joy, when you hear the dastardly brutes of Poles throwing your son into the flames, when your son shrieks under the knife and the burning pitch. Oh, I know you! You would be glad to rise from your grave and fan the flames under him with your cap!"

"Stay, Katherine. Come, my precious Ivan; let me kiss you! No, my child, no one shall touch a hair of your head. You shall grow up to the glory of your country; you shall fly like a whirlwind at the head of the Cossacks, with a fine velvet cap on your head and a sharp sabre in your hand. Give me your hand, Father! Let us forget our quarrel. If I have wronged you, I am sorry. Why do you not give me your hand?" said Danilo to Katherine's father, who stood without moving, showing no sign either of anger or reconciliation.

"Father," cried Katherine, embracing and kissing him, "please don't be so merciless. Forgive Danilo. He will never offend you again."

"For your sake only I forgive him, daughter," he replied, kissing her, a strange glitter in his eyes.

Katherine shuddered faintly; the kiss and the strange glitter in his eyes seemed uncanny to her. She leaned her elbows on the table, at which Danilo was bandaging his wounded arm, wondering if he had done right and like a Cossack in asking forgiveness for something for which he was not to blame.

IV

Day dawned, but there was no sunshine: the sky was overcast and a drizzling rain was falling on the fields, the woods and the broad Dnieper. Katherine woke up, but she did not feel happy: her eyes were tear-stained, and she was restless and vaguely alarmed.

"Oh, dear husband," she said, "I have had such a strange dream!"

"What kind of dream, my darling Katherine?"

"Oh, such a queer dream, and it was as plain as though it were really happening. I dreamt that my father was the very same monster whom we saw at the Captain's house. But please don't pay any attention to this dream. People dream all sorts of silly things! I dreamed that I was standing before him, shivering and frightened, my whole body tortured by every word he spoke. Oh, if only you had heard what he said. . . ."

"What did he say, my precious Katherine?"

"He said, 'Look at me, Katherine! Am I not a handsome man? People talk nonsense when they say that I am ugly. I should make you a fine husband! Look at me, Katherine! Look at my eyes! Can't you see anything there?' Then he looked at me with those fiery eyes of his, and I screamed and woke up."

"Yes, there's much truth in dreams. However, do you know that things aren't so quiet beyond the hills? I shouldn't be surprised if the Poles didn't show up again. Gorobetz has warned me to keep my eyes open. But he needn't have troubled. I am not asleep as it is. My lads have been felling trees during the night and put up a dozen barricades. We shall welcome the soldiers of the Polish king with lead plums and we shall make his gentlemen dance with our sticks!"

"And Father . . . Does he know about this?"

"What do I care whether your father knows about it or not? I'm damned if I can make him out even now. I suppose he must have committed many sins in foreign lands. How else can you explain the way he behaves? He has lived with us for over a month and not once has he made merry like a true Cossack. He would not drink any mead! Do you hear, Katherine, he would not drink the mead I extorted from those cowardly Jews in Brest! Here, lad," exclaimed Danilo, "go down to the cellar, there's a good fellow, and bring me some of that Jewish mead! He won't even drink vodka! The

devil take it, I do believe, Katherine, he doesn't even believe
in the Lord Jesus. Eh? What do you say?"

"The Lord forgive you, Danilo! What are you saying?"

"It certainly is strange, my dear," Danilo went on, taking
the earthenware beaker from the Cossack. "Even the
damned Catholics are partial to vodka. It's only the Turks
who do not drink. Well, Stetsko, did you have a good sip of
mead in the cellar?"

"I just tasted it, sir."

"Tasted it, did you? You lie, you son of a dog! See how
the flies have fallen upon your moustache. I bet you've had
at least half a bucketful. I can see it in your eyes, my lad.
Oh, these Cossacks! What desperate rogues! Ready to
share everything with a comrade, except the bottle; they'll
drain that to the last drop themselves! You know, Katherine,
it's a long time since I was really drunk. Eh?"

"A long time indeed! Why, last . . ."

"All right, all right! Don't be alarmed! I won't drink more
than a beakerful. Here's that Turkish abbot barging through
the door!" he muttered through his teeth, seeing his father-
in-law stooping to get through the door.

"What's the matter, daughter?" the father said, taking
off his cap and adjusting his belt, on which hung a sabre
set with precious stones. "The sun's already high and your
dinner isn't ready!"

"Dinner's ready, Father. It will be served in a minute.
Bring the pot with the dumplings!" Katherine said to the
old maidservant, who was wiping the wooden bowls. "Wait,
I'd better take it out myself," she went on. "You call the
men!"

They all sat down on the floor in a ring: Katherine's father facing the corner with the icons, Danilo on his left,
Katherine on his right, and ten of Danilo's most trusty men
in blue and yellow coats.

"I don't like these dumplings," said Katherine's father,
after eating a little, laying down the spoon. "There's no
flavour in them."

"I daresay you like Jewish stew better," thought Danilo.

"Why do you say there's no flavour in the dumplings?" he went on aloud. "They're not badly made, are they? My Katherine makes dumplings such as our hetman himself does not often taste. And there's no need to despise them. It's a Christian dish. All God's saints and holy men have eaten dumplings."

Katherine's father was silent. Danilo, too, kept his peace. They served wild boar with cabbage and plums.

"I don't like pork," said Katherine's father, helping himself to some cabbage with his spoon.

"Why don't you like pork?" said Danilo. "It's only Turks and Jews who do not eat pork."

Katherine's father knit his brows, looking more angry than ever. He ate nothing but some buckwheat pudding and milk and, instead of vodka, he sipped some black liquid from a flask he kept inside his coat.

After dinner Danilo had a good sleep and only woke at dusk. He sat down at the table to write letters to the Cossack army, while Katherine sat on the low stove, rocking the cradle with her foot. As he sat there, Danilo kept his left eye on his writing and looked out of the window with his right; from the window he could see far in the distance the shining hills and the Dnieper. Beyond the Dnieper stretched the blue ridge of the woods. Overhead glimmered the clear night sky. But it was not the far-away sky or the blue woods that Danilo was admiring: he was watching the spit of land which jutted out into the river and on which the dark mass of the old castle could be made out. He thought he could see a light gleaming in the narrow little window of the castle. But all was quiet. He must have imagined it. All he could hear was the hollow murmur of the Dnieper down below and, from three sides, the resounding thuds of the waves which suddenly came to life. The river was not in its defiant mood. Like an old man, it was merely growling and grumbling. Nothing pleased it. Everything about it had changed. Softly it was waging a war against the hills, the woods and the meadows on its banks.

Now the dark outline of a boat appeared on the wide

expanse of the Dnieper and again a light gleamed and dis-appeared in the castle. Danilo gave a low whistle, and his faithful servant ran in at the sound.

"Stetsko," said Danilo, "grab a sharp sabre and a musket and follow me!"

"Are you going out?" asked Katherine.

"Yes, I'm going out. I have to inspect everything. See that everything's in order."

"But I'm afraid to be left alone. I'm so sleepy, I can't keep awake. What if I should have the same dream again? I am not even sure it was a dream. It seemed so real."

"The old woman will be staying with you and there are Cossacks asleep in the passage and in the courtyard."

"The woman is asleep already and, somehow, I have no confidence in the Cossacks. Listen, Danilo. Lock me in and take the key with you. Then I shan't be afraid. And let the Cossacks lie before the door."

"All right," said Danilo, wiping the dust off his musket and scattering some powder on the gun-lock.

The faithful Stetsko stood already dressed from head to foot in the Cossack harness. Danilo put on his lambskin cap, closed the window, locked and bolted the door, walked quietly out of the courtyard, threading his way among the sleeping Cossacks, and made straight for the hills.

The sky was almost completely clear again. A fresh breeze blew gently from the Dnieper. But for the distant wail of a gull, everything seemed to be dead silent. But soon his ear caught a faint noise. . . . Burulbash and his faithful servant hid quietly behind some bramble bushes which con-cealed one of the barricades of felled trees. Some one in a scarlet coat, with two pistols and a sabre at his side, was coming down the hillside.

"It's my father-in-law," Danilo murmured, watching him from behind the bushes. "Where is he going to at this hour of the night, I wonder? And what is he up to? Don't gape, Stetsko; keep your eyes open and see which way your mis-tress's father takes!"

The man in the scarlet coat went down to the bank of the river and then turned towards the spit of land.

"I thought so," said Danilo. "Gone straight to the sorcerer's den, Stetsko!"

"Yes, sir. Couldn't have gone anywhere else or we should have seen him on the other side. He disappeared near the castle, sir."

"All right, let's get out and follow him. There's something wrong here. Well, Katherine, I warned you that your father was a wicked man. No wonder he never behaves like a true Christian."

Danilo and his trusty servant went quickly across the tongue of land. In another moment they were out of sight. The pitch-black wood around the castle hid them. A soft light appeared at the upper window of the castle. The Cossacks stood below, wondering how to reach it. They could see neither gate nor door. There must be a door in the courtyard; but how were they to get into it? They could hear in the distance the clanking of chains and the dogs running about in the yard.

"Why am I losing time?" said Danilo, seeing a big oaktree by the window. "You stay here," he said to Stetsko, "and I'll climb up the oak; from it I could look straight into the window."

He took off his belt, threw his sabre on the ground, so that it might not clatter, and, catching hold of some branches, lifted himself up. There was still a light at the window. He sat down on a branch close to the window, and, holding on firmly to the tree, he peered in: there was not even a candle in the room and yet it was bathed in a soft light. There were mystic symbols on the walls. Weapons of all kinds were hanging there, but all were strange; neither Turks, nor Crimeans, nor Christians, nor the gallant Swedes ever bore such weapons. Large bats flitted to and fro under the ceiling and their shadows darted over the floor, the door and the walls. Presently the door opened without a sound. Some man in a scarlet coat walked in and went straight up to the table which was covered with a white cloth.

"It is my father-in-law," Danilo murmured, lowering himself a little and clinging closer to the tree.

But his father-in-law was too busy to look whether anyone was watching him through the window. He came in, frowning and out of humour, pulled the cloth off the table, and at once a transparent blue light spread gently through the whole room; but the waves of the pale golden light with which the room had been filled before did not mingle with the blue light, but eddied and dived as in a blue sea and spread out in streaks as though in marble. Then he set a pot on the table and began throwing some herbs into it.

Danilo peered more closely and saw that he was no longer wearing the scarlet coat; instead he was wearing a pair of wide Turkish breeches with pistols in his belt and a strange-looking head-dress inscribed with letters that were neither Russian nor Polish. And even as he looked at his face, his face, too, began to change: his nose grew longer and hung over his lips; in one instant his mouth stretched to his ears; a tooth peeped out from his lips and bent sideways; and he saw before him the same sorcerer who had appeared at the wedding at the Captain's house.

"Your dream was a true dream, Katherine," Danilo thought.

The sorcerer began pacing round the table; the mystic signs on the walls were now changing more rapidly and the large bats flitted more swiftly up and down and to and fro. The blue light grew dimmer and dimmer and at last went out altogether. A tenuous rosy light now filled the room. It seemed to spread through the room to the accompaniment of the soft ringing of bells; then, suddenly, it vanished and darkness covered everything. Nothing was heard but a faint murmur like the gentle whispering of the wind in the peaceful hours of evening as, circling over the mirror-like surface of the water, it bends the silvery willows lower and lower into the waves.

It seemed to Danilo that the moon was shining in the

room and the stars were twinkling, and now and then he
thought he could catch a glimpse of the dark-blue sky, and
he even felt a puff of the cold evening air against his face.
Then Danilo imagined (here he even pulled at his moustache to make sure he was not dreaming) that it was not
the sky he could see in the room, but his own bed-chamber.
There on the walls hung his Tartar and Turkish sabres;
round the walls were the shelves and on the shelves the pots
and bowls and goblets; on the table stood bread and salt;
the cradle hung from the ceiling. . . . But where the icons
were, hideous faces stared; on the low stove . . . but a dense
mist hid everything, and it was dark again, and once again
a rosy light spread through the room to the accompaniment
of the wonderful ringing of bells, and again the sorcerer
stood motionless in his strange turban. The sounds grew
louder and richer, the faint rosy light became brighter, and
something white, like a cloud, hovered in the middle of the
room. And it seemed to Danilo that the cloud was not a
cloud at all, but that a woman was standing there. But
what was she made of? Not of air, surely? And why did
she stand there without touching the floor or leaning on
anything? Why did the rosy light shine through her? Why
were those dancing signs on the wall still visible? Now she
moved her transparent head: her pale blue eyes shone
softly; her hair fell in curls over her shoulders like a light-
grey mist; her lips glowed faintly like the scarcely perceptible red glow of dawn over the white transparent morning
sky; her eyebrows were just two faint dark lines. . . . It
was Katherine! Danilo felt his limbs stiffen. He tried to
speak, but his lips moved without uttering a sound.

The sorcerer still stood motionless in the same place.

"Where have you been?" he asked, and the ethereal figure which stood before him trembled.

"Oh, why did you call me up?" she moaned softly. "I
was so happy. I was in the place where I was born and
where I lived till I was fifteen. Oh, how wonderful it was
there! How green and fragrant was the meadow where I
used to play as a child! And the sweet wild flowers were

the same as ever, and our cottage and the garden! Oh, how my dear mother embraced me! How much love there was in her eyes! She caressed me, kissed my lips and cheeks, combed my fair hair with a fine comb . . . Father," here she fixed her pale eyes on the sorcerer, "why did you murder my mother?"

The sorcerer shook his finger at her menacingly. "Did I bid you speak about it?" he asked, and the ethereal beauty trembled. "Where is your mistress now?"

"My mistress Katherine has fallen asleep, and I was so glad I took wing and flew away. I have yearned to see my mother for such a long time. I was suddenly fifteen again. I felt so light, like a bird. Why have you summoned me?"

"You remember all I said to you yesterday?" asked the sorcerer in so soft a voice that Danilo found it hard to catch his words.

"I remember, but what would I not give to forget it! Poor Katherine, she doesn't know as much as her soul knows, does she?"

"It is Katherine's soul," thought Danilo, but still he dared not stir.

"Repent, Father! Is it not terrible that after every murder you commit the dead rise up from their graves?"

"Don't mention that to me again!" the sorcerer interrupted her menacingly. "I shall insist that you carry out my wish. I shall make you do what I want. Katherine shall love me!"

"Oh, you are a monster and not my father!" she moaned. "No, it shall never be as you wish. It is true that by your evil spells you have the power to summon a soul and torture it, but only God can make it do what He wills. No, never shall Katherine consent to such an ungodly deed while I am still in her body! Father, a terrible judgment is near at hand! Even if you were not my father, you would never make me betray my husband whom I love and who is true to me. But even if my husband was not true and dear to me, I would not be false to him, for God abominates souls who are faithless and false to their vows."

Here she fixed her pale eyes on the window under which Danilo was sitting and fell silent, still as death.

"What are you looking at? Whom do you see there?" cried the sorcerer.

The wraith of Katherine trembled violently. But already Danilo was on the ground and with his faithful Stetsko was on his way to his native hills.

"Terrible, terrible," he murmured to himself, fear gripping his Cossack heart.

He soon reached his own courtyard where his Cossacks slept as soundly as ever, all but one who sat on guard, smoking a pipe.

The sky was all studded with stars.

V

"Oh, I'm so glad you wakened me!" said Katherine, rubbing her eyes with the embroidered sleeve of her nightgown and observing her husband closely as he stood before her. "What a terrible dream I've had! I could hardly breathe. Oh, I thought I was dying!"

"What sort of dream? Not this one by any chance?" and Burulbash started telling his wife all that he had seen.

"But how did you know it?" Katherine asked in amazement when he finished his story. "But no, no! You told me many things I did not know. No, I certainly did not dream that my father had killed my mother. I did not dream anything of the dead rising from their graves, either. No, I did not dream anything of the kind. Danilo, you're making it up. Oh, what a terrible man my father is!"

"And it is no wonder you did not see everything in your dream. You don't know a tenth part of what your soul knows. Do you know that your father is the Antichrist? Last year when I was getting ready to go against the Crimean Tartars with the Poles (at that time those faithless people were still my allies) the Abbot of the Bratsky Monastery—and he is a holy man, my dear, if ever there was one—told me that the Antichrist had the power to summon the soul of every living man; for when the body is asleep, the soul wanders where it pleases and flies with the archangels about the abode of God. I disliked your father's face from the first. I would not have married you, had I known what kind of a father you had. I should have left you and not taken upon my soul the sin of marrying into the Antichrist's family."

"Danilo," Katherine said, burying her face in her hands and bursting into tears, "what wrong have I done to you? Have I been unfaithful to you, my dear husband? Why then are you so angry with me? Have I not served you truly? Have I ever said a cross word to you when you came home merry from some gay feast? Have I not borne you a black-browed son?"

"Don't cry, Katherine. I know you now and I shall never leave you. It is not you, but your father who has sinned so grievously."

"Please, don't call him my father! He is not a father to me! God is my witness that I disown him; I disown my father! He is the Antichrist. He has renounced God. If he were perishing, if he were drowning, I would not stretch out a hand to save him. If he were dying of thirst after eating some magic herb, I would not give him a drop of water. You are my father!"

VI

The sorcerer sat in a deep cellar at Danilo's house behind a door with three locks and with iron chains on his hands and feet. In the distance above the Dnieper his devilish castle was in flames, and the waves, glowing red as blood, surged and broke against the ancient walls. But it was not for sorcery or any ungodly act that the sorcerer lay imprisoned in the deep cellar. God was his judge. It was for an act of secret treachery that he was imprisoned, for plotting with the enemies of the holy Russian soil to sell the Ukrainian people to the Catholics and burn Christian churches. The sorcerer was cast down. Thoughts black as night filled his head. He had only one more day left to live: tomorrow he would have to take leave of the world; tomorrow his punishment was awaiting him. It would be an act of mercy if he were boiled alive in a cauldron or if his sinful skin were flayed off him. The sorcerer was cast down; his head was bowed. Perhaps he was already repenting in his last hour, but his sins were not such as God would forgive him. Above him was a narrow window, interlaced with iron bars. Clanking his chains, he went up to the window to see if his daughter were passing. She was meek and gentle as a dove; she bore no malice against any man. Would she not take pity on her father? But there was not a soul to be seen. Below the window was the road; no one passed along it. Below the road was the Dnieper; but the river cared for no one: it raged and the monotonous sound of its waves made cheerless music for the prisoner.

Then someone appeared on the road. It was a Cossack. The prisoner heaved a deep sigh. Again the road was deserted. In the distance someone was coming down the hill. A woman's coat was fluttering in the wind. A gold headdress glittered on her head. It was she! He pressed still closer to the window. Now she was coming nearer. . . .

"Katherine, my daughter, have pity on me! Help me, help me!"

She made no reply. She would not listen to him. She did not even turn her eyes towards the prison. She had already passed. She was gone. The whole world was empty. Dismally the Dnieper murmured. Sadness stole into the heart at that sound. But did the sorcerer know anything of such sadness?

The day was drawing to a close. The sun had set. In another moment the last gleam of light in the sky was gone. Now it was evening. It was cool. Somewhere an ox was lowing. Sounds of voices floated from somewhere: people returning from the fields and laughing happily. A boat appeared for a brief moment on the Dnieper and was gone again. . . . No one gave a thought to the prisoner. The silver crescent gleamed in the sky. Somebody was coming along the road from the opposite direction. It was hard to tell in the darkness who it might be. It was Katherine coming back.

"Daughter, for Christ's sake spare one glance at your guilty father. Why, even the savage wolf cubs will never tear their mother to pieces!" She paid no attention to him and walked on. "Daughter, for the sake of your unhappy mother . . ." She stopped. "For the sake of your unhappy mother come here and listen to my last words!"

"Why do you call to me, you renegade? Don't call me daughter! I have disowned all kinship with you. What do you want of me for the sake of my unhappy mother?"

"Katherine, my end is near. I know that your husband means to tie me to the tail of a mare and let me be dragged along the fields until I'm dead. He may even think of a more dreadful punishment for me. . . ."

"But is there a punishment in the world bad enough to atone for your sins? Prepare yourself for it; no one will intercede for you."

"Katherine, it is not the punishment that frightens me, but the torments that await me in the next world. . . . You are innocent, Katherine. Your soul will fly in paradise near the abode of God, but the soul of your renegade father will burn in the everlasting fire that will never be quenched; no drop of dew will descend on it, nor will the wind breathe on it. . . ."

"That punishment I have not the power to abate," said Katherine, turning away.

"Katherine, one more word. You can save my soul. You have no idea how good and merciful God is. You must have heard of the Apostle Paul, what a great sinner he was, but afterwards he repented and became a saint."

"What can I do to save your soul?" said Katherine. "It is not for a weak woman like me to think of it!"

"If only I could get out of here, I'd give up everything. I will repent. I will retire to a cave, put on a rough hairshirt, and spend day and night in prayer. I will give up not only meat, but I will not even taste fish. I shall sleep on bare boards, and I shall pray, pray all the time. And if God in His great mercy will not forgive even a hundredth part of my sins, I'll bury myself up to the neck in the earth, or immure myself into a stone wall. I will take neither food nor drink, and I shall die. All my treasures I will distribute among the monks that they may sing a requiem for me for forty days and forty nights."

Katherine thought it over. "Even if I unlocked the door," she said, "I couldn't possibly take off your chains."

"My chains!" he said scornfully. "You think they have chained me hand and foot, don't you? Oh, no. I threw a mist over their eyes and held out a dry piece of wood instead of hands. Here, have a look: there is not a chain on me now!" he said, stepping into the middle of the cellar. "Even these walls would not have stopped me and I would have gone through them. But your husband does not know what walls these are. They were built by a holy hermit and no evil power can release any one from this prison without unlocking the doors with the very same key with which the saint used to lock his cell. Just such a cell I shall build for myself, great sinner that I am, when I am free again!"

"Listen, I will let you out; but what if you deceive me?" said Katherine, stopping before the door. "What if, instead of repenting, you again become the devil's own accomplice?"

"No, Katherine. I have not long to live. My end is near even if I am not put to death. Do you really believe I shall consign myself to eternal perdition?"

The locks rattled. "Farewell, my dear child. May the merciful God keep and preserve you!" said the sorcerer, kissing her.

"Don't touch me, you abominable sinner! Go, go quickly!" said Katherine.

But he was no longer there.

"I let him out," moaned Katherine, terror-stricken and looking wildly at the walls. "What shall I say to my husband now? I am undone. I'd better bury myself alive!" And bursting into tears, she almost fell on the block on which the prisoner had been sitting. "But I have saved his soul," she said softly. "I have done a good deed which cannot but please God. But my husband . . . I have deceived him for the first time. Oh, how terrible! How hard it will be to lie to him! Someone's coming . . . It is he! My husband!" she exclaimed in despair and fell senseless on the ground.

VII

"It's me, you poor darling! It's me, my sweet child!" Katherine heard when she came round.

She looked up and saw her old maidservant. The old woman was bending over her, muttering something, and, stretching out her withered hand, sprinkled cold water over her.

"Where am I?" Katherine said, sitting up and looking round her. "I can hear the Dnieper in front of me and behind me I can see the hills. Where have you brought me, you old hag?"

"I haven't brought you anywhere. I took you out of that stuffy old cellar, I did. Locked it up with the key so that you don't get into trouble with your husband Danilo."

"But where is the key?" said Katherine, looking at her girdle. "I can't see it."

"Why, my poor child, your husband has taken it off to have a look at the sorcerer."

"At the sorcerer? Oh dear, I'm undone!" Katherine cried.

"May the Lord preserve us from such a calamity, my poor darling. Just keep quiet and no one will know anything about it."

"He's escaped, the cursed Antichrist! Do you hear, Katherine, he has escaped!" said Danilo, coming up to his wife.

His eyes blazed angrily; his sabre shook and rattled at his side. Katherine was paralysed with fear.

"Has someone let him out, dear husband?" she asked in a shaking voice.

"He has been let out all right! The devil has let him out! Look, a log is chained to the wall instead of him. Oh, why

did not God make the devil fear a Cossack's strong hands?
If any of my Cossacks had only thought of doing it and I
got to know about it . . . I'd find no punishment bad
enough for him!"

"And if I . . ." The words were out of Katherine's lips
before she knew what she was saying, and she stopped,
aghast.

"If you had taken it into your head to do such a thing,
you'd no longer be my wife. I'd have sewn you up in a sack
and drowned you in the middle of the Dnieper!"

Katherine caught her breath and she felt her hair stand
on end.

VIII

At a roadside inn near the frontier the Poles had gathered, and for the past two days they had been carousing
there. The inn overflowed with the vermin. They had met,
no doubt, for some raid. Some had muskets; spurs were
jingling, sabres rattling. The Polish gentlemen made merry
and bragged, told tales about their marvellous feats of arms,
mocked at the Orthodox Christians, called the Ukrainian
people their serfs, twirled their moustaches with an air of
importance, and with the same arrogant air sprawled on
the benches, their noses turned up. They had a Catholic
priest among them. He drank and revelled with them and
uttered obscene speeches with his foul mouth. The servants
were no better than their masters. They turned back the
sleeves of their tattered coats and strutted about, as if they
were persons of some importance. They played cards, and
struck each other on the nose with the cards. They had
brought with them other men's wives. Shrieks, fights. . . .
The Polish gentlemen, too, ran wild and played all sorts of
silly tricks: they pulled the Jewish innkeeper by the beard,
painted a cross on his impious brow, fired blank shots at
the women, and danced the Cracovienne with their blas-
pheming priest. Even the Tartars had never behaved in so
disgraceful a manner on Russian soil. God must have willed

it that Russia should suffer such indignities for her sins! In the general hubbub people could be heard talking of Danilo's homestead beyond the Dnieper and of his beautiful wife. . . .

The band of cut-throats were not there for any good!

IX

Danilo sat at the table, his head propped up on his hand, thinking. Katherine sat on the low stove, humming a song.

"I don't know why, but I'm feeling sad, Katherine," said Danilo. "My head aches and my heart aches. Oh, I'm so weary, weary! I think my death must be near."

"Why don't you come and put your head on my bosom, dear husband? Why do you harbour such black thoughts?" Katherine thought, but she dared not speak her thoughts aloud. She was too conscious of her guilt to accept her husband's caresses.

"Listen, Katherine," said Danilo, "promise me not to desert our son when I am gone. God will never grant you any happiness either in this world or in the next if you forsake him. Hard will it be for my bones to rot in the damp earth, but harder still will it be for my soul."

"What are you saying, dear husband? Was it not you who laughed at us, weak women? And now you talk like a weak woman yourself. It's much too early for you to talk of death!"

"No, Katherine, I feel that I have not long to live. I don't know, my life is no longer what it used to be. Everything is so sad. Oh, the years of my adventurous youth, how they come back to me! But they have gone for good, never to return. He was living then, the pride and glory of our army, old Konashevich, the Ukrainian hetman! I can still see those Cossack regiments, as though they were passing before my eyes now. Oh, what a glorious time it was, Katherine, what a glorious time! The old hetman sitting on a black horse, his golden mace gleaming in his hand, the soldiers of his regular army standing around him and the red sea of the

Dnieper Cossacks astir on every side! The hetman began to speak and every man in that vast army of foot and horse stood still as if rooted to the ground. The old man wept when he told us of the old days and battles of long ago. Oh, if you only knew, Katherine, how valiantly we fought the Turks in those days! You can still see the scar on my head which I received in those battles. Four bullets pierced me in four places, and not one of the wounds has quite healed. The gold we took in those days! The Cossacks filled their caps with precious stones. What horses, Katherine, oh, what fine horses we drove away with us in those days! Never, never shall I fight like that again! Not that I have grown old or that my body has grown feeble, but the Cossack sword drops out of my hand. There seems nothing more left for me to do, and I don't know what I live for. There is no order in the Ukraine: the colonels and the captains fight each other like dogs. There is no recognised chieftain over them all. Our gentry are aping the Polish fashions and they have also grown crafty as the Poles. They have even sold their souls, accepting the Uniat faith. The Jews are oppressing the poor. . . . Oh, those days, those days, the days that are gone! Where are you, the years of my youth? Here, lad, go to the cellar and bring me a jug of mead. Let me drink to the happy times that have gone and to the years that will never come back!"

"How shall we receive our guests, sir? The Poles are approaching from the direction of the meadow!" said Stetsko, entering the room.

"I know what they are coming for," said Danilo, rising from his seat. "Saddle the horses, my faithful followers! Put on your harness! Out with the sabres! Don't forget your rations of lead! We must prepare a great welcome for our guests!"

But before the Cossacks had time to mount their horses or load their muskets, the Poles covered the hillside as leaves from the trees cover the ground in autumn.

"Oho, there are certainly enough of them here to avenge our injuries!" cried Danilo, looking at the fat Polish gentlemen, who were swaying haughtily on their gold-harnessed horses in the front ranks of the advancing Poles. "It seems that once again I shall be having good sport! Make the best of it, Cossack soul, for the last time. Enjoy yourselves, lads! This is the day we've been waiting for!"

Oh, what sport there was in the hills! What gay revelry! The swords were gambolling, the bullets flying, the horses neighing and prancing. The shouting dazed the brain, the smoke blinded the eye. Everything was in confusion. But a Cossack knew unfailingly where his friend or where his enemy was. A bullet whistled and a gallant rider dropped from the saddle; a sabre flashed and a head rolled in the dust, muttering incoherent words.

But the red top of Danilo's cap could always be seen in the crowd; the golden belt on his blue coat gleamed bright; the mane of his black stallion fluttered in the breeze. He darted hither and thither like a bird, exhorting his followers, waving his Damascus sabre, and cutting down the enemy right and left. Cut them down, Cossack! Have a merry time, Cossack! Cheer your brave heart! Don't look at the gold trappings and the rich coats: trample underfoot the gold and jewels! Spear them, Cossack! Have a merry time, Cossack! But look back! The godless Poles are already setting fire to the cottages and driving away the frightened cattle. And like a whirlwind Danilo turned round, and the cap with the red top was darting now near the cottages and the crowd round him was fast dwindling.

For many hours the Poles fought with the Cossacks. There were not many left of either. But Danilo showed no signs of slackening: with his long spear he knocked Poles out of their saddles and his mettlesome horse trampled more of the enemy underfoot. His courtyard was almost cleared of the enemy; the Poles were taking to their heels; the Cossacks were beginning to strip the dead of their gold coats and rich trappings; Danilo was about to set off in pursuit of the beaten enemy and looked round to call his men—when suddenly he flew into a terrible rage: for he caught sight of Katherine's father. There the sorcerer stood

on the top of a hill, aiming his musket at him. Danilo urged
his horse straight towards him. . . . Cossack, you go to
your doom! . . . There came the crack of a shot, and the
sorcerer vanished behind the hill. Only the faithful Stetsko
caught a glimpse of the scarlet coat and the strange hat.
The Cossack staggered and fell to the ground. The faithful
Stetsko rushed to his master, but his master lay stretched
on the ground, his bright eyes closed. The dark-red blood
spurted from his breast, but he must have become aware
of his faithful servant's presence, for he raised his eyelids
and there was a gleam of recognition in his eyes. "Farewell,
Stetsko. Tell Katherine not to forsake her son, and don't you,
my faithful servants, forsake him, either!" He fell silent. His
gallant soul flew from his noble body; his lips turned blue.
The Cossack slept, never to awaken.

His faithful servant burst out sobbing and waved a hand
to Katherine.

"Come, my lady, come. Your master has had a drop too
much. Here he lies on the damp earth, drunk as a lord. It'll
be a long time before he's sober again!"

Katherine wrung her hands and fell like a sheaf of corn
on the dead body.

"Oh, my husband, is it you lying here with closed eyes?
Get up, my dearest darling; stretch out your sweet hand!
Stand up! Please, look at your Katherine just for once. Open
your lips, say just one little word to me! But you're silent,
you're silent, my noble lord! You have turned blue like the
Black Sea. Your heart beats no more. Why are you so cold,
dear husband? Are not my tears hot enough to warm you?
Is not my weeping loud enough to wake you? Who will
lead your regiments now? Who will ride like a whirlwind
on your black steed? Cry in a mighty voice and wave a
sabre in front of the Cossacks? Oh, Cossacks, Cossacks!
Where is your pride and glory? Your pride and glory is
lying with closed eyes on the damp earth. Bury me in the
same grave as him, bury me with him, I pray! Heap earth
upon my eyes! Press the maple boards upon my white
breasts! I need my beauty no more!"

Katherine wailed and mourned; but a cloud of dust was rising over the road in the distance: old Captain Gorobetz was galloping to the rescue.

X

The Dnieper is beautiful on a calm day when it glides along in full flood, unconstrained and unruffled, through woods and hills. There is not a ripple; not a sound. You look and you cannot tell whether its majestic expanse is moving or not moving, and you almost fancy that it is all made of glass and that, like a blue, mirror-surfaced road, measureless in breadth and endless in length, it winds and twists over a green world. On such a day even the bright sun likes to have a peep at it from its great height and dip its hot beams into its cool glassy waters; and the woods along the banks appear to enjoy nothing better than to see themselves reflected in its waves. Smothered in green foliage, they, and the wild flowers, too, crowd together along the margin of the flowing waters and, bending over, gaze into them, never for a moment tiring of this pastime, never for a moment averting their admiring, radiant glances from the stream, and they smile at it and they greet it, waving their branches. But they dare not look into the Dnieper in midstream; none but the sun and the blue sky gaze into it there. Rarely will a bird fly as far as that. Glorious one! There is no river like it in the world.

Beautiful, too, is the Dnieper on a warm summer night when every living creature is asleep—man, beast, and bird. God alone majestically surveys heaven and earth and majestically shakes His robe of gold and silver, scattering a shower of stars. The stars shine and twinkle over the world and are all reflected together in the Dnieper. The mighty river finds room for them all in its dark bosom. Not one star will escape it, unless indeed it is extinguished in the sky. The black woods, dotted with sleeping crows, and the mountains, rent asunder long ago, which overhang the flowing river, try their utmost to cover it up, if only with their long shadows, but in vain! Nothing in the world could cover up the Dnieper. Blue, deep, deep blue, it flows on and on in a smooth flood at midnight as at midday, and it can be seen far, far away, as far as the eye of man can reach. Playfully snuggling up to the banks, as if seeking for warmth in the chill of the night, it leaves a silvery trail behind, gleaming like the blade of a Damascus sword; but the river, the deep blue river, falls asleep again. The Dnieper is beautiful even then, and no river in the world is like it. But when dark clouds scud like uprooted mountains across the sky, when the black woods sway wildly and are bent to their roots, when the mighty oak is riven asunder, and lightning, zigzagging through the clouds, suddenly lights up the whole world—then the Dnieper is truly terrible. The mountainous billows roar as they dash themselves against the hills, and when, flashing and moaning, they rush back, they wail and lament in the distance. So the old mother of a Cossack laments when she sees off her son as he leaves for the army. A high-spirited, but good lad, he rides off on his black stallion, arms akimbo and cap at a rakish angle; but she, sobbing, runs after him, seizes him by the stirrup, catches his bridle, and wrings her hands over him, shedding bitter tears.

Among the contending waves weird, dark shapes of burnt tree-stumps and boulders can be seen on the projecting tongue of land. And a boat is dashed against the bank, rising and falling as it comes in. What Cossack was so reckless as to take out a skiff when the old Dnieper was raging? Did he not know that the river swallows men like flies?

The boat reached the bank, and out of it stepped the sorcerer. He looked unhappy; bitterly did he resent the funeral the Cossacks had given their slain master. The Poles, too, had paid heavily: forty-four Polish gentlemen in their costly armour and rich coats and thirty-three serfs were left cut to pieces on the battlefield, while the rest were captured with their horses, to be sold to the Tartars.

The sorcerer went down some stone steps between the burnt tree-stumps to a small hut he had dug deep in the earth. He went in softly without making the door creak, put a pot on the table that was covered with a cloth and began throwing some magic herbs into it with his long hands; he then took a pitcher made of some rare wood, scooped up some water with it, and poured it into the pot, moving his lips and muttering some incantations. The room was filled with a rosy light. In this light his face looked horrible: it seemed covered with blood except where the deep wrinkles left lines upon it, and his eyes seemed to blaze with an infernal fire. Villainous sinner! His beard was grey, his face lined with wrinkles; he was all shrivelled, yet he still persevered in his godless design. A white cloud hovered in the room, and something like joy gleamed in his face. But why did he stand rigid all of a sudden with gaping mouth, not daring to stir? Why did the hair of his head stand up? A strange face appeared in the cloud; unbidden and uninvited, it had come to his subterranean home. As the minutes passed, its features grew more and more distinct and its motionless glance more penetrating. The features—eyebrows, eyes, lips—were unfamiliar to him. Never before had he seen them. Nor was there anything fear-inspiring about that face, and yet it filled him with horror. The strange unfamiliar face gazed upon him from the cloud, steadily, unblinkingly. The cloud had vanished, and yet the unfamiliar features of that face showed up more sharply than ever, and the piercing eyes looked hard at him. The sorcerer turned white as a sheet. He uttered a wild scream and overturned the pot. . . . The vision vanished.

XI

"Do not worry, dear sister," said old Captain Gorobetz; "dreams seldom come true."

"Lie down, my dear," said his young daughter-in-law. "I'll fetch a wise woman: no evil power can withstand her. She will drive your fears away."

"Fear nothing," said his son, grasping his sabre. "No one shall hurt you."

Sombrely and with dull eyes Katherine looked at them, not knowing herself what to say. "I have brought this misfortune upon myself," she thought. "It was I who let him out." At last she said: "He gives me no peace. Here I have been ten days with you in Kiev, but I am as unhappy as ever. I thought that at least I would be able to bring up my son in peace to avenge his father's death, but . . . Oh, if you knew how terrible he looked when he appeared to me in a dream! God grant you will never see him! My heart is still pounding. 'I'll kill your son, Katherine,' he shouted, 'if you do not marry me!'" And, bursting into tears, she rushed to the cradle, and the frightened child stretched out its little hands and cried.

The Captain's son boiled with rage when he heard these words and his eyes flashed with anger.

Captain Gorobetz could no longer contain himself. "Let him try coming here, the accursed Antichrist. He'll soon find out if there is still any strength left in an old Cossack's hands. God is my witness," he said, lifting up his keen eyes, "that I hastened to Danilo's help as soon as I learnt of his plight, but I came too late. It was God's will no doubt that I should find him on his cold bed upon which many, aye, many Cossacks have been laid. But, come, don't you think we gave him a worthy funeral? And did we let a single Pole escape with his life? So calm yourself, my dear child. So long as I am alive, or my son, no man will dare harm you!"

Having finished speaking, the old Cossack went up to the cradle, and the child, seeing his red pipe, set in silver, and his pouch with the glittering flints, hanging from a strap, stretched out his arms towards him and laughed.

"He takes after his father," said the old Captain, taking off the pipe and giving it to the child. "He's not out of the cradle, but he already wants to smoke a pipe!"

Katherine sighed softly and began rocking the cradle. They agreed to spend the night together, and after a short time they were all asleep. Katherine, too, fell asleep.

All was quiet in the courtyard and the cottage. Everyone slept except the Cossacks who were keeping watch. Suddenly Katherine woke with a scream, and the others woke, too.

"He's dead! He's been murdered!" she cried and rushed to the cradle.

All surrounded the cradle and they were paralysed with horror when they saw that the child in it was dead. Not a sound did any of them utter, not knowing what to think of so shocking a crime.

XII

Far from the Ukraine, beyond Poland and the populous city of Lemberg, there rises range upon range of immense mountains. Mountain after mountain, they encompass the earth to the right and to the left, as if with chains of stone, and box it up with a wall of rock to protect it from encroachment by the wild and turbulent sea. These mountain ranges stretch into Wallachia and across the Semigrad region, and their enormous pile stands like a horse-shoe between the Galician and the Hungarian peoples. We have no such mountains in our country. The eye is quite powerless to survey them; and on some of their summits no human foot has ever trod. Their aspect is quite amazing: had, one wonders, the frolicsome sea broken away from its wide shores in a storm and thrown up its monstrous waves to a tremendous height, and had they then turned to stone and remained motionless in the air? Or had the heavy stormclouds come tumbling from the sky and blocked up the earth? For they, too, are grey, and their white crests flash and sparkle in the sun.

Until you reach the Carpathian mountains, you may still hear Russian speech, and even beyond the mountains you may here and there hear echoes of our native tongue, but beyond neither speech nor faith is the same. The country there is inhabited by the numerous Hungarian people, and they, too, ride, fight and drink like so many Cossacks; nor are they niggardly with the golden coins in their pockets for their horses' harness or costly coats. There are great and wide lakes among the mountains. They are as still as glass and, like glass, they reflect the bare mountain-tops and their green slopes below.

But who rides through the night on a huge black horse whether the stars shine or not? Who is this giant of superhuman stature who gallops over the mountains, above the lakes, who is reflected with his gigantic horse in the still waters, and throws his vast and terrifying shadow across the mountains? His chased coat of mail glitters; across his shoulder is a pike; his sword clatters against his saddle; his helmet is tilted up; his moustaches are black; his eyes are closed; his eyelashes are drooping—he is asleep! And, asleep, he holds the reins. Behind him sits a young page, and he, too, is asleep, and even in his sleep he holds on to the giant. Who is he? Whither rides he? And why? Who knows? Not one day nor two has he been riding over the mountains. Day breaks, the sun rises, and he is seen no more. Only from time to time do the mountain-people notice a large shadow flitting over the mountains while the sky is clear and no cloud passes across the sun. But as soon as night descends and darkness falls, he becomes visible again and is reflected in the lakes and, quivering, his shadow gallops after him. He has crossed many mountains, and at last he rides up to the top of Krivan. There is no mountain in Carpathia higher than this one. It towers like a monarch over the other mountains. There the rider and his horse stop. The knight sinks into an even deeper slumber and the clouds descend and hide him from view.

XIII

"Hush, woman; don't make such a noise! My baby's asleep. My son cried a long time and now he is asleep. I'm going for a walk in the woods now. . . . What are you looking at me like that for? Oh, how hideous you look: iron pincers are coming out of your eyes! Such long pincers, too, and they are red hot! You must be a witch! Go away, go away, if you are a witch! You will steal my son! How ridiculous that old Cossack Captain is! He thinks I like living in Kiev. No, my husband and my son are here. And, besides, who's going to look after our cottage? I went out so quietly that neither the dog nor the cat heard me. Would you like to grow young again, old woman? It isn't a bit hard: all you have to do is to dance. Like that. See? Just as I'm dancing. . . ." And, having uttered those incoherent sentences, Katherine, her arms akimbo and looking wildly about her, began to dance. With a shriek she tapped with her feet, her silver heels beating spasmodically and out of time. Her black plaits came undone and tossed wildly about her white neck. She darted about the room without stopping, like a bird, waving her hands and nodding her head, and it seemed that she must either collapse on the ground from sheer exhaustion or fall dead.

The old nurse stood mournfully, tears rolling down her wrinkled face; the hearts of the faithful Cossacks were heavy as they looked at their mistress. At last she became exhausted and went on tapping languidly with her feet on the same spot, in the belief that she was dancing the slow Ukrainian turtle-dove dance.

"I have a lovely necklace, boys," she said at length, stopping. "You haven't got one, have you? . . . Where's my husband?" she screamed suddenly, drawing a Turkish dagger from her girdle. "Oh, this is not the knife I need!" she said, tears gushing out of her eyes and her face becoming overcast by a great sadness. "My father's heart is far away: it will not reach it. His heart is wrought of iron. It was forged by a witch in the fire of hell. Why doesn't my father come? Doesn't he know it is time he was stabbed to death? I suppose he expects me to go for him. . . ." And, breaking off, she laughed queerly. "Listen, I've just remembered such a funny thing: I've remembered how my husband was buried. He was buried alive, you know. Oh, it did make me laugh. . . . Listen, listen!" And instead of speaking, she began to sing:

"The cart on the road is covered in blood,
In the cart a brave Cossack's lying;
They cut him down and shot him, and now he's dying.
In his right hand a spear he's holding,
A river of blood from that spear's flowing,
Over the river a plane-tree's growing,
Above the plane-tree a raven's croaking.
A mother for the Cossack's weeping.
Don't weep, Mother, tears you ne'er need shed,
For your son a pretty lady's wed,
A pretty lady, a young bride.
In a field a little cottage stands,
Without doors and without casements long,
And that's the end of my song. . . .
A crayfish with a fish was dancing,
If you don't love me, your mother in an ague'll be
    shaking!"

It was such fragments of songs that she strung together
in a medley of words.

For the past few days she had been living in her cottage.
She would not hear of Kiev; she would not say her prayers;
and she shunned everybody. From morning till night she
wandered about the dark woods. Sharp twigs scratched her
white face and shoulders; the wind tousled her loose plaits;
the dead leaves rustled under her feet—she looked at nothing. At the hour when the glow of sunset fades from the sky,
but before the stars have appeared or the moon is up, people are afraid to walk in the woods. Unbaptised children
claw at the trees and clutch at the branches, sobbing and
laughing, turn somersaults on the roads and the wide
patches of nettles. Maidens who have drowned themselves
in the Dnieper and whose souls are for ever damned come
out of its waves in shoals; their hair streams from their
green heads over their shoulders; with a loud ripple the
water pours from their long hair to the ground; and a
maiden shines through the water as though through a
crystal dress; her lips smile enigmatically, her cheeks blaze,

her eyes enchant the soul: she looks as if she might pine away with love, as if she might kiss her lover to death. . . . Run, Christian! Her lips are ice, her bed—the cold water, her caress deadly: she will drag you into the river. But Katherine looked at no one; in her frenzy she did not fear the water maidens. She ran about with her knife far into the night, searching for her father.

In the early morning a visitor arrived, a handsome man in a scarlet coat, and he inquired after Danilo. He heard their story, wiped the tears from his eyes with his sleeve and shook his head. He said he had fought side by side with Burulbash; side by side they had engaged in mortal combat with the Crimean Tartars and the Turks. Never had he thought that Danilo would meet with such an end. The visitor told them many other things and expressed a wish to see Katherine.

At first Katherine would not listen to anything the visitor told her. But by and by she began to listen to his speeches as though she understood them perfectly. He told her how Danilo and he had lived together like brothers, how once they had hidden under a dam from the Crimeans. . . . Katherine listened and did not take her eyes off him.

"She will recover," the Cossacks thought, looking at her. "This man will cure her! She is listening like one who has already recovered her senses!"

Meanwhile the visitor began describing how Danilo once in confidence had said to him, "Look here, Kuprian. If by the will of God I should die, you take Katherine for your wife. . . ."

Katherine gave him a piercing look. "Ah," she shrieked, "it is he! It is my father!" and she sprang at him with her knife.

For a long time he struggled to snatch the knife from her; at last he did snatch it away, raised it—and a terrible deed was done: the father killed his crazed daughter.

The thunderstruck Cossacks rushed at him, but the sorcerer had already leapt upon his horse and vanished out of sight.

XIV

Outside the city of Kiev an extraordinary miracle happened. All the gentlemen and the hetmans flocked to witness it: suddenly it became possible to see far away to the ends of the earth. Afar could be seen the blue waters of the mouth of the Dnieper, and beyond that the Black Sea was plainly visible. Men who had travelled in foreign lands recognised the Crimea, rising like a mountain out of the sea, and the marshy Sivash. On the right could be seen the Galician land.

"And what's that?" people asked the old men, pointing to the white and grey crests, which loomed far away in the sky, looking more like clouds than anything else.

"Those are the Carpathian mountains!" replied the old men. "Among them there are some that are covered with eternal snow, and the clouds cling to them and spend the night there."

Then a new miracle happened: the clouds which hid the summit of the highest mountain dispersed and on it appeared a horseman in full knightly armour, with his eyes closed. He was plainly visible to all, as though he were only a few yards away.

It was then that one man among that marvelling and frightened multitude leapt on a horse and, looking wildly about him, as though afraid that he might be pursued, he quickly rode off at a gallop. That was the sorcerer. Why was he so panic-stricken? Looking in terror at the strange knight, he recognised the face which had appeared to him unbidden while he was working his spells. He could not have said why he was filled with such dismay at this sight; and, looking apprehensively about him, he rode madly on until he was overtaken by night and the stars began to come out. Then he turned homewards, perhaps to ask the Evil One what that miracle meant. He was just about to leap with his horse over a narrow stream, which ran right across his path, when his horse suddenly stopped in full career, looked round at him and—wonder of wonders!—laughed aloud, both rows of teeth gleaming uncannily in the darkness. The sorcerer's hair stood on end. He uttered a wild scream, wept like one possessed, and turned his horse towards Kiev.

He felt that he was being pursued on all sides. The trees that surrounded him like a dark forest shook their beards and stretched forth their long branches, as though alive, trying to strangle him; the stars seemed to be running ahead of him and pointing to the sinner; the road itself seemed to be racing after him.

The frantic sorcerer hurried to the holy places in Kiev.

XV

A hermit sat alone in his cave before a dimly burning lamp, and he did not take his eyes off the holy book. He had retired to his cave many years ago and he had already made himself a coffin in which he lay down to sleep instead of a bed. The holy man closed his book and began to pray. . . . Suddenly a man of a strange and terrible aspect ran into his cave. The holy man was startled at first at the sight of such a man and he drew back from him. He was trembling all over like an aspen leaf. His eyes rolled wildly and blazed with panic. His misshapen face made one shudder.

"Father, pray! Pray!" he shouted desperately. "Pray for a lost soul!" And he sank to the ground.

The holy hermit crossed himself, took up his book, opened it and, drawing back in horror, dropped it. "There is no mercy for you, terrible sinner that you are! Go, I cannot pray for you!"

"No?" the sinner cried, distraught.

"Look, the holy letters in the book are dripping with blood. . . . There has never been such a sinner in the world!"

"Father, you are mocking me!"

"Go, accursed sinner! I am not mocking you. I am overcome with fear. It is not good for a man to be with you!"

"No, no. You are mocking. Don't pretend. . . . I see you're laughing at me! I can see your old teeth gleaming white!"

And, mad with fury, he sprang at the old hermit and—killed him.

A deep moan rose in the cave and it echoed through the woods and the fields. From behind the woods a pair of gaunt, withered arms with long claws rose in the air, trembled and disappeared.

And now he felt no fear. He felt nothing. Everything was confused. His ears rang, his head spun round as though he were drunk, and everything before his eyes seemed covered with spiders' webs. He leapt upon his horse and rode straight for Kanev, intending to ride from there through Cherkassy direct to the Crimean Tartars, although he hardly knew himself why. He rode one day and another and still Kanev was not in sight. He was on the right road and he ought to have reached it long ago, but there was no sign of Kanev. In the distance he could see the gleaming cupolas of churches. But that was not Kanev. It was Shumsk. The sorcerer was amazed to find himself in quite a different part of the country. He turned back towards Kiev and a day later a city appeared. It was not Kiev, though, but Galich, a city more distant from Kiev than Shumsk. At a loss what to do, he again turned back, but he had the curious feeling that he was still riding in the opposite direction, and always farther and farther away from where he wanted to go. No one in the world could tell what was in the sorcerer's mind; if anyone had seen and known what was there, he would never again have had a quiet night's sleep, neither would he have laughed again for the most of his life. It was not spite, or anger, or fierce resentment. There is no word in the world to describe it. His blood boiled; he was mad with rage; he would have gladly trampled upon the whole world with his horse, seized the whole country from Kiev to Galich, with all the people and everything in it, and drowned it in the Black

Sea. But it was not from spite or malice that he would do it. No, he did not know himself why he wished to do it.

A cold shudder ran through his veins when he saw the Carpathian mountains quite near him, and lofty Krivan capped with grey cloud. His horse still galloped on and was already racing among the mountains. The clouds suddenly lifted, and there before him was the horseman in all his terrible majesty. . . . The sorcerer tried to stop; he tugged at the rein; his horse neighed wildly and, its mane flying, it continued to race towards the horseman. As he saw the motionless horseman stir and suddenly open his eyes, the sorcerer felt everything die within him. But when the dreadful knight saw the sorcerer racing towards him, he laughed, and his wild laugh echoed like thunder through the mountains and resounded in the sorcerer's heart, shaking him to the very core of his being. He felt as if some mighty creature had crawled into him and was walking within him, hammering away at his heart and veins . . . so dreadfully did that laugh resound in him!

The horseman seized the sorcerer with his mighty hand and lifted him into the air. In a trice the sorcerer was dead. He opened his eyes after his death, but he was dead and gazed like a dead man. Neither the living nor the risen from the dead have such a terrible look in their eyes. He rolled his dead eyes from side to side and saw dead men rising up from Kiev, from Galicia and the Carpathian mountains, and they all looked like him.

Pale, terribly pale, one taller than another, one bonier than another, they thronged round the horseman who held his awful prey in his hand. Once more the knight laughed and then he dropped the sorcerer down into the abyss. And all the dead men leapt into the abyss, seized the dead man as he was falling and fastened their teeth into him. Another, taller and more terrible than the rest, tried to rise from the ground, but he could not, for he had not the strength to do it, so huge had he grown in the earth; and if he had risen out of the earth he would have overturned the Carpathian mountains, and the whole of the Semigrad and Turkish lands. He only moved a little and he set the whole earth in a tremor, and many cottages were overturned and many people crushed to death.

A roar is often heard in the Carpathian mountains as if a thousand water-mills were churning up the water with their wheels. It is the sound of dead men gnawing a dead man in the bottomless abyss which no living man has ever seen, for no man dares to go near it. It sometimes happens that the earth trembles from one end to the other: that is, learned men will tell you, because there is a mountain somewhere near the sea from which flames issue and fiery streams flow. But the old men who live in Hungary and Galicia know better and they say it is the dead man who has grown so huge in the earth, trying to rise and shaking the earth.

XVI

A large crowd gathered round a bandore-player in the town of Glukhov, and for the past hour they had been listening to the blind man's playing. No bandore-player sang so well or such wonderful songs. First he sang about the rule of the hetmans, of Sagaydachny and Khmelnitzky, the famous chieftains of the Dnieper Cossacks. Times were different then: the Cossacks were at the height of their glory, they trampled their foes underfoot, and no one dared to hold them up to scorn. The old bandore-player sang merry songs, too, and he turned his sightless eyes upon the crowd as though he could see, and his fingers, with the little sheaths of bone fixed to them, darted about like flies over the strings and the strings seemed to play by themselves; and the people, old men with their eyes fixed upon the ground and young men with their eyes staring at the old singer, dared not even whisper to one another.

"Now," said the old man, "I will sing you about what happened long, long ago."

The people pressed closer and the old man began:

"In times long past when Stephen, famed far and wide as Prince of Semigrad, was king of the Poles, two gallant Cossacks, Ivan and Petro, lived together in amity and love like brothers. 'Whatever you, Ivan, in battle or raid shall obtain, we shall divide in equal parts; when good fortune smiles upon you, I, too, shall be merry; but when dire misfortune befalls one of us, then we both shall share it; if one of us gains rich booty in battle, it shall be shared between us; if the cruel foe takes one of us captive, the other shall sell his goods and chattels for ransom, or else himself go into captivity.' And so it came to pass that whenever they seized cattle and horses from strangers, each of them received his equal share.

"It so fell out that when King Stephen waged war against the Ottoman, he could never prevail in battle, although for three full weeks he stoutly fought the infidel hordes. The Sultan had a Pasha who with only ten of his janissaries put to flight a whole regiment of Poles. The king therefore proclaimed that if a man should be found among his troops who, singlehanded, should bring that Pasha to him dead or alive, he would, as recompense, receive the entire pay of his army. 'Come, brother, let us take the Pasha prisoner,' said Ivan to Petro. So the two Cossacks set off, one one way, one the other.

"Whether or not Petro would have captured the Pasha, there is no telling, but meanwhile Ivan led the Pasha to the king with a rope round his neck. 'Brave fellow!' said King Stephen, and he commanded that Ivan alone be given the pay of the whole army. The king also ordered that Ivan be given any land he might desire, wheresoever it might chance to be, and as many heads of cattle as he should wish. No sooner did Ivan receive the king's reward than he gave half of it to Petro. Petro took his half, but the honour Ivan received from the king rankled in his breast, and in his heart the thought of revenge was planted deep.

"The two knights rode off to take possession of the land beyond the Carpathians that the king had granted to Ivan. The Cossack Ivan had set his little son behind him on the horse, tying him for safety with a rope passed round his own waist. Dusk fell, but they continued on their way. The young child fell asleep; Ivan, too, began to doze. Do not slumber, Cossack, the mountain paths are treacherous! But the Cossack's horse is endowed by nature with a sixth sense, and he can find his way in darkness wherever he may happen to be; nor will he stumble or step off the path. There is an abyss between the mountains, a bottomless chasm, unplumbed by man; as many miles as there are between heaven and earth, are also between the top and the bottom of that great chasm. A narrow path skirts perilously the chasm's edge, so narrow a path that two people can barely ride abreast upon it, but three never. Warily the horse picked his way along that perilous path with the slumbering Cossack on his back, and Petro, in a quiver of excitement and breathless with joy, rode beside him. He looked round, cast a glance into the chasm and thrust his sworn brother over the edge. Horse and Cossack and small child hurtled to their doom together.

"But in his fall the Cossack chanced to grasp a branch, and the horse alone fell to the bottom of the abyss. With his son on his back, Ivan started on his dangerous ascent up the treacherous slope of the precipice; but barely had he reached the top when, looking up, he saw Petro pointing his pike at him to push him back over the precipice. 'Just and merciful Heaven,' Ivan cried, 'far better I had never lifted my eyes than that I had seen my own brother holding his pike ready to thrust me back to my destruction. Stab me, dear brother, stab me with your pike, if God so wills that I should perish here, but spare my child! Take him! Take him, I implore you, for what has an innocent child done to deserve such a cruel death?' But Petro laughed and thrust at him with his pike. Cossack and child fell to the bottom of the chasm. Petro seized his brother's land and cattle and lived like a lord for the rest of his human span. No man had such droves of horses as he, nor flocks of sheep and rams. And Petro died.

"No sooner was Petro dead than God summoned the souls

of the two brothers to appear for judgment before His throne. 'This man, O Ivan,' said God, 'is so great a sinner that it will take me too long to choose a fit punishment for him. Choose thou his proper punishment thyself!' Ivan pondered long what punishment to choose. At length he said, 'This man has done me a great injury. Like Judas, he betrayed his brother; he brought my honourable line to an end and robbed me of all hope of posterity. For a man without an honourable line and without progeny is like a seed that falls upon the ground and perishes in the earth; there is no green shoot to tell the whole world that a seed has been dropped there.

"'Therefore, O Lord, make it so that no issue of his loins may know happiness on earth. Let, I beseech Thee, the last man of his line be the wickedest man on earth, and let each wicked deed of his disturb the peace of his fathers and forefathers in their graves, and, suffering torments unknown in the world before, let them rise from their tombs! But let Judas Petro not have the strength to rise and let him thereby suffer worse torment, and may he bite the earth like one possessed, and may he writhe in agony beneath the ground.

"'And when the hour of retribution comes, when the villainous career of that evil man has in full measure been consummated, raise me, O Lord, from that deep abyss on to the highest mountain, where I may sit mounted on my stallion, and let him come to me, and from that mountain I shall hurl him into the deepest abyss, and let all his dead, all his ancestors, come creeping from every corner of the earth, wherever they lived in their lifetime, to that abyss to gnaw his bones and so repay him for the torments his crimes had made them suffer, and may they gnaw him for ever and for ever. Thrice happy will I be to watch his sufferings! But do not let Judas Petro ever rise from under the ground; let him strive in vain to gnaw the bones of his great-great-grandchild, but let him instead gnaw his own bones, which, growing longer and longer as the years pass, shall make his pains more unbearable still. This will, I am sure, be the worst torture for him, for greater torment knows no man than to long for vengeance, but to be powerless to avenge.'

" 'Terrible is the punishment thou hast devised, O man,' said God, 'but be it as thou hast spoken; but thou too shalt sit on that mountain-top for ever, and never shall thou enter the Kingdom of Heaven whilst thou sittest there on thy horse!' And so it befell as it was spoken, and to this very day the wondrous knight, horsed and accoutred, stands on the highest peak of the Carpathian mountains, watching dead men gnawing the bones of a dead man in the bottomless abyss, and feeling how a dead man's bones are growing larger and larger under the earth, and how he, suffering dreadful agonies, gnaws at his own bones and sets the whole earth shaking fearfully. . . ."

The blind man had long finished his song and he began again thrumming the strings, singing amusing rhymes of Khoma and Yeryoma and Sklyara Stokoza; but his listeners, old and young, did not heed him, and for a long time they stood with bowed heads, their thoughts still full of the dreadful events that happened in the days long gone by.

1830–31

Ivan Fyodorovich Shponka and His Aunt

A MOST unfortunate thing happened to this story. Stepan Ivanovich Kurochka, the person who told it to us, used to come to visit us from Gadyach. Now, I think you ought to know that my memory is simply terrible: whatever you tell me I am quite sure to forget it. Just like pouring water through a sieve. Knowing this weakness of mine, I asked him specially to write it down in a little notebook I keep for the purpose. Well, he has always been good to me, bless him, so he did as I asked and wrote it down for me. I put it into the drawer of my little table. I believe you know it well: it is the one standing in the corner near the door as you enter the room. . . . Oh dear, I quite forgot that you have never been to my house. My wife with whom I have lived for thirty years has never, I am sorry to say, learnt to read and write. Well, so one fine day I noticed that she was baking pasties on some paper. I must tell you, dear readers, that the pasties my wife bakes are simply marvellous; you won't find better pasties anywhere, I warrant you. I just happened to pick up one of these pasties and glance at the paper underneath it and—what do you think I saw? There was some writing on it. It was as if I had known it all along in my heart! I went straight to my little table: half of my notebook was missing! My wife had used the missing pages for her pasties. What was I to do? I could not very well have a fight with her in our old age, could I?

A year ago I happened to drive through Gadyach. Now, I had tied a knot in my handkerchief on purpose so as not to forget to ask Stepan Ivanovich about that story of his. What's more, I promised myself that as soon as I sneezed in the town I must remember to do so. But all in vain. As I drove through the town, I sneezed, blew my nose into my handkerchief, and, of course, forgot all about it. I only remembered it when I had driven six miles from the tollgate. Well, it can't be helped: I have to publish it without the ending. Still, if anyone is very anxious to know how the story ends, he has only to go to Gadyach and ask Stepan Ivanovich. I'm sure he'll be only too glad to tell the story again even if he has to start it from the beginning. He lives not far from the brick church. There is a little lane there: as soon as you turn into it, it is the second or third gate. And this is even better: when you catch sight of a large pole with a quail on it, and a fat peasant woman in a green skirt comes out to meet you (perhaps I ought to tell you that he is a bachelor), then it's his yard. However, you might also meet him in the market place where he is to be found every morning before nine o'clock choosing fish and vegetables for his dinner and talking to Father Antip or to the Jewish tax-farmer. You will recognise him at once, for he is the only one to wear printed cotton trousers and a yellow cotton coat. And here is another sign by which you may recognise him: when he walks he always waves his arms about. I remember our late local assessor, Denis Petrovich, used to say every time he caught sight of him in the distance: "Look, look, here comes a windmill!"

I Ivan Fyodorovich Shponka

It is four years since Ivan Fyodorovich Shponka retired from the army and began to live on his farm of Vytrebenki. When he was still little Vanya he went to the district school in Gadyach, and it is only fair to say that he was a most well-behaved and a most studious boy. The Russian grammar master, Nikifor Timofeyevich Deyeprichastiye*, used to say that if all his boys had been as studious as Shponka, he would not have had to bring his maple-wood ruler into the classroom, for, as he confessed, beating naughty and lazy boys was very tiring work. Vanya's exercise book was always very clean and carefully ruled. Not a smudge anywhere. He always sat quietly at his desk, his arms folded and his eyes fixed on the teacher, and he never stuck bits of paper on to the back of his classmate sitting in front of him, he never cut his desk with his penknife or joined his classmates in their favourite game of squeezing themselves into a bench and pushing the boy at the end off it. Whenever a boy wanted a penknife to clean his pen, he at once turned to Shponka, knowing that he always had one on him, and Ivan Fyodorovich, still little Vanya at the time, took it out of its little leather case, tied on to the buttonhole of his grey uniform, and merely asked not to scrape the pen with the sharp end of the knife, since, as he maintained, that was what the blunt end was for. Such good behaviour soon attracted the attention of the Latin master, whose cough in the corridor was quite sufficient to put the class into a state of mortal terror even before his frieze overcoat and his pockmarked face protruded through the door. This terrible teacher, who always had two birch rods on his desk and half of whose class were always on their knees, made Shponka a prefect, although there were many better pupils in his class.

* Participle

Here we must not omit to acquaint our readers with a certain event which had a great influence on the whole of Shponka's life. One of the pupils who had been entrusted to his care and who was anxious to get him to put *scit* against his name in the class register for some homework he had not even attempted to do, brought a pancake soaked in butter into the class one day. Though Shponka was very keen on meting out justice, he happened to be very hungry that day and the temptation proved too strong for him. He put a book on the desk in front of him, took the pancake, and began eating it. He was so absorbed in this occupation that he did not even notice the dead silence that suddenly fell upon the class. He came to with horror when a dreadful hand, reaching out from a frieze overcoat, caught him by the ear and dragged him out into the middle of the classroom. "Give me the pancake!" said the stern teacher. "Give me the pancake, you villain, I tell you!" He then snatched the buttery pancake with his fingers and flung it out of the window, shouting to the boys who were running about in the schoolyard not to dare pick it up. After that he gave Shponka a good caning across his hands, which was only fair: why did his hands and no other part of his body take the pancake? Be that as it may, but after that Shponka, timid by nature anyhow, became more timid than ever. Perhaps it was just this incident that explained Shponka's great reluctance to join the civil service, for he had learnt by bitter experience that crime did not always pay.

He was nearly fifteen when he passed into the second form where instead of the abridged catechism and the four rules of arithmetic he began to study the unabridged catechism, the book dealing with the duties of man, and fractions. Realising, however, that the further he advanced in his studies, the more difficult they became, and having received the news of his father's death, he spent another two years at school and, with his mother's consent, obtained a commission in the P— infantry regiment.

The P— infantry regiment was quite different from the ordinary run of infantry regiments; and though it was

mostly quartered in villages, it enjoyed a reputation no whit
worse than that enjoyed by many a cavalry regiment. The
majority of its officers drank hard and were very expert at
dragging Jews about by their side locks, in which pastime
they were as proficient as the hussars; a few of them even
danced the mazurka, and the colonel of the P— regiment
never missed an opportunity of remarking on it when talking to someone in society. "Many officers of my regiment,
sir," he used to say, patting his paunch at every word he
uttered, "dance the mazurka. Yes, sir, many of them, a great
many of them." To convince my readers of the high cultural
level of the officers of the P— regiment, we might add that
two of them were terrible gamblers and often lost their uniforms at faro as well as their caps, greatcoats, sword knots,
and even their shirts, a feat that is almost unknown even
among cavalry officers.

Life among such comrades-at-arms did not, however, de-
crease Shponka's timidity. And since he never drank anything stronger than ordinary vodka, of which he had only
a glass before dinner and supper, nor danced the mazurka,
nor played faro, he naturally had to spend most of his free
time in his own company. So it came about that while his
brother officers spent their leisure time visiting small land-
owners in hired carriages, he stayed at home engaged in
occupations that were natural to a gentle and kindly soul
like himself: he either cleaned his buttons, or read his
fortune-telling book, or placed mousetraps in the corners of
his room, or, finally, took off his uniform and lay on his bed.
On the other hand, there was no one more conscientious
than Shponka in the regiment. He drilled his platoon so well
that his company commander always set him up as an example for others. That was why he was so rapidly (only
eleven years after obtaining the rank of ensign) promoted
to the rank of second lieutenant.

It was about that time that he received the news of his
mother's death; his aunt, his mother's sister, whom he knew
only because when he was a little boy she used to bring
him dried pears and very delicious honey cakes of her own

making (she had quarrelled with his mother and that was why Shponka never saw her afterwards), this aunt of his undertook, out of the kindness of her heart, to look after his small estate, of which she had informed him in due course by letter. Thoroughly convinced of his aunt's competence, Shponka carried on with his regimental duties as before. Anyone else in his place, having received so high a rank, would have given himself airs; but pride was totally unknown to him and, having become a second lieutenant, he remained the same Ivan Fyodorovich as he was while being a mere ensign. Having served for four more years after his promotion, an event of so great a significance to him, he was about to leave the Mogilyov Province for Russia with his regiment when he received the following letter:

My dear nephew, Ivan Fyodorovich,

I am sending you your linen: five pairs of socks and four linen shirts of the best quality. I also want to talk to you about business: as you have already got a rank of no small importance, which, I think, you are aware of, and have reached the age when you ought to look after your own affairs, there is no reason why you should carry on with your military career. I am an old woman and you cannot expect me to look after your farm properly; and indeed there are many things I should like to discuss with you personally. Come home, Vanya dear! In expectation of the great pleasure of seeing you, I remain your dearly loving aunt,

                                        Vasilisa Tsupchevska

We have got a most wonderful turnip in our kitchen garden. It is more like a potato than a turnip.

A week after receiving this letter, Shponka wrote the following reply:

Dear Auntie, Vasilisa Kashporovna,

Thank you very much for sending me the linen. My socks especially were terribly old and my batman had to darn them four times as a result of which they have shrunk con-

siderably. I am entirely of the same opinion as you about
the service and I sent in my resignation the day before yesterday. As soon as I get my discharge, I shall hire a coachman. I am sorry I could not carry out your commission with
regard to the wheat seeds, the hard spring wheat: they
have not got any of it in the whole of the Mogilyov
Province. Pigs are mostly fed here on brewers' mash which
is mixed with a little stale beer.

I remain, dear Auntie, your respectful nephew,

Ivan Shponka

At last Shponka received his discharge from the army
with the rank of first lieutenant. He hired a Jewish coachman for forty roubles to take him from Mogilyov to
Gadyach and got into the covered cart just in time to see
the trees flaunting their new green leaves and the whole
earth turning green with fresh verdure and the countryside
full of the fragrance of spring.

II   The Road

Nothing specially remarkable happened on the road. The
entire journey took them over two weeks. Shponka would
probably have arrived much earlier were it not for the fact
that his Jewish coachman was very pious and refused to
travel on the Sabbath, which he spent in prayer all day,
wrapped in his praying shawl. However, as I have already
had the opportunity of observing earlier, Shponka was not
the sort of man to be easily bored. While his coachman
was saying his prayers, he unstrapped his trunk, took out
his linen, and subjected it to a thorough examination to
make sure that it had been properly washed and nicely
folded. He carefully removed the fluff from the new uniform he had had made without shoulder straps, and put it
all back again with the most meticulous care. He was not,
as a rule, very fond of reading, and if he happened to look
into his fortune-telling book sometimes it was because he

liked to find something familiar there, something he had read several times already. So does a city dweller go to his club every day, not in order to hear something new there, but in order to meet those of his cronies with whom he has been accustomed to chat from time immemorial. So does a civil servant read the civil service list with great pleasure several times a day, not for any deep diplomatic reasons, but simply because he enjoys seeing the names of his colleagues in print. "Oh," he repeats hollowly to himself, "Ivan Ivanovich so-and-so! And here am I! H'm!" And next time he reads it again with identical exclamations.

After travelling for two weeks Shponka arrived at a small village seventy-five miles from Gadyach. That was on a Friday. The sun had set when his Jewish coachman drew up at the inn.

This inn was in no way different from other inns of small villages. The traveller is usually regaled there royally with hay and oats just as if he were a post horse. But if he wished to lunch as decent people usually do lunch, he would have to keep his appetite inviolate till a more favourable opportunity. Knowing what to expect, Shponka had provided himself in advance with two bags of rolls and sausages and, ordering a glass of vodka, of which there is no lack at any inn, he sat down to his supper on a bench in front of an oak table firmly dug into the clay floor.

It was just then that he heard the sound of a britzka drawing up at the gates of the inn. The gates creaked open, but the carriage did not drive into the yard for some time. A man could be heard engaged in a violent argument with the old-woman innkeeper. "I'll drive in," Shponka heard him say, "but if a single bedbug bites me in your hovel, I'll thrash you within an inch of your life, you old witch! Damned if I won't! And I shan't given you anything for your hay, either!"

A minute later the door opened and a fat man in a green coat came in, or rather squeezed himself through the door. His head rested stiffly on a short neck, which looked even thicker because of his double chin. He seemed to be one of those people who never worry their heads over trifles and who never have a care in the world.

"How do you do, sir?" he said, catching sight of Shponka. Shponka bowed in silence.

"And may I ask whom I have the honour of addressing?" the fat man went on.

At such an inquiry, Shponka involuntarily rose from his seat and stood to attention, which he usually did when his colonel addressed some question to him.

"Retired First Lieutenant Ivan Fyodorovich Shponka," he replied.

"And may I ask where you are bound for?"

"For my own farm of Vytrebenki, sir."

"Vytrebenki!" the stern interrogator exclaimed. "Allow me, sir, allow me!" he cried, coming up to him and waving his arms about as though someone were preventing him or as though he were pushing his way through a crowd.

Having come up close to Shponka, he threw his arms round him and kissed him first on the right cheek, then on the left and then on the right cheek again. Shponka liked this greeting very much, for his lips received the stranger's huge cheeks as though they were cushions.

"Allow me, sir, to introduce myself," continued the fat man. "I'm a landowner of the same Gadyach district and a neighbour of yours. I live only about three miles from your farm of Vytrebenki in the village of Khortyshche and my name is Grigory Grigoryevich Storchenko. You must pay me a visit in my village of Khortyshche, sir. You must or I won't have anything to do with you. I'm afraid I'm in a bit of a hurry now. Have to attend to some urgent business. . . . And what's this, pray?" he said in a gentle voice to his servant, a young boy in a Cossack coat with patches on his elbows, who had just entered the room and who was putting some bundles and boxes on the table with a bewildered look. "What is this? What is this?" he repeated, his voice growing imperceptibly sterner and sterner. "Did I tell you to put it there, my dear sir? Did I tell you to put it there, you dirty rogue? Get out!" he shouted, stamping. "Wait, you ugly villain! Where is the cellaret with the drinks? Sir," he turned to Shponka, pouring out a glass of homemade brandy, "have a glass of this excellent medicine!"

"No, th-thank you, sir," Shponka said with a stutter. "I —I have already had one."

"I won't hear of it, sir!" cried the landowner, raising his voice. "I won't hear of it! I won't stir from this place until you have drunk it."

Seeing that it was impossible to refuse, Shponka drank it not without pleasure.

"Now, this chicken, sir," the fat landowner went on, cutting it in its wooden box with a knife. "I must tell you that my cook Yavdokha likes to have a drop now and then and that is why her roast chickens tend to be on the dry side sometimes. Hey, boy"—he turned to the boy in the Cossack coat, who had brought in a feather bed and pillows—"make up my bed on the floor in the middle of the room. And see that there is a lot of hay under the pillows. And pull out a flock of hemp from the old woman's distaff to stop my ears with for the night. I must tell you, sir," he addressed Shponka, "that I've been in the habit of stopping my ears for the night ever since that damned incident in a Russian inn when a cockroach crawled into my left ear. Those damned Russians, as I found out later, even eat their cabbage soup with cockroaches in it. I can't tell you what I had been through! My ear kept tickling and tickling—it nearly drove me mad! I was cured by one of our own peasant women. A simple old peasant woman, sir. And what do you think she did? Why, just whispered some incantation over me! What can you say about our doctors after that, sir? In my opinion, they're simply cheating us. Yes, sir, making fools of us. Some of these peasant women know a damn sight more than all these doctors!"

"Indeed, sir, you're absolutely right. These women do indeed——" He stopped short as though unable to find the right word.

Here I may as well explain that Shponka was rather sparing of words. That was, perhaps, caused by his timidity or, perhaps, by his desire to express himself more beautifully.

"Shake up the hay properly—properly!" Storchenko said to his servant. "The hay here is so bad that there's sure to be a twig in it. Allow me, sir, to wish you good night. I'm afraid you won't see me to-morrow: I shall be leaving before daybreak. Your Jew will be keeping his Sabbath because it's Saturday to-morrow, and there's no need for you to get up early. Don't forget what I told you, though: I shan't have anything to do with you if you don't pay me a visit in Khortyshche."

Here Storchenko's valet pulled off his coat and boots, helped him on with his dressing gown, and he sank on to his bed, and it seemed as though one huge feather bed lay down on another.

"Hey, boy, where are you off to, you rascal? Come here, put my counterpane straight! And what about the horses? Have they been watered? More hay! Here, here, under this side! And put the counterpane straight, you blackguard! So—once more—ugh!"

Storchenko heaved two more sighs and let out such a mighty whistle from his nose that the whole room shook; he snored so loudly at times that the old woman, who was dozing on the low stove, kept waking up and looking intently round the room, but seeing nothing, she composed herself and fell asleep again.

When Shponka woke up next morning, the fat landowner was no longer there. That was the only remarkable incident that happened to him on the road. Two days later he was nearing his farm.

As the Jewish coachman drove his jades up the hill, Shponka caught sight of the windmill waving its sails and the row of willows in the valley below, and his heart began to pound violently. Between the willows the water of the pond sparkled gaily and he could feel a fresh breeze rising from it. It was in that pond that he used to bathe a long time ago and it was there that he and the village children used to wade up to their necks in search of crayfish.

The covered cart scrambled up the mound of earth over
the marshy ground by the dam and Shponka saw the old,
familiar little house thatched with reeds and the familiar
apple trees and cherry trees he used to climb surreptitiously
as a boy. As soon as he drove into the yard all manner of
dogs—brown, black, grey, and spotted—came running from
every direction. Some of them rushed barking under the legs
of the horses, others ran to the back of the cart, having
noticed that the axle was smeared with grease; one stood
stock-still near the kitchen, covering a bone with its paw
and barking furiously; another barked from a distance and
kept running to and fro, waving its tail, as if saying, "Look,
good Christians, what a handsome young man I am!" Boys
in dirty shirts came running to stare at the visitor. A sow,
which was taking a walk in the yard with her litter of sixteen little pigs, raised her snout with a searching look and
grunted louder than usual. Wheat, millet, and barley lay
drying in the sun in many heaps on large hempen sheets.
On the roof, too, wild chicory, hawkweed, and other herbs
were laid out to dry.

Shponka was so busy looking at it all that he only came
to when a spotted dog bit the Jewish coachman in the calf.
The house serfs, consisting of the cook, another peasant
woman, and two girls in woollen shifts, now appeared on
the scene and, after first exclaiming, "Why, it's our young
master!" told him that his aunt was planting maize in the
kitchen garden, assisted by the maid Palashka and the
coachman Omelko, who often performed the duties of market gardener and night watchman. But his aunt, who had
caught sight of the matting of the covered cart from a distance, was already there. And Shponka was amazed when
she almost lifted him out of the cart, hardly able to believe
that she was the same aunt who had written to him about
her infirmities and decrepitude.

III   The Aunt

Aunt Vasilisa Kashporovna was about fifty then. She had never married and she used to say that she prized her state of single blessedness above everything in the world. However, as far as I can remember, no one had ever proposed to her. That was because all men felt rather over-awed in her presence and could not summon up enough courage to make her a declaration. "Vasilisa Kashporovna is a woman of character!" her would-be bridegrooms declared, and they were absolutely right, for Vasilisa Kashporovna could put anyone in his place. She made the miller, a confirmed drunkard who was absolutely no good for anything, into a real treasure of a man by just pulling his long tuft of hair every day with her own manly hand and without the application of any other remedy whatsoever. She was of almost gigantic height and proportionately stout and strong. It seemed as though nature had made an unforgivable mistake in making her wear a large dark-brown dress with small pleats on weekdays and a red cashmere shawl on her name days and Easter Sunday instead of the moustache and long jackboots of a dragoon, which would have suited her best. On the other hand, her occupations corresponded perfectly with her appearance: she went rowing by herself, plying the oars more skilfully than any fisherman; she went shooting game birds; she kept constant watch over the haymakers; she knew the exact number of melons and watermelons in the melon field; she took a toll of five copecks from every cart that drove over the mound of earth by the dam; she climbed the pear trees and shook off the pears; she administered beatings to her lazy vassals with her own terrible hand and offered a glass of vodka to the deserving ones with the same terrible hand. Almost at one and the same time she would scold, dye the yarn, run to the kitchen, make *kvas* and honey preserve. She was busy from morning till night and was in time to see to everything. The result of it all was that Shponka's little estate, comprising eighteen serfs according to the last census, was flourishing in every sense of the word. Besides, she doted on her nephew and took good care to save up every copeck for him.

On his return home, Shponka's life underwent a drastic change and followed quite a different path. It seemed as though nature had meant him to administer his estate of eighteen serfs. His aunt herself observed that he would make an excellent farmer, though for the time being she did not allow him to interfere in all the branches of farming. "The lad's still too young," she used to say, although Shponka was in his late thirties. "You can't expect him to know everything!"

However, he, too, kept constant watch over the harvesters and haymakers in the fields, and this occupation filled his gentle soul with ineffable delight. The regular sweep of ten or more shining scythes; the sound made by the grass as it fell in straight rows; the songs of the women harvesters as they rose shrilly into the air, sometimes gay like the welcoming of guests, sometimes mournful like a parting; the tranquil, limpid evening, and what an evening! How fresh and pure was the air! How everything suddenly came to life: the steppe took on red and greenish tints and was ablaze with flowers; quail, bustards, gulls, grasshoppers, thousands of insects, and they all filled the air with their whistling, chirping, buzzing, droning and, suddenly, merged into one harmonious choir; and not for a moment was there silence. Meanwhile the sun was setting and gradually disappearing. Oh, how lovely and fresh! Here and there in the fields campfires were lit and cauldrons put over them, and the moustachioed harvesters sat down round them; the steam rose over the boiled dumplings. The dusk gathered. . . . It is difficult to describe Shponka's feelings at such moments. He forgot everything and joined the harvesters to taste the dumplings he loved so much, and stood motionless on one spot, following with his eyes a gull that disappeared in the sky or counted the stooks of the harvested corn which were dotted all over the field.

In a short time people began to talk of Shponka as a first-class farmer. His aunt could not thank heaven enough for giving her such a nephew and never missed a chance of boasting about him. One day—it happened after the harvest, that is to say, at the end of July—Vasilisa Kashporovna took Ivan Fyodorovich's arm with a mysterious air and said that she wished to discuss a certain matter with him, something she had been revolving in her mind for some time.

"You know, my dear," so she began, "that your farm has eighteen serfs; that, however, is according to the last census; actually I shouldn't be a bit surprised if their number had not grown to twenty-four. But that's not what I was going to talk to you about. You know the wood behind our stream, don't you? And, I suppose, you also know that on the other side of the wood is a large meadow of at least forty acres. There is so much grass on it that the hay could be sold for more than a hundred roubles a year, especially if, as they say, a cavalry regiment is to be stationed in Gadyach."

"Why, of course, Auntie, I know it very well: the grass there is excellent."

"I know it's excellent myself, but do you know that all that land is by rights yours? What are you staring at me like that for? Listen. Do you remember Stepan Kuzmich? But what am I saying? How could you remember him? You were so little then that you could hardly pronounce his name. Dear me! I remember when I came on a visit here at Christmas, just before the fast, and took you in my arms, you nearly made a mess of my dress. Fortunately, I was just in time to hand you over to your nurse Matryona. What a horrible boy you were then! But that's not what I want to talk to you about. In those days the entire land at the other side of our farm and the village of Khortyshche belonged to Stepan Kuzmich. He, I must tell you, began to pay visits to your mother long before you were born, though only when your father was not at home. However, far be it from me to say anything against your mother, God rest her soul, though the poor woman was always unjust to me. But that's not what I want to talk to you about. Be that as it may, only Stepan Kuzmich had made over to you by a deed of gift the land I told you of. But your poor mother, I hope you don't mind me saying so, was a very strange woman. The devil himself—may the Lord forgive me for uttering this nasty word—would not have been able to make her out. Where she put that deed—God only knows. I can't help thinking that that old bachelor Grigory Storchenko has got it. That big-bellied swindler inherited Stepan Kuzmich's estate. I'm ready to bet you anything you like that he had hidden it away."

"Excuse me, Auntie, but isn't it the same Storchenko I got acquainted with at the post station?"

Here Shponka told his aunt about the meeting at the inn.

"Who knows," the aunt answered after a moment's reflection, "perhaps he's not a scoundrel. It's true he only came to live among us sixteen months ago, and it's impossible to find out what a man is like in so short a time. I hear his old mother is a very sensible woman and, they say, a great hand at pickling cucumbers. Her serf girls are wonderfully good at making rugs. But if, as you say, he has been nice to you, you may as well pay him a visit. The old sinner will perhaps listen to the voice of conscience and give you back what doesn't belong to him. I daresay you could drive over there in our britzka, only those damned children have pulled out all the nails at the back. I must tell Omelko to nail the leather properly."

"Whatever for, Auntie? I'll take your shooting brake."

This brought the conversation to an end.

IV   The Dinner

Shponka drove into the village of Khortyshche at dinner time and he began to feel a little apprehensive as he approached the country house. The house was rather long and

not thatched like most of the houses of the local land-
owners, but had a wooden roof. The two barns in the yard
had also wooden roofs; the gates were of oak. Shponka was
like the dandy who, arriving at a ball, sees that everyone
is dressed more elegantly than he. Out of respect, he
stopped his brake near one of the barns and walked to the
front steps of the house.

"Ah, Ivan Fyodorovich!" cried Grigory Storchenko, who
was walking across the yard in a coat and without tie or
braces, but even that seemed too heavy a burden for his
obese figure, for sweat poured all over him. "Why did you
say you'd come and see us as soon as you saw your aunt
and didn't?"

After these words Shponka's lips came into contact with
the already familiar cushions.

"I'm afraid I was kept too busy on my farm. . . .
I've only come for a minute, sir. . . . On business actually. . . ."

"For a minute? Oh no, sir, I won't have that! Hey, boy!"
cried the fat landowner, and the same boy in the Cossack
coat rushed out of the kitchen. "Tell Kassyan to lock the
gates. You hear? Let him lock them properly! And let him
unharness this gentleman's horses at once. Come into the
house, sir. It's so hot here that my shirt's soaking."

On entering the house, Shponka decided not to waste
time and, in spite of his timidity, to launch his attack res-
olutely.

"My aunt, sir," he began, "was so good as to tell me that
the late Stepan Kuzmich's deed of gift . . ."

It is difficult to describe the unpleasant expression that
came into Storchenko's face at these words.

"I'm sorry," he said, "I can't hear a word. I must tell you
that I had a cockroach in my left ear. Those damned Russians have thousands of cockroaches in their cottages. The
agonies I suffered! No pen, sir, can describe it. And it still
tickles. Keeps on tickling. An old woman, you know, did
help me once in a most simple way . . ."

"What I wanted to say is," Shponka ventured to inter-

79

rupt, seeing that Storchenko was trying to change the subject deliberately, "that the deed of gift is mentioned in Stepan Kuzmich's will and that, according to it, I should have——"

"I know that's the sort of thing your aunt would tell you, but it's a lie. I assure you, sir, there's not a word of truth in it. My uncle made no deed of gift. It is true there's some mention of it in his will, but where is it? No one has ever presented it. I'm telling you this because I sincerely wish you well. I assure you the whole thing's a lie!"

Shponka fell silent, thinking that perhaps his aunt had really imagined it all.

"And here comes Mother with my sisters," said Storchenko. "That means that dinner is ready. Come along!"

And he dragged Shponka by the arm into the room in which drinks and snacks were placed on a table.

At the same moment a short old woman, looking exactly like a coffeepot in a cap, entered the room with two young ladies, one fair and the other dark. As a well-bred gentleman, Shponka went up to pay his respect to the ladies, first kissing the old woman's hand and then the hands of the two young ladies.

"This is our neighbour, Ivan Fyodorovich Shponka, Mother," said Storchenko.

The old woman looked very intently at Shponka or, perhaps, it only seemed so to him. However, she was kindness itself. It seemed as though all she wanted was to ask Shponka how many cucumbers his aunt had pickled for the winter.

"Do you drink vodka?" the old woman asked.

"Are you sure you're quite yourself, Mother?" said Storchenko. "What a question to ask a visitor? You should offer him a glass and let him decide for himself whether to drink it or not. What will you have, sir? Centaury or rye vodka? Which do you like best? And what are you standing there for, Ivan Ivanovich?" said Storchenko, turning round.

Shponka saw a man in a long frock coat and a huge stand-up collar coming up to the table with the drinks. His collar covered the whole of his neck so that his head seemed to sit in it as though in a britzka.

Ivan Ivanovich went up to the table with the drinks, rubbed his hands, examined his glass carefully, filled it, held it up to the light, poured the whole of its contents into his mouth and, without swallowing it, rinsed his mouth thoroughly with it first and only then swallowed it. After eating a bit of bread with pickled mushrooms, he turned to Shponka.

"It isn't Mr. Shponka I have the honour of addressing, is it?" he asked.

"Yes, sir," replied Shponka.

"You've changed a lot since I first knew you. Why," Ivan Ivanovich went on, placing his hand about two feet from the floor, "I remember you since you were so high. Your father, God rest his soul, was a most remarkable man. You won't find melons and watermelons like those he used to grow anywhere to-day. Now, take the sort of melons they serve you at the table here," he went on, taking him aside. "What sort of melons are they? It makes you sick to look at them! Believe me, sir, your father's watermelons," he said with a mysterious air, spreading out his arms as though he wished to put them round a huge tree, "were as big as that!"

"Let's go in to dinner," said Storchenko, taking Shponka's arm.

They all went into the dining room. Storchenko sat down in his usual place at the head of the table and tied an enormous napkin round his neck, which made him look like one of those heroic figures barbers are fond of painting on their signboards. Shponka, blushing, sat down at a place pointed out to him opposite the two young ladies, while Ivan Ivanovich took good care to occupy the seat next to him, glad of the opportunity of having someone to whom he could communicate his knowledge of the world.

"You shouldn't have taken the parson's nose, sir," said Mrs. Storchenko, addressing Shponka, who had just been offered a dish by a village waiter in a grey frock coat with a black patch. "This is a turkey. Take the back."

"Please, don't interfere, Mother," said her son. "No one is asking you. You may be sure our guest knows himself what he wants. Take a wing, sir, that one, and the stomach! And why don't you help yourself to some more? Take a leg. What are you gaping at, you there with the dish?" he shouted to the waiter. "Beg the gentleman to take it. Go down on your knees, you scoundrel, and say, Please, take the leg, sir!"

"Please, take the leg, sir!" bawled the waiter with the dish, going down on his knees.

"Good Lord, what sort of a turkey is this!" Ivan Ivanovich said in an undertone with a scornful air, turning to his neighbour. "Is that what turkeys should be like? You should see my turkeys. I assure you that one of them has more fat on it than ten of these. Believe me, sir, it makes me feel sick to look at them as they walk across my yard—so fat are they!"

"Ivan Ivanovich, you're lying!" said Storchenko, who overheard what he was saying.

"Let me tell you, sir," Ivan Ivanovich went on in the same conspiratorial tone, pretending not to have heard what Storchenko had said, "that when I sent them off to Gadyach last year I was offered fifty copecks each. And I refused to take even that."

"Ivan Ivanovich, I tell you you're lying!" said Storchenko, raising his voice and stressing every syllable for the sake of clarity.

But Ivan Ivanovich, pretending that the words did not refer to him at all, went on addressing Shponka, though much more softly.

"Yes, sir, I refused to take it. Not one landowner in Gadyach——"

"Ivan Ivanovich, you're just stupid," Storchenko said in a loud voice. "Ivan Fyodorovich knows it all much better than you and I'm sure he won't believe you."

This time Ivan Ivanovich looked very hurt and, falling silent, began to dispatch the turkey in spite of the fact that it was not as fat as those that made him feel sick to look at.

The clatter of knives, spoons, and plates made conversation impossible for a time, but loudest of all was the noise made by Storchenko as he sucked the marrow of a sheep's bone.

"Have you read Korobeynik's *Journey to the Holy Places?*" Ivan Ivanovich asked Shponka after a pause, thrusting his head out of his britzka. "It's a real delight to one's heart and soul. There are no such books published nowadays. I regret very much not having looked up the year in which it was published."

At the mention of a book Shponka began helping himself diligently to the sauce.

"It's really remarkable, sir, when you consider that a simple artisan went all over those places. Three thousand miles, sir! Three thousand miles! Truly, God himself must have thought him worthy of visiting Palestine and Jerusalem!"

"Did you say, sir," said Shponka, who had been told a great deal about Jerusalem by his batman, "that he had been to Jerusalem?"

"What are you talking about, Ivan Fyodorovich?" Storchenko asked from the other end of the table.

"I just happened to remark, sir, that there are such wonderful places in distant countries," said Shponka, greatly pleased to have managed to utter such a long and difficult sentence.

"Don't you believe him, my dear sir," said Storchenko, who had not really bothered to listen carefully to what Shponka was saying. "He's always telling tall stories!"

Meanwhile the dinner was over. Storchenko, as usual, retired to his room for a nap, and the guests followed his mother and sisters into the drawing room where the table, on which they had left the drinks as they went in to dinner, was now, as if by magic, covered with saucers of different sorts of jams and plates of melons, watermelons, and cherries.

Storchenko's absence could be noticed in everything.
Their hostess became more talkative and revealed, without
being asked, a great number of secret recipes for making
sweetmeats of fruit and berries and for drying pears. Even
the young ladies began to talk; but the fair one, who
seemed to be six years younger than her sister and who was
about twenty-five, was more taciturn.

It was Ivan Ivanovich, however, who was more talkative
and more active than the rest. Convinced that no one would
confuse or shut him up now, he talked about cucumbers,
the planting of potatoes, about how sensible people used
to be in the old days—those of to-day were not a patch on
them!—and about how everything was getting more and
more efficient and resulting in the invention of the most in-
genious things. In a word, he was one of those people who
derive the greatest pleasure from indulging in conversations
about all sorts of entrancing subjects and who go on talking
about everything under the sun. Whenever the conversation
turned upon some important and pious subject Ivan Ivanovich heaved a sigh after every word, nodding his head
slightly; but if it turned upon farming, he thrust his head
out of his britzka and pulled such faces that one could guess
from them alone how to make pear wine, how big were the
melons he was talking about, and how fat were the geese
that ran about his yard.

At last, towards the evening, Shponka succeeded with
great difficulty in taking his leave. And in spite of his com-
pliant character and his host's insistence that he should
stay the night, he stuck to his decision to go and he did go.

V *His Aunt's New Scheme*

"Well? Have you got the deed from the old villain?"

This was the question with which Shponka was met by
his aunt, who had been waiting for him impatiently for several hours on the front steps and who, at last, could no
longer resist rushing out of the gates.

"No, Auntie," said Shponka, alighting from the cart. "Mr. Storchenko hasn't got the deed."

"And you believed him? He's lying, the damned rogue! One day I'll go and see him myself and thrash him with my own hands. Oh, I'll render some of his fat for him, I will! However, I think we'd better discuss the matter first with the clerk of our district court to see whether we could issue a writ against him. . . . But that's not what I want to talk to you about. Well, was it a good dinner?"

"Yes, a very good one, Auntie."

"Well, what did they give you? Tell me. I know the old woman is very good at running her kitchen."

"We had cheesecakes with sour cream, Auntie. Sauce with pigeons, stuffed ones. . . ."

"And did you have turkey with plums?" asked the aunt, who was a past master at preparing that dish.

"We had turkey, too. . . . The young ladies, Mr. Storchenko's sisters, are quite pretty, especially the fair one."

"Oh?" said the aunt, looking intently at Shponka, who blushed and dropped his eyes. A new idea flashed through her mind. "Well?" she asked eagerly, with interest. "What kind of eyebrows has she got?"

We ought to explain here that the aunt judged a woman's beauty first of all by her eyebrows.

"Her eyebrows, Auntie, are exactly the same as you told me you had when you were young. And she has small freckles all over her face."

"Oh!" said the aunt, pleased with Shponka's remark, though it had never occurred to him to pay her a compliment by it. "What dress did she wear? Though, I daresay, you won't find such thick material nowadays as my dress is made of. But that's not what I want to talk to you about. Well, did you say anything to her?"

"How do you mean? Me, Auntie? You're not really thinking——"

"And why not? There's nothing strange about it, is there?

It's God's will! Perhaps it's your fate to live in wedlock with her."

"I don't know how you can say a thing like that, Auntie. This shows that you don't know me at all. . . ."

"Well, now he's offended!" said his aunt. "The lad's still young," she thought to herself. "Doesn't know anything. They must be brought together. They must get better acquainted."

Here the aunt left Shponka and went to have a look into the kitchen. But ever since then she could think of nothing but of seeing her nephew married as soon as possible and of nursing her great-nephews. Her head was full of plans for the preparations for the wedding, and it was noticed that she bustled about the house more than ever, but that everything she did turned out worse rather than better. Often when making a pie, which she never trusted Cook to do, she forgot herself and, fancying that a little child was standing beside her and asking for a bit of the pie, she would absent-mindedly hold out her hand with the best bit to him, and the watchdog, taking advantage of this heaven-sent opportunity, seized the tasty morsel and brought her out of her reverie by his loud champing, for which he was always beaten with a poker. She even gave up her favourite occupations and did not go hunting, especially after she had shot a crow instead of a partridge, a thing that had never happened to her before.

At last, four days later, everyone saw the britzka hauled out of the barn into the yard. The coachman Omelko, also market gardener and night watchman, had been knocking with a hammer since early morning, fastening the leather to the back of the carriage and driving off the dogs who kept licking the wheels. I deem it my duty to acquaint my readers with the fact that it was the very same britzka Adam used for his travels, so that if anyone should try to pass off another britzka for Adam's, it is an absolute lie and his britzka is a counterfeit one. It is a mystery how it managed to save itself from the flood. It must be assumed that Noah built a special barn for it in his ark. I regret very much not being able to describe what it looked like. It will suffice to say that Vasilisa Kashporovna was highly satisfied with its architecture and always expressed her regrets that old carriages were no longer in fashion. The very construction of the britzka, a little on one side, that is to say, its right side much higher than its left, appealed to her greatly, for, as she used to say, this made it possible for a short person to get into it from one side and a tall one from the other. However, there was room inside the britzka for five short persons and three as tall as the aunt herself.

About midday Omelko, having finished with the britzka, led three horses out of the stables, horses that were only a little younger than the britzka, and began harnessing them with a rope to that majestic equipage. Shponka and his aunt, one from the left side and the other from the right, got into the britzka, and it rolled off. The peasants they met on the road stopped respectfully at the sight of so magnificent a carriage (the aunt seldom drove out in it), took off their caps, and bowed low. Two hours later the carriage stopped before the front steps—I think it is hardly necessary to add: before the front steps of Mr. Storchenko's house. Storchenko himself was not at home. His mother and the two young ladies met their visitors in the dining room. Shponka's aunt went up to her with a majestic step and, putting one foot forward with great dexterity, said in a loud voice:

"I'm very glad, madam, to have the honour of paying my respects to you in person. And, together with my respects, allow me to thank you for the hospitality you have extended to my nephew, who cannot find words to express his appreciation. Your buckwheat, madam, is first class. I saw it as I drove up to your village. May I ask how many stooks you get from an acre?"

After which there was a general exchange of kisses. When they sat down in the drawing room, their hostess began:

"I'm afraid I cannot tell you anything about the buckwheat. That is my son's province. I have long since given up doing anything about it. Besides, I shouldn't be able to: I'm too old. In the old days, I remember, our buckwheat used to reach as high as a man's waist, but now goodness only knows what it is like. Though, mind you, I am told that everything is much better now."

Here the old lady heaved a sigh. And some outside observer might have recognised in that sigh the sigh of the eighteenth century.

"I've heard, madam, that your serf girls make excellent rugs," said Vasilisa Kashporovna, touching the old lady upon her most sensitive spot by her remark.

At these words Mrs. Storchenko seemed to brighten up and off she went, telling them how to dye yarn and how to prepare the threads for it. From the rugs the conversation quickly turned to the pickling of cucumbers and the drying of pears. In short, within less than an hour the two ladies became so absorbed in their conversation that they were talking as though they had known each other for years. Indeed, Vasilisa Kashporovna even began to talk to her about many things in so low a voice that Shponka could not hear what they were saying.

"Won't you have a look at it yourself?" said their hostess, getting up.

Vasilisa Kashporovna and the young ladies got up after her and they were all about to go to the serf girls' room. The aunt, however, signalled to Shponka to remain and whispered something in the old lady's ear.

"Mashenka," said Mrs. Storchenko, turning to the fair-haired young lady, "stay and talk to our guest and see he isn't bored."

The young lady stayed behind and sat down on the sofa. Shponka sat on his chair as though he were sitting on thorns, blushing and dropping his eyes; but the young lady apparently did not notice it at all and she remained sitting calmly on the sofa, absorbed in the examination of the walls and the windows or following with her eyes the cat which was scurrying about timidly under the chairs.

Shponka plucked up a little courage and was about to

start a conversation, but it seemed that he had lost all his words on the road. He could not think of anything, however much he tried.

The silence lasted for about a quarter of an hour. The young lady still remained sitting as before.

At last Shponka plucked up courage.

"There are a great many flies in the summer, ma'am," he said in a half-trembling voice.

"Yes, ever so many," replied the young lady. "My brother purposely made a flyflap out of mother's old slipper, but there are still lots of them."

Here the conversation again came to an end and Shponka could not find anything more to say, however much he racked his brains.

At last their hostess with his aunt and the dark girl returned. After exchanging a few more words, Vasilisa Kashporovna said good-bye to the old lady and her daughters in spite of the repeated invitations to stay the night. The old lady and her two daughters came out on the front steps to see their visitors off and they waved for a long time to the aunt and her nephew who kept looking out of their carriage.

"Well, what did you talk about when you were left alone with the young lady?" the aunt asked on their way home.

"Maria Grigoryevna is a very modest and well-behaved girl," said Shponka.

"Listen, I want to talk to you seriously. You will, God be praised, be thirty-eight soon. Your rank is excellent. It's time to think of children. You must get yourself a wife."

"Good heavens, Auntie!" cried Shponka, frightened. "A wife? No, thank you, Auntie. . . . You're making me feel ashamed. . . . I've never been married before. . . . I wouldn't know what to do with her!"

"You will, my dear boy, you will!" the aunt said with a smile, and she thought to herself: "No wonder! The lad's still young. He knows nothing!" And she went on aloud: "No, my dear boy, you won't find a better wife than Maria

Grigoryevna. And, besides, you liked her very much, didn't you? I've already discussed it all with the old woman. She will be very pleased to have you as her son-in-law. It's true we don't know what that old sinner Grigory Grigoryevich will say. But we won't take any notice of him, and if he tries to refuse to part with her dowry, we'll drag him into court. . . ."

At that moment the britzka drove up to their yard and the ancient nags came to life again, scenting the proximity of the manger.

"Listen, Omelko, first of all let the horses have a good rest and don't you take them to the horse pond as soon as you've unharnessed them. They're too hot. Well, my boy," she went on, as she climbed out of the carriage, "I advise you to think it over carefully. I have to go to the kitchen now. I forgot to tell Solokha to get our supper ready and I shouldn't be surprised if that good-for-nothing slut never thought of it herself."

But Shponka stood there as if thunderstruck. It was true that Maria Grigoryevna was not at all a bad-looking girl, but to marry her! That seemed so strange, so fantastic to him that he could not think of it without feeling frightened. To live with a wife! It was incomprehensible. He would not be alone in his room, but there would always be the two of them! Sweat broke out on his face the more he became absorbed in his thoughts.

He went to bed earlier than usual, but hard as he tried, he could not fall asleep. At last longed-for sleep, that universal bringer of peace, came; but what a sleep! He had never had such incoherent dreams. First he dreamed that everything was whirling noisily around him, and he was running, running as fast as his legs would carry him—now he was at his last gasp. . . . Suddenly someone caught him by the ear. "Ouch! Who is it?" "It's me, your wife!" a voice shouted in his ear. And he woke up. Then he imagined that he was already married, that everything in their home was so queer, so strange: a double bed stood in his room instead of a single one. His wife was sitting on a chair. He felt strange; he did not know how to approach her, what to say to her, and then he noticed that she had the face of a goose. Turning away, he saw another wife, also with the face of a goose. He turned in another direction, and there was a third wife. Behind—still another wife. Here he was seized with panic and rushed into the garden; but there it was hot. He took off his hat and—saw a wife sitting in his hat. He put his hand in his pocket for his handkerchief and— there was a wife in his pocket, too; he took some cotton wool out of his ear and—there, too, sat a wife. . . . Then he suddenly began hopping on one leg, and his aunt, look- ing at him, said with a dignified air: "Yes, you must hop on one leg now because you are a married man." He went towards her, but his aunt was no longer his aunt, but a belfry. And he felt that someone was dragging him by a rope up the belfry. "Who's dragging me?" he asked plain- tively. "It's me, your wife. I'm pulling you because you are a bell." "No, I'm not a bell, I'm Ivan Fyodorovich!" he screamed. "Yes, you are a bell," said the colonel of the P— infantry regiment, who was passing by. Then he dreamed that his wife was not a human being at all, but a sort of woollen material, and that he went into a shop in Mogilyov. "What sort of material would you like?" said the shop- keeper. "You'd better take a wife, sir. It's the most fash- ionable material. Very good material, indeed, sir. Everyone is having frock coats made of it now." The shopkeeper measured and cut out his wife. Shponka took her under his arm and went off to a Jewish tailor. "No," said the Jew, "that's bad material. No one has frock coats made of it now. . . ."

Shponka kept waking up in terror and almost in a fainting condition. Cold sweat poured from his brow.

As soon as he got up in the morning, he turned at once to his fortune-telling book, at the end of which the virtuous bookseller, out of the goodness of his heart and with no selfish motive, had put an abbreviated dream interpreter.

But he could find nothing there that in the least resembled his incoherent dream.

Meanwhile quite a new scheme matured in his aunt's head, of which you will learn in the next chapter.

1831

The Portrait

PART ONE

NOWHERE WAS there so great a crowd of people as before the little art dealer's shop in Pike's Yard, one of the many markets in St. Petersburg. This little shop had indeed a most varied assortment of curiosities: the pictures were mostly painted in oils, covered with a dark-green varnish, in dark-yellow, tawdry frames. A winter landscape with white trees, a red evening sky, looking like the reflection of some conflagration, a Flemish peasant with a pipe and a broken arm, looking more like a turkey with frills than a human being—those were their usual subjects. To these must be added a few engraved portraits: the portrait of Hozreva-Mirza, the Persian prince and special envoy, in a lambskin cap, and portraits of generals with crooked noses in three-cornered hats. In addition, the doors of such shops are usually hung with all sorts of illustrated popular ballads, printed on large sheets of paper, which bear witness to the native talent of the Russian. On one of them was the fairy princess Miliktrissa Kirbityevna, on another the City of Jerusalem, with houses and churches unceremoniously bedaubed with red paint, which also covered part of the street and two praying Russian peasants in mittens. As a rule, not many people purchased any of these works of art, but hundreds were eager to look at them. Some shiftless footman would be quite sure to stop and gape at them, holding in his hands dishes from the restaurant with the dinner for his master, whose soup would be cold by the time it was served. An old soldier in a greatcoat would be gazing at them, this king of hawkers with a few penknives for sale; or a market woman from Okhta with a basketful of shoes. Each one would show his admiration in his own way: the peasants usually poked their fingers; the hawkers examined them with a serious air; servant lads and apprentices laughed and teased each other about the coloured caricatures; old footmen in frieze overcoats looked at them simply because they had to gape at something; and the market women, young Russian peasant women, hurried towards such a shop by instinct, eager to hear what the people were gossiping about and to look at what the people were looking at.

At this time Chartkov, a young artist, who happened to be passing by, involuntarily stopped before the shop. His old overcoat and far from fashionable clothes showed that he was a man who had devoted himself to his work with self-denying zeal and had not time to worry about clothes, which always have a mysterious attraction for the young. He stopped in front of the shop and at first began laughing inwardly at those grotesque pictures. At last he began wondering unconsciously what sort of people wanted such pictures. That the Russian people should gape at cheap prints of Yeruslan Lazarevich, or popular figures of fun like Foma and Yeryoma, or "The Glutton" or "The Drunkard," did not strike him as particularly strange; the subjects were, after all, familiar and intelligible to the people. But who were the purchasers of those ridiculous, clumsily painted, dingy oil paintings? Who wanted these Flemish peasants, these red and blue landscapes, which showed some pretensions to a higher level of art, but which merely succeeded in expressing the depth of its degradation? They did not even seem to be the works of a precocious child, for, if they were, one would have perceived in them a certain intensity of feeling in spite of the caricature of an art which the whole picture conveyed. But all one found in them was a total lack of talent, the dull-witted, feeble, decrepit incompetence of a born failure that impudently thrusts himself among the arts, whereas his true place is among the meanest of the crafts, a failure that is true to his calling, however, and introduces the tricks of his trade even into the world of art. The same colours, the same mannerisms, the same unimaginative, bungling and clumsy hand, which one would have thought belonged to an automaton rather than to a living man! . . .

He stood before those grimy pictures a long time without even thinking of them any more, while the owner of the shop, a drab little man in a frieze overcoat and with a face that had not been shaved since Sunday, talked to him for some time, bargaining and discussing prices before even finding out what his prospective customer fancied and what he was likely to buy.

"For those peasants, sir, and for the little landscape painting I'd take two pounds. What wonderful brushwork! It fairly hits you in the eye! Just got them from the warehouse. The varnish isn't dry yet. Or take that one, sir—the winter landscape! Thirty bob. The frame itself is worth more. What a lovely winter landscape, sir!" Here the art dealer struck a light blow on the canvas as further proof of the fine quality of the winter landscape. "Shall I tie them up together and take them to your place? Where do you live, sir? Here, boy, give me some string!"

"Wait a moment; not so fast!" said the artist, recovering with a jolt as he saw the enterprising dealer beginning in good earnest to tie up the pictures with a piece of string. Feeling a little ashamed, though, not to take anything at all after standing so long in the shop, he added, "Wait a moment. I'll have a look round. Perhaps there is something I'd like to have."

Stooping, he began picking up from the floor the faded,

dusty old paintings, thrown together in a heap, which the shopkeeper apparently did not consider to be of any great value. There were among them old family portraits of people whose descendants could most probably no longer be traced anywhere; pictures of quite unknown people on torn canvases and frames that had lost their gilding; in fact, all sorts of trash. But the artist began examining them carefully, thinking to himself, "I might find something worth while here." He had heard many stories of the discovery of paintings of the great masters among the rubbish of popular print shops.

The art dealer, seeing that his customer was likely to be busy for some time, stopped fussing over him and, assuming his usual attitude and proper gravity of demeanour, again took up his position at the open door of his shop, inviting the passers-by to come in, waving his hand towards his pictures. "Come right in, sir! Have a look at my pictures! Lovely pictures! Come in, come in! Just got them from the warehouse!" he shouted until he was hoarse and generally in vain. Then he had a long talk with a rag merchant, standing opposite at the door of his little shop, and at last remembering that he had a customer in his shop, turned his back on the people in the street and went inside.

"Well, sir," he addressed the artist, "have you found anything?"

The artist had been standing without moving for some time before a portrait in a huge and once magnificent frame, upon which, however, only a few gleaming spots of gilt remained. It was the portrait of a man with a face the colour of bronze, rather haggard and with high cheekbones; the features of his face seemed to have been caught by the artist in a moment of a sudden spasmodic movement and there was a terrific force in them that could not possibly belong to a man of a northern latitude. The fiery tropical sun was clearly imprinted upon them. A wide oriental robe was draped round him. However damaged and dusty the portrait was, Chartkov could see the unmistakable hand of a great artist as soon as he removed the dust from the face.

The portrait had apparently been left unfinished; but the firmness of hand with which it had been painted was astonishing. The eyes were particularly striking; the artist seemed to have applied to them the full power of his brush and all his painstaking care. They seemed to glare at you, glare at you out of the portrait, destroying its harmony by their uncanny vitality. When Chartkov carried the portrait to the door, the eyes stared at him with even greater intentness. They produced almost the same impression on the people in the street. A woman who stopped behind him cried, "He looks at you as if he was alive!" and drew back. A curious, uncomfortable feeling, a feeling which he could hardly explain to himself, took hold of the young artist, and he put the portrait down on the floor.

"Well, sir, won't you take this portrait?" asked the owner of the shop.

"How much?" said the artist.

"Well, I don't want to make a profit on it, sir. Shall we say six shillings?"

"No."

"Well, what would you offer me for it, sir?"

"One and sixpence," said the artist, preparing to go.

"Dear me, what a price to offer! Why, the frame alone is worth more than one and sixpence! Seems to me you don't really want to buy it. Come back, sir, come back! Just add another sixpence. No? All right, all right! Take it for one and six. It's practically giving it away, but seeing that you are my first customer today . . ." He made a gesture which seemed to say, "Ah well, so be it! It's giving a fine picture away!"

It was thus that Chartkov quite unexpectedly became the owner of the old portrait, and almost at the same instant he could not help reflecting, "Why have I bought it? What do I want it for?" But there was nothing he could do about it. He took one and sixpence out of his pocket, gave it to the art dealer, took the portrait under his arm and went home. On the way he remembered that the one and sixpence he had given for it was the last one and sixpence he had in the world. His thoughts at once took on a gloomy cast. He cursed himself for being such a fool, and at the same time he felt a listless void inside him. "Damn, what a rotten world it is!" he said, expressing the typical feeling of a Russian whose affairs have just about touched rock bottom. And he walked on mechanically with hurried steps, feeling totally indifferent to everything. The red glow of sunset still lingered over half the sky; the houses which faced that way were faintly illuminated by its warm light, while the cold, bluish radiance of the moon was getting stronger. Light, half-transparent shadows, cast by the houses and the feet of pedestrians, fell upon the ground in long, narrow bars. The artist was already glancing more and more frequently at the sky, which was irradiated by a kind of faint, translucent, uncertain light, and almost at the same moment there burst from his lips the words, "What a delicate tone!" and "Damn it, what a nuisance!" The portrait kept slipping from under his arm and he was continually putting it back and quickening his pace. Dog-tired, and covered with perspiration, he at last dragged himself home to Fifteenth Row of Vassilyev Island. With difficulty he climbed up the stairs, wet with slops and adorned with the footprints of cats and dogs, and he was out of breath by the time he reached the door of his flat. There was no reply to his knock at the door: his servant, whose name was Nikita and who always wore a blueshirt, was not at home. He leant against the window, resigned to wait patiently for the return of Nikita, whom he employed as his Jack of all trades: his model, his paint grinder and his sweeper of floors which he usually dirtied immediately with his boots. At last he heard the lad's footsteps behind him. While his master was away, Nikita spent all his time in the street. It took him a long time to get the key into the key-hole which he could hardly see because of the darkness. At last the door was opened. Chartkov entered the hall, which was terribly cold, like all the halls of artists' flats, not that it seems to matter to them much. Without handing his overcoat to Nikita, he went into his studio—a large, square room, though with rather a low ceiling, with window-panes covered with hoar-frost, filled with all sorts of artist's lumber: bits of plaster-of-Paris arms, frames covered with canvas, sketches begun and discarded, draperies hung on chairs. Feeling terribly tired, he threw off his overcoat, put the portrait absent-mindedly between two small canvases, and flung himself on a narrow sofa, of which it could hardly be claimed that it was covered with hide, because the row of brass nails which had once fastened the hide to the frame of the sofa had long since detached themselves, leaving the upholstery also detached, so that Nikita pushed dirty socks and shirts and all the dirty linen under it. Having stretched as much as it was possible to stretch on so narrow a sofa, he at last called for a candle.

"There is no candle, sir," said Nikita.

"What do you mean, there is no candle?"

"We had no candle yesterday, either," said Nikita.

The artist remembered that they had indeed had no candle the night before, and he calmed down and fell silent. He let Nikita help him with his undressing, and put on his worn, old dressing-gown.

"The landlord's been here again, sir," said Nikita.

"Oh? Came for his money I suppose. I know," said the artist, dismissing the subject with a wave of the hand.

"But he wasn't alone, sir," said Nikita.

"Who was with him?"

"Dunno, sir. Looked like a policeman to me."

"What did he want to bring a policeman for?"

"Dunno, sir. He said, sir, it was because your rent had not been paid."

"Well, what about it?"

"Dunno what about it, sir. Only he says, 'If he can't pay,' he says, 'he'd better clear out of the flat.' They'll be coming again tomorrow, both of 'em, sir."

"Let them come," said Chartkov with mournful indifference, feeling completely out of humour with the whole world.

Chartkov was a talented young man of great promise;

there were odd moments when his brush seemed suddenly to show that he possessed keen observation, intense perception, and a quick impulse to get closer to nature.

"Take good care, my dear fellow," his art master used to say to him; "you have talent, and it would be a thousand pities if you ruined it. The trouble with you is that you're so confoundedly impatient. If you get interested in something, if you happen to take a fancy to something, you get so entirely absorbed in it that everything else is just of no account to you; you don't want even to look at it. Take care you don't become a fashionable artist. Even now your colours seem to be getting out of hand. Much too slick those colours of yours are, if you don't mind my saying so. Your drawing, too, lacks strength. Sometimes it is very weak. No lines. Running after fashionable light effects. You seem to be mainly working for effect. Watch out or one day you'll find yourself a mere imitator of the English school. And another thing. You're getting too much attracted by the fashionable world. I have seen you sometimes wearing an expensive scarf round your neck, a beautifully polished hat. Mind, I don't say it isn't a tempting prospect. Start painting fashionable pictures, become a fashionable portrait painter, and all your money worries are at an end: you'll get lots of money. But remember, my dear fellow, that is the way to ruin your talent, not to develop it. Take great care over every picture you paint. Take your time over it; think it over carefully. Forget about fine clothes. Let others rake in the money; your time will come!"

The professor was partly right. There were indeed moments when our artist wanted to enjoy himself, to show off, in fact to display in some way his youthful exuberance. But in spite of that he could take himself in hand. At times, as soon as he got hold of his brush, he could forget everything, and he would only put it down reluctantly, as one waking from a beautiful dream. It is true that he was as yet incapable of understanding the whole depth of Raphael, but he was already under the spell of the swift, mighty brush of Guido, lingered before the portraits of Titian, was enrap-

tured by the Flemish painters. He was still unable to see
through the darkened surface of the old painters; but he
already saw something in them, though in his heart he dis-
agreed with his professor's view that the art of the old
masters was unattainable by the modern painter. It seemed
to him that in some ways the nineteenth century had got
ahead of them; that the imitation of nature had somehow
or other become more brilliant, more vivid, and more close.
He was reasoning in this instance as youth always reasons,
youth that has already achieved something and realises it
in the pride of its inner consciousness. Sometimes he could
not help feeling annoyed when some foreign painter, a
Frenchman or a German, created a general stir, although
he was not always even a professional painter, but just a
showman, who by the smartness of his brushwork and the
brightness of his colours amassed a fortune in no time. He
did not think of this when absorbed in his work, for then
he forgot food and drink and the whole world; but when
he felt the pinch of necessity, when he had not enough
money to buy paints and brushes, when the importunate
landlord came ten times a day to demand the rent for the
flat. It was then that the lot of the rich fashionable painter
appealed so powerfully to his hungry imagination; it was
then that the thought, which often flashes through the
mind of a Russian, also flashed through his mind: give it
all up and take to drink just out of sheer vexation of spirit
and spleen. And now he was almost in that mood.

"Yes, have patience, have patience!" he muttered, irrita-
bly. "But there is an end even to one's patience! Have
patience! And where will I get the money for my dinner
tomorrow? No one will lend me any. And if I were to take
all my drawings and paintings to an art dealer, he wouldn't
give me more than sixpence for them. I suppose they have
been of some use to me. I realise that. None of them has
been a waste of time. Each of them has taught me something. But what's the use of it? Sketches, rough drafts. It
can go on for ever. And who'd buy any of my pictures
never even having heard my name? And who wants studies

from the antique or from life? Or my unfinished Psyche's
Love, or the interior of my room, or Nikita's portrait, a
damn sight better though it is than the portraits of some
of the fashionable painters? Why take all this trouble; why
waste my time, like a beginner, on the elementary rules of
my art, when I could easily do something that will make
me as famous as the rest of them and earn as much money
as they do into the bargain?"

Having said this, the artist suddenly shuddered and grew
pale; a horribly contorted face was looking at him from
behind one of his canvases. Two terrible eyes were gazing
intently at him as though about to devour him; the lips
seemed sternly to enjoin silence. Terrified, he was about to
cry out and call Nikita, whose loud snoring he could hear
from the hall; but suddenly he stopped and laughed. The
feeling of terror disappeared in an instant. It was the portrait he had bought and completely forgotten. The moonlight which filled the room fell upon the portrait and in-
vested it with an uncanny vitality. He began examining and
wiping it. Dipping a sponge in water, he rubbed it over the
portrait a few times, washed off almost all the accumulated
and encrusted dirt, hung it on the wall before him and
admired more than ever its extraordinarily fine technique;
almost the whole face seemed to have come to life, and
the eyes looked at him in a way that made him shudder
involuntarily and retreat a few steps, exclaiming in an as-
tonished voice, "By Jove, it looks at you with human eyes!"
He suddenly remembered the story he had heard from his
professor a long time ago of a portrait of Leonardo da
Vinci's. The great master had worked on it for several years
and still regarded it as unfinished, but in spite of that it
was, according to Vasari, generally acclaimed as a finished
masterpiece. The most finished thing about it was the eyes
which amazed Leonardo's contemporaries; even the tiniest,
hardly visible veins in them were not overlooked and were
reproduced on the canvas. But here, in the portrait that
now hung on the wall before him, there was something uncanny. This was no longer art; it destroyed the harmony

of the portrait itself! Those eyes were living, human eyes! They seemed to have been cut out of a living man and put in there. Here there was no longer any of that sublime feeling of joy that encompasses the soul at the sight of the work of an artist, however terrible the subject chosen by him might be; the sensation he received from looking at this portrait was rather one of joylessness, painfulness and anxiety. "What's the matter?" the artist could not help asking himself. "After all, it is only something copied from life, a picture painted from a model! Then why on earth should it give me this strangely unpleasant feeling? Or is a faithful, slavish imitation of nature such an offence that it must affect you like a loud, discordant scream? Or if you paint a thing objectively and coolly, without feeling any particular sympathy for it, must it necessarily confront you in all its terrible reality, unillumined by the light of some deep, hidden, unfathomable thought? Must it appear to you with the reality which reveals itself to a person who, searching for beauty in man, picks up a scalpel and begins to dissect a man's inside, only to find what is disgusting in man? Why is it that simple, lowly nature appears in the work of one artist as though illumined by some magic light and you never get the sensation of anything low? On the contrary, you seem to derive a certain enjoyment from it, and life afterwards seems much more placid and calm. And yet the same kind of subject appears in the work of another artist as low and sordid, though he is no less true to nature. The truth is that there is nothing in it that sheds a lustre upon it. It is just like a landscape in nature; however beautiful it may be, something seems to be missing in it, if there is no sun in the sky."

He again went up to the portrait to examine those wonderful eyes more closely, and to his horror he noticed that they were actually looking at him. That was no longer a copy from nature; it was the kind of life that might have lit up the face of a dead man risen from the grave. Whether it was the moonlight which brought with it the phantasmagoria of a dream world and clothed everything in shapes so different from what it appeared in broad daylight, or whether there was another reason for it, he became suddenly (he himself hardly knew why) frightened of remaining alone in the room. He walked slowly away from the portrait, turned away from it and tried not to look at it, but, try as he might, he could not help looking at it now and again furtively out of a corner of an eye. At last he even became frightened to walk about in the room; he had the odd feeling that at any moment somebody else would be walking behind him, and he began casting apprehensive glances over his shoulder. He was not a coward, but his imagination and his nerves were extremely sensitive, and that evening he could not have explained to himself what he was so afraid of. He sat down in a corner of the room, but even there he could not help feeling that someone would any minute be peering over his shoulder into his face. Even Nikita's loud snoring which came from the hall did not dispel his fear. At last he rose quietly from his place and, without raising his eyes, went behind the screen, where he undressed and went to bed. Through a chink in the screen he could see the whole room, which was flooded with moonlight, and straight in front of him he saw the portrait hanging on the wall. Those eyes were fixed upon him steadily, more terribly and more significantly than ever, and it seemed they would not look at anything but him. Feeling strangely ill at ease, he decided to get up and cover up the portrait. He jumped out of bed, snatched up a sheet and, walking up to the portrait, covered it up entirely. That done, he went back to bed in a more composed frame of mind.

He could not sleep and his thoughts turned upon the miserable lot of a painter, the thorny path which lay before him in this world. Meanwhile his eyes looked involuntarily through the chink in the screen at the portrait wrapped in the sheet. The moonlight emphasised the whiteness of the sheet, and it seemed to him that the terrible eyes were gleaming through the cloth. Panic-stricken, he began to peer more keenly at the portrait, as though wishing to con-

vince himself that it was all imagination. But . . . good
gracious, what was that? He could now see plainly, very
plainly indeed, that the sheet had vanished and . . . the
portrait was all uncovered and, without paying the slightest attention to anything round it, it was looking straight
at him—no, not at him, but into him, right into him! . . .
His heart began to pound violently. The next thing he saw
was that the old man began moving, and presently he
pressed both his hands against the frame. Then he raised
himself on his hands and, thrusting out his legs, jumped
out of the frame . . . Through the chink in the screen he
could now see the empty frame. He could hear footfalls
in the room, footfalls which were drawing closer and closer
to the screen. The artist's heart began pounding even more
violently. Panting, and hardly able to breathe for fear, he
expected to see the old man glancing from behind the
screen any minute. And almost immediately he did indeed
glance from behind the screen, his bronze face looking not
a bit different, and rolling his big eyes. Chartkov tried to
scream, but his voice failed him; he tried to move, but his
limbs were paralysed. With a gaping mouth he gazed
breathlessly at this terrible phantom of enormous height,
wearing a curious kind of flowing oriental robe, and waited
to see what it would do next. The old man sat down almost at his feet and pulled something out from between
the folds of his wide robe. It was a bag. The old man undid
it, and, picking it up by the bottom, shook it. Heavy packets
in the shape of large rolls of coins fell on the floor with
a dull thud; each roll was wrapped in blue paper, and
each was clearly marked: 1,000 sovereigns. Thrusting his
long, bony hands out of his wide sleeves, the old man began
unwrapping the rolls. There was a gleam of gold. However
deeply the artist had been disturbed in his mind, and however terror-stricken he was, he could not help looking with
avidity at the gold, staring motionless as it came out of
the paper in the bony hands of the old man, gleaming and
ringing dully and faintly, and as it disappeared when the
old man wrapped it up again. Then he noticed one roll of

coins that had rolled farther away than the rest and was lying near the top of the bed where he could easily reach it with his hand. He grasped it almost convulsively and glanced in terror at the old man to see whether he had noticed it or not. But the old fellow seemed to be too busy to see anything. He collected all his packets, replaced them in the bag and, without even looking at him, retired behind the screen. Chartkov's heart beat wildly as he listened to the sound of the retreating footsteps in the room. He clasped the little packet more firmly in his hand, quivering in every limb, and suddenly he heard the footsteps coming back, nearer and nearer, to the screen: the old man must have discovered that one of the rolls was missing. And in another moment Chartkov saw him looking in again from behind the screen. In despair he clasped the packet in his hand with all the strength at his command, exerted every effort to make some movement, uttered a scream and . . . woke up.

He was bathed in a cold sweat; his heart was pounding away as fast as could be, his chest tightened, as though his last breath was about to leave it. "Was it only a dream?" he said, clasping his head with both his hands; but the amazing vividness of that apparition was not like a dream. For it was *after* he had awakened that he saw the old man disappearing inside the frame of the portrait, and he even caught a glimpse of the skirt of his wide robe, and he could still feel that only a minute ago he had been holding some heavy packet in his hand. Moonlight filled the room, and from the dark corners it picked out in one place a canvas, in another a plaster-of-Paris hand, in a third a piece of drapery left on a chair, in a fourth a pair of trousers and dirty boots. It was only then that he became aware of the fact that he was no longer lying in bed, but was standing in front of the portrait. How he had got there he could not for the life of him say. What surprised him even more was that the portrait was all uncovered and there was certainly no sheet to be seen anywhere. Paralysed with terror, he stood motionless before it and, as he gazed at it, he saw a pair of living human eyes fixing him with their stare. Cold sweat broke out on his brow; he wanted to run away, but his feet seemed to be rooted to the ground. And he could see that it was no longer a dream, for the old man's face began to stir and his lips began to protrude towards him, as though they wished to suck him dry. . . . With a loud shriek of despair he leapt back—and woke up.

"Was this, too, a dream?" His heart was beating so violently that it seemed about to burst. He groped round him with his hands. Yes, he was lying in bed in precisely the same position in which he had fallen asleep. There was the screen before him; moonlight flooded the room. He could see the portrait through the chink in the screen, covered with the sheet as he had left it before going to bed. So this, too, was a dream! But his clenched fist still felt as though something had been inside it. His heart was beating strongly, almost terrifyingly; the weight on his chest was unbearable. He fixed his eyes on the chink in the screen and looked steadily at the sheet. And now he could see clearly that the sheet began to unfold as though a pair of hands were struggling behind it, trying to throw it off. "Good Lord, what is all this?" he cried, crossing himself in despair, and woke up.

So this, too, was a dream. He jumped out of bed, half-crazed and bewildered, and he could not explain what was happening to him: whether he was suffering from the after-effects of a nightmare, or whether he had become the victim of the devil; whether he was feverish or delirious, or whether he had seen a real apparition. In an attempt to calm his overwrought nerves and to still his throbbing blood which pulsated feverishly through his veins, he went up to the window and opened the little ventilating pane. The cool breeze, blowing across his face, revived him. Moonlight was still lying on the roofs and white walls of the houses, though little clouds were now scudding more frequently across the sky. All was still; only at rare intervals could he hear the faint, distant creaking of a cab, the driver of which must have fallen asleep on his box in some out-of-the-way lane, lulled by his lazy nag while waiting for a belated fare. He went on gazing for a long time, his head thrust out of the window. Signs of the approaching dawn were already perceptible in the sky; at last he felt drowsy, shut the ventilating pane, left the window, went back to bed and was soon sound asleep.

He woke up very late. He had a splitting headache and he felt sick like a man suffering from coal-gas poisoning. It was a dull, dismal day; a thin drizzle of rain was falling outside and the moisture was coming through the crevices of the windows against which pictures and primed canvases were piled. Sullen and disgruntled like a wet cockerel, he sat down on his tattered sofa, without an idea in his head what to do or how to set about doing anything. At last he remembered his dream. The more of it he recalled, the more depressingly real it became in his imagination, and he even began to wonder whether it had been a dream or a hallucination. Had it not been something more than that? A vision perhaps? He pulled down the sheet and examined the dreadful portrait in the light of day. The eyes, it was true, were rather strikingly alive, but there was nothing in them to make him feel nervous; all that had remained of his terrors of the night was quite an unaccountable feeling of uneasiness. Yet even now he was not sure that it had only been a dream. He could not help feeling that among the different incidents in his dream there was some appalling fragment of reality. There was, for instance, something in the look of the old man and in the expression of his face which seemed to say that he had paid him a visit during the night; his hand still felt the weight of the heavy packet, as though someone had only snatched it away a minute ago. He had the odd feeling that if only he had held on to it more firmly the packet would have remained in his hand after he had awakened.

"Lord, if only I had a little bit of that money!" he murmured, fetching a deep sigh, and in his imagination he could see those packets again, each inscribed alluringly: 1,000 sovereigns, tumbling out of the bag. They opened

up, the gold gleamed, then they were wrapped up again.
. . . He was sitting on his torn sofa, his eyes staring vacantly
at nothing, unable to tear his thoughts away from so
fascinating a vision, like a child sitting in front of some
particularly delectable sweet with his mouth watering as he
watches others at the table eating it.

Presently there came a knock at the door which brought
him back to reality with a disagreeable bump. His landlord came in, together with the district police inspector,
whose appearance, as is well known, is more disturbing to
people of small means than the face of a petitioner is to the
wealthy.

The landlord of the small house where Chartkov lived belonged to the class of persons who are commonly owners of
houses somewhere in Fifteenth Row in Vassilyev Island,
in the Petersburg district, or in some remote corner of
Kolomna—persons who are to be found in great numbers all
over Russia and whose character is as difficult to describe
as the colour of a threadbare frock-coat. In his young days
he had been a captain in the army, and was also often employed in civil affairs, a big bully and a great believer in
flogging; he was rather efficient in a way, though stupid,
and a bit of a dandy. But in his old age all those striking
peculiarities of his character became merged into a kind of
uniform dullness. He had been a widower for some time;
he had been in retirement for some time; he was no longer a
dandy; and he had even left off bragging and bullying. All
he cared for now was his cup of tea and an opportunity of
gossiping over it. He used to spend his time pacing his
room, snuffing the candle end, calling upon his tenants
punctually at the end of each month for the rent, and, key
in hand, would go into the street to have a look at the roof
of his house. He routed the caretaker several times a day
out of his den where he usually sneaked off to sleep; in
short, he was a retired army officer who, after a gay and
dissolute life and after years of being jolted about in post-
chaises, was left with only a few insipid, conventional
habits.

"You can see for yourself, sir," said the landlord to the police officer with a deprecatory wave of the hands. "He just doesn't pay his rent. Just doesn't pay!"

"What do you expect me to do if I have no money," said Chartkov. "Can't you wait a little longer? I'll pay you."

"I'm afraid, sir, I can't wait," said the landlord crossly, waving the key in his hand. "I'm used to decent tenants, sir. Lieutenant-Colonel Potogonkin has been living in my house for seven years; Anna Petrovna Bukhmisterova has rented the coach-house and the stables with two stalls, keeps three servants—that's the kind of tenants I have. I am not in the habit, sir, of having trouble with my tenants about the rent, and that's the truth. Will you please be so good as to pay at once or look for another place!"

"Well, sir, if you've undertaken to pay, you have to pay," said the police inspector with a slight shake of the head, pushing a finger between the buttons of his uniform.

"But what am I to pay him with? That's the question. You see, I haven't got a penny."

"In that case, sir, you'd better satisfy Ivan Ivanovich by giving him some of your pictures," said the police officer. "He might agree to be paid in pictures."

"No, sir, thank you very much! No pictures for me. I might have considered it if this gentleman's pictures were anything decent, something you could hang on a wall, such as a general with a star, or a portrait of Prince Kutuzov, but look at those pictures of his! There, if you please, is a portrait of a peasant, a peasant in a shirt, a portrait of his servant, the young feller who grinds his paints for him. Now fancy painting a portrait of that oaf! I shall give him a good thrashing one day; he's been removing all the nails from my bolts, the rascal! . . . Look at the kind of things he paints. There's a picture of his room. Now what I'd like to know, sir, is why if he must paint his room he doesn't tidy it up first. Look at that! Painted it with all the filth and rubbish on the floor! See what a mess he's made of my flat? I tell you, sir, some of my tenants have been living in my house for over seven years! Gentlemen, sir, colonels!

Anna Petrovna Bukhmisterova. . . . No, sir, there's no worse tenant in the world than an artist. Lives like a pig and doesn't pay his rent! It's just a scandal, sir!"

And the poor artist had to listen patiently to all this. Meanwhile the police inspector amused himself by an examination of the pictures and sketches, showing at once that he had a much more sensitive imagination than the landlord and that his soul was not altogether impervious to artistic impressions.

"Ah," he said, poking a finger into a picture of a nude, "nice bit of goods that. . . . And what's that black mark doing under the nose of this fellow here? Been taking too much snuff, or what?"

"Shadow," Chartkov muttered gruffly, without looking at the policeman.

"But you should have put it somewhere else, sir," said the police officer. "Shows up too much under the nose. And whose portrait is that?" he went on, going up to the portrait of the old man. "Looks a bit of a horror, don't he? Wonder if he really did look so terrifying. Good gracious me! Seems to look through you, don't he? Makes your flesh creep. Who was your model?"

"Oh, some man . . ." said Chartkov.

He stopped short without finishing the sentence, for at that moment there was a loud crack. The police inspector must have grasped the frame of the portrait too firmly between his fingers, and, a policeman's grip being notoriously clumsy, the moulding at the side broke and fell into the hollow frame with the exception of one piece, which dropped out together with a packet wrapped in blue paper, which fell with a heavy thud on the floor. Chartkov's eyes immediately caught the inscription on the roll: 1,000 sovereigns, and he flew like mad to pick it up. Seizing it, he clasped it convulsively in his hand, which sank with the weight.

"I could have sworn I heard the jingling of money," said the police officer, who had heard the noise of something falling on the floor, but was not quick enough to see what it was owing to the lightning rapidity with which Chartkov picked up the roll of gold coins.

"What has it got to do with you whether I have anything or not?"

"All it's got to do with me, sir, is that you have to pay your landlord at once the rent you owe him. You seem to have the money, but you don't want to pay him. Isn't that so?"

"All right, I'll pay him today."

"But why didn't you pay him before, sir? Why give your landlord all this trouble? Why waste the time of the police, sir?"

"I didn't want to touch that money. I shall pay him in full this evening and I'm leaving his flat tomorrow. I don't want to stay with such a landlord!"

"Well, it seems he'll pay you all right, sir," said the police officer, turning to the landlord. "But if he doesn't satisfy you in full this evening, he'll have to take the consequences, artist or no artist."

Having delivered this warning, the police inspector put on his three-cornered hat and walked out into the passage, followed by the landlord, whose head was lowered as though he were sunk in deep meditation.

"Thank God they've gone at last," said Chartkov as he heard the front door closing behind his visitors.

He looked out into the passage and, wishing to be left entirely alone, sent off Nikita on some errand. Then he locked the front door, and returning to the studio, began unwrapping the packet with trembling hands and a wildly beating heart. The packet contained gold sovereigns, all new and red hot. Almost beside himself, the painter sat down in front of the heap of gold, asking himself all the time whether he were not seeing it in a dream. There were exactly one thousand sovereigns in the roll, which before he had unwrapped it looked exactly as he had seen it in his dream. He turned the coins over in his hand for some time, examining them, and unable to regain his composure. Stories came crowding into his mind of hidden treasures, cabinets with secret drawers, left by grandfathers to their spendthrift grandchildren in the firm belief that the money would restore their fortunes. It occurred to him that some grandfather might have wished to leave his grandson a present and had hidden it in the frame of a family portrait. Full of such wildly romantic ideas, he wondered whether there were not some mysterious connexion here with his own fate, whether the existence of the portrait was not in some way connected with his own existence, and whether the very fact of its acquisition by him was not due to some kind of predestination. He began examining the frame of the portrait with particular interest. There was a hollowed-out space at the side of the frame, so skilfully and neatly closed up by a little board that if the heavy hand of the police officer had not smashed through it, the gold coins would have remained undisturbed for ever. Looking closely at the portrait, he was again struck by the high quality of its workmanship and the extraordinary treatment of the eyes: they no longer frightened him, and yet every time he looked at them he could not help experiencing a curiously unpleasant sensation. "Well, sir," he apostrophised the portrait mentally, "I don't know whose grandfather you are, but I'm going to put you behind glass all the same and I'll get you a fine gilt frame for having been so good to me." Then he put his hand on the heap of gold coins which lay before him, and his heart began beating fast at the touch.

"What shall I do with them?" he thought, looking at the big pile of gold sovereigns on the table. "Now I have nothing to worry about for at least three years. I can shut myself up in my room and work. I have enough money to pay for my paints, my dinners, my teas, my rent, everything! No one will worry me or interfere with my work; I can buy myself an excellent lay-figure, order a plaster torso, model some legs and feet, set up a Venus, get myself copies of the most famous pictures. And if I go on working for the next three years, without hurry or fuss, without caring a hoot whether my pictures sell or not, I can knock the whole lot of them into a cocked hat, and I can become an excellent painter into the bargain!"

That was what he was saying to himself at the prompting of his reason; but within him another voice was making itself heard louder and louder. And when he looked at the gold again, his twenty-two years and his ardent youth said something quite different to him. For now everything he had hitherto been looking upon with such envious eyes was within his reach; now he could have everything that had made his mouth water in the past, everything he had only been able to admire from a distance. Oh, how his young heart began to throb at the mere thought of it! To be dressed in the height of fashion, to be able to afford a real feast after so long a fast, to be able to rent a fine flat, to go to the theatre any time he liked, or to a pastrycook's, or to . . . and so on and so forth. He picked up the money, and in another instant he found himself in the street. The first thing he did was to go to a fashionable tailor and get himself dressed in the smartest clothes, dressed like a man of fashion from head to foot; and having got himself fitted out, he kept admiring himself incessantly, like a child. Next he bought all sorts of scents and pomades; then he rented the first magnificent flat on Nevsky Avenue he came across, without haggling over the price. He further acquired (quite by the way) an expensive *lorgnette* and (also quite by the way) a huge quantity of various cravats, many more than he would ever be likely to use. He then visited a hair-dresser's and had his hair curled; drove twice in a carriage through the main thoroughfares of the city without rhyme or reason; went into a pastrycook's and gorged himself on sweets; and, finally, treated himself to a dinner at one of the most select French restaurants in town about which the rumours that had reached him were as vague as the rumours about the Chinese Empire. There he had dinner in grand style, looking rather disdainfully at the other diners and constantly arranging his curled locks in the mirror. He drank a bottle of champagne which till now he had also known chiefly by hearsay. The wine went to his head and he left the restaurant in high feather, as though he were Old Nick's best friend, as the Russian saying has it. He strutted along the pavement, ogling everyone through his *lorgnette*. On the bridge he caught sight of his old professor and darted past him with his nose in the air, leaving the poor professor quite flabbergasted, rooted to the spot, an interrogation mark frozen on his face.

The same evening all his things, everything he possessed in the world—his easel, his canvases and his pictures—were moved to his new magnificent flat. Putting the best of them in the most conspicuous places and the worst in some obscure corner, he walked about for hours from one handsome room to another, continually looking at himself in the mirrors. His soul yearned with an irresistible desire to become famous overnight and show the world what a fine fellow he was. He could already hear the cries, "Chartkov, Chartkov, Chartkov! Have you seen Chartkov's latest? What sureness of touch! What intense perception of truth! What amazing speed! What genius!" He paced the rooms in a state of growing exultation, carried away by the wonderful vistas that opened up before him. Next day, taking ten gold sovereigns with him, he went to see the editor of a popular daily whom he intended to ask for his kind assistance. The journalist received him very cordially, immediately addressed him as "my dear fellow," pressed both his hands, made a careful note of his name and address, and on the very next day there appeared in the paper, below a notice of some newly invented tallow candles, the following article under the heading:

CHARTKOV'S REMARKABLE GENIUS

"We are sure that every cultured reader of our paper will be glad to hear of the wonderful acquisition our capital has just made, an acquisition that is highly desirable from every point of view. No one, we venture to think, will deny that we have among us many handsome men and many beautiful and charming ladies, but so far we have lacked the means of immortalising them in paint so that posterity may admire them as much as we do. We are now glad to be able to state that this omission has been made good. An artist has at last been found who combines everything that is required for so high and responsible a task. No beautiful lady need any longer despair of being depicted in all her grace and charm, light, airy, lovely, and bewitching as a butterfly fluttering over spring flowers. The respectable head of a large family can now behold himself surrounded by all its members. The merchant, the warrior, the citizen, the statesman—everybody can now pursue his work or profession with fresh zeal. We would like to give them one word of advice, though: *Do not delay your visit to the studio of this remarkable artist!* Go there immediately, wherever you are or whatever you happen to be doing, whether you are out for a drive in your carriage, or on your way to visit a friend or a cousin, or doing some shopping in one of our large emporia. The artist's magnificent studio (Nevsky Avenue, number so-and-so) is filled with portraits from his brush, portraits that we do not hesitate to say are worthy of a Van Dyck or a Titian. It is hard to know what to admire most: the truth with which a likeness has been caught, the resemblance to the original, or the quite extraordinary and amazing brightness and freshness of the painting as a whole. We congratulate this artist: all glory to him! We wish you every success, Andrey Petrovich! (The journalist must have cultivated a familiar style.) May you make yourself and your country famous! We for one know how to value you, and we are sure that great popularity and with it also great riches—much as some of our fellow-journalists seem to despise the latter—will be your reward."

The artist read this notice with unconcealed delight. His face brightened; he was beginning to be talked of in print— that was quite a new experience to him, and he re-read the notice a few times. He felt greatly flattered by the comparison with Van Dyck and Titian. He also liked the phrase, "We wish you every success, Andrey Petrovich!" To be addressed in print by his Christian name was an honour that he had never known before. He began pacing the room quickly, ruffling his hair, sitting down in a chair for a minute and then jumping up again and sitting down on the sofa. He tried to imagine how he would receive the ladies and gentlemen who came to sit for him, and he walked up to a canvas and began making all sorts of grand gestures with the brush over it in an attempt to discover which of them lent more grace to his hand. On the following day his doorbell rang. He ran to open the door. A lady, preceded by a footman in a livery with a fur lining, entered, followed by a girl of eighteen, her daughter.

"Are you Mr. Chartkov?" the lady asked.

The artist bowed.

"The papers have been writing such a lot about you. I'm told your portraits are simply marvellous!" Having said this, the lady raised her *lorgnette* to her eyes and went quickly to look at the walls, on which, however, there was nothing to be seen. "But where are your portraits?"

"Oh, I've had them removed," said the artist, somewhat taken aback. "I've only just moved into this flat and—er—I'm afraid they're still on the way. . . . Haven't arrived yet."

"Have you been to Italy?" asked the lady, eyeing him through her *lorgnette,* having found nothing else to look at.

"No, ma'am, I haven't been to Italy. I—er—wanted to go, but I've had to put it off for the time being, I'm afraid. . . . Won't you sit down? Here are arm-chairs. You must be tired. . . ."

"No, thank you. I've been sitting a long time in the carriage. Ah, there it is! At last I can see one of your works!" cried the lady, running to the opposite wall and looking through her *lorgnette* at his sketches, studies, interiors and portraits which were standing on the floor. "*C'est charmant, Lise. Lise, venez ici!* Look, an interior in the style of Teniers. Do you see? Everything is a most frightful disorder: a table, a bust on the table, a hand, a palette. Look at the dust, my dear! How wonderfully the dust has been painted! *C'est charmant!* And there's a painting of a girl washing her face

—quelle jolie figure! Oh, Lise, Lise, look at that jolly young peasant! A peasant in a Russian shirt! Look, my dear, a peasant! So you don't confine yourself to portraits, do you?"

"Oh, that's nothing. . . . Just a few studies. Been amusing myself. . . ."

"Tell me, what is your opinion of our modern portrait painters? It's true, isn't it, that we haven't got anyone today who can be even compared with Titian? They haven't the same strong colours . . . that . . . that . . . I'm afraid I can't express it in Russian." (Chartkov's first visitor was a great admirer of painting and had rushed through all the art galleries in Italy with her *lorgnette*.) "But M. Zéro; ah, what a wonderful painter! What marvellous genius! I find there is even more subtlety in his faces than in Titian's. Haven't you heard of M. Zéro?"

"I'm afraid I haven't."

"M. Zéro! Oh, what a genius! He painted a picture of my daughter when she was only twelve. You must come to see us. Lise, you must show Mr. Chartkov your album. You know, we came to see you today so that you could start on her portrait at once."

"Why, yes . . . of course . . . I . . . I can start at once."

And in a twinkling he pulled out the easel to the middle of the room, put a canvas he had ready on it, picked up his palette and fixed his gaze on the pale face of his visitor's daughter. If he had been a judge of character, he would have at once discerned in it the dawning of a childish passion for balls, the first signs of boredom during the long periods of waiting before and after dinner, the eagerness to show herself in a new dress in public, the heavy traces of her uninspired application to the various arts which her mother insisted that she should study to improve her mind and refine her feelings. But all the artist saw in this delicate little face was an almost porcelain transparency of skin, so irresistible to the brush; a charming, faintly perceptible languor; a slender, lovely, gleaming neck; and an aristocratic slenderness of figure. And he was already triumphing beforehand as he thought how he would show off the lightness and brilliance of his brushwork, for until now he had painted only the harsh features of coarse models, or the severe lines of ancient sculptures, or made copies of some classical masters. He could see already in his mind's eye how this sweet little face would look on canvas.

"You know," said the lady with quite a rapturous expression on her face, "I'd very much like to . . . You see, she's wearing an ordinary dress now. . . . Well, I don't mind telling you that I shouldn't like her to be painted in a dress which we're so used to. I should like her to be dressed quite simply and to sit in the shade of a tree, with fields in the background or just a wood. You see, I don't want anything that might suggest that she is about to go to a ball or some fashionable party or something of the sort. . . . Our balls, you know, have such a devastating effect on the spirit; so deadening, I mean. . . . They destroy all that remains of our feelings. . . . What I want is simplicity, as much simplicity as possible."

(Alas! From the faces of both mother and daughter it could be clearly perceived that they had spent so much of their energy in dancing at balls that they had almost turned into wax figures.)

Chartkov set to work. He put his sitter in the best possible position, got a rough idea what he was going to do, waved the brush in the air, making a few rapid mental notes, different points of composition, screwed up his eyes a little, retreated a few steps to look at the girl from a distance, and in one hour finished the rough sketch of the portrait. Feeling satisfied with it, he began painting in earnest, feeling carried away by his work. He seemed to have forgotten everything, even that he was in the presence of two aristocratic ladies, and lapsed sometimes into certain artistic mannerisms, such as ejaculating all sorts of sounds, humming a tune from time to time, as is usual with an artist who becomes engrossed in his work. With one movement of his brush and without the slightest ceremony he made his sitter raise her head, which she at last could hardly keep still for a moment, for she was beginning to show unmistakable signs of fatigue.

"That'll do," said the mother. "That's quite enough for the first sitting."

"Just another touch," pleaded the artist, completely forgetting himself.

"No, thank you so much. It's really time we went. Lise, three o'clock!" she said, taking out a watch, suspended on a gold chain from her waist and exclaiming, "Goodness, how late!"

"Please just give me one more minute!" said Chartkov in the innocent and imploring voice of a little boy.

But the lady was not at all disposed to humour his artistic demands on this occasion and promised to stay longer another time instead.

"What a pity," Chartkov thought to himself. "I was just getting into my stride!"

And he could not help remembering that no one ever interfered with him or stopped him in his studio on Vassilyev Island. Nikita used to sit for hours in the same pose without moving—he could have gone on painting him for ever; he would even fall asleep in the same pose. And feeling rather out of humour, Chartkov put down his brush and palette on a chair and stopped rather vaguely before the canvas. A compliment paid him by the society woman roused him from his reverie. He flew to the door to see them off; on the staircase he received an invitation to dinner for the next week. He returned to his flat looking very cheerful. He thought the woman of fashion exceptionally charming. He had always looked upon such beings as something unapproachable, beings born for the sole purpose of driving along the street in magnificent carriages with liveried footmen and gorgeous coachmen and casting glances of cold indifference on some poor devil trudging along on foot in a cheap, shabby cloak. And suddenly one of those beings had actually been to see him in his rooms; he was painting a portrait of her daughter; he had been invited to dinner to an aristocratic house. He felt so pleased and delighted that he celebrated his first success by an excellent dinner, an evening show and another ride in a carriage through the city for no particular purpose.

During the following days it never occurred to him to carry on with his ordinary work. He was only making ready for the next visit, waiting impatiently for the bell to ring. At last the aristocratic lady with her charming, pale daughter arrived. He made them sit down, pulled out the easel with a certain bravado and an affectation of social airs and graces, and set to work on the girl's portrait. The sunny day and the bright light helped him a great deal. In the sweet face of his sitter he saw much that, if only he succeeded in catching it and putting it on canvas, would lend great distinction to the portrait. He perceived that he could make an exceptionally good job of it if only he could carry out fully his present conception of what his picture should be like when finished. His heart even began beating a little faster when he felt sure that he would be able to bring something out that no one seemed to have noticed in a face before. He became so absorbed in his work that he was aware of nothing but his painting, completely oblivious of the fact that his sitter was a person of quality. With ever mounting excitement, he saw how marvellously well he managed to bring out those subtle features and the almost transparent flesh tints of the seventeen-year-old girl. He caught every shade, the slight sallowness, the almost imperceptible blueness under the eyes, and he was even about to put in the little pimple on her forehead, when he suddenly heard her mother's voice over him, "Gracious me, you're not going to put that in, surely? That's quite unnecessary," she said. "And in a few places you got it a little too yellowish, don't you think? Here, for instance; and there it looks as if she had some dark spots on her skin. . . ." The artist tried to explain that the dark spots and the yellow tint blended so well because they brought out the soft, pleasing tones of the face. But he was told that they did not bring out any tones and did not blend at all, and that he was merely imagining it.

"But," said the artist good-naturedly, "please let me add just a touch of yellow here. Just in this one place."

But he was not allowed to do anything of the sort, it being announced that Lise was a little indisposed that day, that she never was sallow and that her complexion had indeed always been remarkably fresh. Sadly he began removing what his artistic instinct had made him put on the canvas. Many almost imperceptible touches disappeared and with them the resemblance to the original partly disappeared also. Apathetically he began imparting to the portrait that conventional colouring which is daubed on mechanically and which transforms even faces drawn from life into those coldly ideal faces one finds only in the sketches of art students. But the society woman was pleased that the unflattering tints had been completely eliminated. She merely expressed her surprise that the work was taking so long, adding that she was told that he usually finished a portrait in two sittings.

After they had gone, Chartkov stopped for a long time before the unfinished picture, gazing stupidly at it, while his head was full of those soft, feminine features, those shades and ethereal tones, he had observed and which his own brush had so pitilessly removed. Being full of them, he took the portrait off the easel and began looking for the head of Psyche he had sketched roughly on a canvas a long time ago but had put away somewhere. He found it. It was a lovely girlish face, cleverly drawn but completely idealised, with the cold conventional features which did not seem to belong to any living body. Having nothing else to do, he now began going over it, retracing on it everything he had happened to observe in the face of his aristocratic sitter. The features, shades and tones caught by him appeared on it in a refined form in which they occasionally appear on the paintings of an artist who, having made a close study from nature, moves away from it and creates a work of art which is like it and yet independent of it. Psyche began to come to life and the as yet faintly dawning idea began gradually to be clothed into a visible body. The type of the face of the young society girl was unconsciously transferred to Psyche's face and through this it received a unique individuality which entitles a work of art to be considered as truly original. He seemed to have made use of certain idiosyncrasies of his sitter and of the whole impression of her as created in his mind, and he kept working on it, and for the next two days did nothing else.

It was while he was working on this picture that the ladies arrived again. He did not have time to take the picture off the easel and, seeing it, the two ladies uttered a cry of joy, throwing up their hands in amazement.

"Lise! Lise! Look, how extraordinarily like you! *Superbe! Superbe!* What a clever idea to dress her in a Greek costume. Oh, what a pleasant surprise!"

The painter did not know how to disillusion them, seeing that they were so pleased with being deluded. Feeling rather ashamed, he said, without looking at them, "This is Psyche. . . ."

"You mean you painted her as Psyche? *C'est charmant!*" said the mother with a smile, and her daughter smiled, too. "Don't you think, Lise, you look really lovely as Psyche? *Quelle idée délicieuse!* But what a work of art! It's . . . it's a Correggio! I have of course read and heard about you, but to tell you the truth I never thought you had such a talent. You simply must paint my portrait, too!"

It was quite evident that the mother also wanted to be painted as some kind of Psyche.

"What am I to do with them?" thought the artist. "If they have set their hearts on it, let Psyche be what they imagine it to be." And aloud he said, "Would you mind posing for a few more minutes? I want to touch up a few things."

"Oh, I'm afraid you might. . . . I mean, the picture looks so like her now!"

But the artist realised that she was afraid he might add some yellow tints on the face, and he reassured her, saying that he would only add a little more brilliance and expression to the eyes. To be quite just, he felt rather ashamed of himself and he wanted to impart just a little more similitude to the portrait for fear that otherwise he might be accused of being guilty of a barefaced fraud. And the features of the pale young girl did in the end appear more clearly in Psyche's face.

"That's enough!" said the mother, who was beginning to fear that the portrait might show too close a resemblance to her daughter.

The artist was generously rewarded: smiles, money, and compliments were showered upon him. He had his hand pressed in real gratitude; he was invited to dinners; in short, he was overwhelmed with a thousand flattering encomiums.

The portrait created a sensation in town. The society woman showed it to her friends, and everybody was in raptures over the art with which the painter had succeeded in preserving the likeness of the original and at the same time adding beauty to it. The last remark was of course made not without a touch of malice. The artist was suddenly snowed under with work. It seemed as though the whole town wanted to be painted by him. His doorbell rang continuously. This might, on the one hand, have turned out to be rather a good thing for him, for it provided him with endless opportunities for practice by the sheer diversity and multiplicity of the faces of the sitters. But, unfortunately, they all belonged to a class of people whom it was very difficult to manage, people who were always in a hurry, always busy, or who belonged to the polite world and, consequently, were more busy than anyone else and therefore impatient to excess. They all demanded that his work should be both good and quick. The artist realised that it was absolutely impossible to finish any portrait and that he would have to substitute cleverness, rapidity and superficial brilliance for everything else. To capture merely the general expression as a whole and not to probe with his brush into the finer details—in fact, he found it almost impossible to follow nature to the bitter end. Moreover, nearly all his sitters made all sorts of stipulations of one kind or another. The ladies demanded that as a rule only soul and spirit should be shown on their portraits, that in certain circumstances the rest should be completely ignored, that all the angularities should be rounded off, all the defects touched up and even, if possible, eliminated altogether. What they wanted, in fact, was that their faces should be generally admired, if not indeed that men should fall in love with them at first sight. As a result, many ladies, when posing, assumed expressions that quite startled the artist. One tried to give her face a melancholy cast; another tried to look dreamy; a third was quite determined to make her mouth look as small as possible and she screwed it up so much that it finally turned into a point not bigger than a pinhead. And in spite of all that, they all wanted their portraits to be like them, demanding, moreover, that he should make them look artless and natural. The men were no whit better than the women. One insisted that his profile should express strength and energy; another wanted his eyes to be raised and to look inspired; a Lieutenant of the Guards demanded that Mars should be plainly visible in his eyes; a civil servant was absolutely set on having more frankness and nobility in his face and that one of his hands should rest on a book bearing the clearly legible inscription: "He Always Upheld Truth."

At first all these demands threw the artist into a cold sweat: he felt that all that had to be carefully considered and thought over, and yet he was given precious little time to do it in. At last he realised what it was all about and found the whole thing as easy as anything. Two or three words were enough to give him a pretty good idea what his sitter wanted to be portrayed as. If one showed a partiality for Mars, he thrust Mars into his face; if someone else had an ambition to look like Lord Byron, he obliged him with a Byronic pose and profile. If the ladies wished to be shown as Madame de Stael's heroine Corinne, or Lamotte-Fouqué's heroine Undine, or as Aspasia, he was only too glad to please them all, throwing in a plentiful supply of good looks on his own account, which, as the whole world knows, can do no harm and will make up for any want of resemblance.

Soon he began to marvel himself at the amazing rapidity and smartness of his brush. And it is unnecessary to add that all his sitters were in raptures about his portraits and proclaimed him a genius.

Chartkov became a fashionable painter in every sense of the word. He was invited to dinners; he escorted society women to picture galleries and even went for drives with them. He was always immaculately dressed, and was heard again and again to express the opinion that an artist must belong to society, that he had to uphold the honour of his profession, that artists as a rule dressed like cobblers, that their manners were atrocious, that they had no idea of good taste, that they lacked every social refinement, and that they were, in fact, utter boors. At home, in his studio, everything was now very tidy and spotlessly clean. He employed two magnificent footmen; he had a large following of well-groomed pupils; he changed a few times a day into all sorts of morning coats; he had his hair waved regularly; gave a great deal of attention to improving his deportment with different types of callers; devoted much time to beautifying his appearance in every possible way so as to make the best and most pleasing impression upon the ladies; in short, very soon it was quite impossible to recognise in him that modest and unassuming artist who had once worked so obscurely in his miserable little flat on Vassilyev Island. About art and artists he now expressed very decided opinions; he affirmed that too much merit had been allowed the old masters and that all the painters could paint before Raphael was herrings and not human figures; that the idea that in them one could feel the presence of some divine spirit existed merely in the imagination of their admirers; that many works of Raphael himself were far from perfect and that the fact that they were still considered masterpieces was due merely to the influence of tradition; that Michelangelo was a cheap braggart because he merely wanted to show off his knowledge of anatomy, that there was not a jot or tittle of grace about him, and that real brilliance, real power of subtle drawing, real splendour of hue, could be found only among the modern painters. And here, quite naturally, he thought it necessary to make a few personal observations. "I can't understand," he used to say, "why some artists are so keen on slaving and drudgery. In my opinion a man who wastes several months on a picture isn't an artist at all. He is simply a hack. I can't believe he really possesses any talent at all. A genius works boldly, rapidly. Take myself, for instance," he declared, usually addressing one of his visitors. "This picture took me only two days to paint; that little head I did in one day; that one in a couple of hours; and that one in just over one hour. No, I must say quite frankly that I do not recognise anything as art that is produced laboriously, stroke by stroke. That's not art; that is craft!" So he harangued his visitors, and his visitors marvelled at the strength and cleverness of his brush, uttered cries of surprise on hearing how little time it had taken him to produce his pictures, and afterwards told each other, "That man's got talent, real talent! Just look at him when he's speaking! How his eyes flash! *Il y a quelque chose d'extraordinaire dans toute sa figure!*"

The artist was flattered to hear such opinions expressed about him. When a notice praising his work appeared in some journal, he was as pleased as Punch about it, though this praise had been bought with his own money. He carried the press cutting about with him wherever he went, showing it with assumed casualness to his friends and acquaintances, as though it were something of no importance to him, and this really pleased him in a sort of good-natured, ingenuous way. His fame spread, his works and orders multiplied. He was even beginning to weary of the same kind of portraits and faces, whose profiles and poses he now knew by heart. He lost all zest in his work, painting portraits without any particular enthusiasm, drawing a rough sketch of a head and leaving the rest to his pupils. Before then he had tried at any rate to find some kind of new pose for every sitter; he did his best to startle and stun his public by the forcefulness of his style of painting and by

the ease with which he achieved his effects. But now even
that gave him no more pleasure. His brain was weary of
planning and thinking. He just could not go on doing it
and, anyway, he had not the time: his rather dissipated
mode of living and the polite society in which he tried to
play the part of a man of the world—all that distracted him
too much and left him no leisure either for thought or work.
His hand lost its cunning, his paintings became cold and
lifeless, and without noticing it himself he lapsed into monotonous, well-defined and long-worn-out forms. Monotonous, cold, eternally neat and tidy and, as it were, but-
toned-up faces of Civil Servants and army officers did not
give much scope to his brush, which was beginning to forget how to draw magnificent draperies, forceful movements
and passions. As for composition, dramatic effect and its
lofty purpose—not a trace of it remained. All he saw was a
uniform or a corsage or a frock-coat, before which art wilts
and imagination withers. His work lost even all ordinary
distinction, and yet it was still popular, although real art
experts and artists merely shrugged their shoulders when
they saw his latest paintings. Some who had known Chartkov before were puzzled, for they could not understand
how his talent, the signs of which were quite unmistakable
at the beginning, could have vanished so completely, and
they tried in vain to solve the mystery of how a man could
have lost his gifts in the heyday of his power.

But the self-satisfied artist, intoxicated by his success, did
not hear this criticism. He was already approaching the
age when his mind and his habits were settling down into
a rut: he began to put on flesh and was visibly expanding
in girth. In the papers and journals he was already coming
across the adjectives *distinguished* and *honoured* coupled
with his name: "Our honoured Andrey Petrovich. . . . Our
distinguished Andrey Petrovich. . . ." He was already being offered important posts in the Civil Service, invited to
serve on boards of examiners and on committees. He was
already beginning, as is usual when a man reaches the age
of discretion, to take the part of Raphael and the old

masters, not because he had convinced himself entirely of their transcendent merits, but because he enjoyed throwing them in the teeth of the younger artists. He was already beginning, as is the habit of men of his age, to accuse all young people indiscriminately of immoral and vicious trends of thought. He was already beginning to believe that everything in the world was achieved by simple methods, that there was no inspiration from above, and that everything must be subject to one strict rule of precision and uniformity. He had, in fact, reached the age when anything showing the slightest flash of inspiration is condemned and frowned upon, when even the mightiest chord reaches the spirit feebly and does not pierce a man's heart with its sound, when the touch of beauty no longer fans the virgin forces into fire and flame, but all burnt-out feelings respond more easily to the jingle of gold, hearken more attentively to its seductive music and little by little allow themselves unconsciously to be lulled to sleep by it. Fame cannot give pleasure to a man who has stolen it, to one who does not deserve it; it never fails to produce a thrill only in those who are worthy of it. For this reason all his feelings and desires became obsessed with gold. Gold became his passion, his ideal, his terror, his joy, his aim. The bundles of banknotes grew in his coffers, and, like every one who succumbs to the dreadful fascination of money, he became a bore; he was no longer interested in anything that did not bring in money; he became a miser for no reason at all, a vicious hoarder. He was in danger of becoming one of those strange human beings one meets in such large numbers in our callous world: human beings who are regarded with horror by men full of life and passion, to whom they seem to be walking coffins with a corpse where their hearts should be. But one event which occurred just then gave him so powerful a shock that all his dormant vitality was reawakened.

One day he found a note on his table in which the Academy of Art invited him, as one of its distinguished members, to go and give his opinion on a new painting sent

from Italy by a Russian artist who had been pursuing his
art there. The painter was one of his old fellow students
who had from his earliest years devoted himself passionately
to art and who had been working at it like a slave, his
fiery spirit entirely dedicated to it. He had left his friends
and relations, abandoned the mode of life to which he had
become accustomed and which was dear to him, and hurried off to the country under whose beautiful skies art
comes to full fruition, to the lovely city of Rome, the very
name of which makes the ardent heart of an artist beat
faster and more vigorously. There he buried himself in his
work like a recluse and allowed no diversions to distract him.
He did not care whether people discussed his character or
not; whether he did or did not cut a figure in society;
whether his manners were polished or not; whether his
poor, shabby clothes brought the profession of an artist
into disrepute. He cared even less whether his fellow artists
were angry with him or not. He scorned everything. He
gave himself up entirely to his art. He never wearied of
visiting the art galleries, and he would stand for hours before the works of the great masters, studying every aspect
of their genius and following every movement of their magic
brush. He never finished anything without comparing his
work several times with the work of these great teachers
and without drawing from them a silent, yet eloquent les-
son for himself. He never took part in noisy discussions and
controversies; he neither defended nor condemned the
purists. He gave every man his due and extracted from everything what was beautiful and true. He ended up by
taking for his teacher one great master only—the divine
Raphael, like a great poet who, after reading many works
of every kind, full of many wonderful and sublime passages,
leaves Homer's *Iliad* on his table as his constant book of
reference, having discovered that it contains everything one
can wish, and that there is nothing in the whole world that
cannot be found in it expressed to perfection. And so he
had gained from the study of his great master's works a
sublime conception of creative art, an intense beauty of

thought, and the superb loveliness of a divinely inspired brush.

When Chartkov entered the room, he found a large crowd of people already gathered before the picture. A profound silence, so rare among a large crowd of art lovers, this time pervaded the room. He hastened to assume the grave air of a connoisseur and approached the picture. But, dear God, what was it he saw?

Pure, perfect, lovely as a bride, the work of the artist stood before him. Modest, divine, innocent, and simple as genius itself, it towered over him. It was as though those heavenly figures, amazed at the multitude of eyes turned upon them, had modestly lowered their lovely eyelashes. The art experts studied the work of the new, unknown artist with a feeling of sheer astonishment. All seemed united in it: a study of Raphael, which was reflected in the high nobility of the composition, and a study of Correggio, which was expressed in the finished perfection of the artist's brush. But what appeared more powerfully than anything was the firmness of conception that emanated from the very soul of the artist himself. Every detail of the picture was pervaded by it: in everything law and innate strength was evident. Everywhere could be discerned that liquid roundness of lines, which nature alone seems to possess, which only the eye of the creative artist can see, and which in a copyist merely becomes angular. The artist, it could be plainly seen, had first of all absorbed everything he had received from the outside world and stored it up in his mind, and it was from there, from that living fountain of his spirit, that he had drawn it, transforming it into one harmonious, triumphant song. Even the uninitiated could now see how measureless is the gulf that separates creative art from a mere copy from nature. It is almost impossible to describe the unusual stillness which had fallen against their will upon all those whose eyes were fixed on the picture. Not a murmur could be heard, not a sound. Meanwhile the picture seemed every minute to assume grander and grander proportions; it seemed to become a thing apart, growing more brilliant and more and more wonderful until at last it was transformed into one flash of inspiration, into a blinding instant of time, the fruit of a thought that had descended to the artist from heaven, an instant compared with which the whole life of man is but a preparation. Involuntary tears filled the eyes of the visitors who had crowded round the picture and were about to roll down their cheeks. It was as if all tastes, all the arrogant, wrongheaded aberrations of taste had blended into one silent hymn of praise in honour of a divine work of art.

Chartkov stood motionless and with parted lips before the picture, and when at last the visitors and the art experts burst into talk and began discussing the merits of the painting, when at last they turned to him with a request to tell them what he thought of it, he came to himself. He tried to assume an air of indifference, tried to repeat the usual platitudes of dry-as-dust artists, something like, "Of course I don't want to run him down. The man certainly has talent and there is something in the picture which shows that he had certain ideas he wanted to express, but so far as the chief thing is concerned . . ." And then, needless to say, to utter the few words of praise which have damned many an artist. He wanted to do this, but the words died on his lips, and instead tears burst from his eyes, discordant sobs broke from his lips and he rushed out of the room like one distracted.

For a moment he stood motionless in the middle of his magnificent studio. All his senses seemed numbed. His whole being, every living part of him, had been awakened all at once, as though his youth had come back to him, as though the dead embers of his genius had burst into flame again. The scales suddenly fell from his eyes. O Lord, and to have ruined, so pitilessly ruined, the best years of his life, to have stamped out, to have quenched the spark of divine fire that perhaps glowed in his breast and that would perhaps by now have developed into greatness and beauty which, too, might have wrung tears of admiration and gratitude. And to have ruined it all, to have ruined it all without pity! It seemed as though at that moment all those impulses and strivings he had once known had revived in his soul all of a sudden. He snatched up a brush and approached a canvas. Beads of perspiration came out on his brow. One desire took hold of him and only one thought filled his brain: he longed to paint a fallen angel. No idea could have been more in harmony with his present frame of mind. But, alas, his figures, attitudes, groupings, and thoughts looked forced and disconnected as they appeared on the canvas. For his painting and his imagination had too long conformed to one pattern, and his feeble attempts to escape the limits and fetters he had laid upon himself merely showed up his faults and blunders. He had disdained the long and wearisome stairway of the gradual accumulation of knowledge of the fundamental laws of art— the stairway to future greatness. He felt irritated, dejected, dismayed. He ordered all his latest works to be taken out of his studio, all those lifeless fashionable pictures, all those portraits of hussars, society women and state councillors. He then shut himself up in his studio, gave strict orders that no one should be admitted, and became absorbed in his work. He set to work with infinite patience, as though he were a young art student. But how mercilessly, how thanklessly did his brush expose his shortcomings! At every step he was pulled up by his ignorance of the most elementary rules; his failure to master a simple and quite unimportant mechanical process damped all his enthusiasm and stood like an insurmountable obstacle in the way of his imagination. His hand unconsciously returned to the trite and commonplace forms to which it was so well accustomed: hands folded in one set way, head not daring to depart by an inch from the usual angle, even the folds of the garment following conventional lines and refusing to obey and drape themselves round a body in an unfamiliar position. And he knew it, he knew it! He felt it! He saw it all himself!

"But, good Lord, did I ever possess any talent?" he said at last. "Was I not mistaken?" And as he pronounced these words, he walked up to his old paintings which he had produced in so pure and unmercenary a spirit in that wretched flat of his in the lonely Vassilyev Island, far from the noisy crowds, far from all splendour and abundance, far from all sorts of cravings. He went up to them now and began examining them carefully. As he did so, all the details of his former poor existence came back to him. "Yes," he exclaimed in despair, "I had talent! I can see the traces of it everywhere! Everywhere there are signs of it!"

He stopped dead and suddenly trembled all over: his eyes met the motionless stare of the old man whose remarkable portrait he had bought in Pike's Yard. The old man's eyes seemed to be staring at him, boring through him! The portrait had been covered up all that time, concealed behind a stack of other pictures. He had forgotten all about it. But now after all the fashionable portraits and pictures which had filled the studio had been removed, it emerged, as though by design, together with the other pictures of his youth. As he recalled every detail of that strange incident of his life, as he recalled that in a way it was that strange portrait that was the cause of his transformation, that the hoard of money he had received in so miraculous a manner had awakened in him all those vain desires and passions which had destroyed his talent—as he recalled all that, he almost went off his head. He immediately ordered the hateful portrait to be taken out. But his mental excitement was not allayed by the mere fact of the removal of the portrait: his whole being, all his emotions were shaken to their foundations, and he suffered that dreadful torture which sometimes appears as a rare exception in nature when a man of small talent tries to fill a space too big for him and fails miserably; the kind of torture which in a young man may lead to greatness, but which in a man who should long ago have left the phase of idle dreams behind him is transformed into futile yearning; that terrible torture which renders a man capable of the most frightful crimes. He became obsessed with a horrible envy, an envy that bordered upon madness. His face became contorted with hatred when he saw a work that bore the stamp of genius. He ground his teeth and devoured it with a basilisk glance. A plan, the most monstrous plan ever conceived by man, was devised in his mind, and he threw himself into carrying it out with all the energy of a man possessed. He began buying up all the best works of art that came into the market. Having spent a fortune on a picture, he took it up carefully into his studio and there he flung himself upon it with the fury of a tiger, slashing it, tearing it, cutting it to pieces, stamping on it, and roaring with delighted laughter as he did so. The vast wealth he had amassed provided him with all the means for gratifying this fiendish passion. He opened his bags of gold. He unlocked his chests. No monster of ignorance ever destroyed so many wonderful works of art as were destroyed by this fierce avenger. At his appearance at an auction, everyone despaired of obtaining any work of art. It seemed as if the heavens in their wrath had sent this awful scourge into the world expressly for the purpose of depriving it of all harmony. This horrible passion threw a most horrible shadow upon his face: he now always looked at the world with jaundiced eyes. Scorn of the world and everlasting denial were stamped on his features. It was as though the terrible Demon of Pushkin's poem had been reincarnated in him. Words of venom and bitter reproof poured from his lips unceasingly. He walked through the streets like some harpy and, seeing him from a distance, all his acquaintances did their best to avoid him, for to meet him was enough to poison the whole day for them.

Fortunately for the world and for art, such a highly strung and violent life could not last long: the intensity of his passion was too abnormal and vast for his feeble strength. He began suffering more and more from fits of raving madness which, finally, took the form of a most dreadful disorder. A high fever combined with a galloping consumption took hold of him with such fierceness that in three days he was reduced to a shadow of his former self. To this were added all the symptoms of incurable madness. Sometimes it took several men to restrain him. He began to be haunted by the long-forgotten, living eyes of the strange portrait, and in those moments his insane fury was truly horrible. All the people who stood round his bed seemed to him like dreadful portraits. The portrait was doubled and quadrupled before his eyes; all the walls seemed to be hung with portraits, and their unmoving, living eyes were gazing fixedly upon him. Terrible portraits glared at him from the ceiling and from the floor; the room widened and lengthened endlessly to make room for more and more of those staring eyes. The doctor who had undertaken to treat him, and who had heard something of the strange story of his life, tried hard to find some connexion between the hallucinations of his brain and the events of his life, but without success. The sick man understood nothing and felt nothing except his own frightful agonies, and only uttered bloodcurdling screams or babbled incoherently. At length his life came to an end in a final—and this time silent—paroxysm of suffering. His corpse looked horrible. Nothing could be found of his great wealth; but the discovery of the savagely torn-up masterpieces, which must have cost millions, made people realise the terrible purpose they had served.

PART TWO

Many carriages, chaises and cabs were standing before the entrance of a house in which an auction was taking place of the possessions of one of those wealthy art lovers who have an easy, comfortable life and gaily tread the primrose path of dalliance, acquiring quite innocently the reputation of art patrons and very amiably spending millions on works of art of all kinds, millions accumulated by their well-to-do, business-like fathers and grandfathers and, as often happens, even by their own hands during the early days of their life. Such patrons of the arts, needless to say, no longer exist; for our nineteenth century has long ago

acquired the dull physiognomy of a banker whose sole delight is his millions, and those, too, in the shape of figures
in ledgers. The long drawing-room was filled with a most
miscellaneous crowd of people who had swooped down like
birds of prey on an abandoned corpse. Here was a regular
flotilla of Russian merchants from the Arcade as well as
from the less fashionable markets, all in dark-blue coats of
German cut. Their looks, the expression of their faces, were
somehow more grave, more independent; they showed no
trace of that excessive and rather extravagant servility
which is so characteristic of a Russian shopkeeper in the
presence of a customer in his shop. Here they were not so
eager to parade their courtesies, in spite of the fact that
in the same room were many of those aristocrats before
whom, in any other place, they were ready to kowtow and
sweep away the dust they themselves had brought in on
their boots. Here they were completely at ease, fingered
books and pictures without the slightest ceremony in their
eagerness to find out the quality of the goods, and boldly
outbid the noble art experts. Here were many inveterate
frequenters of public auctions who seemed to have made it
a rule of their lives to be present at an auction every morning instead of having lunch at home; aristocrats who fancied themselves as art experts, and who deem it their duty
never to miss a chance of adding to their collections and
who anyway have nothing else to do between twelve and
one o'clock; finally, the gentlemen whose clothes were as
poor as their pockets were empty and who appear every
day at an auction without any mercenary aim but just out
of curiosity, to see who will bid more and who less, who
will outbid whom, and to whom the goods will be knocked
down. A large number of pictures were scattered all over
the room without any attempt at classification, among
pieces of furniture and books with the monogram of their
former owner who most probably never had the laudable
curiosity to look into them. Chinese vases, marble table-
tops, modern and antique furniture with curved lines,
adorned with the paws of griffons, sphinxes and lions, gilt

and not gilt, chandeliers, sconces—all this lay about in confused heaps on the floor, not arranged in order as in shops. It was a veritable chaos of the fine arts. The feeling we generally get at an auction is rather uncomfortable: it all looks too much like a funeral procession. The room in which it takes place is rather gloomy; the windows are obstructed with furniture and pictures and give very little light; the silent faces and the funereal voice of the auctioneer, who keeps knocking with his little hammer and chanting a requiem for the poor arts which have met here under such strange circumstances. All this seems to emphasise even more the general unpleasant atmosphere of the place.

The auction was apparently in full swing. A whole crowd of eminently respectable people were huddled together in one spot and seemed to be very excited about something, each one trying to outbid the other. From every side came the words, "Rouble, rouble, rouble." They did not even give the auctioneer time to repeat the last bid which had already grown to four times the original offer. The crowd was excited about a portrait which could not but attract the attention of anyone with the most rudimentary knowledge of painting. The hand of a master was clearly discernible in it. The portrait had quite clearly been restored several times as well as revarnished, and showed the features of some oriental gentleman in a wide robe and with an unusual, strange expression on his face, though the people who crowded round it were most of all struck by the remarkable vitality of his eyes. The longer a person looked at them, the more did they seem to bore right through him. This peculiarity, this extraordinary whim of the artist, attracted the attention of almost everyone. Many of the bidders for the picture had had to withdraw from the sale, for the price offered for it was quite incredible. There remained only two well-known aristocrats, great collectors of paintings, who seemed equally determined to secure the picture. They were both in a ferment of excitement and they would have most certainly gone on outbidding each other till the picture was knocked down for quite a fantastic price, if one of the men who had been examining it had not said, "Allow me, gentlemen, to interrupt your competition for a while. You see, I perhaps more than anyone else have a right to the picture." These words immediately drew the attention of everybody in the room to the speaker. They were uttered by a tall and slender man of about thirty-five, with long black hair. His pleasant face, full of a kind of gay light-heartedness, showed a character free of all worldly care; there was no pretence to fashion in his dress: everything about him indicated the artist. He was, in fact, the artist B., whom many people in the room knew personally.

"However strange my words may sound to you," he went on, seeing that everybody in the room was looking at him, "you will, I think, admit, if you will be so kind as to listen to my little story, that I had every right to speak them. Everything convinces me that this is the portrait I am looking for."

A quite natural curiosity took possession of almost everybody in the room, and even the auctioneer himself stopped short, openmouthed and with raised hammer, prepared to listen. At the beginning of the story many people quite involuntarily turned again and again to have a look at the portrait, but as the story got more and more interesting everyone's gaze was directed only at the artist.

"I suppose you all know that part of the town which is called Kolomna," he began. "Everything there is quite unlike any other part of St. Petersburg. There we are no longer in a capital city, and not even in the provinces. Indeed, as you walk through the streets of Kolomna, you seem to feel all the desires and passions of youth leaving you. There the future seems never to bother to look in; there everything is quiet, silent, dead; there everything is suggestive of retirement from active life, everything is in strange and striking contrast to the movement and noise of a capital city. The people who live there are for the most part retired Civil Servants, widows, poor people, people who seem at one time or another to have had some acquaintance with the Supreme Court and who have therefore sentenced themselves to life imprisonment in that district; cooks no longer in service who spend the whole day in the street markets, gossiping in the small grocers' shops with the shop-keepers, and who every day spend a few pence on a little coffee and a quarter of a pound of sugar, and, lastly, that class of people who can be summed up by the word ashen-grey, people whose clothes, faces, hair, and eyes have a kind of dingy, ashen appearance, like a day which is neither sunny nor stormy, but something betwixt and between: a slight mist covers everything and robs every object of its sharp outlines. Here, too, we may add the retired titular councillors and the retired military men with an eye miss-ing and a swollen lip. These people are entirely apathetic. They go about without looking at anything; they are silent and yet do not seem to be thinking of anything. You won't find much in their rooms, except perhaps sometimes a bottle of pure Russian vodka, which they go on sipping all day without any particular enthusiasm and without any strong rush of blood to their heads that follows too much drinking, such as the young German artisan likes to indulge in on a Sunday, that dare-devil of the slums who is the sole mon-arch of the pavement after midnight.

"Life in Kolomna is terribly dull; you rarely come across a carriage in its streets, except perhaps one carrying the actors to and from the theatre, which alone breaks the uni-versal silence by its clatter and loud din. Here almost every one goes on foot, and a cab very often crawls along at a snail's pace without a fare, but with a bundle of hay for its bearded nag. You can easily find a flat there for ten shillings a month, with morning coffee thrown in. Widows with pensions form the aristocracy in that part of the town; they behave with the utmost propriety, sweep their rooms at fairly frequent intervals and discuss with their lady friends the dearness of beef and cabbage; very often they share their rooms with their young daughters, silent, mute, though sometimes quite good-looking creatures, with dis-gusting lap dogs and clocks with dismally ticking pendu-lums. Then there are the actors whose meagre pay does not allow them to live in any other part of the town, free and easy folk, living, like all artists, as they please. At home they sit about in their dressing-gowns, repairing a pistol, or gluing together out of cardboard all sorts of things that might come in useful in the house, or playing draughts or cards with their friends, and so spend the whole morning and do almost the same thing in the evening, except occasionally with the addition of a glass of punch. Besides these grand seigneurs and aristocrats of Kolomna, there is the usual small fry. It is as difficult to name or number them as it is to enumerate the multitude of insects in stale vinegar. Among them you will find old women who are constantly saying their prayers; old women who are constantly drinking; old women who both pray and drink; old women who eke out a miserable existence by means that pass all understanding, who, like ants, drag all sorts of things on their backs, such as old clothes and linen, from Kalinkin Bridge to the old junk market to sell them there for tuppence-half-penny; in fact, you will find there the very dregs of humanity whose position even a benevolent economist would find it hard to improve.

"I mention all this just to let you see how often these poor people are driven by necessity to obtain some immediate, temporary help by resorting to borrowing; for the presence of such people usually attracts a certain type of money-lender who settles among them and supplies them with small loans on any kind of security at a high rate of interest. These small money-lenders are a hundred times more hard-hearted than any big money-lender, for they live in the slums among a poverty-stricken population clad in rags that the rich money-lender who only deals with people who drive about in carriages never sees. This is why every human feeling dies in them so soon.

"Among these money-lenders there was one. . . . But perhaps I'd better tell you straight away that the events I am about to relate occurred in the last century in the reign of the late Empress Catherine II. You will, of course, realise that since then the very appearance of Kolomna and the life of its inhabitants have greatly changed. Well, among these money-lenders there was a certain person, a remarkable man in every respect, who had settled in that part of the town a long time ago. He went about in a flowing oriental robe. His dark complexion revealed his southern origin; but what his nationality actually was, whether he was an Indian, a Greek, or a Persian, no one could say for certain. His great, almost gigantic height; his dark, haggard, scorched face with a complexion that was indescribably repulsive; his large eyes blazing with an unnatural fire; his thick, beetling eyebrows, set him rather sharply apart from all the ashen-grey inhabitants of the capital. His very house was different from the small wooden houses of that district. It was a stone building of a type which the Genoese merchants had at one time built in large numbers, with irregular windows of different sizes, iron shutters, and bolts and bars. This money-lender differed from every other money-lender in that he was willing to advance any sum to anybody, from a poor old lady to the most extravagant courtier. Very often splendid equipages used to stop in front of his house, and sometimes the head of some gorgeously dressed court lady would look out of their windows. As usual, it was rumoured that his iron chests were filled to the very top with gold, jewellery, diamonds and all sorts of pledged articles of great value, but at the same time he was not by any means as greedy of gain as other money-lenders. He lent money very readily, and seemed to fix the dates of repayment very fairly; but by some curious methods of arithmetic he made the repayments work out at enormous rates of interest. So at any rate it was rumoured. But what was really strange and what amazed many people was the fate of all those who borrowed money from him: for all of them came to an unhappy end. Whether it was simply the sort of thing people said about him, or some absurd superstitious talk, or rumours spread with the intention of harming him, was never discovered. But a few facts which occurred within a short time of each other and for everybody to see, were certainly very remarkable and could not easily be forgotten.

"Among the aristocracy of that day one young man rapidly attracted general attention. He belonged to one of the best families and had distinguished himself in the service of his country while still very young. He was a warm admirer of everything that was true and noble, a patron of learning and the arts, a man who had in him the making of a Mæcenas. Soon he was worthily rewarded by the Empress who had appointed him to an important office which corresponded exactly with his wishes and in which he could do much for learning or any other worthy cause. The young statesman surrounded himself with artists, poets and men of learning. He wished to give work to all, to encourage all. He undertook a large number of useful publications at his own expense, placed many orders, offered many prizes to encourage art and science, spent thousands on it all, and in the end found himself financially embarrassed. But, full of noble impulses, he would not give up his work. He raised money by borrowing wherever he could and finally came to the Kolomna money-lender. Having obtained a considerable loan from him, this man within a short time changed completely: he became an embittered persecutor of art and learning, venting his spite particularly on young scholars and artists. He could only see the bad side of whatever was written or published, and he twisted every word round to mean something the writer never intended it to mean. Unfortunately the French Revolution happened just at that time. He used it as an excuse for all sorts of wickedness. He began discovering revolutionary tendencies in everything; he began suspecting subversive intentions in everything. His suspicions grew so much that finally he began suspecting even himself; he began fabricating terrible and unjust accusations against innocent people and brought unhappiness and ruin upon thousands. It goes without saying that such acts in the end came to the ears of the Empress herself, who was terribly shocked, and full of the nobility of mind and spirit which is so great an ornament of crowned heads, she uttered words which unhappily were not recorded at the time and preserved for us, but the deep sense of which impressed itself upon the hearts of many. The Empress observed that it was not under a monarchical form of government that the high and noble aspirations of the human mind were trampled upon, and the finest achievements of the human mind, poetry and the arts, despised and persecuted; on the contrary, it was the monarchs and the monarchs only who had been their patrons; that the Shakespeares and Molières flourished under their gracious protection, while Dante could not find a corner for himself in his republican birthplace; that real geniuses arose during the time when kings and kingdoms were at the topmost pinnacle of their power and glory and not at the time of ugly political disturbances and republican terror which had so far not given a single poet to the world; that poets must be held in honour, for they brought peace and sweet contentment to the heart of man, and not troubles and discontent; that scholars, poets, and all those who were actively engaged in the arts were the diamonds and pearls in the crown imperial, for it was by them that the reign of a great monarch was glorified and made immortal. In a word, the Empress, when speaking those words, was divinely beautiful. Old men, I remember, could not recall that speech without tears. All took an interest in that affair. To the honour of our national pride be it said that in the Russian heart there always abides a fine impulse to take the side of the persecuted. The statesman who had forfeited the confidence of his Sovereign was punished in an exemplary manner and dismissed his post. But he could read a much worse punishment in the faces of his fellow countrymen: utter and universal scorn. Nothing could adequately describe the sufferings of his vain spirit; his pride, his disappointed ambitions, his ruined hopes, all combined to torture him, and his life came to an end in dreadful attacks of raving madness.

"Another striking example of the baneful influence of the money-lender also occurred in the sight of all. Among the many lovely women of our northern capital at that time, one was universally acclaimed as the loveliest of them all. Her beauty was an exquisite blend of our northern beauty with the beauty of the south, a gem that makes its appearance only rarely in the world. My father used to tell me that he had not seen any woman to equal her in his life. Everything seemed united in her: riches, intelligence, and great charm of soul. Many men sought her hand in marriage, and foremost among them was Prince R., one of the best and most honourable of all young noblemen of that time, handsome of face and of a noble, chivalrous character, the ideal hero of novels and women, a Grandison in every respect. Prince R. was passionately, madly in love, and his love was fully reciprocated. But the girl's parents did not consider him a good match for their daughter. The ancestral estates of the prince had ceased to be his property long ago; his family was in disfavour at court, and the bad state of his affairs was known to all. Suddenly the prince left the capital for a time, as though for the purpose of improving his affairs, and after a short time he returned a rich man who could now afford to live in great style and luxury. Splendid balls and parties made him known at court. The father of the beautiful girl gave his consent and one of the most fashionable weddings in town soon took place. What was the real reason of so sudden a change in the affairs of the bridegroom, and where he had obtained such great wealth no one could say for certain; but it was whispered that he had entered into some kind of agreement with the mysterious usurer and received a loan from him. Be that as it may, the wedding was one of the great social events of the season. The bride and the bridegroom were the objects of general envy. Every one knew how deeply in love they were, and how constant their love was, and how much they must have suffered during their long separation, and how great their virtues were. Romantic ladies already painted in rosy colours the great happiness that was in store for the young people. But everything fell out quite differently. In one year a terrible change took place in the husband. His character, until then so fine and noble, was poisoned with suspicion, jealousy, intolerance and all sorts of insane humours. He became his wife's tyrant and torturer and, what no one could have foreseen, was guilty of the most abominable acts of cruelty, going so far as to beat her. In only one year people found it difficult to recognise the woman who so recently had been such a radiant beauty and had had crowds of the most devoted admirers. At last, unable to bear her treatment any longer, she first broached the subject of a divorce. Her husband flew into a terrible rage at the mere mention of it. In his first outburst of fury he forced his way into her room with a knife and he would without a doubt have stabbed her there and then, if he had not been seized and restrained. In a fit of raving madness and despair he turned the knife against himself—and ended his life in the most horrible agonies.

"In addition to these two instances, which occurred before the eyes of the whole world, many more instances were told of similar happenings among the lower classes, all of which had ended tragically. In one instance, an honest, sober man became a drunkard; in another a shopkeeper's assistant robbed his employer; in a third a cabby, who had for years plied his trade honestly, murdered his fare for a few pence. It was of course impossible that such happenings, sometimes retailed with all sorts of embellishments, should not have struck terror in the hearts of the humble inhabitants of Kolomna. No one doubted that the usurer was possessed of the devil. It was said that he often made such demands that the poor wretches who came to him for a loan fled from him in horror, not daring to repeat them to anyone afterwards; that his money possessed the power of becoming incandescent and burning through things, and that it was all marked with strange symbols. All sorts of fantastic tales were told about him. And perhaps the most remarkable thing of all was that the entire population of Kolomna, the entire world of poor old women, low-grade Civil Servants, small-part actors, and all the small fry we have mentioned earlier, would rather suffer any hardships

and privations than apply to the terrible money-lender for
a loan. There were even cases of old women who had actually died of starvation, preferring to starve to death rather
than destroy their souls. Any one meeting him in the street
shrank back in horror and threw frightened glances over his
shoulder a long time at the receding, immensely tall figure.
In his appearance alone there was so much that was uncommon that people could not help ascribing supernatural
powers to him. Those powerful features, so deeply chiselled
that no living man has ever had any features like them;
that torrid bronze complexion; that excessive thickness of
the eyebrows; those unbearable, terrible eyes, even the long
folds of his oriental robe—everything seemed to say that the
passions of other men paled before the passions that stirred
in his body. My father always used to stand motionless
when meeting him and each time he could not help saying
to himself, 'A devil, a real devil!' But I'd better introduce
you to my father who, by the way, is the real subject of
my tale.

"My father was a remarkable man in many ways. He
was an artist the like of whom you do not often meet, a
self-taught artist, who without the help of teachers or a
school had discovered in his own soul the rules and laws of
art, driven only by his passion for perfection and walking
(for reasons which he himself perhaps did not know) along
one path only, the path along which his spirit led him. He
was one of those born geniuses whom our contemporaries
so often contemptuously dismiss by the word 'amateur' and
who are never disheartened by sneers or failure, whose
strength and zeal are, on the contrary, constantly renewed,
and who in spirit go far beyond those works which had
earned them the title of 'amateur.' By his own innate, lofty
instinct he perceived the presence of an idea in every object;
he grasped the meaning of the words: historic painting; he
grasped why a simple drawing of a head, a simple portrait
of Raphael, Leonardo da Vinci, Titian, and Correggio could
be called historic painting, while a huge canvas of an historical subject was still nothing more than a *tableau de*

genre, despite all the artist's pretensions to historical painting. Both inner inclination and personal conviction guided his brush to religious subjects, the highest and the very last step of the sublime in art. He did not know the meaning of personal ambition or bad temper, so inseparable a part of the character of many a painter. He was a man of great firmness of character, honest, frank, even rude, with somewhat rough manners, but with more than a touch of pride in his soul, who always spoke of people both indulgently and critically. 'Why should I care what they think?' he used to say. 'It isn't for them I am working. I'm not painting my pictures for a drawing-room. He who understands me will thank me. It's no use blaming a man of the world for understanding nothing about painting: instead he understands everything about cards, is a good judge of wine or a horse—what more does a gentleman want? I daresay if he tried one thing and then another and started getting clever he'd become a confounded nuisance! To each his own: let each man mind his own business. So far as I'm concerned, I prefer a man who tells me frankly that he doesn't know anything about art rather than one who plays the hypocrite and pretends to know what he doesn't know and only succeeds in making trouble and being a damned nuisance generally!' He worked for very little pay, that is to say, for a pay which was just sufficient to keep his family and to permit him to carry on with his work. Moreover, he never refused to help anyone who was in real need, and especially to hold out a helping hand to a poor brother artist. He believed with the simple, reverent faith of his fathers, and that was perhaps why a lofty, exalted expression appeared as though by itself on all the faces he painted, an expression which even the most brilliant artists of his time never succeeded in reproducing, however hard they might try. At last, by unremitting labour and perseverance in the path he had marked out for himself, he even began to win the respect of those who had before decried him as an amateur and as a self-taught, 'home-made' artist. He was always getting commissions for pictures from churches, and he was

never without work. One of his pictures in particular occupied all his thoughts. I can't remember what its subject
was; all I know is that he had to introduce the Prince of
Darkness into it. He pondered long what kind of a face to
give him, for he wanted that face to express all that weighs
down and oppresses man. While thinking about it, the face
of the mysterious money-lender would occasionally flash
through his mind and he could not help saying to himself,
'That's the man I ought to take as my model for the devil.'
Imagine his surprise, therefore, when one day, while working in his studio, he heard a knock at the door and almost
immediately the terrible usurer entered. A cold shiver ran
down my father's spine in spite of himself.

"'You're a painter?' the money-lender asked my father
without ceremony.

"'Yes,' said my father, bewildered and wondering what
was to come next.

"'All right. I want you to paint my portrait. I don't know,
but I may possibly be dead soon. I have no children and
I don't want to die completely. I want to live. Can you
paint a portrait that will look alive in every detail?'

"My father thought, 'Couldn't be better. The fellow is
asking me himself to use him as a model of the devil for
my picture!' So he agreed. They came to terms and arranged the times of the sittings, and the very next day my
father, taking his palette and brushes, was already at the
usurer's place.

"The high wall surrounding the courtyard, the dogs, the
iron doors, the bolts and bars, the arched windows, the
chests covered with strange rugs, and, last but not least,
the extraordinary master of the house himself who sat motionless before him—all that produced a strange impression
upon my father. The lower part of the windows was, as
though on purpose, covered and blocked up, so that the
light came in only from the top. 'Damn it, how wonderfully
his face is lighted up now!' my father said to himself, beginning to paint breathlessly, as though afraid lest the favourable light should vanish. 'What terrific power!' he went

on speaking to himself. 'If I'm successful in getting him even half as well as he is now, he'll kill all my saints and angels: they'll all pale into insignificance before him! What devilish power! He'll simply jump out of my canvas, even if I am only just a little true to nature. What amazing features!' he went on repeating to himself, working away with redoubled zeal, and soon he was able to see himself how certain features were already beginning to be transferred to the canvas. But the closer he got to them, the more he became oppressed by a strange, uncanny feeling of dread, which he could not himself explain. However, he decided in spite of it to pursue, with the most scrupulous exactitude, every inconspicuous feature and expression. First of all he applied himself to portraying his eyes. There was so much force in those eyes that it seemed absurd even to attempt to reproduce them as they were. But he made up his mind to discover their minutest feature and shade and thus to solve their mystery. . . . However, as soon as he began painting them and delving deeper and deeper into them as he proceeded with his work, there arose in his heart such a strange revulsion, he felt such an inexplicable prostration of soul, that he was forced again and again to lay down his brush for a time and then start afresh. But at last he could endure it no longer. He felt that those eyes pierced his very soul and filled it with indescribable alarm. This feeling became much stronger next day and the day after. He became frightened. He threw down his brush and told the money-lender bluntly that he did not intend to go on with the painting of his portrait. The change that came over the sinister usurer at those words had to be seen to be believed. He fell at my father's feet, imploring him to finish his portrait, pleading that his fate and his continued existence in the world depended on it, saying that my father had already caught with his brush his living features and that if he would reproduce them faithfully his life would in some supernatural way remain in the portrait and because of that he would not die completely, and finally urging that it was absolutely necessary for him to remain in the world. My father was terrified by these words: they seemed so utterly inexplicable and horrible to him that he dropped his brushes and his palette and rushed out of the usurer's house.

"He was worried about it all that day and the following night, but next morning he got the portrait back from the money-lender. It was brought by a woman, the only human being the usurer kept as a servant, who told my father that her master did not want the portrait, that he did not intend to pay anything for it, and that he was therefore returning it. On the evening of the same day my father learnt that the money-lender had died and was about to be buried according to the rites of his religion. All that seemed inexplicably strange to him. But from that day a marked change showed itself in my father's character: he grew restless and ill at ease, and he was unable to understand the reason for it. Shortly afterwards he did something which no one would have expected of him. For some time the paintings of one of his pupils had begun attracting the attention of a small circle of art experts and art lovers. My father always considered that he had talent and for that reason he did all he could to help him. But suddenly he felt jealous of him. The general interest taken in his work and the discussions which it provoked became unbearable to him. Then to his utter annoyance he learnt that his pupil had been commissioned to paint a picture for a rich church which had been recently rebuilt. That was the last straw! 'No, I shan't let that youngster triumph over me!' he said to himself. 'It's a bit too soon for you, my boy, to lick your elders. Thank God, there is still some strength left in me. Let's see who will lick whom!' And this straightforward and honourable man began scheming and intriguing, a thing he had hitherto abhorred, until at last he succeeded in getting the church authorities to declare an open competition for the picture, so as to give other artists a chance of sending in their pictures. Then he shut himself up in his studio and began working feverishly at his picture. It seemed as if he wished to give all he had, to sacrifice his last ounce of strength, to it. And indeed it turned out one of his best works. No one doubted that he would win the competition. All the pictures were sent in, and, compared with my father's picture, all the others were as day is to night. Then suddenly one of the members of the committee of judges (I think he was a person in holy orders) made a remark which rather surprised everybody. 'There is doubtless a great deal of talent in the picture of this artist,' he said, 'but there is no saintliness in the faces; on the contrary, there is even something demonic in their eyes, as though some evil feeling has guided the hand of the artist.' All looked at the picture, and they could not help agreeing with the justice of these words. My father rushed up to his painting, as though anxious to make sure whether what he considered an offensive remark was justified or not, and perceived with horror that he had given the usurer's eyes to almost every face in his picture. They all gazed with such demon-like intensity that he could not help shuddering himself. His picture was rejected, and to his great mortification he learnt that his pupil's picture had been accepted. It is impossible to describe his fury when he returned home. He nearly assaulted my mother, drove all his children away, broke his brushes and smashed his easel, took the picture of the money-lender off the wall and ordered a fire to be lit in the fireplace, intending to cut it up and burn it. But just as he was about to destroy the picture a friend of his came in, an artist like my father, a very jovial fellow, who was always in high spirits, never hankered after fame, worked away happily at anything that happened to come his way, and was never happier than at a dinner or a party.

"'What are you doing? What do you want to burn?' he said, going up to the portrait. 'Why, man, this is one of your best works! It's the money-lender who recently died, isn't it? It's a real masterpiece! You certainly hit him straight between the eyes! Gosh, got right into them, haven't you? I bet in real life his eyes never looked like that!'

"'Well, let's see what they'll look like in the fire!' said

my father, and he seized the portrait and was about to throw it in the flames.

" 'Wait a minute, for God's sake!' said his friend, restraining him. 'If it's got on your nerves so much, give it to me!'

"At first my father would not agree, but at last he let himself be persuaded, and his jovial friend took the portrait away with him, pleased as anything with his new acquisition.

"After he had left, my father suddenly felt much happier, as though with the removal of the portrait a heavy load had been taken off his mind. He was now himself surprised at his spite and jealousy and the quite apparent change in his character. Thinking over his behaviour towards his pupil, he felt deeply grieved at heart and said, not without a feeling of inward anguish, 'It was God who punished me; my picture deserved to be rejected. It had been planned with the idea of ruining a fellow artist. A fiendish feeling of envy stimulated my brush, so is it any wonder that a fiendish feeling was also reflected in it?' He immediately went in search of his former pupil, clasped him to his heart, asked his forgiveness, and did his best to make amends. He went on working as happily as before, but his face grew much more pensive. He said his prayers more frequently, became more taciturn, and never spoke disparagingly about people again; even the rather coarse exterior of his character somehow became softer and more gentle. Something else soon gave him another shock. He had not seen the friend who had carried off the portrait for some time. He was thinking of going to find out how he was, when his friend quite unexpectedly entered his studio. After the usual greetings his friend said:

" 'I say, old man, now I understand why you wanted to burn that picture. Damn it, there's certainly something uncanny about it. . . . I don't believe in witchcraft, but, say what you like, there certainly is some evil power in it. . . .'

" 'What do you mean?' asked my father.

" 'Well, ever since I hung it up in my room I've felt so unsettled, so worried, so depressed, as though I was contemplating murder or something. I never knew what insomnia meant, but now I began to suffer not only from insomnia. . . . I have had such awful dreams. . . . I really hardly know if they were dreams or something quite different. It was as if the devil himself was trying to strangle me, and all the time that damned old fellow was sure to bob up somewhere. My dear chap, I simply can't tell you the sort of state I was in. Nothing like it ever happened to me before. All that time I was walking about like a madman: obsessed with fears, expecting something awful to happen to me any moment. I felt I couldn't say a friendly word to anyone, speak frankly to any man, just as though some spy was at my elbow all the time. And it was only after I had given the portrait to my nephew, who kept asking for it, that I felt as if a heavy weight had been lifted from my shoulders. I was a happy man once more, and I still am, as you see. Well, old chap, you certainly dished up the devil himself this time!'

"My father listened to his story with rapt attention and then asked, 'Has your nephew still got the portrait?'

" 'Heavens, no! He couldn't stand it, either,' replied the jovial artist. 'I tell you the soul of that usurer must be in that portrait: he seems to be jumping out of the frame, walking about the room and, according to my nephew, doing all sorts of uncanny things. I'd have thought he had gone off his head, if I hadn't had a somewhat similar experience myself. He sold it to a collector, who I understand couldn't put up with it, either, and got rid of it to someone else.'

"This story made a deep impression upon my father. He was now worried in good earnest, became oppressed with melancholy thoughts, and at last persuaded himself that his brush had been the tool of the devil and that part of the usurer's life had somehow or other really passed into the portrait and was now plaguing and tormenting people, instilling all sorts of devilish ideas into their minds, leading an artist astray, inflicting terrible tortures of envy and jealously, and so on and so forth. Three severe blows that he experienced one after another a short time later—the sudden deaths of his wife, his daughter, and his little son—he looked upon as a punishment from above and he made up his mind to retire from the world immediately. As soon as I was nine years old, he placed me at the school of the Academy of Art and, after settling his debts, he withdrew to a lonely monastery where he soon took monastic vows. There he amazed the monks by the austerity of his life and his strict observance of all the monastic rules. The Father Superior, having learnt about his skill as a painter, demanded that he should paint the principal icon in the monastery church, but the humble brother categorically refused, saying that he was unworthy to touch his brush, that it had been contaminated, and that he had first to purify his soul with hard work and mortification of the flesh to be once more worthy of undertaking such a task. They did not want to force him to paint the picture, while he increased the rigors of his monastic life as much as possible until even such a life did not satisfy him, for he did not consider it sufficiently austere. So with the blessing of the Father Superior he went into the wilderness to be entirely alone. There he built himself a hut with the branches of trees, fed only on raw roots, hauled large stones from one place to another as a penance, stood on the same spot with his hands raised to heaven from sunrise to sunset and recited his prayers all the time. He seemed in fact to have applied himself to finding and experiencing every possible degree of suffering and attaining to that state of self-immolation, examples of which can be only found in the Lives of the Saints. In this manner he mortified his flesh a long time, for several years, strengthening it only by the living grace of prayer. One day at last he returned to the monastery and said to the Father Superior, 'Now I'm ready. If God wills, I shall bring my labour to an end.' He selected as the subject of his picture the Birth of Jesus. He worked on it for a whole year, without leaving his cell, and barely sustaining himself on the coarse monastic fare, and praying incessantly. At the end of the year the picture was ready. It was indeed a miracle of art. I need hardly tell you that neither the Father Superior nor the monks knew much about painting, but even they were struck by the singular holiness of the figures. The feeling of divine humility on the face of the Blessed Virgin as she bent over the Child; the profound intelligence in the eyes of the Holy Child, as though they already saw something from afar; the solemn silence of the Magi, amazed by the Divine Miracle and prostrating themselves at His feet; and, finally, the indescribably holy stillness which pervaded the whole picture—all this was presented with such harmonious strength and great beauty that its effect was magical. All the brethren fell on their knees before the new icon and the Father Superior, deeply moved, said, 'No, man could never produce such a picture with the aid of human art alone; a holy, divine power has guided your brush and the blessing of Heaven rested upon your labours.'

"Just at that time I finished my course at the Academy, was awarded a gold medal and with it the joyful hope of a journey to Italy—the greatest ambition of a twenty-year-old artist. All I had to do was to take leave of my father, whom I had not seen for the past twelve years. I don't mind confessing that I had even forgotten what he looked like. I had of course heard some talk about the austerity and holiness of his life and was prepared beforehand to meet a recluse of a forbidding exterior, a man who had renounced the world and become a complete stranger to it, a man who knew nothing except his cell and his prayers, a man exhausted and shrivelled from eternal fasts and vigils. Imagine my surprise therefore when I saw before me a fine-looking, almost inspired old man! There was no trace of exhaustion on his face: it shone with the brightness of heavenly joy. A beard, white as snow, and thin, almost ethereal, hair of the same silvery hue fell picturesquely over his chest and the folds of his black frock, almost to the rope with which his poor monastic garb was girded; but still more remarkable to me was to hear from his lips such words and thoughts which, I don't mind telling you, I shall treasure in my heart

for the rest of my life and I sincerely hope that every one
of my fellow artists will do the same.

" 'I was waiting for you, my son,' he said when I went
up to him for his blessing. 'There is a path before you which
you will henceforth follow all through your life. Your path
is plain; do not turn away from it. You have talent; talent
is one of the most precious of God's gifts—do not destroy it.
Examine, study carefully everything you see, pursue your
art and master it, but in everything try to find its inward
meaning, and most of all endeavour to obtain an understanding of the high mystery of creation. Blessed are those
who possess it, for there is nothing in nature too low for
them. Indeed, a creative artist is as great in little things as
in great things; in things that are despicable, he finds nothing to despise, for the beautiful spirit of Him who made
them shines invisibly through them, and whatever is despicable is in fact clothed in glory, for it has gone through
the purifying fire of His spirit. It is in art that man finds an
intimation of heavenly paradise, and for this reason alone
art is higher than anything. And as a life spent in the calm
contemplation of God is higher than a life spent in the tur-
moil of the world, so is creation higher than destruction.
As an angel is, by the pure innocence of his bright soul
alone higher than all the vast power and proud passion of
Satan, so is a great work of art greater than anything else
in the world. Sacrifice everything to it and love it with all
your heart, not with the passion of earthly lust, but with a
gentle, heavenly passion; for without it man is powerless to
raise himself above the earth and incapable of uttering the
sweet sounds of contentment and peace. For a great work of
art comes into the world to bring peace of mind and reconciliation to all. It is incapable of sowing the seeds of discontent in the soul of man, but everlastingly aspires to God like
an uttered prayer. But there are moments in a man's life,
dark moments . . .' He paused and I could not help noticing that his bright countenance became suddenly overcast, as though obscured for a moment by a cloud. 'There
is one incident in my life,' he said, 'I cannot explain. Even

to this day I cannot understand what that strange being was whose portrait I painted. It surely must have been some manifestation of the devil. I know the world denies the existence of the devil, and I will therefore not speak of him. I will only say that it was with repugnance that I painted him, that at the time I felt no love for my work. I tried to force myself to be true to nature by stifling every human emotion in me. No, that was not a work of art, and it is because of that that the feelings aroused by it in all who look at it are unruly feelings, riotous, restless, turbulent feelings, not the feelings of an artist, for even in times of general alarm an artist remains tranquil and at peace. I am told this portrait is passing from hand to hand, spreading feelings of dissatisfaction and discontent, giving rise in an artist to a feeling of envy, jealousy and black hatred towards his fellow artists, to wicked desires to persecute and oppress. May the Almighty keep and preserve you from these evil passions! There is nothing more dreadful than they. Far better to endure all the anguish of the worst persecution than to inflict even a semblance of persecution on any man. Keep your heart pure, my son. He who has a spark of genius in him must be purer in soul than the rest of mankind. For much will be forgiven an ordinary man that will not be forgiven him. A man who goes out of his house dressed in bright holiday clothes has only to be splashed by a spot of dirt from under a wheel for people to crowd round him, point a finger at him, and talk of his slovenliness, while the same people do not even notice the great number of spots on the week-day clothes of other passers-by. For stains on week-day clothes are never seen!'

"He blessed me and embraced me. Never in my life was I so deeply moved or felt so uplifted in spirit. I clung to his breast with reverence rather than with the feeling of a son and I kissed the scattered strands of his silvery hair. A tear glittered in his eye.

"'My son,' he said to me at the moment of parting, 'I want you to do one thing for me. I expect that one day you will come across the portrait I told you of. You will have no difficulty in recognising it by the remarkable eyes and their unnatural expression. Destroy it, I beg you, destroy it at all costs!'

"I promised him solemnly to do as he wished. What else could I have done? For fifteen years I have never happened to come across anything that remotely resembled the description of the portrait my father had given me, when all of a sudden at this auction . . ."

Here without finishing his sentence the artist turned to the wall to have another look at the portrait. The crowd of listeners did the same at the same instant, searching for the strange portrait with their eyes. But to their amazement it was no longer on the wall. A low murmur went through the crowd, followed almost immediately by the word "stolen" pronounced distinctly by several people. Someone had succeeded in filching it, taking advantage of the fact that the attention of the listeners had been distracted by the story. And for a long time the people in the auction room looked perplexed, wondering whether they had really seen those uncanny eyes, or whether it was merely an illusion, a vision that had flashed across their eyes tired by the long examination of old pictures.

1841–42

Nevsky Avenue

THERE IS nothing finer than Nevsky Avenue, not in St. Petersburg at any rate; for in St. Petersburg it is everything. And, indeed, is there anything more gay, more brilliant, more resplendent than this beautiful street of our capital? I am sure that not one of her anaemic inhabitants, not one of her innumerable Civil Servants, would exchange Nevsky Avenue for all the treasures in the world. Not only the young man of twenty-five, the young gallant with the beautiful moustache and the immaculate morning coat, but the man with white hair sprouting on his chin and a head as smooth as a billiard ball, yes, even he is enthralled with Nevsky Avenue. And the ladies . . . Oh, for the ladies Nevsky Avenue is a thing of even greater delight! But is there anyone who does not feel thrilled and delighted with it? The gay carriages, the handsome men, the beautiful women—all lend it a carnival air, an air that you can almost inhale the moment you set foot on Nevsky Avenue! Even if you have some very important business, you are quite certain to forget all about it as soon as you are there. This is the only place in town where you meet people who are not there on business, people who have not been driven there either by necessity or by their passion for making money, which seems to have the whole of St. Petersburg in its grip. It really does seem that the man you meet on Nevsky Avenue is less of an egoist than the man you meet on any other street where want and greed and avarice can be read on the faces of all who walk or drive in carriages or cabs. Nevsky Avenue is the main communication centre of the whole of St. Petersburg. Anyone living in the Petersburg or Vyborg district who has not seen a friend on the Sands or the Moscow Tollgate for years can be sure to meet him here. No directory or information bureau will supply such correct information as Nevsky Avenue. All-powerful Nevsky Avenue! The only place in St. Petersburg where a poor man can combine a stroll with entertainment. How spotlessly clean are its pavements swept and, good gracious, how many feet leave their marks on them! Here is the footprint left by the clumsy, dirty boot of an ex-army private, under whose weight the very granite seems to crack; and here is one left by the miniature, light as a feather, little shoe of the delightful young creature who turns her pretty head towards the glittering shop-window as the sun-flower turns to the sun; and here is the sharp scratch left by the rattling sabre of some ambitious lieutenant—everything leaves its imprint of great power or great weakness upon it. What a rapid phantasmagoria passes over it in a single day! What changes does it not undergo in only twenty-four hours!

Let us begin with the early morning when all St. Petersburg is filled with the smell of hot, freshly baked bread and is crowded with old women in tattered clothes who besiege the churches and appeal for alms to the compassionate passers-by. At this time Nevsky Avenue is deserted: the stout shopkeepers and their assistants are still asleep in their fine linen shirts, or are lathering their noble cheeks, or drinking coffee; beggars gather at the doors of the pastry-cooks' shops where the sleepy Ganymede, who the day before flew about like a fly with the cups of chocolate, crawls out with a besom in his hand, without a cravat, and flings some stale pasties and other leavings at them. Workmen are trudging through the streets: occasionally the avenue is crossed by Russian peasants, hurrying to their work in boots soiled with lime which not all the water of the Yekaterinsky Canal, famous for its cleanness, could wash off. At this time it is not proper for ladies to take a walk, for the Russian workman and peasant love to express themselves in vigorous language that is not even heard on the stage. Sometimes a sleepy Civil Servant will walk along with a brief-case under his arm, if the way to his office lies across Nevsky Avenue. It can indeed be stated without fear of contradiction that at this time, that is to say, until twelve o'clock, Nevsky Avenue does not serve as a goal for anyone, but is merely a means to an end: it is gradually filled with people who have their own occupations, their own worries, their own disappointments, and who are not thinking about it at all. The Russian peasant is talking about the few coppers he earns; old men and women wave their hands about or talk to themselves, sometimes with picturesque gestures, but no one listens to them or even laughs at them except perhaps the boys in brightly coloured smocks who streak along Nevsky Avenue with empty bottles or mended boots. At this time you can please yourself about your dress. You can wear a workman's cap instead of a hat, and even if your collar were to stick out of your cravat no one would notice it.

At twelve o'clock Nevsky Avenue is invaded by tutors and governesses of all nationalities and their charges in cambric collars. English Johnsons and French Coques walk arm in arm with the young gentlemen entrusted to their parental care and explain to them with an air of grave decorum that the signboards over the shops are put there to tell people what they can find inside the shops. Governesses, pale misses, and rosy-cheeked mademoiselles walk statelily behind slender and fidgety young girls, telling them to raise a shoulder a little higher and to walk straighter. In short, at this time Nevsky Avenue is a pedagogic Nevsky Avenue. But the nearer it gets to two o'clock in the afternoon, the fewer do the numbers of tutors, governesses, and children grow, until finally they are crowded out by their loving fathers who walk arm in arm with their highly-strung wives in gorgeous, bright dresses of every imaginable hue. These are by and by joined by people who have by that time finished all their important domestic engagements, such as talking to their doctors about the weather and the small pimple that has suddenly appeared on their nose; or enquiring after the health of their horses and the children, who, incidentally, seem always to be showing great promise; or reading in the papers the notices and important announcements of the arrivals and departures; or, lastly, drinking a cup of tea or coffee. They are soon joined by those upon whom enviable fate has bestowed the blessed calling of officials on special duties as well as by those who serve in the Foreign Office and who are particularly distinguished by their fine manners and their noble habits. Dear me, what wonderful appointments and posts there are! How they improve and delight the soul of man! But, alas, I am not in the Civil Service myself and so am deprived of the pleasure of appreciating the exquisite manners of my superiors. Every one you now meet on Nevsky Avenue is a paragon of respectability: the gentlemen in long frock-coats with their hands in their pockets; the ladies in pink, white and pale blue redingotes and hats. You will meet here a most wonderful assortment of side-whiskers, a unique pair of whiskers, tucked with astonishing and extraordinary art under the cravat, velvety whiskers, satiny whiskers, and whiskers black as sable or coal, the latter, alas, the exclusive property of the gentlemen from the Foreign Office. Providence has denied black whiskers to those serving in any other ministry, and to their great mortification they have to wear red whiskers. Here you come across moustaches so wonderful that neither pen nor brush can do justice to them, moustaches to which the best years of a lifetime have been devoted—the objects of long hours of vigil by day and by night; moustaches upon which all the perfumes of Arabia have been lavished, the most exquisite scents and essences, and which have been anointed with the rarest and most precious pomades; moustaches which are wrapped up for the night in the most delicate vellum; moustaches for which their possessors show a most touching affection and which are the envy of all who behold them. Thousands of different sorts of hats, dresses, multicoloured kerchiefs, light as gossamer, to which their owners sometimes remain faithful for two whole days, dazzle every eye on Nevsky Avenue. It looks as if a sea of butterflies have risen from flower stalks and are fluttering in a scintillating cloud above the black beetles of the male sex. Here you meet waists such as you have never seen in your dreams: slender, narrow waists, waists no thicker than the neck of a bottle, waists which make you step aside politely whenever you meet them for fear of injuring them by some awkward movement of your elbow; your heart is seized with apprehension and terror lest these most delightful products of art and nature should be snapped in two at the merest breath from your lips. And the ladies' sleeves you meet on Nevsky Avenue! Oh, what lovely sleeves! They remind you a little of two balloons, and it really seems as though the lady might suddenly rise in the air were she not held down by the gentleman walking beside her; for it is as delightfully easy to lift a lady in the air as it is to lift a glass of champagne to the lips.

Nowhere do people bow to each other with such exquisite and natural grace as on Nevsky Avenue. Here you meet with a unique smile, a smile which is perfection itself, a smile that will sometimes make you dissolve with pleasure, sometimes make you bow your head with shame and feel lower than the grass, and sometimes make you hold up your head high and feel higher than the Admiralty spire. Here you meet people who talk about the weather or a concert with an air that is the acme of good breeding and with a dignity that is full of the sense of their own importance. Here you meet a thousand of the oddest characters and witness a thousand of the oddest incidents. Oh dear, the strange characters one meets on Nevsky Avenue! There are, for instance, many people who when they meet you will be quite sure to stare at your boots and, when you have passed, turn round to have a look at the skirts of your coat. I have not discovered the reason for it yet. At first it occurred to me that they must be bootmakers, but I was wrong, of course: they are for the most part Civil Servants from different ministries, many of whom are very able men who can draw up excellent reports from one ministry to another, or they are people who spend their time taking walks or reading the papers in cafés; they are, in fact, highly respectable people. In this thrice-blessed hour between two and three o'clock in the afternoon when the entire capital seems to be taking a walk on Nevsky Avenue, it becomes the greatest exhibition of the best productions of man. One displays a smart overcoat with the best beaver, another a nose of exquisite Grecian beauty, a third most excellent whiskers, a fourth a pair of most ravishing eyes and a perfectly marvellous hat, a fifth a signet ring on a most charming little finger, a sixth a foot in a delightful little shoe, a seventh a cravat that arouses your admiration, an eighth a moustache that takes your breath away. But at the stroke of three the exhibition closes and the crowds begin to dwindle. . . .

At three o'clock there is a fresh change. Spring suddenly descends on Nevsky Avenue: it is covered with Civil Servants in green uniforms. Hungry titular, court and other councillors walk as fast as they can. Young collegiate registrars, provincial and collegiate secretaries do their best to promenade along Nevsky Avenue with a dignified air which seems to belie the fact that they have been sitting in an office for six solid hours. But the elderly collegiate secretaries and titular and court councillors walk along quickly with bowed heads: they cannot spare the time to gaze at passers-by; they have not yet completely torn themselves away from their office worries; their thoughts are still in a terrible jumble; their heads are full of whole archives of business begun and still unfinished; instead of signboards they see for a long time a cardboard file with papers or the fat face of the head of their department.

Nevsky Avenue

From four o'clock Nevsky Avenue is empty and you will scarcely meet a single Civil Servant there. Some sempstress from a shop will run across Nevsky Avenue with a box in her hand; or some unfortunate victim of a philanthropic court registrar, thrown upon the mercy of the world in a frieze overcoat; or some eccentric visitor to whom all hours are alike; or some tall, thin Englishwoman with a reticule and a book in her hand; or some workman, a Russian, in a high-waisted coat of twilled cotton, with a very narrow beard, who lives from hand to mouth all his life, a man of tremendous energy, his back, arms and legs working away as he walks deferentially along the pavement; or sometimes a humble artisan—you will meet no one else on Nevsky Avenue at that time.

But once let dusk fall upon the houses and streets, and the policeman, covered with a piece of matting, climb up his ladder to light the street lamp, and engravings which do not venture to show themselves in daylight appear in the low shop-windows, and Nevsky Avenue comes to life again and everything begins to stir; it is then that the mysterious time comes when the street lamps invest everything with an alluring, magic light. You now meet a great many young men, for the most part bachelors, in warm frock-coats and overcoats. There is a certain purposefulness or something that resembles some purpose in the air at this time. It is something that is very difficult to account for: everybody seems to be walking much faster, everybody seems to be strangely excited. Long shadows flit over the walls and the road, their heads almost touching the Police Bridge. Young collegiate registrars, provincial and collegiate secretaries walk up and down the Avenue for a long time; but the elderly collegiate registrars, and the titular and court councillors mostly sit at home, either because they are married and have families, or because their German cooks who live with them are masters of the culinary art. You meet here the same elderly gentlemen who at two o'clock in the afternoon were walking along Nevsky Avenue with such admirable decorum and dignity. Now you will see them vying with the young collegiate registrars in overtaking some lady to peep under her hat, a lady whose full lips and cheeks plastered with rouge many of the strollers find so irresistibly attractive, especially shop managers, handicraftsmen, and merchants in frock-coats of German cut, who walk in groups and usually arm in arm.

"I say," cried Lieutenant Pirogov on such an evening, catching hold of the arm of the young man who was walking beside him in a cut-away coat and cloak, "did you see her?"

"Yes, I did. What a lovely creature! A perfect Bianca of Perugino!"

"Who are you talking about?"

"Why, that girl, the girl with the dark hair and those wonderful eyes. Oh, what lovely eyes! What poise, what a glorious figure, what a perfect profile!"

"I'm talking about the blonde who passed her in that direction. Why don't you go after the dark one if you like her so much?"

"What do you mean?" exclaimed the young man in the cut-away coat, reddening. "As if she was one of the women who stroll about Nevsky Avenue in the evening! She must be a woman of high society," he went on with a sigh. "Why, her cloak alone must be worth eighty roubles!"

"Don't be an ass," said Pirogov, giving him a violent push in the direction in which the brightly-coloured cloak was fluttering. "Go on, you idiot, or you'll miss your chance! I'll go after the blonde!"

The two friends parted company.

"We know what you are, all of you!" thought Pirogov to himself with a conceited and self-confident smirk, convinced that no woman in the world could resist him.

The young man in the cut-away coat and cloak went rather nervously and tremulously in the direction in which the brightly coloured cloak was fluttering in the distance, lit brilliantly every time it drew near a street lamp and shrouded in darkness the moment it receded from it. His heart beat fast, and he unconsciously quickened his pace.

The thought that he might have some claim on the attention of the beautiful girl who was disappearing in the distance never occurred to him; and still less could he accept the horrid implication of the coarse hint thrown out by Lieutenant Pirogov. All he wanted was to see the house of that ravishing creature who seemed to have flown down on Nevsky Avenue straight from heaven and who would most probably fly away no one could tell where. Oh, if only he knew where she lived! He walked so fast that he continually pushed dignified, grey-whiskered gentlemen off the pavement.

This young man belonged to a class of people so rare in our country as to be looked upon as phenomenal. These people are no more citizens of St. Petersburg than the people we see in a dream are part of the world of reality. This quite exceptional class of people is particularly uncommon in a city where the inhabitants are either Civil Servants, shopkeepers, or German artisans. He was an artist. A strange phenomenon, is it not? A St. Petersburg artist! An artist in the land of snows! An artist in the land of the Finns, where everything is wet, flat, monotonous, pale, grey, misty! . . . These artists are not at all like the Italian artists, proud and fiery, like Italy and her skies; on the contrary, they are mostly inoffensive, meek men, shy and easygoing, devoted to their art in an unassuming way, drinking their tea with a couple of friends in a small room, modestly discussing their favourite subject, and satisfied with the minimum of food and comfort. They employ some old beggar woman for their model, keeping her posing for six full hours just to transfer her impassive, numb and miserable expression on the canvas. They like to paint interiors of their rooms with every kind of litter lying about: plaster-of-Paris hands and feet, coffee-coloured with dust and age, a broken easel, a discarded palette, a friend playing the guitar, walls covered with paint, and an open window through which you can catch a glimpse of the pale Neva and poor fishermen in red shirts. Everything they paint has a greyish, muddy tint—the indelible imprint of the north. But for all that they labour over their pictures with real enjoyment. They are very often men of talent, and if they were breathing the air of Italy their talent would probably have opened up as freely, as widely, and as splendidly as a plant that has been taken out into the open air after being kept indoors for a long time. They are generally rather timid folk: a star and a fat epaulette throw them into such confusion that they automatically reduce the prices of their pictures. Sometimes the desire for smart clothes proves too strong for them, but for some reason a handsome coat never seems right on them, looking like a new patch on old clothes. Very often they will wear an excellent cut-away coat and a dirty cloak, or an expensive velvet waistcoat and a frock-coat covered with paint: just as on one of their unfinished landscapes you will sometimes see a nymph drawn with her head upside down; not finding any other place, the artist painted it on the old priming of another of his works on which he had once spent so many happy hours. An artist of this sort never looks you straight in the face, and if he does look at you it is with dull, rather vacant eyes. He does not transfix you with the keen stare of an observer, or with the penetrating hawk-like glance of a cavalry officer. This is because while looking at your features he at the same time sees the features of some plaster-of-Paris Hercules which stands in his room; or he may be thinking of a picture he is planning to paint. This often makes it extremely difficult to make any sense of his replies, which at times indeed are quite incomprehensible; and the fact that he is constantly thinking of several things at once merely increases his natural shyness.

The artist Piskarev, the young man we have described, belonged to this class of people. He was a very shy and inoffensive fellow who carried within his breast the seeds that at a favourable opportunity might one day have blossomed into flower. He sped after the girl who had struck him with such wonder, with a secret dread in his heart, and he seemed surprised at his own impertinence. The unknown girl, upon whom all his thoughts and feelings were now concentrated and whom he did not for a moment lose sight of, suddenly turned her head and looked at him. Oh, dear God, what heavenly features! Her enchanting forehead of such dazzling whiteness was framed by hair as lovely as an agate. They curled, those wonderful tresses, and some of them, straying from under the hat, brushed against her cheek, suffused with the most delicate, fresh colour, brought on by the chill of the evening. Her lips held the delightful promise of ineffable bliss. Whatever remains of the memories of childhood, whatever excites the imagination and gives birth to a gentle mood of inspiration in a room lighted only by a glimmering lamp, seemed to have become fused, blended and reflected on the sweet lips of the unknown beautiful girl. She looked at Piskarev, and his heart fluttered in dismay at that look: there was anger in her eyes and indignation on her face at so impertinent a pursuit; but even anger was enchanting on her lovely face. Overcome with shame and shyness, he stopped dead, his eyes fixed on the ground. But no! He just could not give up that divine creature without even knowing where the shrine was to which she had come down to dwell!

These were the thoughts that passed through the head of the young dreamer, and he made up his mind to follow her. But to make sure he did not annoy her again, he kept at a great distance from her, looked idly about him, stared hard at the signboards, without however losing sight of a single movement of the fair stranger. There were fewer people about now, and the street became much quieter. The beautiful girl looked round again, and this time it seemed to him as if a ghost of a smile had flitted across her lips. He trembled all over, unable to believe his eyes. No, it just could not be true! It must have been the deceptive light of the street lamp which had produced that illusion of a smile on her face! Or was it his own imagination that was making a fool of him? He could scarcely breathe for excitement; everything in him was transformed into a kind of half-realised, tremulous agitation. All his feelings seemed to have caught fire suddenly, and a mist seemed to spread itself before his eyes. The pavement, he felt, was moving at a terrific speed under him; the carriages with their galloping horses stood still; the bridge stretched and was about to break in the centre of its arch; the houses were upside down; a sentry-box came reeling towards him; and the halberd of the constable, together with the gilt letters of some signboard and the scissors painted upon it, flashed across his very eyelash. And all this was produced by a single glance, by one turn of a pretty head. He saw nothing, he heard nothing, he heeded nothing: he only followed the light footprints of her lovely feet, trying in vain to slow down the rapid pace of his own feet, which flew in time with the beating of his heart. Sometimes he was overwhelmed with doubt: did that expression on her face really mean that she did not object to his following her? And then he would stop for a moment, but the beating of his heart, the irresistible force and the tension of all his feelings drove him on and on. He did not even notice the four-storied building which loomed suddenly in front of him, or the four rows of lighted windows that glared at him all at once, and he was brought to a sudden halt by the iron railings of the front steps which seemed to rush violently at him. He saw the unknown girl run up the steps, turn round, put a finger against her lips, and make a sign to him to follow her. His knees shook; his feelings, his thoughts, were aflame; joy like a flash of lightning pierced his heart, bringing with it the sensation of sharp pain. No, it was certainly not a dream! Oh, how much happiness could be crowded in one brief moment! What a lifetime of ecstasy in only two minutes!

But was it not all a dream? Was it possible that she who with one glance could make him sacrifice his life for her, that she who made him feel so overpoweringly happy if he so much as went near the house where she lived—was it possible that she was really being so nice and kind to him? He flew up the stairs. No earthly thought troubled him; no earthly passion blazed within him. No! At that moment he was pure and without stain, like a chaste youth

who still yearned for some vague, spiritual love. And what
in a dissolute man would have awakened lust, made his
desires even more holy. The confidence that such a weak,
beautiful creature reposed in him, that confidence meant
that he must treat her as a knight used to treat the lady
whose favour he wore in the lists, and that he must obey
her commands like a slave. All he longed for at that moment was that her commands should be as hard to carry
out as possible and preferably be fraught with great danger, so that he might fly to carry them out with greater
zeal. He did not doubt that an event both mysterious and
of the highest moment compelled the unknown girl to place
her trust in him, and that he would most probably be asked
to perform some important service, and he felt sure he possessed the necessary strength and determination for anything.

The staircase went round and round and his thoughts
whirled round and round with it. "Mind the step!" A voice
like a heavenly harp sounded above him and sent a fresh
thrill through him. On the dark landing of the fourth floor
the unknown girl knocked at a door; it was opened and
they went in together. They were met by a rather attractive-
looking woman with a candle in her hand, who gave Piskarev such a strange and impudent look that he could not
help dropping his eyes. They entered a room, and the artist
saw the figures of three women in different corners. One
was laying out cards; another was sitting at the piano and
strumming with two fingers a pitiful travesty of some ancient polonaise; the third was sitting before a mirror and
combing out her long hair, and made no attempt to dis-
continue her toilette at the entrance of a stranger. A sort
of disagreeable disorder, to be found only in the untidy
room of a bachelor, reigned everywhere. The furniture,
which was fairly good, was covered with dust; a spider had
spread his web over the ornamental moulding in one of
the corners of the ceiling; through the door of another room
that was ajar he caught a glimpse of a shiny spurred boot

and the red braid of a uniform; a man's loud voice and a woman's laugh resounded without any restraint.

Good God, where had he got to? At first he refused to believe it, and he began scrutinising the different objects that filled the room. But the bare walls and the uncurtained windows did not indicate the loving care of a housewife, and the faded faces of these wretched creatures, one of whom sat down right in front of him and examined him as coolly as if he were a dirty spot on someone's dress— all that convinced him that he had got to one of those foul places where vice begotten of the spurious education and the terrible overcrowding of a big city takes up its abode, a place where man sacrilegiously crushes and holds up to scorn all that is sacred and pure and all that makes life beautiful, and where woman, the beauty of the world and the crown of creation, becomes a strange and equivocal creature, losing with the purity of her heart all that is womanly and adopting in a way that can only arouse disgust the impudent manners of man, and so ceasing to be the weak and lovely creature that is so different from ourselves.

Piskarev looked at the girl with amazement, as though still wishing to convince himself that it really was the same girl who had so bewitched him and who had made him follow her from Nevsky Avenue to this place. But she stood before him as beautiful as ever; her hair was as lovely; her eyes seemed no whit less heavenly. She was fresh: she was only seventeen! It could be seen that it was not long that abominable vice had had her in its clutches, for it had as yet not dared to touch her cheeks; they were so fresh and suffused with such a delicate rosy bloom—oh, she was beautiful!

He stood motionless before her and was almost on the point of letting himself be deceived again in a kind of well-meaning, good-natured way as he had let himself be deceived a short while ago, had not the beautiful girl, bored by his long silence, given him a meaning smile, looking straight into his eyes. That smile of hers was full of such

pathetic impudence that it was as strange and out of place
on her face as a look of piety is on the vicious face of a
corrupt official or a ledger in the hands of a poet. He shuddered. She opened those sweet lips of hers and said something, but it was all so stupid, so vulgar. . . . Just as if
the loss of innocence must needs bring with it the loss of
intelligence, too. He did not want to hear any more. Oh,
he was so absurd! He was as simple as a child! Instead
of making the best of the circumstance that the girl seemed
to like him, instead of being glad of such an opportunity,
as doubtless many a man would have been in his place,
he fled out of that house, leaping down the stairs like a
frightened wild animal, and rushed out into the street.

With his head bent low and his hands lying lifelessly in
his lap, he sat in his room, like a beggar who has found
a priceless pearl and almost immediately dropped it into
the sea. "Such a beautiful girl! Such divine features! And
where? In what kind of a place? . . ." That was all he
could bring himself to say.

And, indeed, we are never so moved to pity as at the
sight of beauty touched by the corrupting breath of vice. If
ugliness were the companion of vice, it would not matter so
much, but beauty, sweet beauty which in our thoughts we
associate only with purity and innocence!

The beautiful girl who had so bewitched poor Piskarev
was indeed a most extraordinary and singular phenomenon.
Her presence in that ghastly place and among those contemptible people seemed even more extraordinary. Her
features were so faultlessly formed, the whole expression of
her lovely face was marked by such nobility, that it was
impossible to believe that vice had already got its terrible
claws into her. She should have been the priceless pearl,
the whole world, the paradise, the dearest possession of a
loving and devoted husband; she should have been the
lovely, gentle star of some small family circle, where her
slightest wish would have been anticipated even before she
opened her sweet lips. She should have been the belle of
the crowded ball-room, on the shining parquet, in the glit-

ter of candles; she would have been divine when surrounded by the silent adoration of a crowd of admirers, prostrate at her feet. But alas! Instead she had been flung into the abyss to the accompaniment of loud, demonic laughter, by some terrible whim of a fiendish spirit, eager to destroy the harmony of life.

Overcome by a feeling of poignant pity, the artist sat disconsolately before a guttered candle. It was past midnight, the clock on the tower struck half-past twelve, and he still sat motionless, neither asleep, nor fully awake. As if taking advantage of his immobility, sleep was beginning to steal gently over him. The room had almost entirely disappeared, only the flickering light of the candle still penetrating the world of dreams into which he was fast sinking, when a sudden knock at the door made him shudder violently and sit up. The door opened and a footman in a rich livery walked in. Never before had a rich livery made its appearance in his lonely room and at such an unusual time, too. . . . He did not know what to make of it, and he eyed the footman with impatience and ill-disguised curiosity.

"The lady you visited a few hours ago, sir," said the footman with a courteous bow, "asked me to say that she wished to see you and sent her carriage to fetch you."

Piskarev was speechless with amazement. "A carriage, a footman in a livery! No, it can't be! There must be some mistake. . . ."

"I'm afraid you must have come to the wrong place," he said rather shyly. "Your mistress must have sent you to fetch someone else and not me."

"No, sir, I've made no mistake. Did you not, sir, accompany a young lady to a house in Liteynaya Street, to a room on the fourth floor?"

"Yes, I did."

"Well, in that case, sir, will you please come quickly? My mistress is most anxious to see you and she begs you to come straight to her house."

Piskarev ran down the stairs. Outside a carriage was indeed waiting for him. He got into it, the door was slammed, and the carriage sped noisily over the cobbled road. A panorama of lighted shops with bright signboards passed swiftly across the windows of the carriage. Piskarev was wondering all the time what the explanation of this adventure could be and was unable to find an answer to the mystery. A house of her own, a carriage, a footman in a rich livery. . . . All this could hardly be reconciled with the room on the fourth floor, the grimy windows and the discordant piano. The carriage stopped in front of a brightly lighted entrance, and he was immediately struck by the long row of carriages, the talk of the coachmen, the brilliantly lit windows and the strains of music. The footman in the rich livery helped him out of the carriage and escorted him deferentially to a hall with marble columns, with a doorkeeper smothered in gold braid, fur-coats and cloaks lying about, and a brightly burning lamp. An airy staircase with shining banisters, fragrant with all sorts of perfumes, led to the rooms upstairs. Already he was ascending it, already he had gone into the first large room, when he grew frightened and drew back at the sight of such crowds of people. The extraordinary diversity of faces completely bewildered him: it seemed as though some demon had chopped up the whole world into thousands of pieces and then mixed them all indiscriminately together. The gleaming shoulders of the women, the black frock-coats, the chandeliers, the lamps, the airy floating gauzes, the ethereal ribbons, and the fat double-bass which peeped out from the railings of the magnificent orchestral gallery—everything looked splendid to him. He saw all at once so many highly respectable old gentlemen and middle-aged gentlemen with stars on their evening coats, or ladies stepping with such grace, pride and poise over the parquet floor, or sitting in rows; he heard so many English and French words; moreover, the young gentlemen in black evening dress were so full of noble airs, spoke with such suave dignity or kept silent with such grave decorum, that they seemed quite incapable of saying anything *de trop;* they made jokes with so grand an air, smiled so respectfully, wore such superb whiskers, knew so well how to display their elegant hands while straightening their cravats. The ladies were so ethereal, so utterly and divinely vain, so full of rapture, they so enchantingly cast down their eyes that . . . But Piskarev's humble look as he leaned against a column was enough to show that he was utterly confused. At that moment the crowd surrounded a group of dancers. They were whirling round, draped in transparent creations of Paris, in garments that seemed to be woven out of air; their lovely feet touched the floor without any apparent effort and they could not have looked more ethereal if they had walked on air. One among them was lovelier, more dazzling and more gorgeously dressed than the rest. An indescribably subtle taste was expressed in her whole attire, and yet she did not seem to be aware of it herself, as though it all came to her naturally and of its own accord. She looked and did not look at the crowd of spectators who surrounded the dancers; she lowered her long, lovely eyelashes indifferently, the dazzling whiteness of her face still more dazzling; and as she bent her head a light shadow fell across her ravishing brow.

Piskarev tried hard to push through the crowd to have a better look at her, but to his intense annoyance a huge head of curly black hair kept getting continually in his way; moreover, he was wedged so tightly in the press of people that he did not dare either to move forward or to step back for fear of treading on the toes of some Privy Councillor. But at last he did succeed in forcing his way to the front. He glanced instinctively at his clothes to make sure that they were tidy, and to his horror he saw that he was wearing his old coat which was stained all over with paint. In his haste to leave he must have forgotten to change into proper clothes. He blushed to the roots of his hair and stood there with downcast eyes, praying for a chance to get away. But there was no possibility of getting away, for Court Chamberlains in resplendent uniforms formed an impenetrable wall behind him. He wished he were miles away from the beautiful girl with the lovely brow and eyelashes, and he raised his eyes fearfully to see whether she were looking at him, and, good Lord, she stood facing him! . . . But what was that? What was that? "It is she!" he cried almost at the top of his voice. And, indeed, it was she. It was the girl he had met on Nevsky Avenue. The girl he had followed to her house.

Meanwhile she raised her long eyelashes and looked at everybody in the room with her bright eyes. "Oh, how beautiful she is, how beautiful!" was all he could utter with bated breath. Her eyes roamed slowly round the circle of men, each of whom seemed eager to attract her attention, but she soon withdrew them with a bored and fatigued air and, as she did so, her eyes met Piskarev's eyes. Oh, what bliss! What heavenly joy! His happiness was so overwhelming that it threatened to destroy him, to kill him outright! She made a sign to him: not with her hand, nor with an inclination of her head; no, it was in her eyes, in those entrancing eyes of hers, that he read this sign, and so subtle and imperceptible was it that no one could see it, no one but he. Yes, he saw it! He understood it! The dance went on for a long time; the languid music seemed at moments to fade and die away entirely, but again and again it burst forth in shrill, thunderous notes; at last—the end. She sat down, her bosom heaving under the light cloud of gauze; her hand (goodness, what a divine hand!) dropped on her knees, crushing her ethereal dress under it, and the dress under her hand seemed breathing music, and its delicate lilac hue made her lovely hand look more dazzlingly white than ever. Oh, all he wanted was just to touch it, and nothing more! He had no other desires; they would be sheer impertinence! . . . He stood behind her chair, not daring to speak, not daring to breathe.

"Were you bored?" she said. "I was awfully bored, too. You hate me, don't you?" she added, lowering her eyelashes.

"Hate you? I . . . Why . . ." Piskarev, completely taken aback, was about to say, and he would no doubt have poured forth a stream of quite meaningless words, if at that moment a Court Chamberlain with a beautifully curled shock of hair had not come up and engaged her in conversation, his talk sparkling with wit and compliment. He displayed rather charmingly a row of good teeth, and every witticism he uttered knocked a sharp nail into the young artist's heart. Fortunately, a stranger at last approached the Court Chamberlain with some sort of question.

"Oh, what a frightful nuisance this is!" she declared, raising her heavenly eyes at him. "I think I'd better sit down at the other end of the room. I'll wait for you there!"

She swept through the crowd and disappeared. He pushed his way after her like a man possessed, and in a twinkling he was there.

Yes, it was she. She sat like a queen, fairer and lovelier than all, and her eyes were searching for him.

"You're here?" she asked softly. "I'll be frank with you. I expect the circumstances of our meeting must have seemed strange to you. Did you really imagine I could belong to that contemptible class of human beings among whom you met me? I suppose you can't help thinking my actions rather strange, but I will reveal a secret to you. Will you promise," she said, looking straight into his eyes, "never to betray it?"

"Yes, oh yes, I promise!"

But at that moment an elderly gentleman walked up, began speaking to her in a language Piskarev could not understand, and offered her his arm. She cast an imploring glance at Piskarev and indicated to him by a sign that she wanted him to remain there and wait for her; but he was much too impatient to obey any command, even one that came from her lips. He went after her, but the crowd parted them. He lost sight of her lilac dress and he rushed from room to room in great agitation, pushing every one he met unceremoniously out of his way. But in every room important-looking gentlemen were sitting at card tables, plunged in dead silence. In a corner of one room some elderly people were engaged in an argument about the superiority of military to civil service; in another a group of people in magnificent dress-coats were making disparaging remarks on the voluminous labours of a hard-working poet. Piskarev became suddenly aware that a distinguished-looking gentleman had buttonholed him and was submitting an eminently fair observation he had made to the artist's criticism; but Piskarev pushed him rudely away without even noticing that he wore a very high order round his neck. The artist rushed into another room, but she was not there; into a third—she was not there, either. "Where, oh where is she? Give her to me! Oh, I can't live without another look at her! I must, I simply must know what she wanted to tell me!" but all his search was in vain. Worried and exhausted, he stood desolately in a corner and watched the crowds; but his eyes had become strained by then and everything seemed blurred and indistinct. At last the walls of his room became clearly visible to him. He raised his eyes. Before him stood the candlestick with the light flickering in the socket; the whole candle had burnt out and the melted tallow had spread all over the table.

So he had been asleep! Oh, dear, what a wonderful dream that was! And why had he wakened? Why had he not waited another minute? She would quite certainly have come again! The cheerless dawn shed its dull, unpleasant light through his window. The room was in such a terrible, untidy mess. . . . Oh, how disgusting reality was! How could it even be compared with a dream? He undressed quickly and got into bed, wrapping himself up in a blanket, anxious to recapture even for an instant the dream that had vanished. And he did fall asleep almost immediately, but the dream he dreamed was not the one he longed for: one moment Lieutenant Pirogov appeared with his pipe, another the Academy caretaker, then some Regular State Councillor, then the head of the Finnish woman who had sat for him for a portrait, and the like absurdities.

He lay in bed till midday, trying to fall asleep and see her again in his dreams; but she did not appear. Oh, if only he could have seen her lovely features for one minute;

if only he could have heard again the faint rustle of her dress; if only he could have caught a fleeting glimpse of her bare arm, white and dazzling like driven snow!

Dismissing everything, forgetting everything, he sat there looking utterly crushed and forlorn, full only of his dream. He never thought of touching anything; his eyes stared lifelessly and without a glimmer of interest at the window that looked out into the yard where a dirty water-carrier was sprinkling water that froze in the air, and the bleating voice of the rag-and-bone man resounded stridently, "Ol' clo' for sale! Ol' clo' for sale!" Everyday life and reality fell jarringly upon his ear. He sat like that until evening, and then he went eagerly back to bed. He struggled long with sleeplessness, but at last he got the better of it. Again a dream; a stupid, horrid dream. "O Lord, have mercy upon me! Show her to me for one minute! Just for one minute, O Lord, I beseech Thee!" Again he waited for the evening; again he fell asleep; again he dreamed of some Civil Servant, who was a Civil Servant and a bassoon at the same time. Oh, this was intolerable! At last she appeared! Yes, yes. . . . Her sweet little head, her curls. . . . She was looking. . . . But oh, only for a moment, for the briefest possible moment! Again a mist, again some silly dream!

In the end the dreams became his whole life, and from that time his life underwent a curious change: he, as it were, slept when he was awake and kept awake when he was asleep. Anyone seeing him sitting dumbly before an empty table, or walking along the street, would have taken him for a sleep-walker, a somnambulist, or for a man ruined by drink. He stared vacantly in front of him; his natural absent-mindedness increased, until at last all feeling and emotion were completely banished from his face. He revived only at the approach of night.

Such a condition undermined his health, and his worst time came when sleep began to desert him altogether. Anxious to save the only treasure he still possessed, he did all he could to regain it. He had heard there was one unfailing remedy against insomnia: all he had to do was to take opium. But where was he to get opium? He then remembered a Persian shopkeeper he knew who sold shawls and who pestered him for a picture of a beautiful girl. He decided to go to him, thinking that the Persian would be sure to supply him with opium.

The Persian received him sitting on a divan with his legs crossed under him.

"What do you want opium for?" he asked the painter.

Piskarev told him about his insomnia.

"All right, I'll get you the opium," said the Persian, "but paint me a beautiful girl. And, mind, I want that girl to be really beautiful, with black eyebrows and eyes as big as olives, and me lie beside her smoking my pipe. She is to be beautiful, remember! She must be a real beauty!"

Piskarev promised everything. The Persian went out for a minute and came back with a little bottle with some dark liquid, poured some of it very carefully into another bottle, which he gave to Piskarev with instructions not to use more than seven drops in a tumbler of water. The painter seized the precious phial greedily and rushed straight back home. He would not have parted with that little bottle of opium for a king's ransom.

When he got home he poured a few drops into a glass of water and, swallowing it, went to bed.

Oh, what bliss! What joy! There she was! There she was again! But how different she looked! Oh, she was lovely as she sat at the window of that bright country house! How simple her dress was—a simplicity in which only a poet's fancy is clothed! And her hair. . . . How plain her coiffure was and how lovely! How it suited her! A small kerchief was thrown lightly round her slender neck; everything about her revealed a mysterious, indefinable sense of good taste. How sweetly, how beautifully she walked! How musical was the rustle of her plain dress and the sound of her footsteps! How lovely her arm encircled by a bracelet of hair!

"Do not despise me! I'm not the sort of woman you take me for. Look at me! Look at me closer. Tell me now, do you really think I'm capable of doing what you think I do?"

"No, no! Of course not! Let anyone who thinks so, only let him . . ."

But just at that moment he woke! He was deeply touched, lacerated, tortured, and his eyes were brimming with tears! "Far better you had never existed, far better you had never been born, but had merely been the creation of an inspired artist! I'd never have left the canvas; I'd have stood before it always, looking at you and kissing you! I'd have lived and breathed with you, as the most beautiful dream, and then I should have been happy! I should have had no other desires! You would have been my guardian angel, and to you I would have prayed when I went to sleep at night and when I awoke in the morning, and it would have been you I'd have waited for if ever I had to paint saintliness and godliness. But now . . . Oh, how terrible my life is! What's the good of her being alive? Is the life of a madman pleasant to the friends and relations who once loved him? O Lord, what an awful thing life is! A perpetual clash between dream and reality!"

Such thoughts occupied him almost continuously. He thought of nothing else; he hardly touched any food; and with the impatience, with the passion of a lover he waited for the evening when once more he would see the vision he longed for. The concentration of all his thoughts upon one subject at last began to exercise so powerful an influence over his whole existence as well as over his imagination that the longed-for dream came to him almost every day, but the situation in which he saw the girl he loved was always the exact opposite of reality, for his thoughts were as pure as the thoughts of a child. It was through these dreams of his that their subject seemed to become in some way purer and was so completely transformed.

The doses of laudanum inflamed his mind more than ever, and if there ever was a man in love to the last extremity of madness, violently, dreadfully, annihilatingly, rebelliously in love, that unhappy man was he!

Of all his dreams one delighted him more than any other.

He dreamt that he was in his studio. He was happy, and it was with real pleasure that he was sitting at his easel with the palette in his hand. And she was there, too. She was his wife. She sat beside him, leaning her sweet little elbow on the back of his chair and watching him work. Her eyes, languid and heavy, disclosed such a huge load of bliss. Everything in the room breathed of paradise; everything was so bright, so beautifully tidy! O Lord, and now she leaned her sweet little head on his bosom! . . . Never had he dreamt a better dream. After it he got up feeling refreshed and less abstracted than before. Strange thoughts came into his head. "Perhaps," he thought, "she has been drawn into her life of vice against her own will by some terrible accident. In her heart of hearts she is perhaps anxious to repent; she is perhaps herself longing to escape from her awful position. And can I suffer her to go to her ruin with callous indifference when all I have to do is to hold out a hand to save her from drowning?" His thoughts went even further. "No one knows me," he said to himself, "and, anyway, no one dares say anything about me. If she really repents, if she expresses her genuine sorrow and contrition and agrees to change her present way of life, I will marry her. I ought to marry her and I shall probably do much better than any other man who marries his housekeeper or often the most contemptible of creatures. For my action will be wholly disinterested and it may also turn out to be great, since I shall restore to the world one of its beautiful ornaments."

Having conceived this rather rash plan, he felt the colour returning to his cheeks; and, going up to the looking-glass, he was appalled to see how hollow his cheeks had become and how pale his face was. He began dressing with great care; he washed, smoothed his hair, put on his new cutaway coat and a smart waistcoat. Then, flinging his cloak over his shoulders, he went out into the street. Inhaling the fresh air, he felt a new man, like a convalescent who decides to go out for a walk for the first time after a long illness. His heart was beating fast as he approached the street where he had not been since his first fatal meeting with the girl.

He spent a long time looking for the house, for his memory seemed to have failed him. He walked twice along the street, uncertain before which house to stop. At last one looked familiar to him. He ran quickly up the stairs and knocked at the door. The door opened and . . . who came out to meet him? Why, his ideal, his mysterious idol, the original of his dreams, his life, the sum and substance of his existence, she in whom he lived so dreadfully, so agonisingly, so blissfully—she stood before him, she herself! He trembled, hardly able to stand on his feet from weakness, so overwhelmed was he with happiness. She stood before him as lovely as ever, though her eyes looked sleepy, though a pallor had spread over her face, which was no longer as fresh as before; but still she was beautiful.

"Oh, it's you!" she said on seeing Piskarev and rubbing her eyes (it was two o'clock in the afternoon). "Why did you run away from us that evening?"

He sank into a chair, feeling too faint to stand, and looked at her.

"I've only just got up. They brought me home at seven this morning. I was dead drunk," she added with a smile.

Oh, if only she had been dumb, if only she had been unable to speak at all rather than utter such words! In a flash she had shown him her whole life. He could see it as clearly as though it had passed before him in a panorama. But, in spite of that, he decided with a heavy heart to try and see whether his admonitions would have any effect upon her. Plucking up courage, he began explaining her awful position to her in a voice that shook, but which was at the same time full of passionate conviction. She listened to him with an attentive air and with the feeling of wonder we display at the sight of something strange and unexpected. She glanced with a faint smile at her friend who was sitting in a corner and who had stopped cleaning a comb and was also listening with rapt attention to the new preacher.

"It's true I'm poor," said Piskarev at last, after a long and highly instructive homily, "but we will work, we'll do our best, both of us, to improve our position. Surely nothing can be more agreeable than the feeling that our success will be due entirely to our own efforts. I will do my painting, and you shall sit beside me and inspire me in my work. You can do some embroidering or some other kind of needlework, and we shall have all we need."

"How do you mean?" she interrupted with an expression of undisguised scorn. "I'm not a washerwoman, or a dressmaker! You don't expect me to work, do you?"

Oh, she could not have described the whole of her mean and contemptible life better than in those words! A life full of idleness and emptiness, the true companions of vice.

"Marry me!" her friend, who till then had sat silent in a corner, interjected with an impudent air. "When I'm married I will sit like this!" she declared with a stupid grimace on her pathetic face, to the great amusement of the beautiful girl.

Oh, that was too much! That was more than he could bear! He rushed out of the room, too stunned to feel or think. He felt dazed and wandered about all day stupidly, aimlessly, seeing nothing, hearing nothing, feeling nothing. No one knew whether he had slept anywhere that night or not, and it was only on the following day that by some blind instinct he staggered back to his room, looking terrible, haggard and pale, with his hair dishevelled and signs of madness in his face. He shut himself up in his room, let no one in and asked for nothing. Four days passed, and his locked room was not opened once. At last a week passed, and still his room remained locked. People knocked at his door and began calling him, but there was no reply; in the end they broke down the door and found his lifeless body with the throat cut. From his convulsively outspread arms and his terribly contorted face it was evident that his hand had been unsteady and that he must have suffered a long time before his sinful soul had left his body.

So perished the victim of a mad passion, poor Piskarev,

the gentle, shy, modest, childishly good-natured man, who carried a spark of genius in his breast which might with time have blazed forth into a great bright flame. No one shed any tears over him; there was no one to be seen by his dead body, except the ordinary figure of the district police inspector and the bored face of the police surgeon. Quietly and without any religious service, his body was taken to Okhta, and the only man who followed it was a night watchman, an ex-soldier who did indeed weep, but only because he had had a glass of vodka too many. Even Lieutenant Pirogov did not come to pay his last respects to the poor luckless artist upon whom during his lifetime he had conferred his exalted patronage. However, he had other business to attend to, being involved in rather an extraordinary adventure. But let us turn to him. I do not like corpses and dead men and I always feel rather ill at ease when my path is crossed by a long funeral procession, and an old crippled soldier, dressed like some Capuchin, takes a pinch of snuff with his left hand because he is carrying a torch in his right. The sight of a rich catafalque and a velvet pall always depresses me terribly, but my feeling of depression is mingled with grief whenever I see the bare, pine coffin of some poor wretch being taken to the cemetery on a cart and only some old beggar woman, who had met it at the crossroads, following it because she has nothing else to do.

I believe we left Lieutenant Pirogov at the moment when he parted from Piskarev and went in pursuit of the blonde. This blonde was a very slender and an exceedingly attractive little creature. She stopped before every shop and gazed at the belts, kerchiefs, earrings, gloves and all sorts of pretty trifles in the shop-windows. She was never still, she kept looking in all directions, and was continually casting glances behind her. "You'll be mine, my pretty one!" Pirogov murmured complacently, as he continued to pursue her, hiding his face in the collar of his greatcoat to make sure that none of his friends recognised him. But I suppose

we ought really to tell our readers a little more about
Lieutenant Pirogov.

Before saying anything about Lieutenant Pirogov, however, we must say something about the circle to which he
belonged. There are army officers in St. Petersburg who
form a kind of middle class of their own. You will always
find them at a dinner or at a party given by some State
Councillor or Regular State Councillor who has achieved
his rank by forty years of hard work. One or two pale
daughters, colourless like St. Petersburg itself and with the
first bloom of youth perhaps a little worn off, the tea-table,
the piano, the improvised dances—all this is inseparable
from the bright epaulette glittering in the lamplight between the refined, fair-haired young lady and the black
frock-coat of her brother or of some friend of the family.
To infuse a little life into those apathetic misses or to make
them laugh is one of the hardest tasks in the world: one
has to be a real artist to do that. But perhaps one need not
be an artist at all, but merely possess the knack of saying
something that is neither too clever, nor too funny. One
has, in short, to be an adept in the small talk which the
ladies like so much. Now the gentlemen in question must
be given the credit of possessing this special gift for making
these insipid beauties laugh and listen to them. "Oh, do
stop! Aren't you ashamed to say such silly things!" are often
their highest reward. You very rarely, indeed hardly ever,
meet these gentlemen in high society. From there, alas, they
are elbowed out ruthlessly by those who in those circles
pass for aristocrats. On the whole however, they enjoy the
reputation of being cultured and well-bred men. They are
fond of discussing literature; they praise the editor Bul-
garin, the poet Pushkin, and the journalist Grech, and speak
with undisguised contempt of the popular writer A. A.
Orlov, who is the constant butt of their wit. They never miss
a public lecture, whatever its subject, whether on book-
keeping or even forestry. You can rely on always finding
one of them at the theatre, whatever the play, unless indeed it be some vaudeville portraying the lives of the lower

classes, such as "Filatka and Miroshka—the Rivals, or Four Wooers and One Girl," which greatly offends their fastidious taste. Otherwise they are always to be found at the play. In fact, they are the best customers of a theatrical manager. They are particularly fond of fine verses in a play, and they greatly enjoy calling loudly for the actors. Many of them, by teaching in State establishments or coaching people to pass examinations for State establishments, can with time afford their own carriage and pair. Then their social circle becomes much wider and in the end they get to the stage when they marry a merchant's daughter who can play the piano and brings with her a dowry of a hundred thousand or thereabouts, in cash, and a large number of bearded relations. As a rule, however, they can never achieve such an honour till they have served long enough to have reached the rank of colonel. For the Russian bearded gentry, in spite of the fact that the smell of cabbage soup may linger about their beards, do not on any account want to see their daughters married to any man unless he is a general, or at least a colonel. Such are the main characteristics of this sort of young man. But Lieutenant Pirogov had a large number of talents which were all his own. He could, for instance, recite excellently the verses from Ozerov's *Dimitry Donskoy* and Griboyedov's *The Misfortune of Being Too Clever,* and he was an absolute master of the art of blowing smoke from his pipe in rings, so that he could string a dozen of them together, one on top of the other. He also could tell the amusing story about a cannon being one thing and a unicorn another in a most inimitable way. It is perhaps a little difficult to enumerate all the talents fate had lavished with so generous a hand upon Pirogov. He liked to talk about an actress or a dancer, but not as crudely as a young second lieutenant usually discourses on the same subject. He was very proud of his rank, to which he had only lately been promoted, and though occasionally as he lay down on the sofa he would murmur, "Vanity of vanities, all is vanity! What though I am a lieutenant?" he was, as a matter of fact, very pleased with his new dignity. He often alluded to it in conversation in a roundabout way, and once when he met some Government clerk whom he did not think sufficiently respectful to him, he stopped him at once and pointed out to him in a few trenchant words that he was a lieutenant and not some ordinary officer. He did his best to put it the more eloquently as two very good-looking ladies were passing at the time. In general Pirogov displayed a passion for the fine arts and patronised and in every possible way encouraged the artist Piskarev, which, however, might have been mainly due to his great desire to see his manly countenance portrayed on canvas. But enough of Pirogov's qualities. Man is so wonderful a creature that it is quite impossible to enumerate all his virtues, and the more you scrutinise him the more new characteristics you discover in him, and a description of all of them would go on for ever.

And so Pirogov went on pursuing the blonde, trying from time to time to attract her attention by addressing some questions to her, to which she replied rather brusquely, stiffly and inaudibly. They passed through the dark Kazan Gates and entered Meshchanskaya Street, a street of tobacconists and grocery shops, of German artisans and Finnish nymphs. The blonde ran faster and darted into the gates of a rather dirty-looking house. Pirogov went after her. She ran up a narrow, dark staircase and went in at a door, through which Pirogov boldly followed her. He found himself in a big room with black walls and a soot-covered ceiling. A heap of iron screws, locksmith's tools, shining coffee-pots and candlesticks lay on the table; the floor was littered with iron and copper filings. Pirogov realised at once that it was an artisan's lodging. The fair stranger darted through a side-door into another room. For a moment Pirogov wondered what to do next, but, following the Russian practice, he decided to carry on. He found himself in a room which was quite unlike the first, a very neatly furnished room, showing that the master of the house was a German. He was struck by a really extraordinary scene.

In front of him sat Schiller, not the Schiller who wrote

Wilhelm Tell and *The History of the Thirty Years' War,*
but the well-known Schiller, the tinsmith of Meshchanskaya
Street. Beside Schiller stood Hoffmann, not the writer Hoffmann, but the very excellent bootmaker of Officer Street,
a great friend of Schiller's. Schiller was drunk and was sitting on a chair, stamping and shouting something in an
excited voice. All this would not have surprised Pirogov.
What did surprise him was the extraordinary attitude of
the two men. Schiller was sitting with his head raised and
his rather thick nose thrust out, while Hoffmann was holding this nose between forefinger and thumb and flourishing
his cobbler's knife over it, only missing it by a fraction
of an inch. Both gentlemen were talking in German, and
for this reason Lieutenant Pirogov who only knew how to
say *Guten Morgen* in German, could not make out what was
happening. However, what Schiller was saying was this:

"I don't want a nose! I have no use for it!" he said, waving his hands. "I spend three pounds of snuff a month on
my nose. And I get it in some rotten Russian shop, for a
German shop does not keep Russian snuff. I pay forty
copecks a pound to the dirty Russian shopkeeper, which
makes one rouble and twenty copecks a month or fourteen
roubles and forty copecks a year. How do you like that,
Hoffmann, my dear friend? Fourteen roubles and forty
copecks on my nose alone! And on holidays I usually take
rappee, for I'm damned if I'm going to take that rotten
Russian snuff on a holiday. In a year I use two pounds of
rappee at two roubles per pound. Six and fourteen makes
twenty roubles and forty copecks on snuff alone! That's
sheer robbery, my dear fellow, highway robbery! Am I
right, Hoffmann, dear friend of mine?" Hoffmann, who was
also drunk, answered affirmatively. "Twenty roubles and
forty copecks!" Schiller went on. "Damn it, man! I'm a
Swabian German. I have a king in Germany! I don't want a
nose! Cut off my nose! Here, take it!"

And but for the sudden appearance of Lieutenant
Pirogov, Hoffmann would quite certainly have cut off
Schiller's nose, for he had already placed the knife in posi-

tion as though he were going to cut out a piece of leather for a sole.

Schiller was greatly annoyed that an unknown and uninvited man should have prevented him from carrying out his plan of getting rid of his expensive nose. Although he was in a blissful state of intoxication, he, besides, felt that in his present position and under such circumstances he cut rather a poor figure. Meanwhile Pirogov said with a slight bow and with his usual courtesy, "Excuse me, sir. . . ."

"Get out of here!" Schiller replied with long-drawn-out emphasis.

Pirogov felt rather disconcerted. He was not used to being spoken to in such a way. A smile which was just about to appear on his face vanished at once, and he said with a note of hurt dignity, "I'm afraid, sir—er—You evidently haven't noticed, sir, that—er—that I'm an officer!"

"An officer? What's an officer? I'm a Swabian German, I am. I can be an officer myself!" said Schiller, banging the table with his fist. "A year and a half you're a cadet, two years—a lieutenant, and tomorrow you're an officer! But I don't want to be an officer! That's what I do to an officer—phew!" and Schiller held out his open hand and blew on it.

Lieutenant Pirogov realised that there was nothing left for him to do but to withdraw, but he could not help resenting such treatment which was hardly complimentary to his rank. He stopped a few times on the stairs, as though wishing to summon enough courage and to think of a way to make Schiller feel sorry for his insolence. In the end, however, he decided that it was possible to excuse Schiller because of his quite undeniable state of intoxication. Besides, he remembered the charming blonde, and he made up his mind to forget the whole incident.

Early next morning Lieutenant Pirogov again appeared in the tinsmith's workshop. In the first room he was met by Schiller's pretty wife, who asked him in a rather severe voice, which incidentally went very well with her sweet little face, "What do you want?"

"Ah, good morning, my dear! Remember me? Oh, you sweet little rogue, what lovely eyes you've got!" said Lieutenant Pirogov, who at the same time was about to chuck her very prettily under the chin with his forefinger.

But the blonde uttered a frightened cry and asked him again very severely, "What do you want?"

"What do I want, my dear? Why, all I want is to see you, of course!" said Lieutenant Pirogov with a very charming smile, going up closer to her; but noticing that the timid blonde was about to slip through the door, he added, "I want to order some spurs, my dear. Do you think your husband could make me a pair of spurs? Not that a man wants any spur to love you, my sweet. What a man wants is a bridle rather than a spur. What lovely hands you've got!"

"I'll call my husband!" said the blonde and went out.

Lieutenant Pirogov was the perfect gentleman in declarations of that kind.

A few moments later Schiller came in looking rather sleepy, for he had only just woken up after the orgy of the previous day. Seeing Pirogov, he recalled rather vaguely the incident of the day before, that is to say, he could not remember exactly what had happened, but he had an idea that he had behaved rather stupidly, and so he gave the officer a very stern look.

"I'm afraid I can't take less than fifteen roubles for a pair of spurs," he declared, wishing to get rid of Pirogov; for, being a respectable German, he felt ashamed to look at any person who had seen him in an undignified position. Schiller liked to drink without any witnesses, with two or three friends, and at such times he used to shut himself up even from his own workmen.

"Why are you charging me so much?" Pirogov asked, politely.

"German work," said Schiller very coolly, stroking his chin. "A Russian will charge you two roubles for them."

"All right," said Pirogov. "Just to show you how much I

like you and how much I desire your acquaintance, I'll pay you fifteen roubles."

Schiller thought it over for a moment. As an honest German craftsman he felt a little ashamed to have asked so much, and, wishing to put the officer off, he said that he could not possibly have them ready before a fortnight. But Pirogov agreed to that without raising a single objection.

The German considered it. He was wondering how best to do the work so that it should really be worth fifteen roubles. Meanwhile the blonde came into the workshop and began looking for something on the table, which was covered with coffee-pots. The lieutenant took advantage of the tinsmith's abstraction to go up to his wife and press her arm, which was bare to the shoulder.

Schiller did not like that at all.

"*Mein' Frau!*" he exclaimed.

"*Was wollen Sie doch?*" said the blonde to her husband.

"*Gehn Sie* to the kitchen!" said her husband.

The blonde went out.

"In a fortnight then?" said Pirogov.

"Yes, sir, in a fortnight," said Schiller, reflectively. "I'm very busy now."

"Good-bye. I'll call again."

"Good-bye, sir," replied Schiller, locking the door after him.

Lieutenant Pirogov made up his mind not to abandon his quest in spite of the fact that the German woman had quite openly rebuffed all his advances. It never occurred to him that any woman could resist him, particularly as his good manners and his brilliant rank gave him the right to expect every possible consideration from the fair sex. We feel bound, however, to state that Schiller's wife, for all her good looks, was rather a stupid woman. Not that stupidity in a pretty woman is to be despised; on the contrary, it greatly enhances her charms. At any rate, I have known many husbands who were in raptures over the stupidity of their wives, finding it the best proof of their child-like in-

nocence. Beauty works perfect wonders. Far from produc-
ing a feeling of disgust, all her intellectual shortcomings
become somehow extraordinarily attractive in a beautiful
woman; even vice seems only to add to her charm. But let
her beauty vanish and a woman will have to be twenty
times as clever as a man to inspire respect, let alone love.
Anyway, however stupid Schiller's wife was, she was faithful to her vows, and Pirogov would therefore have found
it extremely difficult to succeed in his bold enterprise; but
the greater the obstacles, the sweeter the victory, and he
found the blonde more and more fascinating every day. He
began paying frequent visits to Schiller to see how the work
on his spurs was progressing, so that in the end Schiller
got sick and tired of it. He did his best to finish the spurs
as quickly as possible, and at last they were ready.

"Oh, what fine workmanship!" exclaimed Lieutenant
Pirogov when he saw the spurs. "How wonderfully they're
made! I'm sure our general himself hasn't got such fine
spurs!"

Schiller felt very flattered. There was quite a merry
twinkle in his eyes and he forgave Pirogov everything. "A
Russian officer," he thought, "is a clever fellow!"

"I suppose you couldn't make me a sheath for a dagger
or something, could you?"

"Why, of course, sir," said the German with a smile.

"Excellent! Do make me a sheath for a dagger then. I'll
bring it to you. I have a very fine Turkish dagger, but I'd
like to have another sheath for it."

This was just like a thunderbolt to Schiller. He knit his
brows, thinking, "What a fool I am!" and inwardly cursing
himself for being responsible for Pirogov's second order. But
he felt it would be dishonest to refuse it now, particularly
as the Russian officer had been so nice about his work. So
after shaking his head, he agreed to do the sheath. But the
kiss which Pirogov impudently imprinted on the blonde's
lips as he went out left him utterly bewildered.

I think it will not be out of place here to make the reader
a little better acquainted with Schiller.

Schiller was a real German in the full sense of the word. Even at the age of twenty, when the Russian lives without a care for the morrow, Schiller had already planned his future in a most thorough and methodical way and never under any circumstances did he deviate from the course he had set himself. He resolved to get up at seven, to lunch at two, to be punctual in everything, and to get drunk every Sunday. He resolved to save a capital of fifty thousand in ten years, and this was as certain and irrevocable as fate itself, for a Civil Servant will sooner forget to peep into his chief's ante-room to see if he is in than a German will consent to break his word. Under no circumstances did he increase his expenses, and if the price of potatoes went up, he did not spend a penny more on them, but merely bought less potatoes, and though such a regime often resulted in his being hungry, he soon got used to it. His exactness was such that he made it a rule never to kiss his wife more than twice in twenty-four hours, and to make sure he did not kiss her three times he never put more than one teaspoonful of pepper in his soup. On Sundays, however, this rule was not so strictly observed, for then Schiller drank two bottles of beer and one bottle of cummin brandy, which he always abused. He did not drink like an Englishman, who bolts the door immediately after dinner and gets dead drunk in solitude. On the contrary, like a German, he always drank in merry company, either with Hoffmann the shoemaker or with Kuntz the carpenter, also a German and a great drunkard. Such was the character of the worthy Schiller who now found himself in a devilishly awkward fix. Although he was a German and therefore a little phlegmatic, Pirogov's behaviour aroused in him a feeling which was very much like jealousy. He racked his brains, but could not think how to get rid of this Russian officer. Meanwhile Pirogov, smoking a pipe in the company of his brother officers (for so Providence seems to have decreed that wherever there are officers there are also pipes), alluded rather self-importantly and with an agreeable smile on his lips to the little intrigue with a pretty German lady, with whom, according to him, he was on very intimate terms, though as a matter of fact he had almost given up all hope of ever having his way with her.

One day he was walking along Meshchanskaya Street, staring at the house adorned with Schiller's signboard with coffee-pots and *samovars* on it, when, to his great delight, he beheld the pretty head of Mrs. Schiller looking out of the window and watching the passers-by. He stopped, blew her a kiss and said *Guten Morgen*. The blonde bowed to him as to an old friend.

"Is your husband at home?"

"Yes, he's at home."

"And when isn't he at home?"

"He's never at home on Sundays," replied the foolish little blonde.

"That's not bad," thought Pirogov to himself. "I must remember that."

Next Sunday he descended like a bolt from the blue on Schiller's establishment. Schiller, as his wife had said, was not at home. His pretty wife looked rather frightened, but on this occasion Pirogov behaved with the utmost discretion, treated her with great respect, and, bowing very courteously, paraded all the elegance of his slender figure in his close-fitting uniform. He joked very agreeably and politely, but the silly little German woman replied to all his remarks only in monosyllables. At last having tried every approach he could think of and seeing that nothing seemed to amuse her, he suggested that they should dance. The pretty German woman immediately agreed, for German women are very fond of dancing. Pirogov, in fact, pinned all his hopes on that, for, in the first place, dancing was something that gave her pleasure; secondly, it gave him the opportunity of displaying his figure and dexterity; and, thirdly, he could get much closer to her in dancing, for he could put his arm round her and lay the foundations for everything that was to come; in short, he was sure that such a propitious start was bound to lead to complete success.

He chose for their first dance a gavotte, knowing that the Germans like a slow, sedate dance. The pretty German woman stepped out into the middle of the room and lifted her entrancing little foot. This attitude so enchanted Pirogov that he immediately started kissing her. Mrs. Schiller screamed, but this merely increased her charm in Pirogov's eyes, who smothered her with kisses. Suddenly the door opened and in walked Schiller with Hoffman and Kuntz the carpenter. All these worthy artisans were as drunk as lords.

I leave it to the reader to imagine Schiller's anger and indignation.

"You're an impertinent fellow, sir!" he shouted, boiling over with indignation. "How dare you kiss my wife, sir? You're a scoundrel, sir, and not a Russian officer! Damn it, Hoffmann, my dear fellow, I'm a German, and not a Russian pig, aren't I?" Hoffmann nodded. "Oh, I'm not going to be made a cuckold! Take him by the collar, Hoffmann, there's a good fellow! I'm not going to put up with it," he went on brandishing his arms about violently, his face the colour of his red waistcoat. "I've been living in St. Petersburg for eight years! I have a mother in Swabia and an uncle in Nuremberg. I'm a German, I am, and not some horned beast! Strip him, Hoffmann, my dear friend! Off with his clothes! Hold him by his arms and legs, *Kamarad* Kuntz!"

The Germans seized Pirogov by his arms and legs. In vain did the lieutenant try to defend himself against them; the three German artisans were the most stalwart specimens of German manhood in St. Petersburg, and they treated him with such an utter lack of ceremony and civility that I cannot find words in which to describe this highly regrettable incident.

I am sure that next day Schiller was in a high fever, that he was shaking like an aspen leaf and expecting any minute the arrival of the police, and that he would have given anything in the world if what had happened the previous day had been a dream. However, what was done could not be undone. But nothing could compare with Pirogov's anger and indignation. The very thought of so terrible an insult made him furious. Siberia and the lash seemed to him the least punishment Schiller deserved. He rushed back home so that, having dressed, he could go at once to the general and report to him in the most lurid colours the outrage committed on his person by the German artisan. At the same time he meant to send in a written complaint to the General Staff, and if the punishment should still be unsatisfactory, he resolved to take the matter further and, if need be, further still.

But the whole thing somehow petered out most strangely; on the way to the general, he went into a pastry-cook's, ate two pastries, read something out of the *Northern Bee,* and left with his anger somewhat abated. The evening, moreover, happened to be particularly cool and pleasant and he took a few turns on Nevsky Avenue; by nine o'clock he calmed down completely and it occurred to him that it was hardly wise to disturb the general on a Sunday, especially as he was quite likely to be out of town. And so he went instead to a party given by one of the directors of the Auditing Board, where he found a very agreeable company of Civil Servants and army officers. There he spent a very pleasant time and so distinguished himself in the mazurka that not only the ladies but also the gentlemen were in raptures over it.

What a wonderful world we live in! I could not help reflecting as I strolled along Nevsky Avenue the other day and as I recalled these two incidents. How strangely, how mysteriously does fate play with us! Do we ever get what we want? Do we ever attain what all our endeavours seem to be specially directed to? Everything seems to happen contrary to our hopes and expectation. Fate rewards one man with a pair of splendid horses, and you see him driving about in his carriage, looking bored and paying no attention to the beauty of his trotters, while another man whose heart is consumed with a passion for horseflesh has to go on foot and get all the satisfaction he can by clicking his tongue whenever a fine trotter is led past him. One man has an excellent cook, but unhappily nature has endowed him with so small a mouth that he cannot possibly take more than two pecks, while another has a mouth as big as the arch of the General Headquarters, but, alas, he has to be content with a German dinner of potatoes. How strangely does fate play with us all!

But strangest of all are the incidents that take place on Nevsky Avenue. Oh, do not trust that Nevsky Avenue! I always wrap myself up more closely in my cloak when I walk along it and do my best not to look at the things I pass. For all is deceit, all is a dream, all is not what it seems. Take that gentleman who is strolling about in the immaculate coat. You think he is very rich, don't you? Not a bit of it: he carries all his wealth on his back. You may think that those two fat men who have stopped in front of the church that is being built are discussing its architecture. But you are wrong. They are merely discussing those two sitting crows facing each other so strangely. You may fancy that that enthusiast who is waving his arms about is complaining to his friend about his wife who threw a ball out of a window at an officer who was a complete stranger to him. Not at all: he is talking of Lafayette. You think those ladies . . . but the ladies are least of all to be trusted. And please don't look so often into the shop-windows: the trinkets displayed there are no doubt very beautiful, but there is a strong odour of money about them. And may the Lord save you from peeping under the hats of the ladies! However much a cloak of a beautiful girl may flutter in the distance, I, for one, will never follow it to satisfy my curiosity. Away, away from the street lamp, for heaven's sake! Pass it quickly, as quickly as you can! You'll be lucky if all you get is a few drops of stinking oil on your new suit. But, even apart from the lamp-post, everything is full of deceit. It lies at all times, does Nevsky Avenue, but most of all when night hovers over it in a thick mass, picking out the white from the dun-coloured houses, and all the town thunders and blazes with lights, and thousands of carriages come driving from the bridges, the outriders shouting and jogging up and down on their horses, and when the devil himself lights all the street lamps to show everything in anything but its true colours.

1834

The Nose

I

A MOST extraordinary thing happened in Petersburg on the twenty-fifth of March. The barber, Ivan Yakovlevich, who lives on the Voznessensky Avenue (his surname is lost, and even on his signboard, depicting a gentleman with a lathered face and bearing the inscription: "Also lets blood," no surname appears)—the barber Ivan Yakovlevich woke up rather early and inhaled the smell of hot bread. Raising himself a little in bed, he saw that his wife, a highly respectable lady who was very fond of a cup of coffee, was taking out of the oven some freshly baked bread.

"I won't have coffee today, my dear," said Ivan Yakovlevich. "Instead I'd like some hot bread with onions."

(That is to say, Ivan Yakovlevich would have liked both, but he knew that it was absolutely impossible to ask for two things at once; for his wife disliked such absurd whims.)

"Let the fool eat bread," his wife thought to herself. "All the better for me: there'll be an extra cup of coffee left." And she flung a loaf on the table.

After putting on, for propriety's sake, his frock coat over his shirt, Ivan Yakovlevich sat down at the table, sprinkled some salt, peeled two onions, picked up a knife, and, assuming a solemn expression, began cutting the bread. Having cut it in two, he had a look into the middle of one of the halves and, to his astonishment, noticed some white object there. Ivan Yakovlevich prodded it carefully with the knife and felt it with a finger. "It's solid," he said to himself. "What on earth can it be?"

He dug his fingers into the bread and pulled out—a nose! Ivan Yakovlevich's heart sank: he rubbed his eyes and felt it again: a nose! There could be no doubt about it: it was a nose! And a familiar nose, too, apparently. Ivan Yakovlevich looked horrified. But his horror was nothing compared to the indignation with which his wife was overcome.

"Where have you cut off that nose, you monster?" she screamed angrily. "Blackguard! Drunkard! I shall inform the police against you myself. What a cutthroat! Three gentlemen have told me already that when you are shaving them you pull so violently at their noses that it is a wonder they still remain on their faces!"

But Ivan Yakovlevich was more dead than alive. He recognised the nose as belonging to no other person than the Collegiate Assessor Kovalyov, whom he shaved every Wednesday and every Sunday.

"Wait, my dear, I'll wrap it in a rag and put it in a corner: let it stay there for a bit and then I'll take it out."

"I won't hear of it! What do you take me for? Keep a cutoff nose in my room? You heartless villain, you! All you know is to strop your razor. Soon you won't be fit to carry out your duties at all, you whoremonger, you scoundrel, you! You don't expect me to answer to the police for you, do you? Oh, you filthy wretch, you blockhead, you! Out with it! Out! Take it where you like, only don't let me see it here again!"

Ivan Yakovlevich stood there looking utterly crushed. He thought and thought and did not know what to think.

"Damned if I know how it happened," he said at last, scratching behind his ear. "Did I come home drunk last night? I'm sure I don't know. And yet the whole thing is quite impossible—it can't be true however you look at it: for bread is something you bake, and a nose is something quite different. Can't make head or tail of it!"

Ivan Yakovlevich fell silent. The thought that the police might find the nose at his place and charge him with having cut it off made him feel utterly dejected. He could already see the scarlet collar, beautifully embroidered with silver, the sabre—and he trembled all over. At last he got his trousers and boots, pulled on these sorry objects, and, accompanied by his wife's execrations, wrapped the nose in a rag and went out into the street.

He wanted to shove it under something, either under the seat by the gates or drop it, as it were, by accident and then turn off into a side street. But as ill luck would have it, he kept coming across people he knew, who at once addressed him with the question: "Where are you off to?" or "Who are you going to shave so early in the morning?"—so that he could not find a right moment for getting rid of it. On one occasion he did succeed in dropping it, but a policeman shouted to him from the distance, pointing to it with his halberd: "Hey, you, pick it up! You've dropped something!" And Ivan Yakovlevich had to pick up the nose and put it in his pocket. He was overcome by despair, particularly as the number of people in the streets was continually increasing with the opening of the stores and the small shops.

He decided to go to the Issakiyevsky Bridge, for it occurred to him that he might be able to throw it into the Neva. But I'm afraid I am perhaps a little to blame for not having so far said something more about Ivan Yakovlevich, an estimable man in many respects.

Ivan Yakovlevich, like every other Russian working man, was a terrible drunkard. And though every day he shaved other people's chins, he never bothered to shave his own. Ivan Yakovlevich's frock coat (he never wore an ordinary coat) was piebald; that is to say, it was black, but covered all over with large brown, yellow, and grey spots; his collar was shiny; and instead of three buttons only bits of thread dangled from his coat. Ivan Yakovlevich was a great cynic, and every time the Collegiate Assessor Kovalyov said to him: "Your hands always stink, Ivan Yakovlevich," he would reply with the question: "Why should they stink, sir?" "I don't know why, my dear fellow," the Collegiate Assessor would say, "only they do stink." And after taking a pinch of snuff, Ivan Yakovlevich would lather him for that all over his cheeks, under the nose, behind his ears, and under his beard, in short, wherever he fancied.

This worthy citizen had in the meantime reached Issakiyevsky Bridge. First of all he looked round cautiously, then he leaned over the parapet, as though anxious to see whether there were a great many fishes swimming by, and as he did so he stealthily threw the rag with the nose into the river. He felt as though a heavy weight had been lifted from his shoulders: Ivan Yakovlevich even grinned. Instead of going to shave the chins of civil servants, he set off towards an establishment which bore the inscription: "Tea and Victuals," intending to ask for a glass of punch, when he suddenly noticed at the end of the bridge a police inspector of noble exterior, with large whiskers, with a three-cornered hat, and with a sabre. He stood rooted to the spot; meanwhile the police officer beckoned to him and said: "Come here, my man!"

Knowing the rules, Ivan Yakovlevich took off his cap some way off and, coming up promptly, said: "I hope your honour is well."

"No, no, my good man, not 'your honour.' Tell me, what were you doing there on the bridge?"

"Why, sir, I was going to shave one of my customers and I just stopped to have a look how fast the current was running."

"You're lying, sir, you're lying! You won't get off with that. Answer my question, please!"

"I'm ready to shave you two or even three times a week, sir, with no conditions attached," replied Ivan Yakovlevich.

"No, my dear sir, that's nothing! I have three barbers

who shave me and they consider it a great honour, too.
You'd better tell me what you were doing there!"

Ivan Yakovlevich turned pale. . . . But here the incident
is completely shrouded in a fog and absolutely nothing is
known of what happened next.

II

Collegiate Assessor Kovalyov woke up fairly early and
muttered, "Brrr . . ." with his lips, which he always did
when he woke up, though he could not say himself why
he did so. Kovalyov stretched and asked for the little looking glass standing on the table. He wanted to look at the
pimple which had appeared on his nose the previous evening, but to his great astonishment, instead of his nose, he
saw a completely empty, flat place! Frightened, Kovalyov
asked for some water and rubbed his eyes with a towel:
there was no nose! He began feeling with his hand and
pinched himself to see whether he was still asleep: no, he
did not appear to be asleep. The Collegiate Assessor
Kovalyov jumped out of bed and shook himself: he had no
nose! He immediately told his servant to help him dress
and rushed off straight to the Commissioner of Police.

Meanwhile we had better say something about Kovalyov
so that the reader may see what sort of a person this Collegiate Assessor was. Collegiate Assessors who receive that
title in consequence of their learned diplomas cannot be
compared with those Collegiate Assessors who obtain this
rank in the Caucasus. They are two quite different species.
Learned Collegiate Assessors . . . But Russia is such a wonderful country that if you say something about one Collegiate Assessor, all the Collegiate Assessors, from Riga to
Kamchatka, will most certainly think that you are refer-
ring to them. The same, of course, applies to all other
callings and ranks. Kovalyov was a Caucasian Collegiate Assessor. He had obtained that rank only two years earlier
and that was why he could not forget it for a moment;
and to add to his own importance and dignity, he never

described himself as a Collegiate Assessor, that is to say, a
civil servant of the eighth rank, but always as a major, that
is to say, by the corresponding rank in the army. "Look
here, my good woman," he used to say when he met a
peasant woman selling shirt fronts in the street, "you go
to my house—I live on Sadovaya Street—and just ask: Does
Major Kovalyov live here? Anyone will show you." But if
he met some pretty little minx, he'd give her besides a secret
instruction, adding: "You just ask for Major Kovalyov's
apartment, darling." And that is why we, too, will in future
refer to this Collegiate Assessor as Major Kovalyov.

Major Kovalyov was in the habit of taking a stroll on
Nevsky Avenue every day. The collar of his shirt front was
always extremely clean and well starched. His whiskers
were such as one can still see nowadays on provincial district surveyors, architects, and army doctors, as well as on
police officers performing various duties and, in general, on
all gallant gentlemen who have full, ruddy cheeks and are
very good at a game of boston: these whiskers go right
across the middle of the cheek and straight up to the nose.
Major Kovalyov wore a great number of cornelian seals,
some with crests and others which had engraved on them:
Wednesday, Thursday, Monday, and so on. Major Kovalyov
came to Petersburg on business, to wit, to look for a post
befitting his rank: if he were lucky, the post of a vice-
governor, if not, one of an administrative clerk in some important department. Major Kovalyov was not averse to
matrimony, either, but only if he could find a girl with a
fortune of two hundred thousand. The reader can, therefore, judge for himself the state in which the major was
when he saw, instead of a fairly handsome nose of moderate
size, a most idiotic, flat, smooth place.

As misfortune would have it, there was not a single cab
to be seen in the street and he had to walk, wrapping himself in his cloak and covering his face with a handkerchief,
as though his nose were bleeding. "But perhaps I imagined
it all," he thought. "It's impossible that I could have lost
my nose without noticing it!" He went into a pastry cook's

for the sole purpose of having a look at himself in a mirror. Fortunately, there was no one in the shop: the boys were sweeping the rooms and arranging the chairs; some of them, sleepy-eyed, were bringing in hot cream puffs on trays; yesterday's papers, stained with coffee, were lying about on tables and chairs. "Well, thank God, there's nobody here," he said. "Now I can have a look." He went timidly up to the mirror and looked. "Damn it," he said, disgusted, "the whole thing is too ridiculous for words! If only there'd be something instead of a nose, but there's just nothing!"

Biting his lips with vexation, Kovalyov went out of the pastry cook's and made up his mind, contrary to his usual practice, not to look or smile at anyone. Suddenly he stopped dead in his tracks at the front doors of a house; a most inexplicable thing happened before his very eyes: a carriage drew up before the entrance, the carriage door opened, and a gentleman in uniform jumped out and, stooping, rushed up the steps. Imagine the horror and, at the same time, amazement of Kovalyov when he recognised that this was his own nose! At this extraordinary sight everything went swimming before his eyes. He felt that he could hardly stand on his feet; but he made up his mind that, come what may, he would wait for the gentleman's return to the carriage. He was trembling all over as though in a fever. Two minutes later the nose really did come out. He wore a gold-embroidered uniform with a large stand-up collar, chamois-leather breeches, and a sword at his side. From his plumed hat it could be inferred that he was a State Councillor, a civil servant of the fifth rank. Everything showed that he was going somewhere to pay a visit. He looked round to the right and to the left, shouted to his driver, who had driven off a short distance, to come back, got into the carriage, and drove off.

Poor Kovalyov nearly went out of his mind. He did not know what to think of such a strange occurrence. And, indeed, how was it possible for a nose which had only the day before been on his face and which could neither walk nor drive—to be in a uniform! He ran after the carriage which, luckily, did not go far, stopping before the Kazan Cathedral.

He hastened into the cathedral, pushing his way through the crowd of beggarwomen with bandaged faces and only two slits for the eyes, at whom he used to laugh so much before, and went into the church. There were only a few worshippers inside the church; they were all standing near the entrance. Kovalyov felt so distraught that he was unable to pray and he kept searching with his eyes for the gentleman in the State Councillor's uniform. At last he saw him standing apart from the other worshippers. The nose was hiding his face completely in his large stand-up collar and was saying his prayers with the expression of the utmost piety.

"How am I to approach him?" thought Kovalyov. "It is clear from everything, from his uniform, from his hat, that he is a State Councillor. I'm damned if I know how to do it!"

He went up to him and began clearing his throat; but the nose did not change his devout attitude for a moment and carried on with his genuflections.

"Sir," said Kovalyov, inwardly forcing himself to take courage, "Sir——"

"What do you want?" answered the nose, turning round.

"I find it strange, sir, I—I believe you ought to know your proper place. And all of a sudden I find you in church of all places! You—you must admit that——"

"I'm sorry but I can't understand what you are talking about. . . . Explain yourself."

"How can I explain it to him?" thought Kovalyov and, plucking up courage, began: "Of course—er—you see—I—I am a major and—and you must admit that it isn't right for—er—a man of my rank to walk about without a nose. I mean—er—a tradeswoman selling peeled oranges on Voskressensky Bridge can sit there without a nose; but for a man like me who expects to obtain the post of a governor, which without a doubt he will obtain and—er—besides, being received in many houses by ladies of good position, such as Mrs. Chekhtaryov, the widow of a State Councillor, sir, and many others—er—— Judge for yourself, sir, I mean, I—I don't know"—Major Kovalyov shrugged his shoulders—"I am sorry but if one were to look upon it according to the rules of honour and duty—er—you can understand yourself, sir——"

"I don't understand anything, sir," replied the nose. "Please explain yourself more clearly."

"Sir," said Kovalyov with a consciousness of his own dignity, "I don't know how to understand your words. It seems to me the whole thing is perfectly obvious. Or do you wish —I mean, you are my own nose, sir!"

The nose looked at the major and frowned slightly.

"You are mistaken, sir. I am *myself*. Besides, there can be no question of any intimate relationship between us. I see, sir, from the buttons of your uniform that you are serving in a different department."

Having said this, the nose turned away and went on praying.

Kovalyov was utterly confounded, not knowing what to do or even what to think. At that moment he heard the agreeable rustle of a lady's dress; an elderly lady, her dress richly trimmed with lace, walked up to them, accompanied by a slim girl in a white dress, which looked very charming on her slender figure, and in a straw-coloured hat, as light as a pastry puff. Behind them, opening a snuffbox, stood a tall flunkey with enormous whiskers and quite a dozen collars on his Cossack coat.

Kovalyov came nearer, pulled out the cambric collar of his shirt front, straightened the seals hanging on his gold watch chain and, turning his head this way and that and smiling, turned his attention to the ethereal young lady who, like a spring flower, bent forward a little, as she prayed, and put her little white hand with its semi-transparent fingers to her forehead to cross herself. The smile on Kovalyov's face distended a little more when he caught sight under her pretty hat of a chin of dazzling whiteness and part of her cheek, suffused with the colour of the first spring rose. But suddenly he sprang back as though he had burnt himself. He recollected that, instead of a nose, he had absolutely nothing on his face, and tears started to his eyes. He turned round, intending to tell the gentleman in uniform plainly that he was merely pretending to be a State Councillor, that he was a rogue and an impostor and nothing else than his own nose. . . . But the nose was no longer there: he had managed to gallop off, no doubt to pay another visit. . . .

That plunged Kovalyov into despair. He left the church and stopped for a moment under the colonnade, carefully looking in all directions to see whether he could catch sight of the nose anywhere. He remembered very well that he wore a hat with a plume and a gold-embroidered uniform; but he had not noticed his cloak, nor the colour of his carriage, nor his horses, nor even whether he had a footman behind him and, if so, in what livery. Besides, there were so many carriages careering backwards and forwards that it was difficult to distinguish one from another. But even if he had been able to distinguish any of them, there was no way of stopping it. It was a lovely, sunny day. There were hundreds of people on Nevsky Avenue. A whole flowery cascade of ladies was pouring all over the pavement from the Police Bridge to the Anichkin Bridge. There he saw coming a good acquaintance of his, a civil servant of the seventh rank, whom he always addressed as lieutenant colonel, especially in the presence of strangers. And there was Yaryzhkin, the head clerk in the Senate, a great friend of his, who always lost points when he went eight at boston. And here was another major, who had received the eighth rank of Collegiate Assessor in the Caucasus, waving to him to come up. . . .

"Oh, hell!" said Kovalyov. "Hey, cabby, take me straight to the Commissioner of Police!"

Kovalyov got into the cab and kept shouting to the driver: "Faster! Faster!"

"Is the Police Commissioner at home?" he asked, entering the hall.

"No, sir," replied the janitor. "He's just gone out."

"Well, of all things!"

"Yes, sir," the janitor added, "he's not been gone so long, but he's gone all right. If you'd come a minute earlier, you'd probably have found him at home."

Without taking his handkerchief off his face, Kovalyov got into the cab and shouted in an anguished voice:

"Drive on!"

"Where to, sir?" asked the cabman.

"Straight ahead!"

"Straight ahead, sir? But there's a turning here: to right or to left?"

This question stumped Kovalyov and made him think again. A man in his position ought first of all apply to the City Police Headquarters, not because they dealt with matters of this kind there, but because instructions coming from there might be complied with much more quickly than those coming from any other place; to seek satisfaction from the authorities of the department in which the nose claimed to be serving would have been unreasonable, for from the nose's replies he perceived that nothing was sacred to that individual and that he was quite capable of telling a lie just as he had lied in denying that he had ever seen him. Kovalyov was, therefore, about to tell the cabman to drive him to Police Headquarters, when it again occurred to him that this rogue and impostor, who had treated him in such a contumelious way, might take advantage of the first favourable opportunity and slip out of town, and then all his searches would be in vain or, which God forbid, might go on for a whole month. At last it seemed that Heaven itself had suggested a plan of action to him. He decided to go straight to a newspaper office and, while there was still time, put in an advertisement with a circumstantial description of the nose so that anyone meeting it might bring it to him at once or, at any rate, let him know where it was. And so, having made up his mind, he told the cabman to drive him to the nearest news-paper office and all the way there he kept hitting the cab-man on the back with his fist, repeating, "Faster, you rogue! Faster, you scoundrel!" "Good Lord, sir, what are you hit-ting me for?" said the cabman, shaking his head and flick-ing with the rein at the horse, whose coat was as long as a lap dog's. At last the cab came to a stop and Kovalyov ran panting into a small reception room where a grey-haired clerk, in an old frock coat and wearing spectacles, sat at a table, with a pen between his teeth, counting some coppers.

"Who receives advertisements here?" cried Kovalyov. "Oh, good morning!"

"How do you do?" said the clerk, raising his eyes for a moment and dropping them again on the carefully laid out heaps of coppers before him.

"I should like to insert——"

"One moment, sir, I must ask you to wait a little," said the clerk, writing down a figure on a piece of paper with one hand and moving two beads on his abacus with the other.

A footman with galloons on his livery and a personal ap-pearance which showed that he came from an aristocratic house, was standing beside the clerk with a note in his hand. He thought it an opportune moment for displaying his knowledge of the world.

"Would you believe it, sir," he said, "the little bitch isn't worth eighty copecks, and indeed I shouldn't give even eight copecks for her, but the countess dotes on her, sir, she simply dotes on her, and that's why she's offering a hundred roubles to anyone who finds her! Now, to put it politely, sir, just as you and me are speaking now, you can never tell what people's tastes may be. What I mean is that if you are a sportsman, then keep a pointer or a poodle, don't mind spending five hundred or even a thousand roubles, so long as your dog is a good one."

The worthy clerk listened to this with a grave air and at the same time kept counting the number of letters in the advertisement the footman had brought. The room was full

of old women, shop assistants, and house porters—all with
bits of paper in their hands. In one a coachman of sober
habits was advertised as being let out on hire; in another
an almost new, secondhand carriage, brought from Paris in
1814, was offered for sale; in still others were offered for
sale: a serf girl of nineteen, experienced in laundry work
and suitable for other work, a well-built open carriage with
only one spring broken, a young, dappled-grey, mettlesome
horse of seventeen years of age, a new consignment of
turnip and radish seed from London, a summer residence
with all the conveniences, including two boxes for horses
and a piece of land on which an excellent birchwood or
pinewood could be planted; there was also an advertisement
containing a challenge to those who wished to purchase old
boot soles with an invitation to come to the auction rooms
every day from eight o'clock in the morning to three o'clock
in the afternoon. The room, in which all these people were
crowded, was very small and the air extremely thick; but
the Collegiate Assessor Kovalyov did not notice the bad
smell because he kept the handkerchief over his face and
also because his nose was at the time goodness knows
where.

"Excuse me, sir," he said at last with impatience, "it's
very urgent. . . ."

"Presently, presently," said the grey-haired gentleman,
flinging their notes back to the old women and the house
porters. "Two roubles forty copecks! One moment, sir! One
rouble sixty-four copecks! What can I do for you?" he said
at last, turning to Kovalyov.

"Thank you, sir," said Kovalyov. "You see, I've been
robbed or swindled, I can't so far say which, but I should
like you to put in an advertisement that anyone who brings
the scoundrel to me will receive a handsome reward."

"What is your name, sir?"

"What do you want my name for? I'm sorry I can't give
it to you. I have a large circle of friends: Mrs. Chekhtaryov,
the widow of a State Councillor, Pelageya Grigoryevna
Podtochin, the widow of a first lieutenant. . . . God forbid

that they should suddenly find out! You can simply say: a Collegiate Assessor or, better still, a gentleman of the rank of major."

"And is the runaway your house serf?"

"My house serf? Good Lord, no! That wouldn't have been so bad! You see, it's my—er—nose that has run away from me. . . ."

"Dear me, what a strange name! And has this Mr. Nosov robbed you of a large sum of money?"

"I said nose, sir, nose! You're thinking of something else! It is my nose, my own nose that has disappeared I don't know where. The devil himself must have played a joke on me!"

"But how did it disappear? I'm afraid I don't quite understand it."

"I can't tell you how it happened. The worst of it is that now it is driving about all over the town under the guise of a State Councillor. That's why I should like you to insert an advertisement that anyone who catches him should bring him at once to me. You can see for yourself, sir, that I cannot possibly carry on without such a conspicuous part of myself. It's not like some little toe which no one can see whether it is missing or not once I'm wearing my boots. I call on Thursdays on Mrs. Chekhtaryov, the widow of a State Councillor. Mrs. Podtochin, the widow of a first lieutenant, and her pretty daughter are also good friends of mine, and you can judge for yourself the position I am in now. I can't go and see them now, can I?"

The clerk pursed his lips tightly which meant that he was thinking hard.

"I'm sorry, sir," he said at last, after a long pause, "but I can't possibly insert such an advertisement in the papers."

"What? Why not?"

"Well, you see, sir, the paper might lose its reputation. If everyone were to write that his nose had run away, why—— As it is, people are already saying that we are publishing a lot of absurd stories and false rumours."

"But why is it so absurd? I don't see anything absurd in it."

"It only seems so to you. Last week, for instance, a similar thing happened. A civil servant came to see me just as you have now. He brought an advertisement, it came to two roubles and seventy-three copecks, but all it was about was that a poodle with a black coat had run away. You wouldn't think there was anything in that, would you? And yet it turned out to be a libellous statement. You see, the poodle was the treasurer of some institution or other. I don't remember which."

"But I am not asking you to publish an advertisement about a poodle, but about my own nose, which is the same as about myself."

"No, sir, I cannot possibly insert such an advertisement."

"Not even if my own nose really has disappeared?"

"If it's lost, then it's a matter for a doctor. I'm told there are people who can fit you with a nose of any shape you like. But I can't help observing, sir, that you are a gentleman of a merry disposition and are fond of pulling a person's leg."

"I swear to you by all that is holy! Why, if it has come to that, I don't mind showing you."

"Don't bother, sir," said the clerk, taking a pinch of snuff. "Still," he added, unable to suppress his curiosity, "if it's no bother, I'd like to have a look."

The Collegiate Assessor removed the handkerchief from his face.

"It is very strange, indeed!" said the clerk. "The place is perfectly flat, just like a pancake from a frying pan. Yes, quite incredibly flat."

"Well, you won't dispute it now, will you? You can see for yourself that you simply must insert it. I shall be infinitely grateful to you and very glad this incident has given me the pleasure of making your acquaintance. . . ."

It may be seen from that that the major decided to lay it on a bit thick this time.

"Well, of course, it's easy enough to insert an advertisement," said the clerk, "but I don't see that it will do you any good. If you really want to publish a thing like that, you'd better put it in the hands of someone skilful with his pen and let him describe it as a rare natural phenomenon and publish it in *The Northern Bee*"—here he took another pinch of snuff—"for the benefit of youth"—here he wiped his nose—"or just as a matter of general interest."

The Collegiate Assessor was utterly discouraged. He dropped his eyes and glanced at the bottom of the newspaper where the theatrical announcements were published; his face was ready to break into a smile as he read the name of a very pretty actress, and his hand went automatically to his pocket to feel whether he had a five-rouble note there, for, in Kovalyov's opinion, officers of the higher ranks ought to have a seat in the stalls—but the thought of his nose spoilt it all!

The clerk himself appeared to be touched by Kovalyov's embarrassing position. Wishing to relieve his distress a little, he thought it proper to express his sympathy in a few words.

"I'm very sorry indeed, sir," he said, "that such a thing should have happened to you. Would you like a pinch of snuff? It relieves headaches, dispels melancholy moods, and it is even a good remedy against haemorrhoids."

Saying this, the clerk offered his snuffbox to Kovalyov, very deftly opening the lid with the portrait of a lady in a hat on it.

This unintentional action made Kovalyov lose his patience.

"I can't understand, sir," he said angrily, "how you can joke in a matter like this! Don't you see I haven't got the thing with which to take a pinch of snuff? To hell with your snuff! I can't bear the sight of it now, and not only your rotten beresina brand, but even if you were to offer me rappee itself!"

Having said this, he walked out of the newspaper office, greatly vexed, and went to see the police inspector of his district, a man who had a great liking for sugar. At his home, the entire hall, which was also the dining room, was stacked with sugar loaves with which local tradesmen had presented him out of friendship. When Kovalyov arrived, the police inspector's cook was helping him off with his regulation top boots; his sabre and the rest of his martial armour were already hung peaceably in the corners of the room, and his three-year-old son was playing with his awe-inspiring three-cornered hat. He himself was getting ready to partake of the pleasures of peace after his gallant, war-like exploits.

Kovalyov walked in at the time when he stretched, cleared his throat, and said: "Oh, for a couple of hours of sleep!" It could, therefore, be foreseen that the Collegiate Assessor could have hardly chosen a worse time to arrive; indeed, I am not sure whether he would have got a more cordial reception even if he had brought the police inspector several pounds of sugar or a piece of cloth. The inspector was a great patron of the arts and manufactures, but he preferred a bank note to everything else. "This is something," he used to say. "There is nothing better than that: it doesn't ask for food, it doesn't take up a lot of space, there's always room for it in the pocket, and when you drop it, it doesn't break."

The inspector received Kovalyov rather coldly and said that after dinner was not the time to carry out investigations and that nature herself had fixed it so that after a good meal a man had to take a nap (from which the Collegiate Assessor could deduce that the inspector was not unfamiliar with the sayings of the ancient sages), and that a respectable man would not have his nose pulled off.

A bull's eye! . . . It must be observed that Kovalyov was extremely quick to take offence. He could forgive anything people said about himself, but he could never forgive an insult to his rank or his calling. He was even of the opinion that any reference in plays to army officers or civil servants of low rank was admissible, but that the censorship ought not to pass any attack on persons of higher rank. The reception given him by the police inspector disconcerted him so much that he tossed his head and said with an air of dignity, with his hands slightly parted in a gesture of surprise: "I must say that after such offensive remarks, I have nothing more to say. . . ." and went out.

He arrived home hardly able to stand on his feet. By now it was dusk. After all these unsuccessful quests his rooms looked melancholy or rather extremely disgusting to him. On entering the hall, he saw his valet Ivan lying on his back on the dirty leather sofa and spitting on the ceiling and rather successfully aiming at the same spot. Such an indifference on the part of his servant maddened him; he hit him on the forehead with his hat, saying: "You pig, you're always doing something stupid!"

Ivan jumped up and rushed to help him off with his cloak.

On entering his room, the major, tired and dejected, threw himself into an armchair and, at last, after several sighs, said:

"Lord, oh Lord, why should I have such bad luck? If I had lost an arm or a leg, it would not be so bad; if I had lost my ears, it would be bad enough, but still bearable; but without a nose a man is goodness knows what, neither fish, nor flesh, nor good red herring—he isn't a respectable citizen at all! He is simply something to take and chuck out of the window! If I had had it cut off in battle or in a duel or had been the cause of its loss myself, but to lose it without any reason whatever, for nothing, for absolutely nothing! . . . But no," he added after a brief reflection, "it can't be. It's inconceivable that a nose should be lost, absolutely inconceivable. I must be simply dreaming or just imagining it all. Perhaps by some mistake I drank, instead of water, the spirits which I rub on my face after shaving. Ivan, the blithering fool, did not take it away and I must have swallowed it by mistake."

To convince himself that he was not drunk, the major pinched himself so painfully that he cried out. The pain completely convinced him that he was fully awake and that everything had actually happened to him. He went up slowly to the looking glass and at first screwed up his eyes with the idea that perhaps he would see his nose in its proper place; but almost at the same moment he jumped back, saying: "What a horrible sight!"

And, indeed, the whole thing was quite inexplicable. If he had lost a button, a silver spoon, his watch, or something of the kind, but to lose—and in his own apartment, too! Taking all the circumstances into consideration, Major Kovalyov decided that he would not be far wrong in assuming that the whole thing was the fault of no other person than Mrs. Podtochin, who wanted him to marry her daughter. He was not himself averse to flirting with her, but he avoided a final decision. But when Mrs. Podtochin told him plainly that she would like her daughter to marry him, he quietly hung back with his compliments, declaring that he was still too young, that he had to serve another five years, as he had decided not to marry till he was exactly forty-two. That was why Mrs. Podtochin, out of revenge no doubt, had made up her mind to disfigure him and engaged some old witch to do the foul deed, for he simply refused to believe that his nose had been cut off: no one had entered his room, and his barber, Ivan Yakovlevich, had shaved him on Wednesday, and during the whole of that day and even on Thursday his nose was intact—he remembered that, he knew that for certain; besides, he would have felt pain and the wound could not possibly have healed so quickly and become as smooth as a pancake. He made all sorts of plans in his head: to issue a court summons against her or to go to see her and confront her with the undeniable proof of her crime. His thoughts were interrupted by a gleam of light through all the cracks of the door, which let him know that Ivan had lighted a candle in the hall. Soon Ivan himself appeared, carrying the candle in front of him and lighting the whole room brightly. Kovalyov instinctively seized his handkerchief and covered the place where his nose had been only the day before so that the stupid fellow should not stand there gaping, seeing his master so strangely transformed.

Ivan had scarcely had time to go back to his cubbyhole when an unfamiliar voice was heard in the hall, saying:

"Does the Collegiate Assessor Kovalyov live here?"

"Come in," said Kovalyov, jumping up quickly and opening the door. "Major Kovalyov is here."

A police officer of a handsome appearance, with whiskers that were neither too dark nor too light and with fairly full cheeks, came in. It was, in fact, the same police officer who, at the beginning of this story, had been standing at the end of Issakiyevsky Bridge.

"Did you lose your nose, sir?"

"That's right."

"It's been found now."

"What are you saying?" cried Major Kovalyov.

He was bereft of speech with joy. He stared fixedly at the police officer who was standing before him and whose full lips and cheeks reflected the flickering light of the candle.

"How was it found?"

"By a most extraordinary piece of luck, sir. It was intercepted just before he was leaving town. It was about to get into the stagecoach and leave for Riga. He even had a passport made out in the name of a certain civil servant. And the funny thing is that at first I was myself inclined to take him for a gentleman. But luckily I was wearing my glasses at the time and I saw at once that it was a nose. You see, sir, I am shortsighted, and if you were to stand in front of me I would just see that you have a face, but would not be able to make out either your nose or your beard or anything else for that matter. My mother-in-law, that is to say, my wife's mother, can't see anything, either."

Kovalyov was beside himself with excitement.

"Where is it? Where? I'll go at once!"

"Don't trouble, sir. Realising how much you must want it, I brought it with me. And the funny part about it is that the chief accomplice in this affair is the scoundrel of a barber on Voznessensky Avenue, who is now locked up in a cell at the police station. I've suspected him for a long

time of theft and drunkenness and, as a matter of fact, he
stole a dozen buttons from a shop only the other day. Your
nose, sir, is just as it was."

At these words, the police officer put his hand in his
pocket and pulled out the nose wrapped in a piece of paper.

"Yes, yes, it's my nose!" cried Kovalyov. "It's my nose all
right! Won't you have a cup of tea with me, sir?"

"I'd be very glad to, sir, but I'm afraid I'm rather in a
hurry. I have to go to the House of Correction from here.
Food prices have risen a great deal, sir. . . . I have my
mother-in-law, that is to say, my wife's mother, living with
me and, of course, there are the children. My eldest, in
particular, is a very promising lad, sir. A very clever boy
he is, sir, but I haven't the means to provide a good education for him—none at all. . . ."

Kovalyov took the hint and, snatching up a ten-rouble
note from the table, thrust it into the hand of the police
officer, who bowed and left the room, and almost at the
same moment Kovalyov heard his voice raised in the street,
where he was boxing the ears of a foolish peasant who had
happened to drive with his cart on to the boulevard.

After the departure of the police officer, the Collegiate
Assessor remained for a time in a sort of daze, and it was
only after several minutes that he was able to recover his
senses, so overwhelmed was he by his joy at the unexpected
recovery of his nose. He took the newly found nose very
carefully in both his cupped hands and examined it attentively once more.

"Yes, it's my nose all right!" said Major Kovalyov.
"There's the pimple on the left side which I only got the
other day."

The major almost laughed with joy. But nothing lasts very
long in the world, and that is why even joy is not so poignant after the first moment. A moment later it grows weaker
still and at last it merges imperceptibly into one's ordinary
mood, just as a circle made in the water by a pebble at
last merges into its smooth surface. Kovalyov began to pon-
der and he realised that the matter was not at an end: the

nose had been found, but it had still to be affixed, to be
put back in its place.

"And what it if doesn't stick?"

At this question that he had put to himself the major
turned pale.

With a feeling of indescribable panic he rushed up to
the table and drew the looking glass closer to make sure
that he did not stick his nose on crookedly. His hands trembled. Carefully and with the utmost circumspection he put
it back on its former place. Oh horror! The nose did not
stick! . . . He put it to his mouth, breathed on it to warm
it a little, and once more put it back on the smooth place
between his two cheeks; but, try as he might, the nose refused to stick.

"Come on, come on! Stick, you idiot!" he kept saying to it.

But the nose, as though made of wood, kept falling down
on the table with so strange a sound that it might have been
cork. The major's face contorted spasmodically. "Won't it
adhere?" he asked himself in a panic. But though he kept
putting it back on its own place a great many times, his
efforts were as unavailing as ever.

He called Ivan and sent him for the doctor, who occupied the best flat on the ground floor of the same house.
The doctor was a fine figure of a man; he had wonderful
pitch-black whiskers, a fresh, healthy wife, he ate fresh
apples in the morning and kept his mouth quite extraordinarily clean, rinsing it every morning for nearly three quar-
ters of an hour and brushing his teeth with five different
kinds of toothbrushes. The doctor came at once. After asking how long it was since the accident, he lifted up Major
Kovalyov's face by the chin and gave a fillip with his
thumb, on the spot where the nose had been, with such
force that the major threw back his head so violently that
he hit the wall. The doctor said that it was nothing and,
after advising him to move away from the wall a little, told
him to bend his head to the right. After feeling the place
where the nose had been, he said: "H'm!" Then he told him
to bend his head to the left, and again said: "H'm!" In con-

clusion he gave him another fillip with the thumb so that
the major tossed his head like a horse whose teeth are being examined. Having carried out this experiment, the doctor shook his head and said:

"No, I'm afraid it can't be done! You'd better remain like
this, for it might be much worse. It is, of course, quite possible to affix your nose. In fact, I could do it right now.
But I assure you that it might be the worse for you."

"How do you like that! How am I to remain without a
nose?" said Kovalyov. "It can't possibly be worse than now.
It's—it's goodness only knows what! How can I show myself with such a horrible face? I know lots of people of
good social position. Why, today I have been invited to two
parties. I have a large circle of friends: Mrs. Chekhtaryov,
the widow of a State Councillor, Mrs. Podtochin, the
widow of an army officer—though after what she did to me
now I shall have no further dealings with her except
through the police. Do me a favour, Doctor," said Kovalyov
in an imploring voice. "Is there no way at all? Stick it on
somehow. It may not be quite satisfactory, but so long as
it sticks I don't mind. I could even support it with a hand
in an emergency. Besides, I don't dance, so that I could
hardly do any harm to it by some inadvertent movement.
As for my gratitude for your visits, you may be sure that
I will recompense you as much as I can. . . ."

"Believe me, sir," said the doctor neither in too loud nor
in too soft a voice, but in a very persuasive and magnetic
one, "I never allow any selfish motives to interfere with the
treatment of my patients. This is against my principles and
my art. It is true I charge for my visits, but that is only
because I hate to offend by my refusal. Of course, I could
put your nose back, but I assure you on my honour, if you
won't believe my words, that it will be much worse. You'd
better leave it to nature. Wash it often with cold water, and
I assure you that without a nose you will be as healthy as
with one. As for your nose, I'd advise you to put it in a
bottle of spirits or, better still, pour two spoonfuls of aqua
fortis and warmed-up vinegar into the bottle, and you'd be

able to get a lot of money for it. I might take it myself even, if you won't ask too much for it."

"No, no," cried the desperate Major Kovalyov, "I'd rather it rotted away!"

"I'm sorry," said the doctor, taking his leave, "I wish I could be of some help to you, but there's nothing I can do! At least you saw how anxious I was to help you."

Having said this, the doctor left the room with a dignified air. Kovalyov did not even notice his face, and in his profound impassivity only caught sight of the cuffs of his spotlessly clean white shirt peeping out of his black frock coat.

On the following day he decided, before lodging his complaint, to write to Mrs. Podtochin a letter with a request to return to him without a fight what she had taken away from him. The letter was as follows:

Dear Mrs. Podtochin,

I cannot understand your strange treatment of me. I assure you that, by acting like this, you will gain nothing and will certainly not force me to marry your daughter. Believe me, I know perfectly well what happened to my nose and that you, and no one else, are the chief instigator of this affair. Its sudden detachment from its place, its flight, and its disguise, first in the shape of a civil servant and then in its own shape, is nothing more than the result of witchcraft employed by you or by those who engage in the same honourable occupations as yourself. For my part, I deem it my duty to warn you that if the aforementioned nose is not back in its usual place today, I shall be forced to have recourse to the protection and the safeguard of the law.

However, I have the honour of remaining, madam, with the utmost respect

Your obedient servant,

Platon Kovalyov

Dear Platon Kuzmich,

Your letter has greatly surprised me. To be quite frank, I never expected it, particularly as regards your unjust reproaches. I wish to inform you that I have never received the civil servant you mention, neither in disguise nor in his own shape. It is true, Filipp Ivanovich Potachkin used to come to see me. And though he did ask me for my daughter's hand and is a man of good and sober habits and of great learning, I have never held out any hopes to him. You also mention your nose. If you mean by that that I wished to put your nose out of joint, that is, to give you a formal refusal, I am surprised that you should speak of such a thing when, as you know perfectly well, I was quite of the contrary opinion and if you should now make a formal proposal to my daughter, I should be ready to satisfy you immediately, for that has always been my dearest wish, in the hope of which

I remain always at your service,

Pelageya Podtochin

"No," said Kovalyov, after he had read the letter, "she had certainly nothing to do with it. It's impossible! The letter is not written as a guilty person would have written it." The Collegiate Assessor was an expert on such things, for, while serving in the Caucasus, he had several times been under judicial examination. "How then, in what way, did it happen? The devil alone can sort it out!" he said at last, utterly discouraged.

Meanwhile the rumours about this extraordinary affair spread all over the town and, as usually happens, not without all sorts of embellishments. At that time people's minds were particularly susceptible to anything of an extraordinary nature: only a short time before everybody had shown a great interest in the experiments of magnetism. Besides, the story of the dancing chairs in Konyushennaya Street was still fresh in people's minds, and it is therefore not surprising that people soon began talking about the Collegiate Assessor Kovalyov's nose which, it was alleged, was taking a walk on Nevsky Avenue at precisely three o'clock in the afternoon. Thousands of curious people thronged Nevsky Avenue every day. Someone said that the nose was in Junker's Stores, and such a crowd of people collected at the stores that the police had to be called to restore order. One enterprising, bewhiskered businessman of respectable appearance, who was selling all sorts of dry pasties at the entrance to the theatre, had purposely made beautiful wooden benches on which it was perfectly safe to stand and invited people to use them for eighty copecks each. One highly estimable colonel, who had left his home earlier than usual so that he could see the nose, pushed his way through the crowd with great difficulty; but, to his great indignation, he saw in the window of the stores, instead of the nose, an ordinary woollen sweater and a lithograph of a girl pulling up her stocking and a dandy, with a small beard and an open waistcoat, peeping at her from behind a tree—a picture that had hung in the same place for over ten years. On stepping back from the window, he said with vexation: "One should not be allowed to create a disturbance among the common people by such stupid and improbable stories."

Then the rumour spread that Major Kovalyov's nose was not taking a walk on Nevsky Avenue but in Tavrichesky Gardens and that he had been there for a long time; in fact, that when the Persian Prince Khozrev Mirza had lived there he had greatly marvelled at that curious freak of nature. A few students of the Surgical Academy set off there. One highly aristocratic lady wrote a letter to the head keeper of the gardens specially to ask him to show that rare phenomenon to her children and, if possible, with instructive and edifying explanations for young boys.

All men about town, without whom no important social gathering is complete, who liked to amuse the ladies and whose stock of amusing stories had been entirely used up at the time, were extremely glad of all this affair. A small section of respectable and well-meaning people were highly dissatisfied. One gentleman declared indignantly that he failed to understand how in our enlightened age such absurd stories could be spread abroad and that he was surprised the government paid no attention to it. This gentleman evidently was one of those gentlemen who would like to involve the government in everything, even in his daily tiffs with his wife. After that—but here again a thick fog descends on the whole incident, and what happened afterwards is completely unknown.

III

The world is full of all sorts of absurdities. Sometimes there is not even a semblance of truth: suddenly the very same nose, which had been driving about disguised as a State Councillor and had created such an uproar in town, found itself, as if nothing had happened, on its accustomed place again, namely, between the two cheeks of Major Kovalyov. This happened on the seventh of April. Waking up and looking quite accidentally into the mirror, he saw —his nose! He grabbed it with his hand—it was his nose all right! . . . "Aha!" said Kovalyov, and nearly went leaping barefoot all over the room in a roisterous dance in his joy. But Ivan, who entered just then, prevented him. He told Ivan to bring in some water for washing at once and, while washing, glanced once again into the mirror: he had a nose! While wiping himself with a towel, he again glanced into the mirror: he had a nose!

"Have a look, Ivan, there seems to be a pimple on my nose," he said, thinking to himself: "Won't it be awful if Ivan were to say, No, sir, there's no pimple and no nose, either!"

But Ivan said: "There's nothing, sir. I can't see no pimple. Nothing at all on your nose, sir."

"That's good, damn it!" said the major to himself, snapping his fingers.

At that moment the barber Ivan Yakovlevich poked his head through the door, but as timidly as a cat which had just been thrashed for the theft of suet.

"Tell me first of all—are your hands clean?" Kovalyov shouted to him from the other end of the room.

"They are clean, sir."

"You're lying!"

"I swear they are clean, sir!"

"Very well, they'd better be!"

Kovalyov sat down. Ivan Yakovlevich put a napkin round him and in a twinkling, with the aid of his brush alone, transformed his whole beard and part of his cheek into the sort of cream that is served in a merchant's home at a name-day party.

"Well, I never!" said Ivan Yakovlevich to himself as he glanced at the nose. Then he bent his head to the other side and looked at the nose sideways. "Well, I'm damned," he went on, looking at the nose for some considerable time. "Dear, oh dear, just think of it!" At last, gently and as cautiously as can only be imagined, he raised two fingers to grasp it by its end. Such was Ivan Yakovlevich's system.

"Mind, mind what you're doing!" cried Kovalyov.

Ivan Yakovlevich was utterly discouraged, perplexed, and confused as he had never been confused before. At last he began carefully titillating him with the razor under the beard, and though he found it difficult and not at all convenient to shave without holding on to the olfactory organ, he did at last overcome all the obstacles by pressing his rough thumb against the cheek and the lower jaw and finished shaving him.

When everything was ready, Kovalyov hastened to dress at once, took a cab, and drove straight to the nearest pastry cook's. On entering, he at once shouted to the boy at the other end of the shop: "Boy, a cup of chocolate!" and immediately went up to the looking glass: he had a nose all right! He turned round gaily and glanced ironically, screwing up one eye a little, at two military gentlemen, one of whom had a nose no bigger than a waistcoat button. After that he set off for the office of the department where he was trying to obtain the post of vice-governor or, if unsuccessful, of an administrative clerk. On passing through the reception room, he glanced into the looking glass: he had a nose all right! Then he went to see another Collegiate Assessor, a man who was very fond of sneering at people, to whom he often used to say in reply to his biting remarks: "Oh, away with you! I know you, Mr. Pinprick!" On the

way he thought: "If the major does not split his sides with
laughter when he sees me, it's a sure sign that everything is
in its proper place." But the Collegiate Assessor showed no
signs of merriment. "It's perfect, perfect, damn it!" thought
Kovalyov to himself. On the way back he met Mrs.
Podtochin and her daughter, greeted them, and was met
with joyful exclamations, which again proved to him that
there was nothing wrong with him. He talked a long time
with them and, taking out his snuffbox deliberately, kept
stuffing his nose with snuff at both entrances for a great
while, saying to himself: "There, I'm putting on this show
specially for you, stupid females! And I won't marry your
daughter all the same. Flirt with her—by all means, but
nothing more!" And Major Kovalyov took his walks after
that as if nothing had happened. He was to be seen on
Nevsky Avenue, in the theatres—everywhere. And his nose,
too, just as if nothing had happened, remained on his face,
without as much as a hint that he had been playing truant.
And after that Major Kovalyov was always seen in the best
of humour, smiling, running after all the pretty ladies, and
once even stopping before a little shop in the Arcade and
buying himself a ribbon of some order for some mysterious
reason, for he had never been a member of any order.

So that is the sort of thing that happened in the northern
capital of our far-flung Empire. Only now, on thinking it
all over, we can see that there is a great deal that is improbable in it. Quite apart from the really strange fact of
the supernatural displacement of the nose and its appearance in various parts of the town in the guise of a State
Councillor, how did Kovalyov fail to realise that he could
not advertise about his nose in a newspaper? I am not saying that because I think that advertisement rates are too
high—that's nonsense, and I am not at all a mercenary person. But it's improper, awkward, not nice! And again—how
did the nose come to be in a loaf of bread and what about
Ivan Yakovlevich? No, that I cannot understand, I simply
cannot understand it! But what is even stranger and more
incomprehensible than anything is that authors should

choose such subjects. I confess that is entirely beyond my comprehension. It's like—no, I simply don't understand it. In the first place it's of no benefit whatever to our country, and in the second place—but even in the second place there's no benefit whatever. I simply don't know what to make of it. . . .

And yet, in spite of it all, though, of course, we may take for granted this and that and the other—may even—— But then where do you not find all sorts of absurdities? All the same, on second thoughts, there really is something in it. Say what you like, but such things do happen—not often, but they do happen.

1835–36

The Overcoat

IN THE department . . . but perhaps it is just as well not to say in which department. There is nothing more touchy and ill-tempered in the world than departments, regiments, government offices, and indeed any kind of official body. Nowadays every private individual takes a personal insult to be an insult against society at large. I am told that not so very long ago a police commissioner (I don't remember of what town) sent in a petition to the authorities in which he stated in so many words that all Government decrees had been defied and his own sacred name most decidedly taken in vain. And in proof he attached to his petition an enormous volume of some highly romantic work in which a police commissioner figured on almost every tenth page, sometimes in a very drunken state. So to avoid all sorts of unpleasant misunderstandings, we shall refer to the department in question as *a certain department*.

And so in *a certain department* there served *a certain Civil Servant*, a Civil Servant who cannot by any stretch of the imagination be described as in any way remarkable. He was in fact a somewhat short, somewhat pockmarked, somewhat red-haired man, who looked rather short-sighted and was slightly bald on the top of his head, with wrinkles on both cheeks, and a rather sallow complexion. There is nothing we can do about it: it is all the fault of the St. Petersburg climate. As for his rank (for with us rank is something that must be stated before anything else), he was what is known as a perpetual titular councillor, the ninth rank among the fourteen ranks into which our Civil Service is divided, a rank which, as every one knows, has been sneered at and held up to scorn by all sorts of writers who have the praiseworthy habit of setting upon those who cannot hit back. The Civil Servant's surname was Bashmachkin. From this it can be clearly inferred that it had once upon a time originated from the Russian word *bashmak*, to wit, shoe. But when, at what precise date, and under what circumstances the metamorphosis took place, must for ever remain a mystery. His father, grandfather, and, why, even his brother-in-law as well as all the rest of the Bashmachkins, always walked about in boots, having their soles repaired no more than three times a year. His name and patronymic were Akaky Akakyevich. The reader may think it a little odd, not to say somewhat *recherché*, but we can assure him that we wasted no time in searching for this name and that it happened in the most natural way that no other name could be given to him, and the way it came about is as follows:

Akaky Akakyevich was born, if my memory serves me right, on the night of 23rd March. His mother of blessed memory, the wife of a Civil Servant and a most excellent woman in every respect, took all the necessary steps for the child to be christened. She was still lying in bed, facing the door, and on her right stood the godfather, Ivan Ivanovich Yeroshkin, a most admirable man, who was a head clerk at the Supreme Court, and the godmother, Arina Semyonovna Byelobrúshkina, the wife of the district police inspector, a most worthy woman. The mother was presented with the choice of three names, namely, Mokkia, Sossia, or, it was suggested, the child might be called after the martyr Khozdazat. "Oh dear," thought his late mother, "they're all such queer names!" To please her, the calendar was opened at another place, but again the three names that were found were rather uncommon, namely, Trifily, Dula and Varakhassy. "Bother," said the poor woman, "what queer names! I've really never heard such names! Now if it had only been Varadat or Varukh, but it would be Trifily and Varakhassy!" Another page was turned and the names in the calendar were Pavsikakhy and Vakhtissy. "Well," said the mother, "I can see that such is the poor innocent infant's fate. If that is so, let him rather be called after his father. His father was Akaky, so let the son be Akaky, too." It was in this way that he came to be called Akaky. The child was christened, and during the ceremony he began to cry and pulled such a face that it really seemed as though he had a premonition that he would be a titular councillor one day. Anyway, that is how it all came to pass.

We have told how it had come about at such length because we are anxious that the reader should realise himself that it could not have happened otherwise, and that to give him any other name was quite out of the question.

When and at what precise date Akaky had entered the department, and who had appointed him to it, is something that no one can remember. During all the years he had served in that department many directors and other higher officials had come and gone, but he still remained in exactly the same place, in exactly the same position, in exactly the same job, doing exactly the same kind of work, to wit, copying official documents. Indeed, with time the belief came to be generally held that he must have been born into the world entirely fitted out for his job, in his Civil Servant's uniform and a bald patch on his head. No particular respect was shown him in the department. Not only did the caretakers not get up from their seats when he passed by, but they did not even vouchsafe a glance at him, just as if a common fly had flown through the waiting-room. His superiors treated him in a manner that could be best described as frigidly despotic. Some assistant head clerk would just shove a paper under his nose without even saying, "Please copy it," or "Here's an interesting, amusing little case!" or something in a similarly pleasant vein as is the custom in all well-regulated official establishments. And he would accept it without raising his eyes from the paper, without looking up to see who had put it on his desk, or whether indeed he had any right to put it there. He just took it and immediately settled down to copy it. The young clerks laughed and cracked jokes about him, the sort of jokes young clerks could be expected to crack. They told stories about him in his presence, stories that were specially invented about him. They joked about his landlady, an old woman of seventy, who they claimed beat him, or they asked him when he was going to marry her. They also showered bits of torn paper on his head and called them snow. But never a word did Akaky say to it all, as though unaware of the presence of his tormentors in the office. It did not even interfere with his work; for while these rather annoying practical jokes were played on him he never made a single mistake in the document he was copying. It was only when the joke got too unbearable, when somebody jogged his arm and so interfered with his work, that he would say, "Leave me alone, gentlemen. Why do you pester me?" There was a strange note in the words and in the voice in which they were uttered: there was something in it that touched one's heart with pity. Indeed, one young man who had only recently been appointed to the department and who, following the example of the others, tried to have some fun at his expense, stopped abruptly at Akaky's mild expostulation, as though stabbed through the heart; and since then everything seemed to have changed in him and he saw everything in quite a different light. A kind of unseen power made him keep away from his colleagues whom at first he had taken for decent, well-bred men. And for a long time afterwards, in his happiest moments, he would see the shortish Civil Servant with the bald patch on his head, uttering those pathetic words, "Leave me alone! Why do you pester me?" And in those pathetic words he seemed to hear others: "I am your brother." And the poor young man used to bury his face in his hands, and many a time in his life he would shudder when he perceived how much inhumanity there was in man, how much savage brutality there lurked beneath the most refined, cultured manners, and, dear Lord, even in the man the world regarded as upright and honourable. . . .

It would be hard to find a man who lived so much for his job. It was not sufficient to say that he worked zealously. No, his work was a labour of love to him. There, in that copying of his, he seemed to see a multifarious and pleasant world of his own. Enjoyment was written on his face; some letters he was particularly fond of, and whenever he had the chance of writing them, he was beside himself with joy, chuckling to himself, winking and helping them on with his lips, so that you could, it seemed, read on his face every letter his pen was forming with such care. If he had been rewarded in accordance with his zeal, he would to his own surprise have got as far as a state councillorship; but, as the office wits expressed it, all he got for his pains was a metal disc in his button-hole and a stitch in his side. Still it would be untrue to say that no one took any notice of him. One director, indeed, being a thoroughly good man and anxious to reward him for his long service, ordered that he should be given some more responsible work than his usual copying, that is to say, he was told to prepare a report for another department of an already concluded case; all he had to do was to alter the title at the top of the document and change some of the verbs from the first to the third person singular. This, however, gave him so much trouble that he was bathed in perspiration and kept mopping his forehead until at last he said, "No, I can't do it. You'd better give me something to copy." Since then they let him carry on with his copying for ever. Outside this copying nothing seemed to exist for him. He never gave a thought to his clothes: his uniform was no longer green, but of some nondescript rusty white. His collar was very short and narrow so that his neck, though it was not at all long, looked as if it stuck a mile out of the collar, like the necks of the plaster kittens with wagging heads, scores of which are carried about on their heads by street-vendors of non-Russian nationality. And something always seemed to cling to his uniform: either a straw or some thread. He possessed, besides, the peculiar knack when walking in the street of passing under a window just at the time when some rubbish was tipped out of it, and for this reason he always carried about on his hat bits of water-melon or melon rind and similar trash. He had never in his life paid the slightest attention to what was going on daily in the street, and in this he was quite unlike his young colleagues in the Civil Service, who are famous as observers of street life, their eagle-eyed curiosity going even so far as to notice that the strap under the trousers of some man on the pavement on the other side of the street has come undone, a thing which never fails to bring a malicious grin to their faces. But even if Akaky did look at anything, he saw nothing but his own neat lines, written out in an even hand, and only if a horse's muzzle, appearing from goodness knows where, came to rest on his shoulder and blew a gale on his cheek from its nostrils, did he become aware of the fact that he was not in the middle of a line, but rather in the middle of the street.

On his arrival home, he would at once sit down at the table, quickly gulp down his cabbage soup, eat a piece of beef with onions without noticing what it tasted like, eating whatever Providence happened to send at the time, flies and all. Noticing that his stomach was beginning to feel full, he would get up from the table, fetch his inkwell and start copying the papers he had brought home with him. If, however, there were no more papers to copy, he would deliberately make another copy for his own pleasure, intending to keep it for himself, especially if the paper was remarkable not so much for the beauty of its style as for the fact of being addressed to some new or important person.

Even at those hours when all the light has faded from the grey St. Petersburg sky, and the Civil Service folk have taken their fill of food and dined each as best he could, according to his salary and his personal taste; when all have had their rest after the departmental scraping of pens, after all the rush and bustle, after their own and other people's indispensable business had been brought to a conclusion, and anything else restless man imposes upon himself of his own free will had been done, and even much more than is necessary; when every Civil Servant is hastening to enjoy as best he can the remaining hours of his leisure—one more enterprising rushing off to the theatre, another going for a stroll to stare at some silly women's hats, a third going to a party to waste his time paying compliments to some pretty girl, the star of some small Civil Service circle, while a fourth—as happens in nine cases out of ten—paying a call on a fellow Civil Servant living on the third or fourth floor in a flat of two small rooms with a tiny hall or kitchen, with some pretensions to fashion—a lamp or some other article that has cost many self-denying sacrifices, such as doing without dinners or country outings; in short, even when all the Civil Servants have dispersed among the tiny flats of their friends to play a stormy game of whist, sipping tea from glasses and nibbling a penny biscuit, or inhaling the smoke of their long pipes and, while dealing the cards, retailing the latest high society scandal (for every Russian is so devotedly attached to high society that he cannot dispense with it for a moment), or, when there is nothing else to talk about, telling the old chestnut about the fortress commandant who was told that the tail of the horse of Falconnetti's statue of Peter I had been docked—in short, even while every government official in the capital was doing his best to enjoy himself, Akaky Akakyevich made no attempt to woo the fair goddess of mirth and jollity. No one could possibly ever claim to have seen him at a party. Having copied out documents to his heart's content, he went to bed, smiling in anticipation of the pleasures the next day had in store for him and wondering what the good Lord would send him to copy. So passed the peaceful life of a man who knew how to be content with his lot on a salary of four hundred roubles a year; and it might have flowed on as happily to a ripe old age, were it not for the various calamities which beset the lives not only of titular, but also of privy, actual, court and any other councillors, even those who give no counsel to any man, nor take any from anyone, either.

There is in St. Petersburg a great enemy of all those who receive a salary of four hundred roubles a year, or thereabouts. This enemy is none other than our northern frost, though you will hear people say that it is very good for the health. At nine o'clock in the morning, just at the hour when the streets are full of Civil Servants on their way to their departments, he starts giving such mighty and stinging filips to all noses without exception, that the poor fellows simply do not know where to put them. At a time when the foreheads of even those who occupy the highest positions in the State ache with the frost, and tears start to their eyes, the poor titular councillors are sometimes left utterly defenceless. Their only salvation lies in running as fast as they can in their thin, threadbare overcoats through five or six streets and then stamping their feet vigorously in the vestibule, until they succeed in unfreezing their faculties and abilities, frozen on the way, and are once more able to tackle the affairs of State.

Akaky had for some time been feeling that the fierce cold seemed to have no difficulty at all in penetrating to his back and shoulders, however fast he tried to sprint across the legal distance from his home to the department. It occurred to him at length that his overcoat might not be entirely blameless for this state of affairs. On examining it thoroughly at home, he discovered that in two or three places, to wit, on the back and round the shoulders, it looked like some coarse homespun cotton; the cloth had worn out so much that it let through the wind, and the lining had all gone to pieces. It must be mentioned here that Akaky's overcoat, too, had been the butt of the departmental wits; it had been even deprived of the honourable name of overcoat and had been called a *capote*. And indeed it was of a most peculiar cut: its collar had shrunk in size more and more every year, for it was used to patch the other parts. The patching did no credit to the tailor's art and the result was that the final effect was somewhat baggy and far from beautiful. Having discovered what was wrong with his overcoat, Akaky decided that he would have to take it to Petrovich, a tailor who lived somewhere on the fourth floor up some back stairs and who, in spite of the disadvantage of having only one eye and pock marks all over his face, carried on a rather successful trade in mending the trousers and frock-coats of government clerks and other gentlemen whenever, that is to say, he was sober and was not hatching some other scheme in his head.

We really ought not to waste much time over this tailor; since, however, it is now the fashion that the character of every person in a story must be delineated fully, then by all means let us have Petrovich, too. To begin with, he was known simply by his Christian name of Grigory, and had been a serf belonging to some gentleman or other; he began calling himself Petrovich only after he had obtained his freedom, when he started drinking rather heavily every holiday, at first only on the great holidays, and thereafter on any church holiday, on any day, in fact, marked with a cross in the calendar. So far as that went, he was true to the traditions of his forebears and in his altercations with his wife on this subject he would call her a worldly woman and a German. Having mentioned his wife, we had better say a word or two about her also; to our great regret, however, we know very little about her, except that Petrovich had a wife, who wore a bonnet, and not a kerchief; there appears to be some doubt as to whether she was good-looking or not, but on the whole it does not seem likely that she had very much to boast of in that respect; at any rate, only guardsmen were ever known to peer under her bonnet when meeting her in the street, twitching their moustaches and emitting a curious kind of grunt at the same time.

While ascending the stairs leading to Petrovich's flat— the stairs which, to do them justice, were soaked with water and slops and saturated with a strong spirituous smell which irritates the eyes and which, as the whole world knows, is a permanent feature of all the back stairs of St. Petersburg houses—while ascending the stairs, Akaky was already wondering how much Petrovich would ask for mending his overcoat, and made up his mind not to give him more than two roubles. The door of Petrovich's flat was open because his wife had been frying some fish and had filled the whole kitchen with smoke, so that even the cockroaches could no longer be seen. Akaky walked through the kitchen, unnoticed even by Mrs. Petrovich, and, at last, entered the tailor's room where he beheld Petrovich sitting on a large table of unstained wood with his legs crossed under him like a Turkish pasha. His feet, as is the custom of tailors when engaged in their work, were bare. The first thing that caught his eye was Petrovich's big toe, which Akaky knew very well indeed, with its deformed nail as thick and hard as the shell of a tortoise. A skein of silk and cotton thread hung about Petrovich's neck, and on his knees lay some tattered piece of clothing. He had for the last minute or two been trying to thread his needle and, failing every time, he was terribly angry with the dark room and even with the thread itself, muttering under his breath, "Won't you go through, you beast? You'll be the death of me yet, you slut!" Akaky could not help feeling sorry that he had come just at the moment when Petrovich was angry: he liked to place an order with Petrovich only when the tailor was a bit merry, or when he had, as his wife put it, "been swilling his corn-brandy, the one-eyed devil!" When in such a state, Petrovich was as a rule extremely amenable and always gave in and agreed to any price, and even bowed and thanked him. It was true that afterwards his wife would come to see Akaky and tell him with tears in her eyes that her husband had been drunk and had therefore charged him too little; but all Akaky had to do was to add another ten-copeck piece and the thing was settled. But now Petrovich was to all appearances sober as a judge and, consequently, rather bad-tempered, intractable and liable to charge any old price. Akaky realised that and was about, as the saying is, to beat a hasty retreat, but it was too late: Petrovich had already screwed up his only eye and was looking at him steadily. Akaky had willy-nilly to say, "Good morning, Petrovich!" "Good morning, sir. How are you?" said Petrovich, fixing his eye on Akaky's hands in an effort to make out what kind of offering he had brought.

"Well, you see, Petrovich, I—er—have come—er—about that, you know . . ." said Akaky.

It might be as well to explain at once that Akaky mostly talked in prepositions, adverbs, and, lastly, such parts of speech as have no meaning whatsoever. If the matter was rather difficult, he was in the habit of not finishing the sentences, so that often having begun his speech with, "This is—er—you know . . . a bit of that, you know . . ." he left it at that, forgetting to finish the sentence in the belief that he had said all that was necessary.

"What's that you've got there, sir?" said Petrovich, scrutinising at the same time the whole of Akaky's uniform with his one eye, from the collar to the sleeves, back, tails and button-holes, which was all extremely familiar to him, since it was his own handiwork. Such is the immemorial custom among tailors; it is the first thing a tailor does when he meets one of his customers.

"Well, you see, Petrovich, I've come about this here, you know . . . this overcoat of mine. The cloth, you know. . . . You see, it's really all right everywhere, in fact, excellent. . . . I mean, it's in fine condition here and—er—all over. Looks a bit dusty, I know, and you might get the impression that it was old, but as a matter of fact it's as good as new, except in one place where it's a bit—er—a bit, you know. . . . On the back, I mean, and here on the shoulder. . . . Looks as though it was worn through a bit, and on the other shoulder too, just a trifle, you see. . . . Well, that's really all. Not much work in it. . . ."

Petrovich took the *capote*, first spread it on the table, examined it for a long time, shook his head, and stretched out his hand to the window for his round snuff-box with a portrait of some general, though which particular general it was impossible to say, for the place where the face should

243

have been had been poked in by a finger and then pasted over with a square bit of paper. Having treated himself to a pinch of snuff, Petrovich held the overcoat out in his hands against the light and gave it another thorough examination, and again shook his head; he then turned it with the lining upwards and again shook his head, again took off the lid with the general pasted over with paper, and, filling his nose with snuff, replaced the lid, put away the snuff-box and, at last, said, "No, sir. Impossible to mend it. There's nothing left of it."

Akaky's heart sank at those words. "Why is it impossible, Petrovich?" he said, almost in the imploring voice of a child. "It's only on the shoulders that it's a bit worn, and I suppose you must have bits of cloth somewhere. . . ."

"Oh, I've got plenty of bits of cloth, sir, lots of 'em," said Petrovich. "But you see, sir, you can't sew 'em on. The whole coat's rotten. Touch it with a needle and it will fall to pieces."

"Well, if it falls to pieces, all you have to do is to patch it up again."

"Why, bless my soul, sir, and what do you suppose the patches will hold on to? What am I to sew them on to? Can't you see, sir, how badly worn it is? You can't call it cloth any more: one puff of wind and it will be blown away."

"But please strengthen it a bit. I mean, it can't be just—er—really, you know . . ."

"No, sir," said Petrovich firmly, "it can't be done. Too far gone. Nothing to hold it together. All I can advise you to do with it, sir, is to cut it up when winter comes and make some rags to wrap round your feet, for socks, sir, are no damned good at all: there's no real warmth in 'em. It's them Germans, sir, what invented socks to make a lot of money (Petrovich liked to get in a word against the Germans on every occasion). As for your overcoat, sir, I'm afraid you'll have to get a new one."

At the word "new" a mist suddenly spread before Akaky's eyes and everything in the room began swaying giddily.

The only thing he could still see clearly was the general's face pasted over with paper on the lid of Petrovich's snuff-box.

"How do you mean, a new one?" he said, still as though speaking in a dream. "Why, I haven't got the money for it."

"Well, sir, all I can say is that you just must get yourself a new one," said Petrovich with callous indifference.

"Well, and if . . . I mean, if I had to get a new one . . . how much, I mean . . ."

"How much will it come to, sir?"

"Yes."

"Well, sir, I suppose you'll have to lay out three fifty-rouble notes or more," said Petrovich, pursing his lips significantly.

He had a great fondness for strong effects, Petrovich had. He liked to hit a fellow on the head suddenly and then steal a glance at him to see what kind of a face the stunned person would pull after his words.

"One hundred and fifty roubles for an overcoat!" cried poor Akaky in a loud voice, probably raising his voice to such a pitch for the first time in his life, for he was always distinguished by the softness of his voice.

"Yes, sir," said Petrovich. "And that, too, depends on the kind of coat you have. If you have marten for your collar and a silk lining for your hood, it might cost you two hundred."

"Now look here, Petrovich . . ." said Akaky in a beseeching voice, not hearing, or at any rate doing his best not to hear, what Petrovich was saying, and paying no attention whatever to the effect the tailor was trying to create. "Please, my dear fellow, just mend it somehow, so that I could still use it a bit longer, you know. . . ."

"No, sir, it will merely mean a waste of my work and your money," said Petrovich.

After such a verdict Akaky left Petrovich's room feeling completely crushed, while the tailor remained in the same position a long time after he had gone, without going back to his work, his lips pursed significantly. He was greatly pleased that he had neither demeaned himself nor let down the sartorial art.

In the street Akaky felt as though he were in a dream. "So that's how it stands, is it?" he murmured to himself. "I really didn't think that it would turn out like that, you know. . . ." Then after a pause he added, "Well, that's that. There's a real surprise for you. . . . I never thought that it would end like that. . . ." There followed another long pause, after which he said, "So that's how it is! What a sudden . . . I mean, what a terrible blow! Who could have . . . What an awful business!"

Having delivered himself thus, he walked on, without noticing it, in quite the opposite direction from his home. On the way a chimney-sweep brushed the whole of his sooty side against him and blackened his shoulder; from the top of a house that was being built a whole handful of lime fell upon him. But he was aware of nothing, and only when some time later he knocked against a policeman who, placing his halberd near him, was scattering some snuff from a horn on a calloused fist, did he recover a little, and that, too, only because the policeman said, "Now then, what are you pushing against me for? Can't you see where you're going? Ain't the pavement big enough for you?" This made him look up and retrace his steps.

But it was not until he had returned home that he began to collect his thoughts and saw his position as it really was. He began discussing the matter with himself, not in broken sentences, but frankly and soberly, as though talking to a wise friend with whom it was possible to discuss one's most intimate affairs.

"No, no," said Akaky, "it's pretty clear that it is impossible to talk to Petrovich now. He's a bit, you know . . . Been thrashed by his wife, I shouldn't wonder. I'd better go and see him next Sunday morning, for after all the drink he'll have had on Saturday night he'll still be screwing up his one eye, and he'll be very sleepy and dying for another drink to help him on his feet again, and his wife won't give him any money, so that if I come along and give him ten copecks or a little more he'll be more reasonable and change his mind about the overcoat, and then, you know . . ."

So Akaky reasoned with himself, and he felt greatly reassured.

Sunday came at last and, noticing from a distance that Petrovich's wife had left the house to go somewhere, he went straight in. To be sure, Petrovich did glower after his Saturday night's libations, and he could barely hold up his head, which seemed to be gravitating towards the floor, and he certainly looked very sleepy; and yet, in spite of this condition, no sooner did he hear what Akaky had come for than it seemed as if the devil himself had nudged him.

"Quite impossible, sir," he said. "You'll have to order a new one." Akaky immediately slipped a ten-copeck piece into his hand. "Thank you very much, sir," said Petrovich. "Very kind of you, I'm sure. I'll get a bit o' strength in me body and drink to your health, sir. But if I were you, sir, I'd stop worrying about that overcoat of yours. No good at all. Can't do nothing with it. Mind, I can promise you one thing, though: I'll make you a lovely new overcoat. That I will, sir."

Akaky tried to say something about mending the old one, but Petrovich would not even listen to him and said, "Depend upon it, sir, I'll make you a new one. Do my best for you, I will, sir. Might even while we're about it, sir, and seeing as how it's now the fashion, get a silver-plated clasp for the collar."

It was then that Akaky at last realised that he would have to get a new overcoat, and his heart failed him. And how indeed was he to do it? What with? Where was he to get the money? There was of course the additional holiday pay he could count on; at least there was a good chance of his getting that holiday bonus. But supposing he did get it, all that money had already been divided up and disposed of long ago. There was that new pair of trousers he must get; then there was that long-standing debt he owed the shoemaker for putting new tops to some old boots; he had, moreover, to order three shirts from the sempstress as well as two pairs of that particular article of underwear which cannot be decently mentioned in print—in short, all the money would have to be spent to the last penny, and even if the director of the department were to be so kind as to give him a holiday bonus of forty-five or even fifty roubles instead of forty, all that would remain of it would be the veriest trifle, which in terms of overcoat finance would be just a drop in the ocean. Though he knew perfectly well, of course, that Petrovich was sometimes mad enough to ask so utterly preposterous a price that even his wife could not refrain from exclaiming, "Gone off his head completely, the silly old fool! One day he accepts work for next to nothing, and now the devil must have made him ask more than he is worth himself!"—though he knew perfectly well, of course, that Petrovich would undertake to make him the overcoat for eighty roubles, the question still remained: where was he to get the eighty roubles? At a pinch he could raise half of it. Yes, he could find half of it all right and perhaps even a little more, but where was he to get the other half? . . .

But first of all the reader had better be told where Akaky hoped to be able to raise the first half.

Akaky was in the habit of putting away a little from every rouble he spent in a box which he kept locked up and which had a little hole in the lid through which money could be dropped. At the end of every six months he counted up the accumulated coppers and changed them into silver. As he had been saving up for a long time, there had accumulated in the course of several years a sum of over forty roubles. So he had half of the required sum in hand; but where was he to get the other half? Where was he to get another forty roubles?

Akaky thought and thought and then he decided that he would have to cut down his ordinary expenses for a year at least: do without a cup of tea in the evenings; stop burning candles in the evening and, if he had some work to do, go to his landlady's room and work by the light of her candle;

when walking in the street, try to walk as lightly as possible on the cobbles and flagstones, almost on tiptoe, so as not to wear out the soles of his boots too soon; give his washing to the laundress as seldom as possible, and to make sure that it did not wear out, to take it off as soon as he returned home and wear only his dressing-gown of twilled cotton cloth, a very old garment that time itself had spared. To tell the truth, Akaky at first found it very hard to get used to such economy, but after some time he got used to it all right and everything went with a swing; he did not even mind going hungry in the evenings, for spiritually he was nourished well enough, since his thoughts were full of the great idea of his future overcoat. His whole existence indeed seemed now somehow to have become fuller, as though he had got married, as though there was someone at his side, as though he was never alone, but some agreeable helpmate had consented to share the joys and sorrows of his life, and this sweet helpmate, this dear wife of his, was no other than the selfsame overcoat with its thick padding of cotton-wool and its strong lining that would last a lifetime. He became more cheerful and his character even got a little firmer, like that of a man who knew what he was aiming at and how to achieve that aim. Doubt vanished, as though of its own accord, from his face and from his actions, and so did indecision and, in fact, all the indeterminate and shilly-shallying traits of his character. Sometimes a gleam would appear in his eyes and through his head there would flash the most bold and audacious thought, to wit, whether he should not after all get himself a fur collar of marten. All these thoughts about his new overcoat nearly took his mind off his work at the office, so much so that once, as he was copying out a document, he was just about to make a mistake, and he almost cried out, "Oh dear!" in a loud voice, and crossed himself. He went to see Petrovich at least once a month to discuss his overcoat, where it was best to buy the cloth, and what colour and at what price, and though looking a little worried, he always came back home well satisfied, reflecting that the time was not far off when he would pay for it all and when his overcoat would be ready.

As a matter of fact the whole thing came to pass much quicker than he dreamed. Contrary to all expectations, the director gave Akaky Akakyevich not forty or forty-five, but sixty roubles! Yes, a holiday bonus of sixty roubles. Whether he, too, had been aware that Akaky wanted a new overcoat, or whether it happened by sheer accident, the fact remained that Akaky had an additional twenty roubles. This speeded up the whole course of events. Another two or three months of a life on short commons and Akaky had actually saved up about eighty roubles. His pulse, generally sluggish, began beating fast. The very next day he went with Petrovich to the shops. They bought an excellent piece of cloth, and no wonder! For the matter had been carefully discussed and thought over for almost six months, and scarcely a month had passed without enquiries being made at the shops about prices, so as to make quite sure that the cloth they needed was not too expensive; and the result of all that foresight was that, as Petrovich himself admitted, they could not have got a better cloth. For the lining they chose calico, but of such fine and strong quality that, according to Petrovich, it was much better than silk and was actually much more handsome and glossy. They did not buy marten for a fur collar, for as a matter of fact it was rather expensive, but they chose cat fur instead, the best cat they could find in the shop, cat which from a distance could always be mistaken for marten. Petrovich took only two weeks over the overcoat, and that, too, because there was so much quilting to be done; otherwise it would have been ready earlier. For his work Petrovich took twelve roubles—less than that was quite out of the question: he had used nothing but silk thread in the sewing of it, and it was sewn with fine, double seams, and Petrovich had gone over each seam with his own teeth afterwards, leaving all sorts of marks on them.

It was . . . It is hard to say on what day precisely it was, but there could be no doubt at all that the day on which Petrovich at last delivered the overcoat was one of the greatest days in Akaky's life. He brought it rather early in the morning, just a short time before Akaky had to leave for the department. At no other time would the overcoat have been so welcome, for the time of rather sharp frosts had just begun, and from all appearances it looked as if the severity of the weather would increase. Petrovich walked in with the overcoat as a good tailor should. His face wore an expression of solemn gravity such as Akaky had never seen on it before. He seemed to be fully conscious of the fact that he had accomplished no mean thing and that he had shown by his own example the gulf that separated the tailors who merely relined a coat or did repairs from those who made new coats. He took the overcoat out of the large handkerchief in which he had brought it. (The handkerchief had just come from the laundress: it was only now that he folded it and put it in his pocket for use.) Having taken out the overcoat, he looked very proudly about him and, holding it in both hands, threw it very smartly over Akaky's shoulders, then he gave it a vigorous pull and, bending down, smoothed it out behind with his hand; then he draped it round Akaky, throwing it open in front a little. Akaky, who was no longer a young man, wanted to try it on with his arms in the sleeves, and Petrovich helped him to put his hands through the sleeves, and—it was all right even when he wore it with his arms in the sleeves. In fact, there could be no doubt at all that the overcoat was a perfect fit. Petrovich did not let this opportunity pass without observing that it was only because he lived in a back street and had no signboard and because he had known Akaky Akakyevich so long that he had charged him so little for making the overcoat. If he had ordered it on Nevsky Avenue, they would have charged him seventy-five roubles for the work alone. Akaky had no desire to discuss the matter with Petrovich and, to tell the truth, he was a little frightened of the big sums which Petrovich was so fond of tossing about with the idea of impressing people. He paid him, thanked him, and left immediately for the department in his new overcoat. Petrovich followed him into the street where he remained standing a long time on one spot, admiring his handiwork from a distance; then he purposely went out of his way so that he could by taking a short-cut by a side street rush out into the street again and have another look at the overcoat, this time from the other side, that is to say, from the front.

Meanwhile Akaky went along as if walking on air. Not for a fraction of a second did he forget that he had a new overcoat on his back, and he could not help smiling to himself from time to time with sheer pleasure at the thought of it. And really it had two advantages: one that it was warm, and the other that it was good. He did not notice the distance and found himself suddenly in the department. He took off the overcoat in the hall, examined it carefully and entrusted it to the special care of the door-keeper. It is not known how the news of Akaky's new overcoat had spread all over the department, but all at once every one knew that Akaky had discarded his *capote* and had a fine new overcoat. They all immediately rushed out into the hall to have a look at Akaky's new overcoat. Congratulations and good wishes were showered upon him. At first Akaky just smiled, then he felt rather embarrassed. But when all surrounded him and began telling him that he ought to celebrate his acquisition of a new overcoat and that the least he could do was to invite them all to a party, Akaky Akakyevich was thrown into utter confusion and did not know what to do, what to say to them all, or how to extricate himself from that very awkward situation. He even tried a few minutes later with the utmost good humour to assure them, blushing to the roots of his hair, that it was not a new overcoat at all, that it was just . . . well, you know . . . just his old overcoat. At last one of the clerks, and, mind, not just any clerk, but no less a person than the assistant head clerk of the office, wishing to show no doubt that he, for one, was not a proud man and did not shun men more humble than himself, said, "So be it! I will give a party instead of Akaky Akakyevich. I invite you all, gentlemen, this evening to tea at my place. As a matter of fact, it happens to be my birthday." The Civil Servants naturally wished him many happy returns of the day and accepted his invitation with alacrity. Akaky tried at first to excuse himself, but everybody told him that it was not done and that he ought to be ashamed of himself, and he just could not wriggle out of it. However, he felt rather pleased afterwards, for it occurred to him that this would give him a chance of taking a walk in the evening in his new overcoat.

That day was to Akaky like a great festival. He came home in a most happy frame of mind, took off his overcoat, hung it with great care on the wall, stood for some time admiring the cloth and lining, and then produced his old overcoat, which had by then gone to pieces completely, just to compare the two. He looked at it and could not help chuckling out loud: what a difference! And he kept smiling to himself all during dinner when he thought of the disgraceful state of his old overcoat. He enjoyed his dinner immensely and did no copying at all afterwards, not one document did he copy, but just indulged himself a little by lying down on his bed until dusk. Then, without dawdling unnecessarily, he dressed, threw the overcoat over his shoulders, and went out into the street.

Unfortunately we cannot say where precisely the Civil Servant who was giving the party lived. Our memory is beginning to fail us rather badly and everything in St. Petersburg, all the streets and houses, has become so blurred and mixed up in our head that we find it very difficult indeed to sort it out properly. Be that as it may, there can be no doubt that the Civil Servant in question lived in one of the best parts of the town, which means of course that he did not live anywhere near Akaky Akakyevich. At first Akaky had to pass through some deserted streets, very poorly lighted, but as he got nearer to the Civil Servant's home the streets became more crowded and more brilliantly illuminated. There certainly were more people in the streets, the women were well dressed and the men even wore beaver collars. There were fewer poor peasant cabmen with their grate-like wooden sledges studded with brass nails; on the contrary, the cabmen were mostly fine fellows in crimson velvet caps with lacquered sledges and bearskin covers, and carriages with sumptuously decorated boxes drove at a great speed through the streets, their wheels crunching on the snow.

Akaky looked at it all as though he had never seen anything like it in his life, and indeed he had not left his room in the evening for several years. He stopped before a lighted shop window and for some minutes looked entranced at a painting of a beautiful woman who was taking off a shoe and showing a bare leg, a very shapely leg, too; and behind her back a gentleman had stuck his head through the door of another room, a gentleman with fine side-whiskers and a handsome imperial on his chin. Akaky shook his head and grinned, and then went on his way. Why did he grin? It might have been because he had seen something he had never seen before, but a liking for which is buried deep down inside every one of us, or because (like many another Civil Servant) he thought to himself, "Oh, those damned Frenchmen! What a people they are, to be sure! If they set their heart on something, something . . . well, something of that kind, you know, then it is something . . . well, something of that kind. . . ." But perhaps he never even said anything at all to himself. How indeed is one to delve into a man's mind and find out what he is thinking about? At last he reached the house where the young assistant head clerk of his office lived.

The assistant head clerk lived in great style: there was a lamp burning on the stairs, and his flat was on the second floor. As he entered the hall, Akaky saw on the floor rows upon rows of galoshes. Among them in the middle of the room stood a *samovar*, hissing and letting off clouds of steam. The walls were covered with overcoats and cloaks, some even with beaver collars and velvet revers. A confused buzz of conversation came from the other side of the wall, and it grew very clear and loud when the door opened and a footman came out with a trayful of empty tea-glasses, a jug of cream and a basket of biscuits. It was evident that the Civil Servants had been there for some time and had already finished their first glass of tea.

After hanging up his overcoat himself, Akaky entered the room, and there flashed upon his sight simultaneously candles, Civil Servants, pipes, card-tables, while his ears were filled with the confused sound of continuous conversation, which came from every corner of the room, and the noise of moving chairs. He stood in the middle of the room, looking rather forlorn and trying desperately to think what he ought to do. But his presence had already been noticed and he was welcomed with loud shouts, and everybody immediately went into the hall to inspect his overcoat anew. Though feeling rather embarrassed at first, Akaky, being of a singularly ingenuous nature, could not help being pleased to hear how everybody praised his overcoat. Then, of course, they forgot all about him and his overcoat and crowded, as was to be expected, round the card-tables set out for whist.

All this—the noise, the talk, and the crowd of people—was very strange and bewildering to Akaky. He simply did not know what to do, where to put his hands and feet, or his whole body; at length he sat down by the card players, looked at the cards, studied the face of one player, then of another, and after a little time began to feel bored and started yawning, particularly as it was getting late and it was long past his bedtime. He tried to take leave of his host, but they would not let him go, saying that they had to drink a glass of champagne in honour of his new overcoat. In about an hour supper was served. It consisted of a mixed salad, cold veal, meat pie, cream pastries and champagne. They made Akaky drink two glasses of champagne, after which he felt that everything got much jollier in the room. However, he could not forget that it was already midnight and that it was high time he went home. To make sure that his host would not detain him on one pretext or another, he stole out of the room and found his overcoat in the hall. The overcoat, he noticed not without a pang of regret, was lying on the floor. He picked it up, shook it, removed every speck of dust from it and, putting it over his shoulders, went down the stairs into the street.

It was still light in the street. A few small grocers' shops, those round-the-clock clubs of all sorts of servants, were still open; from those which were already closed a streak of light still streamed through the crack under the door, showing that there was still some company there, consisting most probably of maids and men-servants who were finishing their talk and gossip, leaving their masters completely at a loss to know where they were. Akaky walked along feeling very happy and even set off running after some lady (goodness knows why) who passed him like a streak of lightning, every part of her body in violent motion. However, he stopped almost at once and went on at a slow pace as before, marvelling himself where that unusual spurt of speed had come from. Soon he came to those never-ending, deserted streets, which even in daytime are not particularly cheerful, let alone at night. Now they looked even more deserted and lonely; there were fewer street lamps and even those he came across were extinguished: the municipal authorities seemed to be sparing of oil. He now came into the district of wooden houses and fences; there was not a soul to be seen anywhere, only the snow gleamed on the streets, and hundreds of dismal, low hovels with closed shutters which seemed to have sunk into a deep sleep, stretched in a long, dark line before him. Soon he approached the spot where the street was intersected by an immense square with houses dimly visible on the other side, a square that looked to him like a dreadful desert.

A long way away—goodness knows where—he could see the glimmer of a light coming from some sentry-box, which seemed to be standing at the edge of the world. Akaky's cheerfulness faded perceptibly as he entered the square. He entered it not without a kind of involuntary sensation of dread, as though feeling in his bones that something untoward was going to happen. He looked back, and then cast a glance at either side of him: it was just as though the sea were all round him. "Much better not to look," he thought to himself, and, shutting his eyes, he walked on, opening them only to have a look how far the end of the square was. But what he saw was a couple of men standing right in front of him, men with moustaches, but what they were he could not make out in the darkness. He felt dazed and his heart began beating violently against his ribs. "Look, here is my overcoat!" one of the men said in a voice of thunder, grabbing him by the collar. Akaky was about to scream, "Help!" but the other man shook his fist in his face, a fist as big as a Civil Servant's head, and said, "You just give a squeak!" All poor Akaky knew was that they took off his overcoat and gave him a kick which sent him sprawling on the snow. He felt nothing at all any more. A few minutes later he recovered sufficiently to get up, but there was not a soul to be seen anywhere. He felt that it was terribly cold in the square and that his overcoat had gone. He began to shout for help, but his voice seemed to be too weak to carry to the end of the square. Feeling desperate and without ceasing to shout, he ran across the square straight to the sentry-box beside which stood a policeman who, leaning on his halberd, seemed to watch the running figure with mild interest, wondering no doubt why the devil a man was running towards him, screaming his head off while still a mile away. Having run up to the police constable, Akaky started shouting at him in a gasping voice that he was asleep and did not even notice that a man had been robbed under his very nose. The policeman said that he saw nothing, or rather that all he did see was that two men had stopped him (Akaky) in the middle of the square, but he supposed that they were his friends; and he advised Akaky, instead of standing there and abusing him for nothing, to go and see the police inspector next morning, for the inspector was quite sure to find the men who had taken his overcoat.

Akaky Akakyevich came running home in a state of utter confusion. His hair, which still grew, though sparsely, over his temples and at the back of his head, was terribly tousled;

his chest, arms and trousers were covered with snow. His old landlady, awakened by the loud knocking at the door, jumped hurriedly out of bed and with only one slipper on ran to open the door, modestly clasping her chemise to her bosom with one hand. When she opened the door and saw the terrible state Akaky was in, she fell back with a gasp. He told her what had happened to him, and she threw up her arms in dismay and said that he ought to go straight to the district police commissioner, for the police inspector was quite sure to swindle him, promise him all sorts of things and then leave him in the lurch; it would be much better if he went to the district police commissioner who, it seemed, was known to her, for Anna, the Finnish girl who was once her cook, was now employed by the district commissioner of police as a nurse, and, besides, she had seen him often as he drove past the house, and he even went to church every Sunday and always, while saying his prayers, looked round at everybody very cheerfully, so that, judging from all appearances, he must be a kind-hearted man.

Having listened to that piece of advice, Akaky wandered off sadly to his room, and how he spent that night we leave it to those to judge who can enter into the position of another man. Early next morning he went to see the district police commissioner, but they told him that he was still asleep. He came back at ten o'clock and again they said he was asleep. He came back at eleven o'clock and was told that the police commissioner was not at home. He came back at lunch-time, but the clerks in the waiting-room would not admit him on any account unless he told them first what he had come for and what it was all about and what had happened. So that in the end Akaky felt for the first time in his life that he had to assert himself and he told them bluntly that he had come to see the district commissioner of police personally, that they had no right to refuse to admit him, that he had come from the department on official business, and that if he lodged a complaint against them, they would see what would happen. The clerks dared say nothing to this and one of them went to summon the commissioner.

The police commissioner took rather a curious view of Akaky's story of the loss of his overcoat. Instead of concentrating on the main point of the affair, he began putting all sorts of questions to Akaky which had nothing to do with it, such as why he was coming home so late, and was he sure he had not been to any disorderly house the night before, so that Akaky felt terribly embarrassed and went away wondering whether the police were ever likely to take the necessary steps to retrieve his overcoat.

That day (for the first time in his life) he did not go to the department. Next day he appeared looking very pale and wearing his old *capote,* which was in a worse state than ever. Many of his colleagues seemed moved by the news of the robbery of his overcoat, though there were a few among them who could not help pulling poor Akaky's leg even on so sad an occasion. It was decided to make a special collection for Akaky, but they only succeeded in collecting a trifling sum, for the clerks in his office had already spent a great deal on subscribing to a fund for a portrait of the director and also on some kind of a book, at the suggestion of one of the departmental chiefs, who was a friend of the author. Anyway, the sum collected was a trifling one. One Civil Servant, however, moved by compassion, decided to help Akaky with some good advice at any rate, and he told him that he should not go to the district police inspector, for though it might well happen that the district police inspector, anxious to win the approbation of his superiors, would somehow or other find his overcoat, Akaky would never be able to get it out of the police station unless he could present all the necessary legal proofs that the overcoat belonged to him. It would therefore be much better if Akaky went straight to a certain Very Important Person, for the Very Important Person could, by writing and getting into touch with the right people, give a much quicker turn to the whole matter.

Akaky Akakyevich (what else could he do?) decided to

go and see the Very Important Person. What position the
Very Important Person occupied and what his job actually
was has never been properly ascertained and still remains
unknown. Suffice it to say that the Very Important Person
had become a Very Important Person only quite recently,
and that until then he was quite an unimportant person.
Moreover, his office was not even now considered of much
importance as compared with others of greater importance.
But there will always be people who regard as important
what in the eyes of other people is rather unimportant.
However, the Very Important Person did his best to increase
his importance in all sorts of ways, to wit, he introduced
a rule that his subordinates should meet him on the stairs
when he arrived at his office; that no one should be admitted to his office unless he first petitioned for an interview,
and that everything should be done according to the
strictest order: the collegiate registrar was first to report to
the provincial secretary, the provincial secretary to the titular councillor or whomsoever it was he had to report to,
and that only by such a procedure should any particular
business reach him. In Holy Russia, we are sorry to say,
every one seems to be anxious to ape every one else and
each man copies and imitates his superior. The story is even
told of some titular councillor who, on being made chief
of some small office, immediately partitioned off a special
room for himself, calling it "the presence chamber," and
placed two commissionaires in coats with red collars and galloons at the door with instructions to take hold of the door
handle and open the door to any person who came to see
him, though there was hardly room in "the presence chamber" for an ordinary writing-desk.

The manners and habits of the Very Important Person
were very grand and impressive, but not very subtle. His
whole system was based chiefly on strictness. "Strictness,
strictness, and *again* strictness!" he usually declared, and at
the penultimate word he usually peered very significantly
into the face of the man he was addressing. There seemed
to be no particular reason for this strictness, though, for the

dozen or so Civil Servants who composed the whole administrative machinery of his office were held in a proper state
of fear and trembling, anyhow. Seeing him coming from a
distance they all stopped their work immediately and,
standing at attention, waited until the chief had walked
through the room. His usual conversation with any of his
subordinates was saturated with strictness and consisted
almost entirely of three phrases: "How dare you, sir? Do you
know who you're talking to, sir? Do you realise who is standing before you, sir?" Still, he was really a good fellow at
heart, was particularly pleasant with his colleagues, and
quite obliging, too; but his new position went to his head.
Having received the rank of general, he got all confused,
was completely nonplussed and did not know what to do.
In the presence of a man equal to him in rank, he was just
an ordinary fellow, quite a decent fellow, and in many ways
even a far from stupid fellow; but whenever he happened
to be in company with men even one rank lower than he,
he seemed to be lost; he sat silent and his position was
really pitiable, more particularly as he himself felt that he
could have spent the time so much more enjoyably. A
strong desire could sometimes be read in his eyes to take
part in some interesting conversation or join some interesting people, but he was always stopped by the thought:
would it not mean going a little too far on his part? Would
it not be mistaken for familiarity and would he not thereby
lower himself in the estimation of everybody? As a consequence of this reasoning he always found himself in a position where he had to remain silent, delivering himself only
from time to time of a few monosyllables, and in this way
he won for himself the unenviable reputation of being an
awful bore.

It was before this sort of Very Important Person that our
Akaky presented himself, and he presented himself at the
most inopportune moment he could possibly have chosen,
very unfortunate for himself, though not so unfortunate for
the Very Important Person.

At the time of Akaky's arrival the Very Important Per-

son was in his private office, having a very pleasant talk
with an old friend of his, a friend of his childhood, who had
only recently arrived in St. Petersburg and whom he had
not seen for several years. It was just then that he was informed that a certain Bashmachkin wanted to see him.
"Who's that?" he asked abruptly, and he was told, "Some
Civil Servant." "Oh," said the Very Important Person, "let
him wait. I'm busy now."

Now we believe it is only fair to state here that the Very
Important Person had told a thumping lie. He was not busy
at all. He had long ago said all he had to say to his old
friend, and their present conversation had for some time
now been punctuated by long pauses, interrupted by the
one or the other slapping his friend on the knee and saying,
"Ah, Ivan Abramovich!" or "Yes, yes, quite right, Stepan
Varlamovich!" However, he asked the Civil Servant to wait,
for he wanted to show his friend, who had left the Civil
Service long ago and had been spending all his time at his
country house, how long he kept Civil Servants cooling their
heels in his anteroom. At last, having talked, or rather kept
silent as long as they liked, having enjoyed a cigar in comfortable arm-chairs with sloping backs, he seemed to remember something suddenly and said to his secretary, who
was standing at the door with a sheaf of documents in his
hand, "Isn't there some Civil Servant waiting to see me? Tell
him to come in, please."

Seeing Akaky's humble appearance and old uniform, he
turned to him and said shortly, "What do you want?" in an
abrupt and firm voice, which he had specially rehearsed in
the solitude of his room in front of a looking-glass a week
before he received his present post and the rank of general.

Akaky, who had long since been filled with the proper
amount of fear and trembling, felt rather abashed and explained as well as he could and as much as his stammering
would let him, with the addition of the more than usual
number of "wells" and "you knows," that his overcoat was
quite a new overcoat, and that he had been robbed in a
most shameless fashion, and that he was now applying to

his excellency in the hope that his excellency might by putting in a word here and there or doing this or that, or writing to the Commissioner of Police of the Metropolis, or to some other person, get his overcoat back. For some unknown reason the general considered such an approach as too familiar. "What do you mean, sir?" he said in his abrupt voice. "Don't you know the proper procedure? What have you come to me for? Don't you know how things are done? In the first place you should have sent in a petition about it to my office. Your petition, sir, would have been placed before the chief clerk, who would have transferred it to my secretary, and my secretary would have submitted it to me. . . ."

"But, your excellency," said Akaky, trying to summon the handful of courage he had (it was not a very big handful, anyway), and feeling at the same time that he was perspiring all over, "I took the liberty, your excellency, of troubling you personally because—er—because, sir, secretaries are, well, you know, rather unreliable people. . . ."

"What? What did you say, sir?" said the Very Important Person. "How dare you speak like this, sir? Where did you get the impudence to speak like this, sir? Where did you get these extraordinary ideas from, sir? What's the meaning of this mutinous spirit that is now spreading among young men against their chiefs and superiors?" The Very Important Person did not seem to have noticed that Akaky Akakyevich was well over fifty, and it can only be supposed, therefore, that if he called him a young man he meant it only in a relative sense, that is to say, that compared with a man of seventy Akaky was a young man. "Do you realise, sir, who you are talking to? Do you understand, sir, who is standing before you? Do you understand it, sir? Do you understand it, I ask you?"

Here he stamped his foot and raised his voice to so high a pitch that it was not Akaky Akakyevich alone who became terrified. Akaky was on the point of fainting. He staggered, trembled all over, and could not stand on his feet. Had it not been for the door-keepers, who ran up to support him, he would have collapsed on the ground. He was carried out almost unconscious. The Very Important Person, satisfied that the effect he had produced exceeded all expectations and absolutely in raptures over the idea that a word of his could actually throw a man into a faint, glanced at his friend out of the corner of his eye, wondering what impression he had made on him; and he was pleased to see that his friend was rather in an uneasy frame of mind himself and seemed to show quite unmistakable signs of fear.

Akaky could not remember how he had descended the stairs, or how he had got out into the street. He remembered nothing. His hands and feet had gone dead. Never in his life had he been so hauled over the coals by a general, and not his own general at that. He walked along in a blizzard, in the teeth of a howling wind, which was sweeping through the streets, with his mouth agape and constantly stumbling off the pavement; the wind, as is its invariable custom in St. Petersburg, blew from every direction and every side street all at once. His throat became inflamed in no time at all, and when at last he staggered home he was unable to utter a word. He was all swollen, and he took to his bed. So powerful can a real official reprimand be sometimes!

Next day Akaky was in a high fever. Thanks to the most generous assistance of the St. Petersburg climate, his illness made much more rapid progress than could have been expected, and when the doctor arrived he merely felt his pulse and found nothing to do except prescribe a poultice, and that only because he did not want to leave the patient without the beneficent aid of medicine; he did, though, express his opinion then and there that all would be over in a day and a half. After which he turned to the landlady and said, "No need to waste time, my dear lady. You'd better order a deal coffin for him at once, for I don't suppose he can afford an oak coffin, can he?"

Did Akaky Akakyevich hear those fateful words and, if he did hear them, did they produce a shattering effect upon

The Overcoat

him? Did he at that moment repine at his wretched lot in life? It is quite impossible to say, for the poor man was in a delirium and a high fever. Visions, one stranger than another, haunted him incessantly: one moment he saw Petrovich and ordered him to make an overcoat with special traps for thieves, whom he apparently believed to be hiding under his bed, so that he called to his landlady every minute to get them out of there, and once he even asked her to get a thief from under his blanket; another time he demanded to be told why his old *capote* was hanging on the wall in front of him when he had a new overcoat; then it seemed to him that he was standing before the general and listening to his reprimand, which he so well deserved, saying, "Sorry, your excellency!" and, finally, he let out a stream of obscenities, shouting such frightful words that his dear old landlady kept crossing herself, having never heard him use such words, particularly as they seemed always to follow immediately upon the words, "your excellency." He raved on and no sense could be made of his words, except that it was quite evident that his incoherent words and thoughts all revolved about one and the same overcoat. At length poor Akaky Akakyevich gave up the ghost.

Neither his room nor his belongings were put under seal because, in the first place, he had no heirs, and in the second there was precious little inheritance he left behind, comprising as it did all in all a bundle of quills, a quire of white Government paper, three pairs of socks, a few buttons that had come off his trousers, and the *capote* with which the reader has already made his acquaintance. Who finally came into all this property, goodness only knows, and I must confess that the author of this story was not sufficiently interested to find out. Akaky Akakyevich was taken to the cemetery and buried. And St. Petersburg carried on without Akaky, as though he had never lived there. A human being just disappeared and left no trace, a human being whom no one ever dreamed of protecting, who was not dear to anyone, whom no one thought of taking any interest in, who did not attract the attention even of a naturalist who never fails to stick a pin through an ordinary fly to examine it under the microscope; a man who bore meekly the sneers and insults of his fellow Civil Servants in the department and who went to his grave because of some silly accident, but who before the very end of his life did nevertheless catch a glimpse of a Bright Visitant in the shape of an overcoat, which for a brief moment brought a ray of sunshine into his drab, poverty-stricken life, and upon whose head afterwards disaster had most pitilessly fallen, as it falls upon the heads of the great ones of this earth! . . .

A few days after his death a caretaker was sent to his room from the department to order him to present himself at the office at once: the chief himself wanted to see him! But the caretaker had to return without him, merely reporting that Akaky Akakyevich could not come, and to the question, "Why not?" he merely said, "He can't come, sir, 'cause he's dead. That's why, sir. Been buried these four days, he has, sir." It was in this way that the news of his death reached the department, and on the following day a new clerk was sitting in his place, a much taller man, who did not write letters in Akaky's upright hand, but rather sloping and aslant.

But who could have foreseen that this was not the last of Akaky Akakyevich and that he was destined to be the talk of the town for a few days after his death, as though in recompense for having remained unnoticed all through his life. But so it fell out, and our rather poor story quite unexpectedly acquired a most fantastic ending.

Rumours suddenly spread all over St. Petersburg that a ghost in the shape of a Government clerk had begun appearing near Kalinkin Bridge and much farther afield, too, and that this ghost was looking for some stolen overcoat and, under the pretext of recovering this lost overcoat, was stripping overcoats off the backs of all sorts of people, irrespective of their rank or calling: overcoats with cat fur, overcoats with beaver fur, raccoon, fox and bear fur-coats, in fact, overcoats with every kind of fur or skin that men have ever made use of to cover their own. One of the de-

partmental clerks had seen the ghost with his own eyes and
at once recognised Akaky Akakyevich; but that frightened
him so much that he took to his heels and was unable to
get a better view of the ghost, but merely saw how he
shook a finger at him threateningly from a distance. From
all sides complaints were incessantly heard to the effect that
the backs and shoulders, not only of titular councillors, but
also of court councillors, were in imminent danger of catching cold as a result of this frequent pulling off of overcoats.
The police received orders to catch the ghost at all costs,
dead or alive, and to punish him in the most unmerciful
manner as an example to all other ghosts, and they nearly
did catch it. A police constable whose beat included
Kiryushkin Lane had actually caught the ghost by his collar on the very scene of his latest crime, in the very act of
attempting to pull a frieze overcoat off the back of some
retired musician who had once upon a time tootled on a
flute. Having caught him by the collar, the policeman
shouted to two of his comrades to come to his help, and
when those arrived he told them to hold the miscreant while
he reached for his snuff-box which he kept in one of his
boots, to revive his nose which had been frostbitten six
times in his life; but the snuff must have been of a kind
that even a ghost could not stand. For no sooner had the
policeman, closing his right nostril with a finger, inhaled
with his left nostril half a handful of snuff than the ghost
sneezed so violently that he splashed the eyes of all three.
While they were raising their fists to wipe their eyes, the
ghost had vanished completely, so that they were not even
sure whether he had actually been in their hands. Since
that time policemen were in such terror of the dead that
they were even afraid to arrest the living, merely shouting
from a distance, "Hi, you there, move along, will you?"
and the ghost of the Civil Servant began to show himself
beyond Kalinkin Bridge, causing alarm and dismay among
all law-abiding citizens of timid dispositions.

We seem, however, to have completely forgotten a certain Very Important Person who, as a matter of fact, was

the real cause of the fantastic turn this otherwise perfectly true story has taken. To begin with, we think it is only fair to make it absolutely clear that the Very Important Person felt something like a twinge of compunction soon after the departure of poor Akaky Akakyevich, whom he had taken to task so severely. Sympathy for a fellow human being was not alien to him; his heart was open to all kinds of kindly impulses in spite of the fact that his rank often prevented them from coming to the surface. As soon as the friend he had not seen for so long had left, he felt even a little worried about poor Akaky, and since that day he could not get the pale face of the meek little Government clerk out of his head, the poor Civil Servant who could not take an official reprimand like a man. In fact, he worried so much about him that a week later he sent one of his own clerks to Akaky to find out how he was getting on, whether his overcoat had turned up, and whether it was not really possible to help him in any way. When he learnt that Akaky had died suddenly of a fever he was rather upset and all day long his conscience troubled him, and he was in a bad mood. Wishing to distract himself a little and forget the unpleasant incident, he went to spend an evening with one of his friends, where he found quite a large company and, what was even better, they all seemed to be almost of the same rank as he, so that there was nothing at all to disconcert him. This had a most wonderful effect on his state of mind. He let himself go, became a very pleasant fellow to talk to, affable and genial, and spent a very agreeable evening. At dinner he drank a few glasses of champagne, which, as is generally acknowledged, is quite an excellent way of getting rid of gloomy thoughts. The champagne led him to introduce a certain change into his programme for that night, to wit, he decided not to go home at once, but first visit a lady friend of his, a certain Karolina Ivanovna, presumably of German descent, with whom he was on exceedingly friendly terms. It should be explained here that the Very Important Person was not a young man, that he was a good husband and a worthy father of a family. Two sons, one of whom was already in Government service, and a very sweet sixteen-year-old daughter, whose little nose was perhaps a thought too arched, but who was very pretty none the less, came every morning to kiss his hand, saying, "*Bonjour, papa.*" His wife, who was still in the prime of life and not at all bad-looking, first gave him her hand to kiss and then, turning it round, kissed his hand. But the Very Important Person, who was very satisfied indeed with these domestic pleasantries, thought it only right to have a lady friend in another part of the town for purely friendly relations. This lady friend was not a bit younger or better-looking than his wife, but there it is: such is the way of the world, and it is not our business to pass judgment upon it. And so the Very Important Person descended the stairs, sat down in his sledge, said to his coachman, "To Karolina Ivanovna," and, wrapping himself up very snugly in his warm overcoat, gave himself up completely to the enjoyment of his pleasant mood, than which nothing better could happen to a Russian, that is to say, the sort of mood when you do not yourself have to think of anything, while thoughts, one more delightful than another, come racing through your head without even putting you to the trouble of chasing after them or looking for them. Feeling very pleased, he recalled without much effort all the pleasant happenings of the evening, all the witty sayings, which had aroused peals of laughter among the small circle of friends, many of which he even now repeated softly to himself, finding them every bit as funny as they were the first time he heard them, and it is therefore little wonder that he chuckled happily most of the time. The boisterous wind, however, occasionally interfered with his enjoyment, for, rushing out suddenly from heaven knew where and for a reason that was utterly incomprehensible, it cut his face like a knife, covering it with lumps of snow, swelling out his collar like a sail, or suddenly throwing it with supernatural force over his head and so causing him incessant trouble to extricate himself from it. All of a sudden the Very Important Person felt that somebody had seized him very firmly by the collar. Turning round, he saw a small-sized man in an old, threadbare Civil Service uniform, and it was not without horror that he recognised Akaky Akakyevich. The Civil Servant's face was white as snow and looked like that of a dead man. But the horror of the Very Important Person increased considerably when he saw that the mouth of the dead man became twisted and, exhaling the terrible breath of the grave, Akaky's ghost uttered the following words, "Aha! So here you are! I've—er—collared you at last! . . . It's your overcoat I want, sir! You didn't care a rap for mine, did you? Did nothing to get it back for me, and abused me into the bargain! All right, then, give me yours now!" The poor Very Important Person nearly died of fright. Unbending as he was at the office and generally in the presence of his inferiors, and though one look at his manly appearance and figure was enough to make people say, "Ugh, what a Tartar!" nevertheless in this emergency he, like many another man of athletic appearance, was seized with such terror that he began, not without reason, to apprehend a heart attack. He threw off his overcoat himself and shouted to his driver in a panic-stricken voice, "Home, quick!" The driver, recognising the tone which was usually employed in moments of crisis and was quite often accompanied by something more forceful, drew in his head between his shoulders just to be on the safe side, flourished his whip and raced off as swift as an arrow. In a little over six minutes the Very Important Person was already at the entrance of his house.

Pale, frightened out of his wits, and without his overcoat, he arrived home instead of going to Karolina Ivanovna's, and somehow or other managed to stagger to his room. He spent a very restless night, so that next morning at breakfast his daughter told him outright, "You look very pale today, Papa!" But Papa made no reply. Not a word did he say to any one about what had happened to him, where he had been and where he had intended to go.

This incident made a deep impression upon the Very Important Person. It was not so frequently now that his subordinates heard him say, "How dare you, sir? Do you realise who you're talking to, sir?" And if he did say it, it was only after he had heard what it was all about.

But even more remarkable was the fact that since then the appearance of the Civil Servant's ghost had completely ceased. It càn only be surmised that he was very pleased with the general's overcoat which must have fitted him perfectly; at least nothing was heard any more of people who had their overcoats pulled off their backs. Not that there were not all sorts of busybodies who would not let well alone and who went on asserting that the ghost of the Civil Servant was still appearing in the more outlying parts of the town. Indeed, a Kolomna policeman saw with his own eyes the ghost appear from behind a house; but having rather a frail constitution—once an ordinary young pig, rushing out of a house, had sent him sprawling, to the great delight of some cabbies who were standing round and whom, for such an insult, he promptly fined two copecks each for snuff—he dared not stop the ghost, but merely followed it in the dark until, at last, it suddenly looked round and, stopping dead in its tracks, asked, "What do *you* want?" at the same time displaying a fist of a size that was never seen among the living. The police constable said, "Nothing," and turned back at once. This ghost, however, was much taller; it had a pair of huge moustachios, and, walking apparently in the direction of Obukhov Bridge, it disappeared into the darkness of the night.

1841

In the Norton Library

LITERATURE

⇛ NORTON CRITICAL EDITIONS ⇚